Assignment Paris

Robert Brightwell

This book is dedicated to Simon Walker, one of my readers, who
suggested a war correspondent as a new central character. I hope he will
forgive the fact that this book bears no relation to the career of a real
correspondent he proposed as a model.

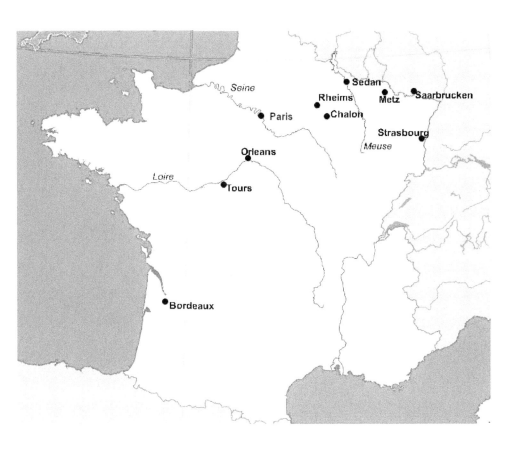

Chapter 1

Clack, clack, clackety-clack, the sound of the telegraph key was like a solo played on a broken piano. On and on it went, the sound seeming to rise and fall in an ungodly rhythm of doom. Twice the man paused as he read my pencilled draft, apprehensive to send on such calamitous content. The first time he muttered to himself, shaking his head. Only a reassuring glance at the pile of franc notes on his desk persuaded him to continue. The second time he turned to stare at me, sweat glistening on his forehead despite the chill of the evening. "Is this really true?" he whispered. I could understand his astonishment. For this gloomy candlelit office was announcing to the world the humiliation of a great nation, the fall of an emperor and an upheaval to the balance of power in Europe. It also confirmed that the whole nature of warfare was changing – the world would never be quite the same again.

The tapping key might have conveyed the facts, the casualty numbers and the political consequences, but it was hard to portray the sheer terror of battle down a wire. A war correspondent is supposed to be impartial, merely observing and calmly reporting on the events around them. Well, it is damn near impossible to be detached when you are surrounded by artillery you cannot see, which is raining down shells all around you. Men were blown apart right in front of me. Looking down, I saw various splashes of blood on my suit. The recollection of recent companions and their grisly demise was seared in my memory. I idly poked a finger at a rip in my jacket, showing just how close I had come to adding my own gore to the mix. There was still mud under my fingernails. Just hours before I had been clawing at the earth under a half-fallen tree like a maddened badger, desperate to find some shelter against the shards of jagged metal ripping through the air all about me.

"Did you not hear the battle?" I asked the telegraphist. "It was only twelve miles away."

The man nodded, pausing in his transmission to gesture at my notes, and stammer, "But…but I never expected this."

I nodded, for few would have predicted what had just happened. Just a single month before France had launched an invasion of Prussia. Their army, full of veterans having fought in North Africa, and with vastly superior weaponry, had been full of confidence. The British papers had carried stories of Prussian towns building defences and preparing for the onslaught. Yet now the exhausted and demoralised French forces had been thrown back into their own territory, bottled up or destroyed. Emperor Napoleon III, who had proudly led his regiments full of *la gloire* over the border, was now a humiliated prisoner of the Prussian king. I smiled ruefully as I remembered my maternal grandfather showing me a battered sword he had picked up during the Battle of Waterloo. He had used it to help vanquish the first Napoleon. History was repeating itself; now I was present to witness the defeat of that emperor's nephew. I was certain then that the war was done. France had no army left and seemed to have little choice but to surrender. How wrong I was. Little did I know that one of the strangest episodes of my career was only just beginning.

There was a scratch from the corner of the room. The flame from the vesta briefly illuminating the face of my colleague, Forbes, before it disappeared behind a cloud of tobacco smoke as he lit his pipe. "The telegraph office will send that across a page at a time," he predicted. "Frank will stop the presses as soon as he gets the first part. The story will run in the morning edition." He chuckled, "Russell will write something much longer, but he will use a courier to get it to London. We have at least a day over the pompous bastards." He grinned wolfishly at the thought.

My companion was immaculately attired in a tweed suit. He was not covered in mud, blood and bullet holes for the very good reason that he had been attached to the Prussian army, along with Russell from *The Times*, who he detested. Willie Russell had made his name reporting from the Crimean War and had nearly brought down the government with his accounts of military incompetence. Now foreign powers saw him as the doyen of journalism and *The Times* as the only important London paper. Our employer, the *Daily News*, was aimed at the middle classes rather than the elite. The price had recently been reduced from thruppence to a penny to drive circulation. To thrive it was vital that we got the news first, so that the paperboys had headlines to shout that would attract the attention of passers-by.

Frank Harrison Hill, the recently appointed editor of the paper, had introduced the new pricing. He was determined that it would succeed, not that he held out much hope of assistance from me. I was only employed under sufferance after an appeal from his brother, my pa. I well remember Uncle Frank leaning over the high lectern he used as a desk. The man had trained for the clergy, and it was not hard to imagine him in the pulpit. "If you are to work here you will not follow the sinful ways of your father," he spouted as he pointed an unwavering ink-stained finger in my direction. "That damn fool has wasted his life on drink and gambling. The first time I see you sink to the same depravities you are out on your ear, kin or not."

On his advice, I had dropped the Hill from my surname and was known in the printworks as Thomas Harrison. Despite this, word must have got out that I was related to the chief. The other correspondents treated me as though I was a spy or toady for my uncle. I was made to feel as welcome as a turd in a trifle.

Christ knows I had tried to make a positive impression. I gave up drink for a whole week and twice even went to the church he frequented to show willing. Then I found a discreet tavern some distance away from the paper, where a chap could enjoy a glass of wine or flagon of ale in peace. It was there I got wind of what I was sure would be my first major story for the paper. I overheard two coachmen talking about a Tory member of parliament, who was dipping his wick in the wife of a leading member of the aristocracy. The *Daily News* supported the new liberal government of Gladstone, and I knew such a scandal would damage their opposition. Being the newly diligent man that I was, I loitered outside the duke's house for two nights until I saw a carriage pulling up near the back entrance, as I had hoped, with a familiar coachman on the box. To further verify the tale, I followed a maid from the house and questioned her when we were alone. At first she would say nothing. It took a silver half-crown coin to loosen her tongue. She admitted it was true and further divulged that the duke was, in turn,

7

neglecting his wife and having an affair with an actress at the Haymarket Theatre. He had seen her public shows ten times, enjoying her private performances even more frequently.

When I presented my copy on the scandal to my uncle, explaining how I had come by the information and checked it, I expected at least grudging praise for my efforts. Instead, the grey eyebrows lowered like a storm cloud over the flinty blue eyes. "A gentleman does not want to read the tattle of servants," he intoned while screwing up my draft article into a ball and tossing it into the bin.

"But it is true. You know the fellow, you must know it is true," I protested.

"I don't doubt it," he agreed. "But where would things end if we published such gossip? Servants would hold sway over their masters' careers. You must raise yourself to higher standards, Thomas. Think like a gentleman."

Well, it is a good job I did not follow his advice. If I had, *The Times* correspondent covering the French would have been with their army rather than the *Daily News*. Instead, as far as I knew, my rival was still languishing in a Paris jail.

I had been surprised to be offered the posting to France at all. When I had been summoned to see my uncle, I had half expected to be dismissed for some as yet unknown infraction of his journalism rules. The editor's office had glass windows so that he could survey his domain, but they also enabled me to see he had company. The stranger was in his early thirties and had the erect bearing of a military man. He also possessed a piercing glare and had noticed my approach long before my chief. I was just wondering if, despite my precautions, I had been followed to the tavern, when my uncle gestured for me to join them.

"This is Archibald Forbes." He introduced the stranger, who, it appeared, had already been told about me. Perhaps that explained his decidedly unimpressed demeanour. "Forbes is to be our new war correspondent," my uncle explained. I felt my shoulders sag slightly with relief, before wondering what on earth this had to do with me. "He has written a number of articles while in the army," my uncle droned on, "and has recently been writing his own journal in London. I am sure he will be an excellent addition to our company at the *Daily News*."

Uncle Frank looked expectantly at me. Evidently, I was to add to this paean of welcome, but all I could think of saying was, "War correspondent? Are we expecting a war?" While there was always a skirmish or two going on somewhere, I was not aware of any great war in the offing. I was also more than a little suspicious of what my involvement was in this meeting. Was I to be some bag-carrying assistant, following him on his travels?

To my surprise it was Forbes who replied. "Have you not been following the news about the Spanish crown, laddie?"

My uncle might well have described me as some incompetent dolt to this newcomer, yet being called "laddie" by a cove a scant ten years older than me irked. "I do not have your venerable experience, sir," I started caustically, "but I do know that there are always revolts and rebellions in Spain. Wasn't the queen forced into exile last year?"

"Aye she was," Forbes grinned as he added, "young *man*." Then he continued, "I agree that more skirmishing in Spain would hardly be newsworthy. But the latest candidate for the Spanish throne is a relative of the Prussian king. The French are insisting that they will not tolerate a Prussian monarch in Spain. Some are threatening war with Prussia if the nominee is not withdrawn."

"But that is just sabre-rattling, surely," I protested. "Neither nation would go to war over something so trivial."

"Mr Forbes thinks they might," interrupted my uncle. "And if they do, we need to be prepared." He looked down at a paper on his desk and I recognised my own handwriting. It was my resume, given to him when I had joined the paper, detailing the many skills I thought I could bring to the world of journalism. "This says that you speak fluent French, is that true?"

I could understand his scepticism as that document was at best creative, while others might consider it downright misleading. My linguistic skills were more passable than fluent like a native, but I nodded eagerly. "I had a good education in languages and ten years ago visited Paris with my grandfather."

My uncle pursed his lips and conceded, "You went to Harrow, I see. At least my brother did not fail you entirely."

It did not seem the right time to tell him that my grandfather had paid for my education. I could not contain my curiosity any longer and blurted out, "What is this about, sir?"

"Whether there is to be a war or not," announced my uncle, "the *Daily News* needs men reporting on what is happening. Mr Forbes has agreed to go to Prussia. I want you to go to Paris."

It is not often that words fail me. Earlier that week I had been reporting on a tortoise competition in Putney, Now I was to go to perhaps the finest capital in the world to report on international affairs. Suspicion swiftly followed joy, for it seemed obvious to me that Paris was by far the plum posting. Yet when I looked at Forbes, he did not seem at all irritated by my good fortune. Instead, there was a look of smug amusement on his features as he watched what must have been a changing array of emotions on mine. "Why are you sending me?" I found myself asking.

"Don't you want to go?" demanded my uncle, his eyebrows rising in surprise. He gestured through the glass windows of his office. "There are a dozen men out there who would give their right arm for this opportunity."

"No, no, of course I want to go," I swiftly countered. There was some catch, I was sure of it, for my uncle was not this generous, but Paris is Paris. I certainly would not be measuring tortoises there.

"I should think so too," he agreed. He paused for a moment and then his tone darkened. "But mark this well: it is essential that you get news to us before our rivals. If *The Times* beats us to the announcement of any new treaties or the declaration of war, then you needn't bother coming back. This is your one chance, Thomas, do not let me down."

With this admonishment ringing in my ears, the meeting came to an end, perhaps before I could ask any more awkward questions. As he showed us both out, my uncle instructed Forbes to impart some advice on my new role. Our new Prussia correspondent was still smiling as we stood on the other side of the glass door. The clatter of the nearby printing presses made it hard to talk easily and so he gestured that we go outside.

"I am missing something," I admitted as we stepped out into the bustle of Fleet Street. "Why do you not want the Paris posting?"

Instead of answering my question, Forbes posed one of his own, "Your uncle does not like you much, does he?"

"It is my father he really hates. Pa inherited what little money there was and then gambled it away. Uncle Frank was furious. With no income, he first studied for the ministry but could not get appointed to a parish that would give him a living. Then he fell to making ends meet with private tutoring before finally becoming a newspaper man." I grinned, "So, I have answered your question. Your turn. Why do you not want the Paris posting?"

Forbes smiled. "It was not offered to me, because your uncle plans to use it to get rid of you." He laughed at the look of surprise on my features and continued, "I would have preferred the Prussia posting anyway. Come, let's get a cab, I want to show you something."

A minute later we were settled in a hansom cab, which he had directed west along the Strand to St James's. He explained that Prussia had already been to war twice in the last six years. In 1864 they had been in an alliance with Austria and had fought and beaten the Danes. Two years later they had turned on their former allies, beating the Austrian army. I vaguely remembered them receiving praise for agreeing generous peace terms with Vienna. On both occasions, Forbes told me, the Prussians had invited members of the press to accompany their army and report freely on what they saw. In contrast, the French government was much more wary of journalists.

Napoleon III had been Emperor of France for eighteen years, eight years longer than his more illustrious uncle. He had previously been president of a French republican government for four years, then retained power in a coup when his term was due to expire. Many Republicans had never been able to forgive this betrayal, which led to a vociferous opposition movement in France. The imperial government tried to control the press by restricting access and increasing censorship. Forbes explained that only the most pliant journalists would be invited to accompany the army, those who would print what they were told to. He doubted any foreign correspondents would be included at all. Telegraph messages to overseas newspapers were likely to be checked by ministry officials before they were transmitted.

"It will be damn near impossible for you to steal a march on rival papers," he told me. "You will be stuck in Paris reading whatever reports French journalists have had approved from the front. And that news will reach London the following day."

"That is assuming that there is a war," I reminded him. "Both France and Prussia will know that if they spend years fighting a war, it will weaken the pair of them. The main beneficiary of such a conflict will be Britain. I can't see them being that foolish – they will no doubt hatch up some compromise." I grinned and added, "Which means I get to enjoy several months in Paris at my uncle's expense."

"You may be right," conceded Forbes. "But I am fairly sure that there will be a war and I will show you why." With that he reached up, rapping his knuckles on the carriage roof, signalling the driver to stop. We had come to a halt in sight of Buckingham Palace. "What do you know about Bismarck, the Prussian chancellor?" he continued as he led us up a side street. I had to confess it was very little. Back then I probably knew more about tortoises from my recent assignment. "He is a wily devil," continued Forbes. "Very little happens in Prussia without his knowledge. The Prussian candidate would not have applied for the Spanish throne without the chancellor's approval. Indeed, I suspect it was probably Bismarck's idea. He would certainly have known that such an appointment would antagonise the French. He seems to have set out to provoke them. Then, of course, there is this." He held out his arm as we turned a corner. There across the street I saw a line of some thirty men waiting patiently for their turn to enter a building. I did at least recognise the flag hanging over the portal.

"Is that the Prussian embassy?" I asked.

"It is. I spent time talking to the men queuing there yesterday. They are getting papers to allow their return to Prussia. Look at their age, they are all in their mid-twenties. Ten years ago the Prussian army was little more than a militia, but the Prussian king is a soldier and has been reforming his forces. All Prussians are now called up to their local regiments when they are twenty to serve for three years. Then, like these men, they are on the reserve for a further four years. Even after that they can still be called up as a member of the militia regiments. Prussia has not yet called up their reserves, but it is clearly preparing for war. Word is reaching Prussians living in England that it is time to return home."

"Would I be right in assuming that there is not a similar queue outside the French embassy?" I ventured.

"We can check if you wish," replied Forbes. "But yesterday there was just an angry Scottish woman shouting to all who would listen that her husband had been wrongly imprisoned in France."

It still made no sense to me. Both nations had large armies with modern weapons; the slaughter in any war would be immense. Yet I could not deny that the Prussians at least seemed to be preparing for such a conflict. I turned to Forbes. "You have done this sort of thing before," I started. "If they do march off to battle, what should I do?"

My companion gave the matter serious thought. "I was a soldier when I submitted articles to papers before, so I went where I was ordered. Most correspondents stayed with the generals. I imagine that Napoleon will march with his armies, so if I were you, I would stick close to him. He will be kept informed of everything that is happening, which means those around him will know too. It is the only way to stay ahead of other journalists in Paris."

"But I thought you said that the French would only allow tame journalists to follow the army and would censor everything that they wrote."

"I did. So you will have to find a way if you want to keep your job."

It says something for my inexperience that back then I did not consider the risks of being blown to pieces by artillery, shot as a spy, buried alive or freezing to death, lost in a forest…all of which I did face. Instead, my biggest concern was merely being arrested and sent back to London!

Chapter 2

Paris was even more beautiful than I remembered. When I had been there ten years before in 1860, many of the wide boulevards and the buildings that lined them were still being built. We had gone to visit the English wife of a dead French officer my grandfather had known somehow during the old wars with France. The widow, I knew as Aunt Eliza, had taken me on tours of the city, which had often required detours around great engineering works for sewers and water pipes. Now all was complete, and it was magnificent.

I had arrived in the city at a huge new railway station. My surly cab driver drove the horse along a scenic route to my hotel to push up his fare and for once I did not mind a jot. We travelled along wide thoroughfares that teemed with strutting soldiers and pretty women enjoying the summer sunshine, for then it was July. Streets were now paved over where the drains lay that I had seen being built before, and elegant crisp new buildings lined each side. There were new parks for Parisians to promenade in while great steel and glass structures called department stores enabled them to buy their hearts' desires. London with its little shops and dark narrow streets seemed very drab in comparison.

Forbes had recommended a hotel that he knew was used by correspondents in Paris. It was near the ornate new opera house that was still under construction, viewed by many as the heart of the city. The hotel front desk was happy to provide a room on sight of the letter of credit I had been given to get funds from local banks during my stay. While my uncle had warned me that he would want a receipt to account for every centime spent, the invoice from the hotel could hide a multitude of sins. He wanted information and the fact was, some sources would have to be entertained on expenses. With that happy thought in mind, as my bags were sent up to my room, I strolled into the hotel bar.

The contingent of British journalists was not hard to find: a group of middle-aged men laughing and joking in English as if they were at a school reunion. Several had the straight bearing of military men, while

14

more had the ruddy complexions of hard drinkers. One was busy regaling the others with a tale of how an elephant had kept stealing his hat when he had been in Abyssinia. When another added to the anecdote, I realised that members of this exclusive coterie must gather like vultures whenever one nation begins to hunt another. This time though there might be no corpse to feed off. A French newspaper lay on the table before them. It was upside down, but I could make out the meaning of the headline: the Prussian noble had withdrawn his candidature for the Spanish throne. It looked like Forbes was wrong after all.

"I'm Harrison from the *Daily News.*" I introduced myself as the laughter from the story subsided.

Most nodded companionably in greeting, but one looked me up and down, his nose wrinkling in distaste. "Harrison… I am not familiar with your work. Have you been a correspondent for long?"

I doubted that the Putney tortoise competition had been big news in Paris and so I was forced to concede that I had worked for the paper for just a couple of months.

"Oh dear," he sneered. "Clearly their new pricing is not working out if Frank can only afford to send cubs to do the work of men." He laughed at his own comment, but I noticed few joined in.

As I hesitated, unsure what to say, another spoke up. "Take no notice of Chalmers. I'm Quin from the *Telegraph.* Here, have this seat beside me. Have you got an artist with you?"

"Er, no," I admitted, noticing now a couple of sketchpads on the table.

"More penny-pinching then," chuckled Chalmers. "And where is Forbes? We heard he had joined your tawdry rag. Has he been let go already?"

"No, he is on his way to Cologne," I muttered defensively.

"Of course he is," spoke up Quin. "The Prussians know how to treat journalists."

"The French know how to treat *some* journalists," countered Chalmers. "You gentlemen will be able to read how the war is progressing from my reports in *The Times.*" He tapped his breast pocket before continuing, "Forbes and the others with the Prussians will be too busy retreating to file any reports."

"Chalmers is the only one of us given accreditation to travel with the army," explained Quin and I understood now why he was less than popular.

"But will there be a war now?" I gestured to the paper on the table before them. "Surely if the prince has withdrawn, then the *casus belli* for conflict has gone."

"I would not be so sure," said Quin passing me the French paper. I managed to read nearly all of it and was astonished to see that the editorial was far from satisfied. It was indignantly insisting that action still be taken to put these upstart Prussians in their place.

When the waiter came, I bought a round of drinks for all and settled into the group. As well as *The Times* and *The Telegraph*, there were representatives from *Pall Mall Gazette*, the *Morning Post*, the *Illustrated London News,* the *Irish Times* and even the *Manchester Evening News*. Several of them had clearly known each other for many years. Like war hounds, they gathered expectantly wherever a sabre was rattled. They were clearly experts in their field and their view was that Forbes was right: a war was still a strong possibility. They were happy to share their experience and advised me to present myself at the war ministry in the morning. This was to get my French government accreditation as a British journalist. I would not be invited to join Chalmers and the army, but at least I would then be included in official briefings.

After a leisurely breakfast at my hotel, I set off for the ministry. My new colleagues had warned me that this would be a long and tedious affair and so on the way I purchased all the latest French newspapers I could find. Then I was directed from one uncomfortable wooden bench to the next as my documentation accumulated the necessary stamps and signatures. As I waited, I set about bringing myself up to date. The papers all reported on the agreement from King Wilhelm of Prussia that his cousin should not be considered for the Spanish throne. At least two papers quoted the French emperor being satisfied that the matter was now resolved. If he was, he was in the minority. The press and several ministers were now seeking guarantees that the Prussians would never interfere in such affairs again. Even the empress, born to Spanish nobility, was said to be indignant. One minister suggested that King William should send a personal letter of 'explanation' to the emperor, although from his tone, only one of grovelling apology would suffice.

After my perusal, I had to agree with my fellow correspondents that the prospect of war remained very real. That at least made the tediously repetitive display of my passport and letters of introduction worthwhile, as I was finally given my certification to show I was an approved foreign correspondent. It was as I left the ministry that I first met Pascal.

"Excuse me, monsieur, but are you by any chance a foreign journalist?"

My brown suit had the cut of an English country gentleman about it and so it was hardly an inspired guess. "Yes I am," I replied warily. "What is it to you?"

"I was wondering if you needed the services of an illustrator." As he spoke, he was opening a large leather portfolio and gesturing at the portrait inside. It was of a French soldier, a wizened old veteran with wrinkles around the eyes from years spent squinting into the desert sun. He gestured over my shoulder and added, "See, monsieur, it is a good likeness."

I turned to look at the sentry standing rigidly to attention at the entrance to the ministry. If his features were frozen, mine were not, for I grinned in surprise. I could see now that the drawing was an extraordinary resemblance, if anything Pascal's soldier was more grizzled than the real thing. "You have a prodigious talent, sir, but…" I had been about to turn him down. The *Daily News* rarely carried illustrations; they had to be engraved and so were time consuming and expensive. Yet as I opened my mouth, fate intervened in the form of a gust of wind. It lifted the corner of the portrait and before either of us could stop it, the paper flipped up in the air and began to make its way down the street.

"Pardon, monsieur," Pascal thrust the leather case in my hands before setting off in pursuit, adding over his shoulder, "I have promised the picture to the sergeant."

He may have said more, but I had long since stopped paying heed. My attention was fully absorbed by the next portrait that had been revealed in the case. How does one judge an artist? Is it the accuracy of the likeness, or the emotions that they convey in paint or in this case a few deft strokes of a pencil on paper? By any measure Pascal had a gift that in my view put him up there with the greats. A woman stared back at me from the case. A tousled, raven-haired beauty, a slight pout to her lips and eyes that carried a brazen challenge. She was wearing a simple chemise, partly unbuttoned so that her left tit poked out invitingly. In short, she gave the impression of exuding lust from every pore. The drawing had certainly excited emotion in me. My mouth was dry with desire and I felt irritated as Pascal returned and started to babble again, interrupting some very colourful imaginings.

He must have given the other drawing to the soldier while I was staring transfixed at his work, but now he resumed his pitch. "Monsieur, I was offering my services as a war artist." Then seeing the cause of my distraction, he grinned and played his ace card. "If you agree, I could introduce you to my model."

I suddenly felt very sure that the *Daily News* could benefit from more illustrations. If they had carried that one on the front page, then its paper boys would have been trampled in a stampede to buy the edition. "You are hired," I agreed, "but only if I manage to leave Paris and join the army." I thought having a Frenchman with me, especially one with such talents, might help ease my path. Yet this was not the issue at the forefront of my mind. "Now, about meeting this model…"

He invited me to join him for dinner at his apartment that evening, at an address just ten minutes' walk from my hotel. I was promised that the model would be present along with a couple of other friends that he wanted me to meet. As we parted, he handed me the drawing that had secured his appointment. After all these years I have it still. It is much smudged from where I had to fold it to keep in my pocket and there is a bloodstain on one corner. Yet it still stirs emotion when I look at it, even now. Perhaps no longer lust, but a lump in my throat at the memories it invokes.

That evening, as I eagerly strolled the boulevards, I braced myself for disappointment. Pascal had if anything exaggerated the rugged features of the soldier and I wondered if he had done the same for the girl. I was just convincing myself that the reality would be some chop-faced harridan, when the door to the apartment swung open and I discovered he had, in fact, done her a grave disservice. She stood just beyond my host's shoulder, and I must have stood there like a stunned bullock for several seconds in awe of her beauty. Finally, Pascal had to grab my arm to pull me over the threshold as he introduced me to Justine…his sister.

His sister! My mind reeled at the thought. What kind of fraternal relationships did French siblings have that enabled him to make such an image? As I recovered from my shock, I was introduced to another couple, but they barely registered in my consciousness. He was a soldier, a Lieutenant Duval, I was reminded later. His wife, Madeleine, was a pretty blonde, and normally deserving of much of my attention and yet that evening she was totally eclipsed. I must have been in a daze. I vaguely recall sitting beside Justine and drinking in her beauty, while trying to impress her when she asked me about being a journalist. The first conversation I clearly remember was when we were all sitting around the dining table. I had asked them what they thought of their emperor. To my surprise, Justine was the first to answer.

"He is a traitor and a tyrant," she declared passionately. "He has betrayed the republic and now he is leading France to tyranny and ruin." There was a weary sigh from Pascal as though this was an argument that they had rehearsed many times before, while from the soldier there came a scoff of derision.

"Nonsense, the emperor has brought pride back to France." Duval turned to me. "We have beaten the Russians alongside you British, we have conquered territory in North Africa and the emperor has personally led forces that defeated the Austrians in Italy. Our army is the best equipped and strongest in the world and that is all down to the emperor."

"Pah, the army, the army," Justine mocked, "He looks after you because you keep him in power. But what about the people? Pascal's magazine was shut down because they would not support the emperor's lies."

"That is shocking," I said hurriedly in agreement as Pascal nodded that this was true. "I take it then that you do not approve of the emperor's ministers trying to humiliate Prussia with their latest demands?"

"Oh no, that is the one thing I do agree with the emperor on," she insisted. "Prussia has insulted France and must be punished." Nods around the table indicated that having divided the diners, I had now united them again on this issue.

"But are you not worried that there might be a war with Prussia? From what I hear, they have a well-trained army that defeated the Austrian forces in little over a month."

"Ah, monsieur, do not be deceived by tales of the great Prussian victory at Sadowa." Duval beamed with pride as he continued, "The Prussians had an advantage there, which they will not have if they are foolish enough to fight us."

"What do you mean?" I asked, curious.

"At Sadowa the Austrians were armed with muzzle loading muskets, which meant that they had to stand to reload and could only fire a maximum of three shots per minute. Against them the Prussians had a breach loading rifle called a needle gun after the firing pin. It can fire twice as fast and while the soldier is lying prone or behind cover. That is why the Austrians were beaten so easily."

"And does the French army have a needle gun?" I enquired, only to see his grin widen even further.

"It does not, monsieur, it has the Chassepot." On seeing my puzzlement, he went on. "It is a vastly superior breech-loading rifle. The maximum range of the needle gun is around five hundred metres, but it fires a heavy bullet, which makes it almost impossible to aim at that distance. It is only accurate to around three hundred metres. The Chassepot fires a smaller bullet, but at a much greater velocity resulting in a flatter trajectory, which makes it easier to aim." I evidently did not look sufficiently impressed with these technical details and so he added something I did understand. "This means that the Chassepot can fire a bullet one thousand five hundred metres, five times the accurate range of the Prussian gun."

"Good grief," I was astonished at the difference. "You will be able to shoot the Prussians long before they can return fire. Do all your soldiers have this new rifle?"

"They do, Monsieur Harrison, and," he lowered his voice conspiratorially before adding, "we have other secret weapons that are even more powerful. That is why we do not mind fighting the Prussians now; it is only a matter of time before they try to copy our advances." I began to feel sorry for Forbes; if he was not careful, there would be bullets buzzing about him like angry hornets. I thought back to those poor devils I had seen queuing outside the Prussian embassy. Some were probably veterans of the Austrian campaign, who thought they knew what to expect. They would be shot down like tin ducks on a fairground stall long before they could bring their own guns to bear.

Duval told me that the French had a different enlistment system to the Prussians. Around a hundred and seventy thousand were recruited each year. Not everyone of military age was called up, it was more a random lottery. If you were unfortunate to be on the list, you could pay someone else to go in your place. Once enlisted, men served for five years in the army and could be called again for a further four years in the reserves. Those who managed to escape call-up still had to serve in something called the Mobile Guard, but these were part-time soldiers. They had only a fortnight's training each year and were able to go home each night.

By then the wine had been opened and the food served. We had a jolly time. I deliberately kept the conversation light to avoid any more arguments around the table. Justine was lively and engaging, with a wide range of interests. She had read several books by Charles Dickens and was intrigued to learn that he had founded the paper I worked for. It had been an enchanting evening and as it drew to a close, I asked if I could see her again.

"I was hoping that you might walk me home," she said, dazzling me with a smile.

"But do you not live here with your brother?" I enquired.

"Pascal is not really my brother, silly," she laughed. "He says that to protect me from unwanted attention." She reached out and touched my arm, "But your attention is quite welcome. I want to hear all about life in London."

My heart soared with joy and as there was still some light, we walked through one of the new parks. She put her arm through mine and her scent competed with bowers of colourful sweet peas. It was turning into an idyllic evening. As I described London at her request, my home city felt a poor comparison to the crisp new uniform architecture of Paris. We left the park and found ourselves in another wide boulevard, illuminated with lines of glittering gas lamps, I could hold myself back no longer. "I know you despise your emperor," I exclaimed as I gestured an arm down the street, "but surely you cannot deny that he has made Paris into a beautiful city."

"Oh yes, he has for the middle and upper classes, we call them the *bourgeoisie*. He has bought the support of soldiers like Pascal with medals and victories and his army now provides protection for the Vatican in Rome. In return the Pope encourages priests to support the emperor. They use their religious superstitions to keep the provincial peasants in line. Now we have fine parks, but what about the people who used to live here? The poor have been driven off, their houses demolished, and they cannot afford to return. They have been forced into slums, which tourists like you never visit." She gave a heavy sigh and concluded, "You are English, you will never understand the real spirit of France."

For the second time that evening I was amazed at how quickly she could fly up into a passion. I had been hoping that she might invite me into her apartment, but now feared that I had blown my chance. "The lower classes suffer terribly in London too," I assured her. "I sometimes help out in a soup kitchen for them." I wracked my brains for some other lies I could add to help me get back in her favour.

She misread the anxiety on my features, for she continued, "I can see from your face that you have a concern for the poor. Perhaps we could meet again? I will take you to Belleville, one of the poverty-stricken quarters. Then you can write an article for your paper telling London what Paris is really like. I am sure your founder, Charles Dickens, would approve."

"Of course," I agreed, resigned now that I would not end that evening in her bed. Yet I had not given up hope of that delight. If she could get so worked up over a slum, I could only imagine the depths of her desires in the boudoir.

Chapter 3

Any possible interest my uncle might have had in an article on the poorer parts of Paris disappeared the next day. Until that point war might have been avoided, but on Thursday the fourteenth of July 1870, the city's only talking point was the Ems Telegram.

This dispatch, sent by one Prussian diplomat to another, concerned their king's meeting with a French official at a place called Ems. It described the king being rude and dismissive to the Frenchman when guarantees had been sought. Quite how such a private message came to be leaked so comprehensively was, at first, a mystery. We later learned that the scheming Bismarck had re-written the message to make it more damning and instructed all embassies to leak it. He was trying to goad the French into fighting. His plan worked perfectly.

I was awoken by a crowd braying under my hotel window. They were shouting for war and demanding that the army march immediately for the Rhine. When I went down for breakfast, I found my colleagues equally jubilant. They showed me the morning editions of the Paris papers, which had printed the telegram in full, along with strident editorials that such an insult must be answered with blood.

The man from the *Pall Mall Gazette* ordered champagne to celebrate our good fortune. "War," he declared, "is when we earn our salt following the clarion call of battle." He at least did not seem to be unduly concerned that he would be following affairs from the luxury of a Paris hotel.

Chalmers, though, could not help reminding us of his advantage. "I will host a farewell party for you all before I leave," he boasted. "Perhaps if you are kind to me, I will send you scraps of news from my bounteous table at the front."

"You can have a scrap from this table if you want," laughed the man from the Manchester paper, as he tossed a bread roll at Chalmers. We all enjoyed our champagne breakfast. Given what I had discovered about the efficacy of the Chassepot, I believed the air of celebration to be entirely justified.

"The Prussians have made a mistake this time," Quin told me as we tucked into bacon and eggs. "I hear the Austrians have been talking to France about an alliance, possibly the Italians too. If that happens then the southern German states such as Bavaria will probably throw in their lot with these allies. The Prussians have been pushing their weight around for too long and making enemies. Now their chickens will come home to roost." He winked and, nodding towards Chalmers, added, "Mark my words, when the French are marching on Berlin, they will want all us journalists with them to record their victory."

We were interrupted by a waiter announcing I had a visitor in the lobby. I knew few people in Paris and left the table half hoping that it was Justine, calling to arrange our next meeting. To my surprise I found the soldier Duval waiting for me. He greeted me warmly before taking me to one side where we could talk in private. "Pascal tells me that you are paying him to be an illustrator," he whispered. I nodded and he went on, "He says that you might pay for important stories, is that true?"

"Well yes, if the story is important," I admitted, wondering where this might lead.

"I can show you one of France's secret weapons. It is in a warehouse near here being repaired, but I need five hundred francs."

"Five hundred francs!" I repeated. That was a huge amount of money. Back then the average worker only earned twenty francs a week. "I am sorry," I told him, "but the maximum I am allowed to pay for a story is a hundred francs." I had just invented the limit, but guessed he would take any money he could get. The papers had announced that the army was being mobilised and soon he would be marching to join his regiment. In the end, when he asked if I knew of any other journalists who could be more generous, we settled on a hundred and fifty francs. He believed the extra cash came from my own pocket, which made him more grateful.

"What I am about to show you is one of France's biggest secrets," he whispered as we hurried down the street. "They are determined that the details of its manufacture do not fall into the hands of the Prussians." He laughed before adding, "but in a few days they will see its awful effect for themselves. So I must make some money now before it is too late." He explained that Madeleine wanted a ring on her finger before he marched to war and without my help, he could not afford one. As we talked, he took a key from his pocket and unlocked the gate to the yard of an engineering business. "There should not be anyone around, they are all marching about the war," he said, before pushing on into a small warehouse.

As I stepped inside, I sensed I would be disappointed. From Duval's fanciful introduction I had no idea what I had been expecting, but the lump under a sheet of canvas in the middle of the space had the shape and dimensions of a fairly standard cannon.

"Are you *sure* this is going to be worth a hundred and fifty francs?" I pressed.

"Behold, monsieur, the Mitrailleuse!" He pulled back the canvas and I remained underwhelmed, for from the side, the gun still looked very like a regular cannon. Seeing my disappointment, Duval gestured for me to join him at the business end of the gun. "Come, Monsieur Harrison, observe the muzzle and you will see its secret. Warily I stepped forward and then finally I did stop in surprise. For instead of one gaping hole for a shell, there were twenty-five of them, arrayed in five rows of five. Each one was bigger than that of a rifle – I reached forward and found I could fit a finger in one easily.

"How far can this gun shoot?" I asked, finally impressed.

"Further than the Chassepot," Duval announced proudly. "Around eighteen hundred metres, just over one of your English miles. The bullets fire one at a time and are very powerful. They would pass through several men or horses if fired into a regiment."

"But how long does it take to reload?" I asked, suspecting that this would be the flaw in the design.

"Come, let me show you." Duval led me to the breech where he demonstrated a screw mechanism that allowed a plate containing twenty-five bullets to be loaded in just a few seconds. "It can fire a hundred and fifty rounds a minute," he boasted as he showed me a crank handle that served as a trigger.

"How many of these guns do you have?" I probed, wondering if this was a rare prototype.

"Two hundred, and we are making more each day. Gunners are being trained for each one and they will train their crews at the front. That way we can keep the secret to as few people as possible. So, monsieur, is this information worth a hundred and fifty francs?" he asked holding out his hand.

It certainly was. Perhaps some of the other correspondents had heard of such a weapon, but I had not, nor had I heard them mention its name. Running my hand over the handle that would release that stream of shot, I tried to imagine its effect in a battle. Just one of them, firing out those great big bullets, could chew up a squadron of cavalry if caught in the open with no cover. There would be not a horseman left if they tried to cover the huge range of the weapon to reach the gun. Two or three batteries of six, I calculated, would be enough to stop an entire attack. The machine could change how battles were fought, and certainly who won them.

I was sure that the Mitrailleuse would make an excellent story for the *Daily News*, especially if Chalmers had not already got wind of its existence for *The Times*. I could not stop myself imagining the impressed glances of the other correspondents when the London papers, featuring my work, arrived in the hotel.

"I hope this is enough to buy a ring," I told Duval as I handed the notes over. "If not, perhaps you can buy one at a discount at a jeweller's in Berlin."

He laughed, "I doubt Madeleine would wait that long."

"When do you leave?" I asked.

"I am not sure. The mobilisation plans are all changing. We were to form up at our regimental depots and then go to the front, but some of those depots are in North Africa and they have decided it would take too long. Now only the reservists will have to go to the depot to collect uniforms and equipment. The rest of us are all to make our way to the front and join our regiments there. I am waiting for them to tell me where my regiment will be."

"Isn't that all likely to be a bit chaotic?" I asked. "Thousands of men milling around the front trying to reach their regiments?"

"Probably," he conceded. "But do not worry, everything was disordered at the start when we fought in Italy. Yet things sorted themselves out and we were still victorious."

I hoped he was right, wished him good luck and prepared to go on my way.

It was as I was going through the door that he gave me the warning. "Monsieur Harrison, whatever you do, do not send your story by telegraph. The government are monitoring it for any mention of the Mitrailleuse and you are certain to be arrested. I would not even post it from your hotel, as they know lots of foreign journalists stay there.

"What? Are you telling me that I have just paid for a story I cannot use?" I demanded, noting that the money had already been tucked away in his tunic.

"Certainly, you can use it," he soothed. "But you should post it in the mail and it would be best not to address your letter to a newspaper. Perhaps to a friend who could forward it on," he suggested. I rushed back to the hotel to write my copy and then went to a post office several streets away to send it. I addressed it to my uncle at his home address and asked him not to use the usual 'From our Paris Correspondent' as the source. It would take several days to reach him, the article to be printed and the paper to arrive back in Paris. I would just have to wait a little longer for the plaudits of my colleagues.

When I joined them in the hotel lounge later, I found that I had missed a briefing from the war ministry. When asked if the French army was ready for war, the minister had insisted that not even a gaiter button was missing. Trains were being requisitioned, plans finalised and soon thousands of men would be heading to the frontier region with the German states. He had further announced that instead of several army groups as originally envisaged, there would now be just one large army group, commanded by the emperor himself.

Once Quin had debriefed me, I shared with him what I had ascertained of the changes to mobilisation plans. We were just debating if things really would go as smoothly as the minister was claiming when a figure half fell through the door into the hotel lounge. It was the correspondent from the *Pall Mall Gazette*. This fellow started his day with a bottle of champagne, moved on to bottles of claret for lunch and dinner, then drank heavily of brandy through the evening, with no sign of intoxication. Yet now he was tighter than a boiled owl and had to be helped into a chair. "Vodka," he gasped by way of explanation. The steward brought him several cups of strong coffee, which he drank as though it was some awful tonic. Eventually revived, he told us what he had learned. There was a Russian nobleman staying at the embassy with whom he had been at school. They had been catching up over old times when secrets were revealed. "Russia has warned Austria that if they mobilise to join the war, Russia will mobilise its army too. Vienna has agreed to stand down. France is on its own."

"Why would Russia do that?" I asked

"Russia is no friend of France after the Crimean War," explained Quin. "There have also been various border disputes between the Russian and Austro–Hungarian empires over their Balkan dominions."

"No," croaked our intoxicated friend. "It is Bismarck. He had it all arranged with the Russians in advance. That is why they moved so quickly." Exhausted by his own revelations, he slumped back on the sofa, his eyes closed.

"My God," murmured Chalmers. "That changes things." As our informant snored, the rest of us began to debate the consequences of his news. The southern German states such as Württemberg, Baden and Bavaria had stayed neutral during the war between Prussia and Austria. France had been hoping that they would join their Franco–Austrian alliance, not least because they would need to march through their territory to reach Prussia. Now at best it looked as though they would remain neutral, although I had a growing suspicion that Chancellor Bismarck would have been at work there too. France had been provoked into declaring war; it was seen as the aggressor, bullying a country that had already made concessions. The London papers we received were all siding with Prussia, a traditional ally, against a Bonaparte-led France. Sandwiched between two warring nations, would the southern German states see France as a friend or an invader?

There was much debate over dinner that evening, which for me continued even after I had retired. As I lay in bed, I could hear Chalmers in the room next to mine laying forth with his opinions. I think he was talking to the man from the *London Illustrated News*, but as the fellow got so few words in, it was hard to be sure. It was a puzzling business. Prussia had to be aware of their great disadvantages in weaponry. The Chassepot rifle had been widely distributed through the French army. Surely a Prussian spy had discovered the existence of the rifle, if not the Mitrailleuse. Yet they were pressing on as though they held all the aces. I just felt glad that I would not be in either army. With luck, I had also secured my first coup as a journalist and then, of course, there was the delectable Justine to pursue. I was beginning to enjoy my life as a war correspondent.

Chapter 4

I arranged to see Justine again that weekend. While I suggested the theatre, she wanted first to take me to the Belleville area of the city, which she insisted would reveal the real Paris. While a tour of a slum was not my idea of a romantic tryst, it was the only way to spend more time in her company and who knew what might follow.

As we entered the narrow streets, I cautiously tucked away my watch. It was the kind of place where a stranger could soon be parted from their valuables. Despite frequent glances around, I saw no villainous coves closing in. Instead, we were soon surrounded by a growing band of snottering brats. They all knew Justine and I learned that she volunteered to teach at a local school. Adults nodded in greeting too; she was clearly a familiar and well-liked face in the vicinity. I was shown into mean streets and alleys where large families lived in single rooms in the run-down dwellings. I readily agreed with her that it was a great contrast to the grander parts of Paris. Yet while I tutted sympathetically, I thought to myself that it was no worse than some of the slums in the east end of London.

"The republic promised equality," she insisted, "but under Napoleon the wealthy get richer and the poor can barely survive. Those grand streets you admire were paved by hungry men working for a pittance to feed their families."

"Perhaps," I agreed. "But after your revolution you just swapped one group of rich men for another. The aristocracy were replaced with generals and marshals and given new titles."

"That is because the old Napoleon overthrew the First Republic and replaced it with an empire. Twice now the people of France have had their republic stolen from them. It cannot be allowed to happen again." I did not understand why she was so interested in politics. Yet she had read various books and pamphlets on it by Jacobins, philosophers as well as some professor called Marx in London. She was convinced that a republic would be a paradise of equality. I did not argue, but the United States was a republic and they still had a division of rich and poor.

I barely cared about the theories she expounded, but I thought she looked beautiful as she did so. Her eyes sparkled with interest and as she waved her arms, a button came undone on her blouse. As I caught a glimpse of the curve of her breast, I could not help but remember Pascal's portrait.

"What do you think about women having the vote?" she suddenly asked me. By that point I was so randy, I would have happily marched behind a banner calling for votes for horses if it would have got her into bed. I was about to make some flippant comment, but saw she was watching me closely. I sensed a lot rested on my reply.

"Well, as I have given up my lodgings to come here, I don't have a vote myself. Most men don't, never mind women." I paused to give the matter serious thought. "You might say I am biased as a newspaper man, but it seems to me that gender should not matter, nor the amount of rent you pay. What should count is an interest in the affairs of government and an understanding of the issues involved." I grinned and concluded, "I would restrict the vote to the literate and well informed, in other words, newspaper subscribers."

She laughed in delight, "Well that might be self-interest, but at least it was well reasoned. I am glad you did not just tell me what you thought I wanted to hear."

By then we were walking back into the city. I was just wondering where to take her for lunch, when she suddenly grabbed my arm. Without warning she pushed me back against a wall and then I felt her lips on mine. I was so surprised it took me a full second to respond, but then my arms were about her and I was kissing back eagerly.

She stepped back laughing – I must have still looked surprised by this sudden turn of events. "Do you think only men can decide when to kiss?" she arched an eyebrow and added, "or who to sleep with, who to marry?"

"I can honestly say I have never been more supportive of female emancipation," I grinned back at her. "Perhaps we should have lunch at my hotel. They could bring it up to my room."

"A French lady never rushes lunch," she reprimanded me before leading the way to a nearby café. It would have been a pleasant meal if

I were not at the boil to get her alone. At least we did not talk any more about the republic. I discovered that Pascal had been one of her lovers. He had drawn her many times, including several nudes, but had now moved on to a new muse. I thought the fellow must be half blind to consider leaving Justine, but resolved to look through his sketch book at the first opportunity. Over the meal I kept her glass topped up with a good white wine, but it had no more effect on her than on the fellow from the *Pall Mall Gazette*.

Eventually we left, with me champing at the bit. I had planned to take her to my hotel, but the route was blocked by a large group of rowdy soldiers. They were drunk, open bottles in their hands, and were insisting that passers-by join them to toast their imminent victories. From the audible squeals, they were taking more than a few liberties with women they encountered. I did not want anyone pawing my girl before me and so we turned away for her apartment. It was above a small bakery and I had never seen a place with more books. There were piles of them on each of the stairs, not that I stopped to read. We were both craving our muttons by then, half undressing each other as we tumbled into the bedroom.

I have to say that Justine took *fraternité* to a whole new level. Perhaps not all those volumes were about politics, I thought, for she taught me things in the bedroom I had never done before with an English girl. She had an unabashed passion for pleasure that took my breath away…literally. By the time we finished I was exhausted. I reflected that if every French woman was like Justine, there would never be war in France. The menfolk would be too tired to lift a rifle.

Afterwards, we drank red wine from teacups, watching through the window as more drunken soldiers passed down the street. Trains were leaving for the frontier now and they were clearly making the most of their last night in the city.

"Will you write the article about Belleville for your paper?" she asked quietly.

"I will, but not until the war is over. My editor will not be interested in it now and I cannot promise that he will publish it even then." I laughed bitterly and added, "In fact, unless I can find a way of following those soldiers to the front, I will probably be fired. The ministry seems determined that I remain in Paris."

"You will succeed. Planchet says that we must use our enemy's tactics against them." She leaned in and kissed me before adding, "and one day I will read your article."

We spent the night together and as we talked during the evening, I came to understand the reason behind her political passions. Her father had been killed during the rioting of the 1848 revolution, the one that had created the Second Republic. She had not even been born then and her pregnant mother had eventually remarried her physician. We made love slowly the next morning as the enticing smell of baking drifted up through the floorboards. The freshest bread, butter and coffee made an excellent breakfast before I reluctantly took my leave.

I was lost in thought as I slowly made my way back to my hotel. In the coming months the people of Belleville would go on to show extraordinary resilience and I did write that article for Justine eventually, although it was nothing like the piece I envisaged then.

I passed a column of troops marching towards a railway station. A score of horse-drawn wagons followed on behind containing equipment that was to accompany them. They at least looked sober compared to the men of the night before. I wondered if there was a Mitrailleuse or two hidden under the canvas covering the carts. My mind turned to the letter still on its way to my uncle. Would it be enough to keep me in employment? It might perhaps buy me another week or two, but Chalmers would soon start sending his reports from the front. *The Times* would be at least a day ahead then. All I would have to offer was information that would appear anyway in the other papers.

When I browsed through the English journals in the hotel lobby, I found an article by Forbes in the *Daily News*. He described defensive earthworks being built around Cologne on the Rhine and cavalry patrols searching for French armies. Women feared ravishment from invaders, particularly the Moorish troops from north Africa, who were thought likely to carry them off as concubines. It was the kind of titillating tale that would play well to the pro-Prussian audience at home.

I spent the rest of the day drafting a piece of my own, describing how the diplomatic situation for France had deteriorated further. Without Austria's support, France needed all its veteran troops, including those stationed in Rome guarding the Papacy. Italy was its only remaining potential ally and ministers had already met to discuss terms. The Italian army was not strong and without access through Austria, would take weeks to reach the front, but France wanted to show it had some international support. Yet Italy's price was too high. They wanted a guarantee that the French would not return to Rome, so that they could seize the city as their capital. This was completely unacceptable to the Pope, who made sure the clergy in France passed on his views. One French bishop fulminated that he would "rather see Prussians in Paris than Italian soldiers in Rome." The emperor could not afford to have the church turn against him and so talk of an Italian alliance was abandoned. France would have to go to war alone.

That evening Chalmers threw his farewell party. He was due to leave with other French correspondents on a train for the front at nine the next morning. Hopes that he might get too drunk to reach the station in time were dashed when we noticed him drinking only soda water. The tedium of staying sober while the rest of us sank into our cups, made him even more scathing than usual. I remember him turning to me as we discussed the Italian issue and enquiring, "Surely you did not cover this in the *Daily News*? I would have thought it far too complex for your readers to understand."

I silently fumed, wondering if I was the only person at that table likely to be sacked for his good fortune. As the evening wore on, I found my mind straying back to the far more pleasurable night before. A bottle of fine port was being passed around the table when something that Justine had said began to nag in my mind. I had not heard before, or since for that matter, of that fellow Planchet she quoted, but the idea of using your enemies' tactics against them was intriguing. Who were my enemies? Chalmers, obviously, as I had to succeed against him. But also the French government, who were stopping me from following him to the front. The seed of an idea began to grow in my mind. Could I do it?

Dare I do it? I joined the others in raising a toast to our host. His smug, self-satisfied sneer in my direction decided things. I had nothing to lose.

I made an excuse to leave the table and was back just half an hour later. I doubt I was missed – most would have thought I was using the jakes. My plan was underway and I could not stop it now even if I wanted to. We turned in around midnight and I lay in bed wondering what the morrow might bring. As things turned out, my scheme was to take effect much faster than I anticipated.

I was awoken by the sharp knock on a door and a demand to open up. "It is the police, monsieur, let us in."

It took me several panicked seconds to realise that it was not my portal being assaulted. Then I heard Chalmers calling out, "What the devil…? It is the middle of the night! How dare you bang on my door. Do you know who I am?" There was the rattle of a key in the lock as a porter must have let the officers in and then more yells of indignation. "This is intolerable…get your hands off me!" The police officer said something I did not catch, but the man from *The Times* was in strident form. "Arrest, you say? We will see what the British ambassador has to say about that. Hang on, at least wait for me to get dressed." But they did not wait. I opened my door a few inches just in time to see him being marched off down the corridor still in his night shirt. He was protesting his innocence and insisting he had to be at the railway station that morning.

I had expected the police to be waiting for him at the train, rather than interrupting his sleep. My aim was to delay his departure for at least a few days. Then, with luck, after some convincing French victories, we would all be able to go to the front together. I doubted Chalmers would be able to explain away the evidence against him in time for the ten o'clock departure. His truthful claim that he knew nothing about the intercepted telegram would be hard to believe. I had filled in the telegraph form in his name, paid over a hundred francs in cash to send it and addressed it to his employer. It gave all the details I had on the Mitrailleuse, but from what Duval had told me, I was confident it would not reach its intended recipient. The ruse was another hefty expense that I doubted my uncle would approve of, yet to me it was money well spent. Then, as I glanced at the door to Chalmers' room, I realised that it could be of even greater value yet.

The police had not bothered to shut it behind them. It was a moment's work to light a candle and go inside. Nearly all of the journalist's clothes were already packed inside two leather trunks. The exceptions were a brown suit and white shirt carefully draped over the back of a chair, ready to put on. Tentatively, I slid my hand inside the jacket and felt for the breast pocket. As I had hoped, I found a bundle of papers. The first was a letter of credit similar to my own, which I put back. The other was a folded document with the lion and unicorn crest of the British government at the top: Chalmers' passport. Next to it was a press accreditation similar to my own, but when I opened it out, a yellow card fell to the floor. It carried the French imperial coat of arms with the eagle in the middle. Written on the card was Chalmers' name alongside a series of stamps and signatures to show that he was permitted to travel to the front and requiring the army to offer him assistance. I looked up and caught sight of myself in the washstand mirror. My teeth glinted in the candlelight as a new scheme came to mind.

Chapter 5

Pascal was nearly as furious as Chalmers had been as I knocked on his window at six that morning. I had already tried the door and got no response. As the curtain flew back, beyond his angry features, I clocked a pretty blonde looking sleepily up at me from underneath a sheet. If she was the new muse, I thought, I would not have wanted to be roused from her either.

"Monsieur, do you know what time it is?" he demanded. I idly wondered why people always ask that when it is patently obvious that you do.

"If you still want to be a war artist, you need to be packed and ready at the eastern station in two and a half hours," I told him.

"But I thought you were not permitted at the front?" he queried, rubbing his face.

"Ah, that is another thing. If anyone asks, my name is Chalmers, Edmund Chalmers, and we work for *The Times*."

We met up again two hours later in front of the Gare de l'Est. The station was another of Napoleon III's impressive new edifices. It was huge and the square outside was already teeming with people, mostly soldiers. Pascal was waiting by the doors with a thick portfolio case for drawing materials and another satchel, which he wore over his shoulder. I was glad he was travelling light. As my stiff leather suitcase bashed into my leg, I was already regretting not bringing something softer. There had been no time to shop for supplies. Since waking my artist, I had enjoyed a brief but very fond farewell with Justine before collecting some cash on my letter of credit. My main fear now was that we would not get away at all. If the authorities had arrested Chalmers, would they have bothered to tell those at the station not to expect him? I was gambling on the fact that they would be far too busy pressing him for an explanation to bother.

As soon as we entered the station, I saw that the odds were in my favour. The place was a teeming cauldron of chaos. Lines of soldiers criss-crossed the concourse, while others stood in crowds around great piles of packs and other kit, blocking the routes to platforms. Civilians were shouting and pushing their way through any gaps they could find to get on and off the trains. On the far side of this hubbub, I spotted a group of men I recognised from ministerial briefings – journalists from the French papers. They were standing beside the first-class carriage of a train, and as I watched, two climbed aboard. I gestured to Pascal and led the way over, pressing between a group of troops who reeked of stale sweat and cheap wine. A harassed army officer was standing near the carriage with a clipboard. He noticed our approach but before he could enquire as to our business, a portly correspondent tugged on his sleeve. The man was insisting that his two steamer trunks be loaded into the luggage car. As the soldier tried to explain that there was no luggage car, the correspondent's resulting indignation provided the perfect distraction for us to climb onto the train unchallenged. It was ridiculously easy and I realised that any of the British correspondents could have done the same. But we were not out of the woods yet. Going down the corridor we passed the compartments containing the French pressmen. Some of them might have known Chalmers and I did not want any awkward questions. We found an empty part of the carriage at the end and slipped gratefully inside. Not that it stayed empty for long.

The door on the platform side swung open and an army major stepped up into the compartment. Instead of demanding to see our papers, he turned and yelled at a sergeant trying to control a column of men marching past. "If they have to vomit, make them do it on the tracks!" He turned to us and shrugged, "Apologies, gentlemen, my men are pigs. I can only hope that they fight as well as they drink."

As he settled into a seat, apparently content that his duties were done, we watched his command stagger past. Several were barely conscious and were being half dragged along by their comrades. Others were still in high spirits, singing at volume despite the heavy packs and rifles they were all carrying. Their uniforms were almost the exact reverse of the ones I was used to seeing in London. Instead of red jackets and dark trousers, most French soldiers wore loose-fitting blue tunics and their trousers were red. The ensemble was topped off with a blue cloth cap. However, the next soldiers to join us wore no uniform at all.

Three young men scrambled into the compartment and settled into the remaining seats. They were well spoken, like boys from a good school, talking excitedly among themselves about how jealous their friends would be. Two of them had what I now recognised as Chassepot rifles, while the third carried a double-barrelled shotgun and wore a battered kepi hat. That was the only piece of uniform amongst the lot of them. While it had a regimental number on the front, the hat looked like it had last seen service long before the boys had been born, for they were barely twenty. They ignored Pascal and me but now one of them noticed the major sitting beside us and saluted awkwardly as he sat down.

"Who the hell are you?" demanded the major.

"We are from the fourteenth detachment of the Paris Mobile Guard," replied one, puffing his chest out with pride.

"Then you should be reporting to your depot for uniforms, equipment and orders," the officer barked. "The army only has supplies for properly trained soldiers at the front."

"Our depot has no supplies or uniforms," said the first lad.

"Or orders," added the one with the shotgun. "No one knows what we should be doing."

"The war will be over long before we could take part," continued the first boy. "So we have taken the depot rifles," he held up his gun, "and we are going to the front by ourselves."

The major sneered in contempt. "So you have had a couple of weekends' drilling in the park and now you think you are fit to join the finest army in the world?" He might have said more, but he was interrupted by the sound of retching from just outside the compartment. A soldier from the finest army in the world was parting company with the contents of his stomach. The major shrugged in resignation. "If you want to peel the uniform off a bloodied corpse and take their equipment, be my guest."

That thought dampened the boys' enthusiasm for a minute or two. We sat in silence for a while and then one of them asked if we too were with the Mobile Guard reserve force. I explained that I was an English journalist with permission to travel, only to have the little squirt with the shotgun give me a lecture about perfidious Albion. He said we had no right to insist that France could not attack Prussia by invading Belgium. He also insisted that everyone knew that Britain wanted Prussia to win. I was saved from arguing by the screech of a steam whistle and with a brutal jolt, the train started to move. We lapsed back into silence. Pascal opened his folder and began a sketch of the boys opposite. In pencil they looked even younger, but I could not fault the likeness.

"Send it to your parents," the major growled when Pascal handed the drawing to its subjects. "That way they will have something to remember you by when you end up on some Prussian bayonet." The man was clearly in a foul mood, which was not helped by the heat of the day. We had all the windows wide open and while the train was moving there was a breeze, which at least made things tolerable.

Unfortunately, we had been travelling less than an hour when the locomotive rattled to a halt. We were headed for the army headquarters at the large fortress town of Metz, a hundred and seventy miles away. I had been hoping that we would arrive by nightfall, but as we were still stuck at midday, that seemed unlikely. By then the carriage was baking like an oven in the full sun. At first no one knew why we had stopped or when we might restart. Eventually, a sergeant came down the train to report that the driver could see another train blocking the track at the next station.

"Why couldn't he just fucking accept the man's apology?" fumed the major. The sergeant looked puzzled, but I guessed the officer's mind was elsewhere and he was referring to his emperor and the concession made by the Prussian king. "All right," the major continued, "let the men off the train to sit in the shade, but don't let any of them wander away."

We all climbed down to stretch out in the cooler shadows. This was the main rail line to the east, but nothing moved on it in either direction for an hour. Then at last the train whistle blew and we could see another train coming west towards us. The soldiers gave a sarcastic cheer as we all climbed back on board. Then we were moving once again.

We stopped twice more that afternoon as we slowly progressed to the frontier. Most sidings already had trains waiting in them. I do not know if they were headed east or west, but the rail network was clearly jammed up. By late afternoon our carriage resembled the interior of a Turkish bathhouse. We had all stripped down to our shirtsleeves, but our clothes were still dripping with sweat. One of the boys sitting opposite had even fainted in the heat, his friends holding his head out of the window to help him recover.

Eventually, we pulled into a siding near a place called Chalon, still around ninety miles short of Metz. The town looked pleasant enough from a distance, but of far more interest just then was the broad river that ran through it. I have never seen soldiers leave a train so fast. The wheels were still moving when the first of them jumped to the trackside and then the whole regiment was running down the embankment towards the cooling water. Those of us in first class could not complain, for we were soon following in their wake. Pascal and I both swam across what turned out to be the River Marne. It was bliss to be cool again. Even the portly French correspondent I had seen earlier had made it down to the bank. He must have got his luggage aboard in the end, for he was clearly travelling in style. He held a silver champagne bucket and, reluctant to plunge in, was using it to tip water over his head.

Soon enough we were hunting around the bank for our discarded shoes and shirts. Then I remembered that I had left all my money and my watch in my jacket on the train. With our possessions retrieved, we made our way into town to find a bed and meal for the night. We were back in the carriage at dawn. The regiment had slept in the field beside the train, so all was ready when the locomotive returned, having been resupplied with water and fuel. We set off in the cool of the morning and managed to travel another fifty miles that day. Twice we passed a small pile of dead horses beside the tracks. Cavalry regiments had been travelling by train too and we guessed that their mounts had died of heatstroke on the way.

After a few more hours we reached a place called Verdun, still thirty miles short of Metz. It was the last large town before our destination and the station and nearby tracks were full of trains. None of them were moving and lines of men had spilled out to sit in the shade. As we once more disembarked, I noticed a column of wagons heading east on a nearby road. I caught Pascal's eye; it was time to change our mode of transport.

A horse-drawn wagon is not normally quicker than a locomotive, but I was sure we would reach Metz faster than the major. The problem with the trains, we gathered from the waggoneer, was that the army had sent huge amounts of supplies down the lines, but no one to unload them. Sidings were blocked up with trains full of Chassepot ammunition or artillery shells, which left less track to get men to the front. The army was now sending companies of men down the line to sort out the problem. We passed one group pushing wooden crates out of a dozen freight carriages, none too gently. I had to hope that they were not artillery shells, or they could have blown themselves to kingdom come.

We came across more signs of confusion as we got closer to Metz the next day. At each major junction there would be a cluster of new handwritten signs nailed to posts, such as '23rd Regiment Depot at Gravelotte', or '15th Artillery Regiment at Augny'. The roads were getting busier too and gun teams would force us to pull to one side of the road as they clattered past. Soldiers in columns or just individuals were streaming in all directions, often asking us if we had seen any signs for their unit. I am sure that I saw depot signs for the 23rd regiment directing soldiers to two different places and wondered how long it would take for one to learn of the other's existence.

Most of the large hotels in Metz were already full, but we managed to find rooms at a lodging house run by some pinch-faced harridan. All of her other guests were in uniform and she glared suspiciously at me in my civilian clothes. Only by offering to pay what I was sure was an extortionate rate, were we able to secure accommodation at all. Pascal had offered to draw her portrait to win her round, but I thought it would take more than his prodigious artistic talent to remove the bitter expression from her features. We had barely been there three hours when we discovered just how mean she could be.

I was enjoying a doze on my bed to escape the heat of the afternoon, when I heard the familiar harsh rap on the door, followed by the demand of a police officer to open up. In my slumber, I thought it was a memory of Paris and was not fully awake until I heard the sharp voice of our host. "I knew it. He will have slipped outside to spy on our army. He said he was English, but his accent sounded German to me."

"I am still here," I called out grumpily as I got up. "I am English and I have a passport to prove it." I let the officer in and showed him my papers. His brow furrowed as he looked at the various ministry stamps and signatures on my press accreditation and the all-important yellow card. I doubt he recognised more than half of them.

"Prussian spies will have fancy papers too," sniped my landlady as he carried out his inspection. "You should take him to the cells." She turned to me and added, "Don't bother asking for a refund on the room. Even if you are English, you are just as bad as King Willie's men. You all want France to lose the war."

"We will have to telegraph Paris for confirmation," concluded the policeman wearily. "But it will take some time as the army has priority on the line."

That was the last thing I needed, for he would swiftly discover that the genuine Chalmers was still in the capital. I had my real passport tucked away in the lining of my coat if my deception was revealed, but by then their suspicions would be heightened. "But surely you can confirm that a train containing journalists from Paris passed through Verdun yesterday? It might even be here by now."

The policeman rubbed his chin doubtfully. "Which French journalists would vouch for you, monsieur?"

I doubted that any of them knew me beyond a vaguely familiar face at a ministry briefing and certainly none could vouch I was Chalmers. "I did not sit with the correspondents…" I admitted.

"There you are!" interrupted the landlady triumphantly. "I told you, he is a Prussian spy. He came here straight from Berlin."

"I came from Paris," I countered irritably. "And if you speak to any of the journalists on that train, they will tell you that we stopped at Chalon. It was so hot that we all went to swim in the river. Oh and one of the correspondents was dousing himself using a silver champagne bucket." The policeman looked impressed with this detail and so I went on, "The train must be getting in soon. Its occupants will confirm my story and will vouch that I am an accredited correspondent. They will all have those same yellow ministry cards." I paused and then added conspiratorially, "It will save you bothering Paris and possibly being reprimanded for detaining me."

I had hoped he might leave me in my room while he made his enquiries, but my host was insistent that I would be on the run the moment he left. Reluctantly, the policeman agreed to take me into custody and so I was to spend my next night in the cells. I could not really complain, for I was to learn that there was a paranoia in the city about Prussian spies. A dozen others had also been arrested and two sentenced to be shot. God knows if any were actually guilty of the charge, but I think my policeman was convinced of my innocence. Pascal was rounded up too and we were given an office to sleep in rather than a cell. I suspect that the supper served was better than that we would have received in the lodging house.

The other correspondents must have arrived by the following morning, for our policeman released us just in time for lunch. He had checked our story but warned us that any foreigners in the town were being treated with suspicion. He was not wrong; over the next few days we witnessed two more correspondents being arrested.

Even though we had passes to join the army, we were repeatedly warned not to attempt to publish anything that could be of use to the enemy. We were also instructed not to go near military camps without permission, but as the whole of Metz was now a military camp this proved impossible. There were large barracks for those manning the great walls all around the city and beyond them, further outer fortresses. On a simple walk down the street one would overhear dozens of soldiers talking about their situation, and most were complaining. Often regiments were short of several companies, who had not yet arrived. Others were waiting for items of uniform or other equipment. There were no ambulances and draught horses were in short supply, as were wagons to move equipment up to the front. Artillery regiments had no idea where their ammunition stockpiles were, while cavalry searched for fodder for their animals.

Much of this missing material had just been left around the railway stations and armouries. Regiments of men had now been detailed to unload the trains so that they did not clog up platforms and sidings, though this effort completely overwhelmed the commissary staff who had made it to Metz. I spoke to one who was close to despair. Some of his men were still to arrive, while others were desperately searching sidings for urgently needed equipment. Meanwhile, every hour, hundreds more boxes were unloaded and piled up, unopened, in any space the soldiers could find.

To avoid suspicion, I let Pascal do most of the talking as we moved about. We walked around the city walls and observed a sea of tents covering the ground beyond. There were parks full of artillery and lines of cavalry as well as many regiments of infantry, including the famed Imperial Guard. We also found some of the more extravagantly dressed troops from North Africa such as the Zouaves with their baggy pantaloons. Talking to the other correspondents, some of whom had better sources than I, the view was that the French had some two hundred thousand men gathered near the frontier. The majority of these were around Metz under the local command of a Marshal Bazaine, but a sizeable portion were further south, with a marshal of Irish heritage called MacMahon.

While the army would never let us print it, most journalists privately concurred that the mobilisation had been chaotic. Many reservists were still to re-join their regiments and apart from the three we had met on the train, there was no sign of the Mobile Guard. According to the major we had travelled with, this was probably a good thing. While the reservists might be out of shape and many had never even fired the new Chassepot, they had all spent years marching under their colours and may well have fought in the Italian campaigns. On the other hand, the Mobile Guard were effectively untrained, with no sense of military discipline and, according to the major, were only likely to get in the way of proper soldiers.

Yet for all its faults, in just two weeks the French had managed to mobilise a huge number of men and get them and a vast amount of equipment up to the frontier. While many soldiers were frustrated that they could not find everything that they wanted, there was also a sense of pride in their achievements so far. The days when soldiers marched to war were long gone. Now it was about the trains and the speed with which they could get men and material to the theatre of operations. All were confident that the Prussians could not have done as well. They had further to travel, across various principalities, and they would have to guard their whole border region, unsure where the French would attack. I was repeatedly assured that over the next few days the crates would all be opened, order restored, and a hole punched through the Prussian defences.

The first indication of this imminent attack came on the twenty-eighth of July, when the emperor arrived in Metz to take overall command. All correspondents were invited the following day to witness him reviewing some of the troops. Napoleon III rode just a short distance to a city square to inspect some immaculately arrayed guards, cavalry and artillery. He was followed by his fourteen-year-old son, known as the prince imperial, who rode a large pony. They stood to take the salute as soldiers paraded their colours before them.

The thing that struck immediately about the emperor was that he did not look well. Instead of a vibrant, energetic leader, he was grey and listless. There had been rumours circulating in Paris when I had arrived that he was suffering from gallstones, although the court insisted it was simply rheumatism. Whatever the cause, it was clearly painful for him to be on a horse, and he dismounted as soon as he decently could. I noticed that a carriage was waiting for the return journey. As his soldiers stood patiently before him, he mounted a dais with the aid of a cane that had been handed to him and made a short speech. The front ranks might have heard it, but I will wager that those at the back did not and neither did we standing to one side. His voice was weak and soft. We could barely detect him speaking at all.

As he retired to his carriage the war minister came over to reiterate what the emperor had said, which was that "wherever the French army marches in Prussia, we will come across the glorious tracks of our fathers. We shall prove worthy of them, for on our success hangs the fate of liberty and civilisation." He was clearly keen to get the quote into the papers as he repeated it twice to be sure we noted it down. When asked about the emperor's health, we were told he was simply tired after

47

a long train journey. Then, to distract from any further questioning along this line, he announced that the first offensive was about to begin and we should prepare to march with the army.

Chapter 6

The fortress town of Metz is only twenty miles from the frontier with the southern German states. As I had feared, Bismark had been at work among them, they had declared for Prussia. With Britain insisting on the protection of Belgian borders to the north and neutral and mountainous Switzerland to the south, the corridor through the southern states was the only route open to the French army to reach Prussian territory. It was roughly a hundred mile gap that both armies would have to fight for or defend. The area was known as the Vosges, it was not flat but a series of rolling hills and valleys, usually running east to west. An Italian correspondent, who may have been talking out of his hat, told me the land had formed that way when the Alps had pushed up from the south.

However it was formed, the route from Metz to the border along the Saint-Avold valley would have taken an averagely fit man one day to cover. It took the French army three. We had not acquired horses – there were none spare to be had – but nor did we need them. I have walked my dog on longer distances than those daily marches. At the end of each day, instead of camping near the side of the road, great divisional bivouacs were constructed some distance off. As a result the army was rarely ready to march again before nine the next morning. Some must have moved down parallel valleys and those of us on foot had to stay off the road, which was reserved for cannon and wagons carrying supplies. Artillery and carts rattled past us, but not with any sense of urgency. There was no sign of the emperor, or his generals and staff officers rushing the army along. It meandered through the countryside as though on a Sunday afternoon stroll. I had not been to war before, but I thought it odd. I would have expected the French to want to push over the border as quickly as possible and before the Prussians could build up any defences.

At the end of the second day we camped on a high escarpment called the Spicheren, which dominated the surrounding countryside. Fewer than three miles to the northeast, between some hills, we could see a cluster of buildings. We were told that it was a town called Saarbrücken in the German state of Baden. This was my first glimpse of German territory and knowing it would be attacked in the morning made this war suddenly seem very real.

We could see little detail through the heat haze of the day beyond a smudge of white walls. One of the other correspondents had brought with him a map of the area and I cursed myself for not thinking to do the same. Saarbrücken was shown as a small and insignificant place, with the Saar River running through the middle of it. We wondered what the map did not show.

The Prussians had to know that the French army was gathering at Metz – that information at least had been printed in various British and French newspapers. This valley was the obvious route into their territory from the city, so they would have dug earthworks and fortifications to protect it. The high ground would be lined with artillery and perhaps overlooking buildings and trenches packed with infantry. I wondered if some Teutonic eye was staring back at us right at that moment, resolute that not a single enemy would pass. The following day promised to be a bloody affair, for there were six French divisions, nearly a hundred thousand men, gathering in the valley below.

I did not sleep well, anxious at what the morrow would hold and my role within it. Forbes and several other correspondents had been soldiers before. The closest I had been to a battle was watching the changing of the guard at Buckingham Palace. The following morning it did indeed seem that I alone was worried. I overheard soldiers talking about teaching the Prussians a lesson and some of the other correspondents were discussing what they would buy in Berlin. Even then there was no great sense of urgency; wagons of supplies were still arriving to top up ammunition limbers and cooking pots.

Gradually, the ranks began to form up in the valley in front of the Spicheren, with sergeants carrying out inspections until all lines were straight and immaculate. The men stood to attention, waiting expectantly for something to happen. On cue a grand coach arrived, riding into the centre of the camp, escorted by Imperial Guard cavalry. Any remaining doubt as to its occupant was allayed by the presence of bewigged footman on the back box, who rushed to lower the steps as it came to a stop. To a roar of acclaim from his army that must have been heard in Saarbrücken, the emperor stepped down from his vehicle and gingerly climbed up into the saddle. Marshal Bazaine rode up beside him and together they trotted their horses into the middle of the jubilant throng. Despite the enthusiasm around them, they both had the demeanour of gaudily dressed undertakers. The emperor was wincing in pain, while his commander's features were set in a permanent scowl of disappointment. Only the prince imperial, following behind on his pony, grinned back and waved to acknowledge the cheers.

The marshal made the announcement, probably to ensure that as many as possible heard it: the emperor was personally to lead his army into German territory. I confess that I was impressed. Even his illustrious uncle rarely led his men from the front and that was before men fought with accurate rifles. I was grateful that the press contingent was not expected to follow his example. We stayed at the rear as, to the sound of bugles and orders, the whole army began to sweep down the valley before us like a huge blue-coated tide. At first they marched in densely packed columns, with their gold regimental eagle standards to the fore. I thought it was only a matter of time before explosive shells began to rain down in their midst.

As we got closer to Saarbrücken, we could see figures on the summit of the two hills that guarded the approach. Sunlight glinted off metal and I imagined them to be the muzzles of weapons pointed in our direction. Yet as I stared eagerly ahead, I could see no sign of other defences and compared to my expectations, the morning remained eerily quiet.

With a mile to go, the infantry re-formed into long loose lines of men. Then the front ranks broke into a jog and swept past on either side of their emperor and generals, yet still not a shot had been fired. I watched in astonishment and stared all around me for any sign that a trap was about to be sprung, but there was nothing.

The front ranks were fewer than five hundred yards away from the defended hilltops when the guns opened fire. Just two paltry cannon let fly at the men in blue, while a crackle of musketry marked where a score of infantry had also appeared to fire down at the approaching army.

51

They were met by a hail of lead in return. Every Frenchman must have had his finger around the trigger, desperate to christen his Chassepot against a Prussian. The hilltop defence barely lasted a minute before its occupants realised that the French were swarming around either side of them to cut off their retreat. Pascal and I had broken into a run too as we saw the enemy break. Racing around the first hill, we were just in time to see a skirmish over the river. It was my first sight of Prussian soldiers and there were far fewer than I had expected. Fifty of them were clustered behind the end of a bridge, a desperate rear-guard to buy time for comrades I could see running away in the distance.

Four French gun batteries were swiftly being set up in response. One was the Mitrailleuse and, like half the army, I looked curiously on to see how formidable this weapon would be. As the deadly handle started to turn, I confess to being awestruck. There was little doubt in my mind then that the French would soon be eating sauerkraut in Berlin. The sound could best be described as similar to an extremely loud police rattle – there was a mechanical evenness about it. As the barrels were discharged they emitted a large plume of smoke in front of the muzzle. I doubt the gunners could see much at all once they had opened fire, but from our vantage point to the side we could watch its gruesome effect. Half a dozen men were flung back like rag dolls, one was nearly torn in half. Others dropped to the ground for cover or cowered behind the walls on the bridge. Even these offered limited shelter, for the huge bullets were knocking great chips of stone out of the parapets. It was only a matter of time before they were whittled away entirely. It was obvious that nothing could survive for long by the river under that fire.

As soon as the deadly rattle paused, the Prussians were up and running, ignoring the Chassepot bullets that still buzzed about them, fatally for some, as they fled. Two more Prussian cannon opened fire from the railway station on the far side of town to cover the retreat. The French cannon switched their aim and soon shells were whistling towards the train platforms, while others fired at real or imagined Prussians in the town itself. As they struck home, we glimpsed terrified occupants scrambling over the fallen masonry to get away.

The emperor had not fallen too far behind his men. I turned as a shout went up that we correspondents were to gather around the prince imperial. The French journalists rushed over eagerly, notebooks in hand. I could see enough from where I was, so stayed put. The lad was standing by one of the batteries, the firing lanyard of a gun in his hand. To the encouragement of those about him, he tugged the cord and the cannon fired a shell into the centre of Saarbrücken. The boy looked delighted as the resulting explosion demolished the corner of a house. Even the emperor momentarily forgot his pain to muster a proud smile, while other staff officers and French journalists applauded enthusiastically. It was as though he had just cut a ribbon to open some civic building. No one gave a thought to the poor sod who had just had his home demolished. One of the emperor's aides shouted that the prince had been 'bloodied in battle'. He beamed at the French journalists expectantly – clearly, he was hopeful they would use the quote.

By then I was far more interested in the retreating Prussians. Their last-ditch defence at the railway station was being overwhelmed and the survivors could be seen running for their lives down the valley beyond. Orders to cease fire were shouted. The battle had lasted barely five minutes. The invasion of the German states had begun.

I was struggling to understand what I had just witnessed. There had been no more than a single battalion of Prussians in Saarbrücken, a few hundred men, supported by a battery of just six guns. Utterly outnumbered, they had been foolhardy to put up any resistance at all, for the outcome was never in doubt. It was incredible that this was all the Prussians could muster. This valley was the obvious route into their territory and yet they had left the door wide open. Several of the French correspondents took this as proof that the Prussian mobilisation was in chaos. "Their army will be strung out on every road and railway track between here and Berlin," one predicted. "Now is the time to drive on into the heartland of their territory before they can recover."

This made logical sense to me. I felt sure that the original Napoleon would have driven his army on to maintain the momentum and element of surprise, but curiously, his nephew did nothing of the sort. The emperor lingered a while to accept a few souvenirs of the victory, then he and his son alighted back into their carriage and headed off in the direction of Metz. I planned to stay where we were, for it was surely only a matter of time before he would return to lead us further east.

While Pascal contented himself with drawing what he could remember of Saarbrücken under fire, I strolled over the river to witness the aftermath of the battle. On what was left of the stone bridge I met a handful of Prussian prisoners being driven the other way. Now familiar with the blue tunics and red trousers of the French, these forlorn figures looked alien in their black uniforms. Particularly their polished black helmets with steel spike protruding from the top. They were all young men, and they stared about them, still in a state of shock at the onslaught they had just experienced. Perhaps they also felt grateful for their relative good fortune as they walked past a score of their dead and wounded comrades on the far bank.

I had seen dead bodies before, of course, mostly from old age or illness and one poor fellow who had been trampled by a horse. But even that grisly memory left me unprepared for what I found. They were the first battle casualties I had ever seen, and the sight horrified me – not that it got any easier in the months and years ahead. The scale of the men's injuries was appalling, far worse than I had anticipated. The big bullets from the Mitrailleuse had torn through bodies with such force that they had partially eviscerated them. I would venture that no man could be hit in the torso and survive, indeed none of the injured looked likely to live. The high velocity slugs from the Chassepot at relatively close range were little better, leaving exit wounds big enough for a fist.

The wounded were gathered up together and laid out on stretchers. A French surgeon was doing his best to bandage them, but it was a hopeless task. Several dead lay nearby and as the French rifled their bodies for valuables, they came across small metal plates tied around each Prussian neck. One was pulled off for closer inspection and I managed to glance at it. Stamped into the thin, cheap metal was a series of letters and numbers. The Frenchman was about to put the curio in his pocket when one of the wounded called out. Gasping in pain, he explained that the tags were there to identify the dead. The fellow's leg had been shattered part way down his thigh. He was bleeding heavily and knew that his own death plate would soon be useful. The French soldier hurriedly retied his trophy back around the neck of its owner.

Just then, my attention was taken by several rifle shots coming from the railway station. I saw injured horses of the Prussian gun battery being despatched and some French gunners examining their enemy's weapons. I strolled over to see for myself. The short stubby affairs were made from steel, compared to the longer bronze barrels of the French. Then I noticed that the Prussian guns also had a breech-loading mechanism. I turned to a nearby artillery officer and gestured at it. "Will these not be able to fire more frequently than your muzzle-loading cannon?"

"Not really," he replied dismissively. "They will still need to be lined up between each shot for accuracy. Steel is more prone to flaws in casting for cannon than bronze, so they also have a tendency to blow up, killing their gunners." The fellow was evidently an expert in his field. As he spoke, he had been using callipers to precisely measure the diameter of the muzzle.

I turned my gaze up the valley; the retreating Prussians were now out of sight. There was no one in the valley beyond the railway station at all. "Should cavalry not be sent to pursue the Prussians?" I asked. "And to check what other forces may be down this valley?"

The officer gave a weary sigh, "You are English, monsieur, is that not so? Perhaps you should leave the management of the French army to the French."

He was right, of course; I had no military experience at all back then. Yet it seemed to me that even a village idiot would want to know where his enemies were and in what strength. Marshal Bazaine, however, showed no such interest and sent not a single scouting party down the valley. Instead, attention turned to building a new camp around the town. Tents sprang up all over the fields between the Spicheren and Saarbrücken and French gun batteries had soon been pulled up on to high ground, replacing the Prussian guns that had fired on our advance.

After my encounter with the artilleryman, I doubted that any French officer would want to hear my opinions, but I was proved wrong when I was invited to the newly erected tent of a Colonel Delafosse. "Ah,

Monsieur Chalmers," he began. He stood to greet me and I nearly looked back over my shoulder before I remembered that Chalmers was me. "On behalf of the war ministry, welcome. I trust you have had every opportunity to witness our glorious victory. Perhaps I can get you a glass of cognac?"

When senior army officers start plying you with drink, you know something is afoot, but I accepted the glass and settled in the chair he indicated. "Your army has been most hospitable," I confirmed. "But I am curious why at least cavalry is not pursuing the Prussians down the valley."

"An excellent question," he beamed at me. "I will ask the marshal for you when I see him. But in the meantime, I wondered if you have given any thought to the despatch you will send to your *Times* newspaper in London?"

"Well, I have not drafted anything yet..." I began, before he interrupted.

"Then I am sure I can be of assistance." The colonel picked up a piece of paper from the table and handed it to me. "Perhaps this could be a starting point. I could arrange to have it telegraphed to your paper immediately. Of course, if you were to make er…changes, then I regret things could take a little longer. The French papers have already agreed to use this suggested wording and the news will be in Paris tomorrow."

I scanned the paper. In many respects it was accurate. The emperor had led his forces, the French had won a victory. Saarbrücken had been captured and the prince imperial had taken part in the battle. Then there was some Gallic guff about French soldiers crying with pride at the resoluteness of the little prince under fire. That was tosh, of course, but there was one far more important glaring inaccuracy. "'A Prussian force of three divisions defeated'," I ventured. "A remarkable achievement given that I have seen hardly any French wounded or dead."

"No one in Paris will complain of low casualty numbers," the colonel replied before adding testily, "I trust we will continue to work together as the army advances towards Berlin. This is just the start of a long campaign that I am sure your readers will be interested to follow." The inference was clear: agree to the draft or I would be travelling no further with the French army.

"Don't worry, Colonel," I grinned at him. "I am happy to sign this draft as suitable for *The Times* and I trust you will send it as soon as possible." What, I wondered, would the editor make of it? First, he was getting reports that his correspondent was under arrest and in Paris. Then that same man was sending spurious reports from the French army. The colonel's main concern was what would be read in Paris and the ministry could control that. But London readers would also get accounts of the battle from Prussian sources. They would swiftly discover that they were quite different.

"I am so pleased we can work together," soothed the colonel. "There is rain forecast for this evening, so I will arrange a tent for you and your artist."

He was as good as his word. That night Pascal and I were comfortably under canvas as a summer storm raged over the battlefield. But if I thought the next day would be a hive of activity as the French finally started to capitalise on their victory, I was set for disappointment. The emperor remained in Metz and from there a steady stream of supply wagons arrived, together with a trickle of reservists re-joining their regiments. It was soon a hot and humid day, the only people moving quickly were couriers galloping between Bazaine's headquarters and the emperor. I must have seen a dozen of them during the day, but the rest and relaxation of the French army was not disturbed.

Most of the French correspondents had returned to Metz to be close to the emperor, but we decided to look around Saarbrücken. Locals clearing away the wreckage of their homes threw hostile glares at passing French soldiers. I was surprised to see that most properties were undamaged. As we crossed the bridge we found several rows of freshly dug graves and saw that a nearby house was being used as a hospital for the wounded of both armies. A large hotel was still open for business and as we were set for at least another night in the area, I booked us two rooms. As I signed the register, I saw a familiar name further up the page. Archibald Forbes had been there just two nights before, which meant he must have been in the town when the French attacked.

A French shell had destroyed the hotel kitchen, but the manager assured us that dinner would be provided. Once he knew I was English, he could not do enough. Everyone knew, he announced, that the British were sympathetic to the Prussian people. It was through the hotel manager that I discovered the St Johann's telegraph. He had waited until Pascal had gone up to his room before he whispered the news. St Johann was a suburb of the town on its eastern side. It had consequently escaped bombardment and, incredibly, the French had not thought to cut the telegraph cable. It was still intact and was regularly sending news of the French army to Baden.

I thanked the fellow and then hurried through the streets, following his directions, hardly able to believe my luck. Sure enough, a wire ran from the building and once I had shown my British passport the telegraphist was keen to help me sent a message. I wrote an accurate account of the attack on the town, explaining that I had witnessed the battle myself, and sent it on to the *Daily News*. The operator even arranged for me to send on some of Pascal's drawings to London, via Baden, too.

A more comfortable night on a proper bed ensued. Then as we enjoyed our mid-morning coffee in the town square, I had another surprise. "I was not expecting to see you here," came a familiar voice. "You have done far better than I expected."

I looked up and was amazed to see that Forbes had returned. My first impulse was to dart a glance east, half expecting hordes of vengeful Prussian troops to appear at the end of the street. Instead, all was quiet. At the next table sat several French officers peaceably drinking wine while three soldiers emerged from a bakery, their arms laden with fresh bread. "What…how are you here?" I stammered.

Forbes grinned at my confusion. Then, nodding at the surrounding soldiery, suggested that we go for a walk to talk in private. "Do you know why the French have not advanced?" he asked me. "The Prussians were expecting them to. I have been staying in a place called Dudweiler just three and a half miles up the valley. We have not seen any French forces, which is just as well as it only has a few companies for defence.

The first sizeable garrison is twelve miles back and they would not have stopped a whole army."

"I have no idea," I told him. "They just seemed to want to make a nominal invasion for the papers in Paris, but then they got cold feet. It is such a wasted opportunity. From the sound of things, they could be halfway to Berlin by now."

"I don't know about that," laughed Forbes. He lowered his voice and added, "The Prussians have four hundred thousand men near the border."

I must have gaped in astonishment. "But that is double the size of the French army." Then I remembered the trains from Paris and shook my head. "You must have that wrong. Even if they did have that number, they would never have all the supplies and ammunition they need. They have further to travel; it would take weeks for an army that size to sort itself out."

"Not a bit of it," my colleague retorted. "You must understand that the Prussians have been preparing for this war for years. They have built three extra train lines to the region to carry men and supplies. They also learned a lesson from the war with Austria and so sent the commissary troops down first to manage the stores as they arrived. Their mobilisation plan was so detailed that every regiment knew in advance which train they would take and their route to the front. I came with them – I have seen the timetables."

"So why did they not defend Saarbrücken?" I challenged.

"Because they did not want to get drawn into a battle before they were ready," Forbes replied evenly. He pulled out his pipe and began to pack it with tobacco. "Right now there are two Prussian armies coming together to the north of here that total a hundred and eighty thousand. To the south is another army of a hundred and twenty-five thousand with more units scattered in between."

I wanted to disbelieve him. The numbers sounded absurd given the distances involved. Yet there was a calm confidence to my colleague's assertions. Then I thought back to Bismarck's careful planning with the Spanish, the Russians and southern German states. He would not have done all that without ensuring that the army was ready too. I had a sudden memory of that queue of young reservists patiently waiting outside the Prussian embassy in London. That had been weeks ago… Suddenly, I knew it was true. In a moment my understanding of the whole war had been turned on its head. I shook my head in amazement. "When I saw the Mitrailleuse at work, I thought we would be chasing your boys all the way to Berlin. Suddenly that city seems a lot further away."

"It works then, the Mitrailleuse?" asked Forbes. "I have heard people say that it is only good for an abattoir, not a battlefield."

"It can turn a battlefield *into* an abattoir," I warned him. "Take my advice and keep well away from the damn things and anyone with a Chassepot rifle. The French have around a hundred thousand men here and in Metz, perhaps a few more now with reinforcements. There are another hundred thousand to the south around Strasbourg, but the French weapons may well even up the score." I shuddered at the memory of the bodies torn apart at the bridge and imagined such slaughter on the scale of a proper battle.

Forbes lit his pipe and puffed contentedly. "You know, between us, we probably know more about the disposition of both armies than either of the commanders." He gave me a warning glare through the smoke before adding, "Not that we can tell them, unless we want to risk being shot as spies." We strolled in silence for a few yards, each taking in what the other had said, before he turned to me again. "I called at the telegraph office. I gather you have already sent an article to Frank."

"Yes, and I have also sent a fictitious one to *The Times* as I am masquerading as their correspondent here."

He chuckled. "If you have got one over that fool Chalmers, we will make a proper war correspondent of you yet."

"I don't know about that. I mean what the hell am I supposed to do now? The French have the best weapons, but the Prussians the greater numbers."

Forbes gave the matter some serious thought. "Frank will expect you to stay with the French army. Find a commander that looks like he knows what he is doing," he advised, "and stick to him like glue."

Chapter 7

The advice Forbes gave me turned out to be easier to follow than I first thought it would be. When I strolled back into the French camp, I found that most of the tents were being struck down, including Marshal Bazaine's. Already columns of men were heading into the hills to our north. I found Colonel Delafosse, already loading his possessions into a cart, and asked him what was happening.

"Monsieur Chalmers, there is no need to worry. You can report to your readers that all is under control."

"So why is the army leaving, where is it going?" I pressed.

Seeing that I was not going to be fobbed off with platitudes, Delafosse paused in his packing to unroll a map. A broad line had been drawn on it from the southern tip of Belgium through Saarbrücken and then along the border as far south as Strasbourg. "We have had reports of Prussian forces gathering to the north," he admitted. "It is heavily wooded land. We cannot be sure of numbers or where they are going. It is unthinkable that French territory could be sullied by an invader and so the emperor has re-deployed his army along this line. Marshal Bazaine will array his forces to the north of here, while General Frossard will defend Saarbrücken. To the south, Marshal MacMahon's forces will hold the line. Once the Prussians are beaten, we will continue our advance. Now, if you will excuse me, I must prepare to return to Metz."

I said nothing of my own recent revelations and watched as the few remaining Paris correspondents prepared to follow the marshal. It struck me that the Prussians were being cunning. Trees would reduce visibility and negate much of the range advantage of the Chassepot. You cannot shoot what you cannot see and the Prussian superiority in numbers would be more telling. I had no wish to blunder around blindly in woods surrounded by trigger-happy or nervous soldiers. No, I would stay where I was, another night in the hotel beckoned. If the Prussians came this way, they would not shell their own town and civilians, I reasoned. I could just allow myself to be captured. My British passport and occupation would see me well treated and I could vouch for Pascal. But then, the following morning, I realised that I had found the officer demonstrating just the type of judgement I was looking for.

General Frossard had watched the rest of the army abandon him to the north. The capture of Saarbrücken had been trumpeted to Paris as a great achievement. For political reasons France wanted to retain this tiny foothold of enemy territory. Yet the town was surrounded by hills that would make it damn difficult to defend. Even a military novice like me could see that if the Prussians got artillery onto the higher ground, they could shell French positions with impunity. Yet just three miles southwest was the huge natural fortress of the Spicheren ridge. It overlooked the land for twenty miles around and was nigh on impregnable. Frossard was an engineer as well as an army officer. To him the advantages of the stronger position were obvious. The morning after his marshal disappeared into the trees, he moved his twenty thousand men back to the Spicheren.

I happily went with him. A man who puts the lives of his men and those of the civilians who accompanied him above the foolish needs of politicians in Paris was just the fellow for me. Not only that, the Prussians would surely know of the Spicheren and so it was the last place that they would attack.

It was a sunny morning as we moved back down the valley. A garrison was left to block the road beside the ridge and more troops guarded a junction covering a road from the northeast as well as the town of Forbach to the west, where supplies were now being stockpiled for the next advance. Frossard certainly knew his business.

Pascal and I joined the rest of the army as it climbed up the shallower slope on the western side. "What do you think will happen?" asked my companion as we stood again atop the Spicheren, staring back east towards the border.

"The Prussians might retake Saarbrücken," I conceded, "but they would be bloody mad to try to attack here."

The face of the escarpment on the German side was over a hundred feet high. The sides were not quite vertical, but you would need both your hands and feet to attempt to climb. With just grass and the occasional patch of scrub to grab at for leverage, there was damn all cover. Even if they somehow made it to the top, the grass summit rose in several levels to the west, giving defenders more clear fields of fire before finally the ground fell away more gently towards a track behind the ridge.

"They will make their move through the forest to the north," I predicted. "They might push the French back there, but we will see how they fare in the open in front of a Mitrailleuse."

Seeing that weapon at work had made a powerful impression on me. Forbes might have been confident in his Prussians, but he had been too busy running for his life during the attack on Saarbrücken to see what damage it could do. The French were getting themselves organised and, while they might not make it to Berlin, back then, I still thought they would give a good account of themselves. My confidence was only slightly shaken when, that evening, we received news of an action fifty miles to the south. A Prussian incursion over the border had captured the French town of Wissembourg.

During the night we could just make out the light of fires on top of the hill overlooking Saarbrücken. Dozens of them had been lit to give the impression that a large French force was still there. In reality, it was just a token garrison, there to warn of any approach of the enemy. I was not surprised when, around nine o'clock the next morning, the single battery on that distant hilltop opened fire. Prussian commanders must have been under a political imperative from Berlin to recover German territory, in the same way that Marshal MacMahon to the south would now be getting orders from Paris to recover Wissembourg. From our high vantage point, we watched as a lone cavalryman galloped up the valley with a report for General Frossard. He did not bother to send a response. He must have anticipated a Prussian sortie and the advance post already had orders to fall back.

By ten o'clock we could see the distant retreat; a battery of horse artillery trotting down the side of the hill towards us, with a company of infantry and some cavalry following on behind. They were in no rush and had travelled over a mile towards us when we began to discern new figures at the far end of the valley. You could barely make out anything without a glass, but their presence was proven by distant gunfire. This was followed instantly by shells exploding amongst the men in blue tunics. We watched as the French battery hauled up to return fire. The artillery men swiftly went about their business, but their shells fell short. The next Prussian salvo killed two horses in one of the French gun teams. There were now only two left, and they might have been wounded. The cannon was abandoned as the rest of the force now hurried towards the valley alongside the base of the Spicheren.

"The Prussian guns have a longer range than the French ones," I concluded to Pascal.

"Yes, but I thought you said that they often blow up." He paused and then pointed, "Never mind that, look over there." He was gesturing down the far end of the valley where dark columns of soldiers were appearing.

"They won't attack," I predicted confidently. "It would be suicidal if they did."

For the next two hours it looked as though I was right. The French rear-guard joined those defending the valley next to the Spicheren, while the Prussians loitered at the Saarbrücken end. Perhaps, I thought, they were trying to work out if the hills were occupied, although the French would have been mad to abandon them. I was surprised that Frossard was not on the summit with us, for it gave a commanding view of miles around. He can't have expected the Prussians to attack either, for we heard he was still at Forbach in the telegraph office. He sent word that he wanted to stay close to the wires for any reports of attacks to the north.

Most of the French army had stood down and my thoughts were turning to lunch, when around noon a sentry shouted out that the Prussians were advancing towards us. We turned and stared, exclaiming in surprise as we realised it was true. However, there was no great concern. The reaction of many was mostly irritation that their meal would now inevitably be delayed.

There must have been some five thousand troops, with four batteries of artillery following on behind. I admit that I felt a thrill of excitement then. The capture of Saarbrücken had been a great anti-climax, especially after the fearful anticipation the night before. It had all been over in a few minutes and I almost felt cheated of the spectacle of a great conflict. But now at last I was to witness a proper battle and see first-hand what war was about. It felt like a professional baptism into my correspondent role. To top things off, I had the perfect vantage point and as far as I could see, the Prussians did not have the slightest hope of victory.

Halfway down the valley they broke formation and spread out in long loose lines with at least a yard or two between each man. The French commander on the Spicheren had his men hold their fire until he was sure that the Prussians were well within range. I heard him laughing as he discussed their enemy's rifle of choice with a group of soldiers. With its heavier bullet, twice the size of the Chassepots', its lower velocity and the fact that they were firing uphill, he thought its range was no more than two hundred and fifty to three hundred yards. "They will struggle to aim accurately even then," he scoffed, before reminding his men that the French rifle would be accurate at five times that distance. They debated whether any of the enemy would reach the Spicheren at all.

 Pascal and I stood at the edge of the escarpment to watch. The Prussians were no more than a mile away now. Their line was curving, with some clearly intending to go round the flank of the ridge, not that they would find much joy there. I could imagine the others staring up at the near vertical sides of the Spicheren in dismay. They must have been cursing the myopic blockhead that had sent them to attack it.

The French artillery batteries opened fire with a sudden ferocity. Explosive shells rained down on the approaching troops, although – unless some of the gunners had loaded solid shot by mistake – there were more than a few duds in their ammunition lockers. The acrid smell of gunpowder filled our nostrils as smoke from the weapons drifted across the hilltop. Then the dull booms were joined by a distinctive staccato rattle. A gunner near me was winding the handle of his Mitrailleuse like a lethal barrel organ, while his assistants called out the aim based on where the bullets struck. At first it was a near impossible endeavour, and the blocks of bullets were sprayed more in hope than anticipation. Yet as the enemy came closer, we could see where shells kicked up the dirt or men fell. The gunners could now hone in on their targets. Some Prussians ran to avoid tracks of bullets coming towards them, only to stumble into a new stream as the barrel was traversed. I watched one fellow march resolutely straight to his doom, perhaps with his eyes closed, only for the last of the twenty-five balls to kick up the turf just beyond his toe.

The infantry was joining in now, kneeling or lying on the ground to aim their Chassepots carefully down into the valley. The cracks of the rifles, rattle of the Mitrailleuse and the boom of artillery around us was deafening. Pascal leaned over to shout in my ear, "I wish I could include sound in my drawings." I could not help but laugh in exhilaration at the scene I was witnessing – I had never experienced anything like it. As a boy I had wanted to be a soldier like my grandfather, but he had been appalled by the idea. The old man had regaled me with enough stories of how he had narrowly escaped death to talk me out of it. Yet despite being at the very heart of a battle, on the top of the Spicheren I felt perfectly safe. Things must have been very different for the poor devils at its base.

Any Prussian with an ounce of common sense would have fled then. Yet these fellows were made of sterner stuff. They had been ordered to attack and so now they broke into a jogging run…towards us. Soon the French cannon could not depress their barrels low enough to hit them. A Mitrailleuse went right up to the edge, three infantrymen hanging on to each wheel as its gunner balanced precariously to fire right down the cliff. Yet if the Prussians thought they would get any relief, they were mistaken. The cliff was lined with infantrymen, pointing Chassepots down at their prey well within range. Pascal and I got back as we were now in their way. It was a good job we did, as minutes later the Prussian batteries opened fire. They had wedged themselves in the valley sides, perhaps to achieve the necessary elevation for their own barrels. It was almost impossible to hit the top edge of a cliff, and most of their shells whistled over our heads. Others exploded against the rock face, sending stone and metal fragments down on their own men trying to shelter under overhangs below.

The noise of battle grew even louder on our flanks now as the Prussians encountered well-prepared defensive positions on either side of the Spicheren. We looked down the northern side, but the treetops hid most of the action from our view. Then Pascal pointed excitedly. "Look, they are running!" he cried. Sure enough, we could see men wearing the distinctive spiked helmets fleeing back in the direction they had come. They had to run the same gauntlet in retreat as they had suffered in their advance. The Prussians safe in hollows against the base of the cliff decided to stay where they were. Perhaps they were waiting for nightfall to move back, or perhaps they knew their commanders better than I did.

That was easily the best battle I witnessed, with my eagle-eyed view and comfortable distance from the blood and gore. The men on the summit of the Spicheren had taken hardly any casualties at all, yet there had to be at least a thousand broken bodies in black uniforms over the valley. A few poor devils were wounded and writhing; some managed piteous cries, which carried up to us in that reflective silence that often follows action. Mercifully, they were in a language I did not understand, although the noise of pain was universal. While things were still fresh in my mind, I took out my notebook and started to write an account of the battle. It was an entirely predictable outcome and I praised Frossard for his foresight. Pascal was drawing the precariously balanced Mitrailleuse from memory – it was an image that would sell well in Paris.

Soldiers around us excitedly exchanged experiences of the battle as they relaxed and drank from their water bottles or gnawed on bread they had kept from breakfast. Cooking fires were rekindled for the delayed meal. Having complimented Pascal on an excellent drawing and finished my notes, I sat back in the sunshine. I was just reflecting that we might soon be back in Saarbrücken if Bazaine had managed to stop the other attacks to the north, when a call went up that the Prussians were coming back.

There was another groan from the hungry at the inconsideration of the Prussians attacking at mealtimes. I jumped up and ran to the edge, staring in disbelief at the sight that met me. Their first foray should have been enough to convince the Prussians that they should attack anywhere *except* around Spicheren. Surely the survivors of that first assault had provided ample reports of the obstacles they faced. Yet some dunderhead commander was refusing to accept that the great Prussian army could be beaten – and he was venturing tens of thousands more lives to prove it. Great dark blocks of men were now pouring into the opposite end of the valley.

Most of the French army were cheering them on, keen to treat them as they had their predecessors. I noticed the French commander looked more apprehensive. He was busily writing despatches to Frossard while riders waited beside him to carry them down to the telegraph office where the general still sat. Perhaps he had already reported his earlier victory and was now summoning reinforcements as a precaution. Yet whatever happened, it was surely a victory postponed rather than lost. For even in greater numbers, I saw no way that the Prussians could conquer the Spicheren.

The early stages of the next assault were much as they had been before, though we mostly kept back from the edge. The Prussians had brought more artillery this time, which they sited beyond the range of ours. While they could accurately fire shells into the rockface and the woods on either side, they still could not drop them down onto the summit itself. The range was much too far for a mortar. Instead, the French began again their bloody hail of shot. I estimated that another thousand men in spiked helmets fell in the approach to our guns and the awful rattle of the Mitrailleuse. The ground in front of the Spicheren was carpeted with their dead, but still they came on. Survivors of the first wave came out of their rock shelters to re-join their comrades and together they launched a fierce assault up a corner of the Spicheren known as the Rotherburg Ridge.

It was a bloody and uneven struggle, the Prussians below barely able to fire their weapons without falling back down the slope, while the French lay over the edge, picking off the enemy at their leisure. A Mitrailleuse was wheeled over, but attracted so much enemy artillery fire, it was forced to withdraw. Other shells peppered the edge of the cliff causing some French casualties and still the Germans pressed on.

If the Prussian commander could have seen what waited for him at the summit, he would surely have given up and saved the lives of virtually all of his command. The French had set up a second gun line with a battery of Mitrailleuse, safely back from the edge that covered the broad swathe of wide-open ground between the ridge and the rest of the Spicheren. Eventually the French commander gave the order to pull back to this new position. A few moments later the first Prussians began to pour over the edge. I watched as one of their officers waved his sword to urge his men on: it was the last thing he did. A cacophonous rattle of rifle and Mitrailleuse swept the ground and men tumbled back down the slope they had fought so hard to climb.

As the afternoon went on, the Prussians made more progress around the flanks. The noise of fighting was intense, although it was difficult to see much through the tree canopy and with gun smoke in the air. Still the French were giving little ground and on occasion driving their enemy before them. In desperation the Prussians sent a troop of cavalry up one hillside path in an effort to clear it. Not a single horseman returned.

By six in the evening, it felt like only a matter of time before the Prussians ordered another withdrawal. If reinforcements from Bazaine arrived, perhaps the French could pursue them all the way back to Saarbrücken and possibly beyond. I was wondering if I would be able to use the telegraph in St Johann again when we heard several French soldiers shouting and pointing from the edge of the escarpment.

The valley out of Saarbrücken came from the northeast and until then the Prussians had all come from that direction. Now, however, gunfire could be heard from the northwest. Another road led that way from further down the Saar River – we had seen a sizeable French force marching there that morning to guard it. If the Prussians broke through it, they could attack the town of Forbach due west, where General Frossard sat near his telegraph, surrounded by warehouses containing a large stockpile of supplies. The plumes of gun smoke from the northwest got steadily thicker, although it was difficult to hear that battle above the noise immediately about us. I noticed the French commander on the Spicheren was also watching the situation anxiously through his

69

glass and sending riders down the shallower slope towards Frossard to find out what was happening. Somehow this new Prussian force must have slipped past Bazaine's soldiers, which were to the north. Surely at least some of them were now marching towards the sound of the guns. If they were to come up behind this new Prussian incursion, an even greater victory could be achieved.

We had been fighting for hours. Amid the chaos, from the top of the Spicheren we could make out that the Prussians who had come from Saarbrücken were now strung out in lines, depleted from an afternoon of fighting. They were making no progress; in fact many were pulling back and the noise of battle was diminishing. But if the combat was ebbing to the northeast, in the northwest it was growing in intensity. Ironically, it became easier to monitor their progress as the light began to fail. Muzzle flashes stood out in the gloom, flickering around the tree canopy. We watched in vain for the arrival of fresh French soldiers. Where the hell was the rest of Bazaine's army? Frossard must have been telegraphing the marshal and any other commander he could reach, begging for assistance. They had to have heard our fight. Surely the marshal would have sent forces to our aid. The chance of a great French triumph was slipping through their fingers. Not only that, the prospect of a defeat was beckoning.

We knew when the battle had reached Forbach, for a stray shot hit one of the crates of ammunition. There was an explosion resembling fireworks at the pleasure gardens. Then more cartridges were ignited. The sound of battle increased tenfold with a roar that must have been heard in Metz. Boxes of shells and bullets let fly their contents randomly about the town and several buildings were set ablaze. We watched anxiously for signs of how the distant battle was progressing. Slowly but surely the distant flashes of light from the fighting were moving west, indicating that the Prussians were still advancing.

By then a grim silence had fallen on the Spicheren. The distant light illuminated faces that stared around at the fighting beneath them as a new realisation dawned. These men and those around the flanks of the mountain had been fighting all day. They had been victorious all day too – Prussian casualties had to be at least double the losses of the

70

French. Yet it was only a matter of time now before the Prussians worked their way round to the gentler slopes of the Spicheren to the south and west. The cliffs that had defended us would then become a trap. As the moon rose in the night sky, a mournful bugle sounded the French army's retreat.

We headed south, stumbling over loose rocks on the slope before we disappeared into the even darker forest at the bottom of the hill. We blundered about, many, including me, trying to come to terms with what had just happened. I had merely been an observer, but for soldiers, particularly those who had lost comrades, the outcome was even more shocking. They felt that they had won their battle, yet they were the ones retreating. When we caught up with those who had fought their way through the chaos at Forbach, the mood was even more bitter. They had been outnumbered and outflanked, fighting a desperate rear-guard action to give the division time to withdraw.

"Where the hell was the rest of the army?" they rightly grumbled. Just a few battalions, they insisted, falling on the rear of the advancing Prussians could have made all the difference. The opportunity for a crushing victory had been turned into a shocking reverse.

We trudged all night through that forest. We were cold, hungry and disorientated, for we had no idea where we were going. It was a struggle to keep our bearings amongst those dark trees. Pascal and I just followed a handful of men we could see in front, ignorant as to where the rest of the division was. To add to our misery, it started to rain. Eventually we came across a hollow where a score of men had given up on their march and thrown themselves down to sleep. Our group turned to join them. I noticed one struggling to light a fire from the damp kindling he could find on the forest floor. I crouched down beside him and reached into my pocket. From my notebook I tore out the pages I had written describing a great French victory and screwed them into a ball. As we watched my words feed the flames, Pascal turned to me and asked, "If we cannot beat the Prussians from a position like the Spicheren, how can we defeat them?"

It was a damn good question.

Chapter 8

In the morning light we were found by a French cavalry patrol. By then there must have been fifty cold, damp men in that hollow. Three had been wounded in the arms and shoulders, but not seriously; Prussian bullets did not create as large a wound as French ones. The horsemen directed us to a small village further south where Frossard's army was regrouping. We left no one behind. The injured were bandaged up and were able to stagger on with the rest of us. No one had any food, and while the soldiers had their cherished Chassepots, few had much ammunition after fighting for most of the previous day. We discovered more bands of soldiers moving in the same direction and eventually found ourselves in a column of several hundred men.

The contrast with the proud army that had marched on Saarbrücken just five days before could not have been greater. Then, bands had been playing and chins tilted high with pride as they envisioned routing their enemies from the field of battle. Now, all musical instruments, along with some artillery and supplies, had been abandoned. Shoulders were slumped and I sensed bitter anger in my new comrades. The mood was not that they had been beaten, but they had somehow been cheated. I knew how they felt. A journalist is supposed to remain impartial, yet I defy anyone to spend weeks in a nation's capital, not to mention time in the bed of one of its more patriotic citizens, as well as march with its army and still not feel some affinity. Forbes felt a similar connection to the Prussians, for he had spoken with some parochial pride about the efficient mobilisation of the German forces. I had shared French hopes of victory, hell I had even written the eulogy on their triumph, yet now all lay in ashes.

Our stomachs rumbled. For most months of the year when an army descended on a small French village, it would have gone hungry. This, however, was August and as we emerged from the forest, we discovered trees heavy with fruit. Farmers watched disconsolately as their plum and apricot trees were picked clean. The apples were still a bit small and sour, but plenty were consumed too. Just then, wafting on the breeze came the aroma of roasting meat. Most cooking pots had been left behind on the Spicheren, but men soon had joints of lamb and pork roasting over bivouac fires in hastily forming regimental depots.

Pascal and I had no battalion to re-join and I doubted the army would go out of its way to feed civilians. We slumped down in the centre of the village and wondered what to do next.

"Paris will be furious when it learns of our defeat," opined my companion. "The last thing they heard was a victory. They will be expecting to hear of the army advancing through Baden and on to Berlin, not giving up French territory."

"There is the loss of Wissembourg too. They certainly will not allow me to send any reports," I agreed. "They will want a victory first, to overshadow what happened on the Spicheren." We wondered what Bazaine was doing. Was he finally marching to avenge our defeat? There was no distant rumble of cannon to disturb that warm summer morning. Equally, there was no sign of pursuit by Prussian scouts either. An army would not have been hard to track, but we could see troops of cavalry still patrolling the forest and rounding up any stragglers.

Men and riders came and went from the largest house, which must have been Frossard's headquarters, as did various villagers, doubtless complaining about the plunder of their livestock and harvest. We did not, therefore, particularly take notice of the officer and escort that came up from the south. Seeing the army bivouacked around the village, a place called Sarreguemines we learned, the young captain reined up. While his escort waited outside, he went into the house to report to the general.

A medical man once told me that nothing spreads through an army faster than dysentery. I replied that he was wrong – bad news travelled far quicker, and so it was that day. While the officer might have been discreet, his escort was not. Soon the contagion of rumour was abroad: the army of MacMahon to the south had been defeated. Later came various embellishments that originated from whispers around the army: the marshal was dead, his army was routed and fleeing to Paris, or his army was surrounded, and we were marching to his relief.

"We will need more supplies and ammunition before we march anywhere," grumbled one soldier at this latest idea.

"Nonsense, we must recapture the Spicheren before we help MacMahon," insisted another. "Much of our artillery is still there."

I watched Frossard's headquarters. Even though we had only heard rumours, a gathering of senior officers there proved that something was afoot. A sentry stood guard at the door, but it was a hot day and the windows were wide open. I gestured at a log store near the side of the building. "Let us sit in the shade over there," I suggested to Pascal. "We might overhear something."

It looked like we were dozing with our hats over our eyes, but my ears were straining for any nugget of information. Unfortunately, all I could make out was the low murmur of voices. The only clear words were when someone shouted out in exasperation, "But dammit, the entire Prussian army cannot be in two places at once." I thought back to what Forbes had told me. It was almost certain that I knew more about the enemy's dispersal than Frossard. Yet I also recalled my colleague's warning to keep such information to myself. On the other hand, by staying silent, I could still be with the French when they blundered into more trouble.

"They have not got a clue what they are up against," I whispered to Pascal. "Perhaps I should tell them."

He shrugged, "As a Frenchman I want to help France, but I do not want to be shot as a spy. We have already been arrested once."

"They would not dare shoot a British journalist," I countered. I was fairly confident of that. At worst I would be thrown out of the country in disgrace. But Frossard struck me as a man with ample common sense. If I was right, he would listen to what I had to say. Making up my mind, I got to my feet. The meeting inside must have broken up, for as I walked around to the front door a stream of senior officers emerged, some still arguing in heated whispers. One gave an order to the sentry, who rushed away on some errand. I cautiously put my head in through the door. To my right a young officer had his back to me, furiously scribbling orders on a pad. He paid no attention to my footsteps as I strolled across the hallway to the open door of a dining room. The table was strewn with maps and a tall grey-haired general stood staring out of the far window, lost in thought.

"Excuse me, sir, I wonder if I might have a word with you," I ventured.

Frossard turned, barely giving me a glance. He sported a moustache and goatee beard like his emperor. When I had glimpsed him before he had exuded energy, but his experience at the Spicheren had sapped that away. He took in my civilian clothes and airily waved back at the door. "If your livestock has been taken by the soldiers, sir, please see the lieutenant outside and he will arrange for it to be paid for.

"No, sir," I started. "I am not a farmer, I am a journalist with the *Daily News* in London."

I got no further before the blue eyes flashed in sudden anger. "Charles," he yelled to the lieutenant in the hallway. "What the hell are you doing out there, letting hacks into my headquarters?" His glare settled on me, "I have no time for interviews, sir, you should have gone back to Metz with Delafosse."

I felt the lieutenant's hand on my arm and hurriedly pulled back. "You don't understand, sir, I am not here to interview you. I want to give you information on the Prussians."

"Wait," Frossard held up a hand to stay his subordinate. Then in a voice heavy with suspicion he looked back at me. "What would a London journalist in France know about the Prussian army?"

I took a deep breath. "My paper has two journalists covering the war, sir. I am assigned to the French army and my colleague, a Mr Forbes, is attached to the Prussian forces. I met Forbes four days ago in Saarbrücken. He told me the disposition of the Prussian army."

The lieutenant sprang back as though I had just dropped a viper on the rug. "And I suppose you betrayed the disposition of our army to him and the Prussians in return," he spat. He looked at his chief, "This is how they managed to outflank us."

"I did not need to tell him anything," I protested. "He was at Saarbrücken when you attacked. He saw the army first-hand and could still see it in the valley two days later. As for where Marshal Bazaine's forces are now, I have no idea."

"In that you're not alone," retorted the general acidly. "So, what can you tell me about the Prussians?"

I told him what Forbes had told me: that the Prussians had two large armies, one in the north and one in the south, both larger than the opposing French forces. When I mentioned the extra train tracks and that in total Forbes thought that they had around four hundred thousand troops in the region, the lieutenant stepped forward again. "This is nonsense, sir," he protested. "This rogue has probably been sent here by the Prussians as a ruse to intimidate us. They cannot possibly have got double the number we have here so quickly."

His general was not so sure. "Have you not wondered why the Prussians provoked us into this war when they knew we had the Chassepot and the Mitrailleuse?" he asked his aide. "I have always thought that they had some advantage of their own and this might be it." He turned to me, "How well do you know this Monsieur Forbes? Could he be lying or easily misled?"

"I met him for the first time a month ago," I admitted. "But we work for the same paper and so there is no advantage to him in misleading me. He also warned me to keep the information to myself. He certainly admires the Prussians, but he is a former soldier himself and so a good judge of their capabilities." I paused, thinking back to that conversation. "I am certain he believed what he told me, even if he had not seen all the soldiers personally."

Frossard nodded and turned to stare down at the maps on his table. Emboldened by his acceptance of what I had told him, I pressed on. "There are rumours running through the army outside that Marshal MacMahon has been defeated. Did he find himself facing a larger Prussian army to the south?"

For a moment the general did not answer, still lost in his thoughts. Then, pointing to a place on his map, he grunted, "It happened here." Leaning over I saw his forefinger next to a place called Frœschwiller. "Everyone will know soon enough," he continued. "MacMahon had a force of over forty thousand defending that part of the border. They fought bravely for eight hours but were damn near encircled. As at the Spicheren, the enemy guns proved to have a longer range and far fewer dud shells. MacMahon did not have the advantage of the hilltop we had and so they lost half their number in casualties and prisoners." He gave a heavy sigh before adding, "He reports that he faced an army of Prussians and Bavarians at least double the size of his force."

I stared at the smudged place name on the map and tried to stop my mind from imagining the slaughter. "Where are the rest of MacMahon's men now?" I asked.

"He is gathering his men together and retreating southwest."

"But surely he should be marching north," I protested. "Your only chance of beating one of the German armies is to combine your forces."

Frossard gave a grim smile. "You do not know this area of France, do you?" he said gesturing to the space north of Frœschwiller. "We are in the Vosges hills. Steep valleys that MacMahon would have to traverse right in front of a much larger enemy force. If they found him, they could easily trap and destroy the rest of his army.

"Then cannot Marshal Bazaine take his army south, around these hills, to unite the French forces?"

"He could," agreed Frossard. "But that would leave Paris open to the Prussians who are facing us here. The emperor could never agree to that."

"So, what are you going to do?" I asked.

"Bazaine is trying to concentrate his forces at Saint Avold, but that is only ten miles southwest of the Prussians in Forbach. My army is in no state to fight again. We will retreat to Metz where I can get them fresh supplies and ammunition. Then the emperor will have to decide what to do next."

We set off again that afternoon, Frossard anxious to put more distance between him and what he now knew was a sizeable Prussian army to his rear. We marched another eight miles that day to reach the town of Puttelange. At least that night we did not have to sleep in the open. The general's aide found us space in a barn, and we were even given some bread smeared with dripping for our dinner. It may have been a generous provision of hospitality, but I noticed a sergeant keeping an eye on us. He even followed me out when I went to use the hastily dug latrine ditch. I suspect that the lieutenant was just ensuring that we did not slip away and join the Prussians with accounts of our conversation with the general.

The next morning we set off directly for Metz. Dark, brooding clouds boiled overhead, matching the mood of the army. By now all had heard of the defeat in the south and word had spread that Bazaine and his army to the north were also pulling back. Men grumbled openly about both their marshal and the emperor. The former for not coming to their aid at the Spicheren and the latter for starting the war with no real plan for winning it. They were resentful and angry: France was being humiliated, its territory invaded and its army was in retreat.

By lunchtime it had started to rain, not a summer shower, but a full deluge that lasted for the rest of the day. We were soon cold and soaked to the skin as we trudged through puddles and slipped in mud. Morale sank even lower and, with it, discipline. Instead of marching in columns the army was now more an armed rabble. We were hungry, too, although an excessive plum consumption was having an unfortunate effect on the digestive system of many, including my own. But when we passed through the centre of one village, we found the bakery door was half off its hinges and the interior had clearly already been ransacked for food.

The next day was at least dry and the thought of food and fresh supplies waiting at our destination kept the men moving on. That night we slept in a meadow. Our clothes had dried on the day's march, but the ground was still damp, and by morning my shirt was clammy again from the morning dew. I lay there as the sun came up, my eyes still closed, enjoying the first warming rays. Around me I could hear grumbles as men got up, some arguing over fires that had gone out or people taking a piss too close to where they were resting. With luck, I thought, we would be within sight of Metz by nightfall and certainly in the city on the morrow. I was daydreaming about a comfortable bed and a roof over my head when suddenly there was a shout: "Look! Prussians!"

I leapt up, half expecting to see a swarm of black-uniformed soldiers charging towards us. Instead, there was a knot of around a dozen horsemen on the top of a hill nearly a mile off. They sat perfectly still, watching us. There had clearly been no pickets posted around our camp, for the French were now running around in alarm, their reaction out of all proportion to the threat. Some ran for their rifles; others furiously stuffed possessions into their packs in preparation for flight. By the time Frossard and a handful of officers had emerged from a nearby barn to see what was happening, several soldiers had readied their rifles and opened fire. It was an extreme range, even for the famed Chassepot, and if the bullets buzzed about the Prussians, they showed no sign of it.

"They are Uhlans," announced a soldier standing next to me. Seeing my blank expression, he clarified, "Prussian lancers. They are the very devils."

"Maybe," I replied. "But I doubt that they will take on the whole army. They must be acting as scouts." I squinted but could barely make out more than silhouettes of men against the rising sun. Still, I was surprised that they had pursued us this far. I had thought the Prussians would be resupplying their armies following their victories and resting their men before resuming their advance. These scouts could not be more than a day's ride in front of their army if they were to keep their generals updated on what was in front of them. I had hoped we would see Metz before any pursuing army but suddenly it was clear: the Prussians were hot on our heels. The Uhlans turned and trotted along a ridge to further extend the range from a score of French rifles. Then one rider detached from the rest and turned to head back east. It would not be long before the Prussian commanders knew where we were.

With no orders necessary, the pace of march that day was considerably faster than the one before. Carts were requisitioned from farms and walking wounded loaded into them to avoid them falling behind. At least once an hour soldiers would dart anxious glances over their shoulders, only to discover that our shadows were still on our trail. Frossard sent some French cavalry back to cover the rear of the column and while the Prussians withdrew a little at that, they remained in view. But even if we had driven them off entirely, it was little challenge to track an army. We were on the road to the largest French city and military citadel in the area, it was not hard to guess where we were going.

There was fresh alarm at midday when a large column of soldiers was spotted to the north. More of our cavalry was sent to investigate, and quickly reported back that it was Bazaine's army on a parallel road. They too had Prussian cavalry trailing them. Late afternoon we spotted a modern fortress on a hill to our left. It had huge thick walls and embankments. Most importantly, a French flag flew from the staff. We all felt considerably more secure when we were on the other side of it. The place was called Queuleu and it guarded the approach to Metz from the southeast. It was part of a ring of forts designed to protect the city – there was a similar fort two miles away covering the northeastern approaches. Despite appearances, however, Queuleu was not fully complete and the fort intended to face due east between them had not yet been constructed. In the end, Bazaine used his army to plug this gap, while we marched on into the city.

Metz was a bastion and had been defending France for centuries. It was built by the broad Moselle River, which provided a natural boundary. Most of the river flowed round it to the west, but channels had been dug around the medieval city walls to provide a moat around the eastern section too. The place was teeming with soldiers; the trainline from Paris must have been busy. Most were reservists trying to re-join their regiments. When they discovered we were the survivors of the Spicheren, they were all over us with questions. "How did you manage to lose?" was the general theme, with a strong implication that the outcome would have been very different if they had been there. Frossard's men were tired, and their pride had been bruised, so it was little surprise to me to see scuffles and brawls break out with their interrogators as they made their way through the streets. Pascal and I ducked away, I wanted a good dinner that did not involve plums and then a comfortable bed for the night.

Chapter 9

"No, monsieur, you cannot send this. Not even a mention of Spicheren is permitted."

I had been kept waiting for half an hour in the telegraph office as my forms were first read and then passed into a back office. This haughty official had eventually emerged, and now tore my draft copy in half in front of me and dropped it into the bin. It was a short factual account of my activities, addressed to my uncle rather than the paper, but I was not surprised at the reaction. Since we had returned to Metz I had met with several of the French correspondents at their hotel. Through them I realised that the country had changed greatly since I was last in the capital.

The Parisian papers were full of outrage, many even demanding the overthrow of the government. I could easily imagine the fury of their readers. They had read reports about the French army throwing back three divisions and marching into German territory. Then when they expected to hear that their army was well on its way to Berlin, they learn it has suffered two calamitous defeats, both on French soil. Far from being the invader, they found themselves as the invaded, their army divided and falling back in confusion. Some papers called for arming the populace and letting the people defend themselves. The idea had been rejected, but all fit, childless men between twenty-five and thirty-five not already in the army, had been called up. The Mobile Guard forces were now being equipped and sent to the front as quickly as possible. While the emperor was hanging on, largely due to the actions of the empress in Paris, a newly recalled legislature had set about replacing many of his ministers. Desperate to shore up their crumbling authority, officials in Metz were imposing even more rigorous censorship. No one could get any news out of France, leaving London readers to rely on Prussian accounts of what was happening.

I am sure that it was not by chance that as I left the telegraph office, I found myself hailed by Colonel Delafosse. "Monsieur, what a pleasure to see you returned safely to Metz."

"Really?" I responded tartly. "I would have thought it would have been more of a pleasure to see me marching to Berlin with your army. Instead, we have been thrown back in defeat and chaos."

"Not at all," he soothed. "There has been no *catastrophic failure*," he stressed the phrase that I had used in my draft to indicate that he had read it. "We have suffered a small unforeseen setback, but these are to be expected in times of war. For you, however, the setback might be a little more permanent."

"What do you mean?" I asked, noting a smugness creep across his features giving me a grim sense of foreboding about his next words.

"Monsieur Chalmers, or should I say Monsieur Harrison, I think for you the war is over. When you went missing from Paris, enquiries were made. The real Monsieur Chalmers was most insistent he was innocent of the crime he was accused of. The telegraph clerk was questioned and his description of the man trying to send information to London matched yours. Monsieur Chalmers has been most indignant. His employer has written to the War Ministry and your own paper, demanding that action is taken. My instructions are to return you to Paris and to give you this telegram."

I took the proffered paper and unfolded it. The contents were everything I had feared. It was from my uncle, fulsomely expressing his displeasure at my behaviour. '*You have disgraced yourself and the paper.*' I could picture the pious satisfaction on his face as he added, '*Against my better judgement I was persuaded to give you a chance, but you have lived down to your poor pedigree. On receipt of this message consider yourself dismissed from the* Daily News.'

The sanctimonious wretch had been looking for an opportunity to get rid of me all along, Forbes had told me as much. Yet while I felt anger and disappointment, there was also a sense of frustration. I had enjoyed the excitement of being a war correspondent and I was sure I could be good at it. Life does not give you many breaks and having an uncle as an editor of a leading paper was one of the few I had been granted. I was damned if I was going to give it up yet. "Did *The Times* publish your story about the three Prussian divisions at Saarbrücken?" I asked Delafosse.

"Yes, it did, although the Prussian-based correspondents soon provided their own versions of the battle. Why do you ask?"

"You know that the real Chalmers would never have agreed to it. You must have got credit for having the London *Times* print your fiction – you owe me for that."

"And what favour do you want in return?" the colonel asked, before adding, "it had better be a small one."

"No favour," I told him, "for it is in your interest too. The British readers only hear about the war from the Prussians, that is why the public sympathises with them. But if this war goes badly for France, you are going to want support from Britain, perhaps to help negotiate a peace. Our politicians will listen to their voters and you want those people switching their support to France. You need British journalists like me with your army to tell your side of things."

"I don't think things are that desperate yet," he countered. "We have suffered a setback, but the emperor and his generals are experienced commanders; they will soon check the Prussian advance. Soon the war will be fought again on German territory."

I noticed that even he did not have the gall to look me in the eye as he spoke this final sentence. "*Two* quite large setbacks," I corrected, "and the Prussians seem to have more soldiers in France than the French. I don't see how you are going to stop them."

Delafosse laughed nervously. "With the reinforcements we have recently received, Marshal Bazaine now commands an army of one hundred and eighty thousand here in Metz. A further reserve army is building up in Chalon and Marshal MacMahon still has a large force to the south. We have more than enough men to throw the Prussians back. Now, what exactly do you want?"

"I want you to pretend that you have not seen me. Leave me to work as a correspondent here in Metz."

"But you have been dismissed!" He gestured to the telegram, which he had clearly read. "You have no paper to write for."

"I want a chance to get my old job back. I lost it in part helping you get your story published and I can be useful again to France." I was begging now and that did not sit comfortably with me. Yet I was asking a military man to disobey orders and he was probably not used to that either. At least he had not dismissed the idea out of hand. He stared at me, considering his response, and I gave him a final prod. "You must have read the Paris papers. You know that the situation is precarious. France needs all the friends it can get."

Slowly, Delafosse nodded. "You may be right," he admitted with a degree of resignation. "Although I doubt your editor will change his mind." He grinned, "If he does not, then there is another British journalist here who I have also *not seen*. He is from the *Pall Mall Gazette*; perhaps they will publish your work.

I returned to my lodgings with my mind in a whirl. If 'Champagne Charlie' was in Metz he would probably buy my information and write his own article. I would be glad of the money, but it would not help me build my own reputation as a war correspondent. To do that I needed my old job back. It seemed to me that Uncle Frank did not hold all the cards. For all his pious preaching, he still had to succeed as a businessman. In the circumstances I doubt he had used the Mitrailleuse article and so most of their war content would have come from Forbes. There would be a whole pack of journalists moving together on the Prussian side and very few exclusives. I had been the only British journalist on the Spicheren and it was an extraordinary tale to tell of how certain victory had been turned into defeat. With Pascal's drawing of those soldiers holding their Mitrailleuse to fire down the cliff on the front page, the *Daily News* would sell out in no time. Back when I was in London, questions were being asked about Frank's penny edition pricing – I knew he needed to make it work. This article would give him the opportunity for extra print runs and higher sales. I just had to get it to him quickly.

I sat down to write, reusing from memory some of the words I had consigned to the flames earlier. Though I say so myself, it was a powerful piece that gave a new and exciting dimension to a battle that had probably already been reported on from the Prussian side. Then I sat down to compose a more delicate note to my uncle. I reminded him of his imperative to get the news before *The Times* got hold of it, suggesting that my actions had been partly at his instigation. I also told him that there were only two British journalists in Metz and if he did not use my material the other paper would. I concluded by saying that if he did print my piece, I would take that as confirmation that my employment had been restored.

Pascal was the obvious person to help me get my article and his drawing to London. Fifteen miles north of Metz was a town called Thionville. From there you could catch a train to Luxembourg and then on to Brussels. From the Belgian capital a mail service ran to London that could deliver letters and parcels in a day. When I put the proposal to him, he was delighted to go. "I have already done two copies of the drawing and sent them to journalists I know in Paris. I can do more on the train and sell them in Brussels too. But how will we know if we have our jobs back at the *Daily News*?"

"Wait in Brussels three days," I told him. "It will take a day for the material to reach London, a day to print and another day for the London newspapers to reach Belgium. If my uncle has not published it by then, send a copy of your picture to the *London Illustrated News* – they are bound to use it."

"What will you do?" asked Pascal.

"I will wait here to see what happens next." I grinned and added, "Anticipating your success, I might even write more articles in the hope that I can use them."

"Be careful, my friend," he urged as he readied to leave.

"Don't worry, I will be fine if I stick close to the emperor. They will make sure no harm comes to him."

It was not hard to guess where the man from the *Pall Mall Gazette* would be. Sure enough, I found him in the bar of the plushest hotel. He had already demonstrated a willingness to sacrifice his liver for the cause of discovering the truth, yet I had read some of his coverage and, even sunk in his cups, he was a better scribbler than most of us. Another former soldier, he kept his readers informed with concise clarity and well-judged opinions.

"Ah, Harrison," he drawled, his slightly unfocussed eyes wrinkled in a smile as he added, "or should I call you Chalmers?" He chuckled, "That was an evil trick you played, although the little prick deserved it.

We will have to keep an eye on you… Waiter, another bottle here and a glass for my friend."

"How long was he in custody?" I asked, settling into the opposite chair.

"Just a couple of days. Then he was out, full of venom, writing letters of complaint to his editor and yours. I heard you were at Spicheren. What do you make of affairs?" I told him what little I knew and the bloodshot eyes watched me steadily. "What do you think the French will do now?" he asked.

"I honestly don't have a clue," I admitted. "They need to combine their armies, but Frossard says that MacMahon cannot come north without risking ambush. I have seen the Paris papers and am certain that if the emperor marches south and leaves the capital exposed to Prussian attack, his regime is bound to fall. I am at a loss to know what they should do."

"Don't worry, you are not alone there. My spies tell me the emperor just paces up and down, smoking furiously and demanding ideas from Bazaine, which he then dismisses. The marshal has been given command of the army here, but Napoleon keeps on interfering. Neither shows any leadership as neither has any kind of plan."

"What is Bazaine like?" I asked. "Frossard was furious he did not come to our aid at the Spicheren. They would have won if he had."

"He is brave," conceded my friend. "He rose up from the ranks, which makes him a popular man of the people to the Republicans, but that also means he spent little time learning tactics." He took a deep draught of freshly poured champagne and concluded, "It does not matter, for sooner or later they will realise that they have no choice. They will have to retreat."

"But why?" I was puzzled. "They have been beaten fighting in the open; surely they would be better off fighting from behind the city walls of Metz."

"Because the Prussians will never be stupid enough to attack Metz. They know a Chassepot will kill at least four or five of their men running over open ground before their own rifles are in range. The fixed batteries in the forts also have a longer range than their field artillery. On the other hand, the Prussians do have enough men to encircle Metz and trap the French army there. They can dig trenches and earthworks for their guns and then they will have the advantage if the French try to break out."

"Well, the Prussians were stupid enough to attack the Spicheren head on. They would have saved thousands of lives if they had only attacked through Forbach," I said. I admit that at the time I thought that Charlie was wrong. With the outer forts keeping the Prussians at bay, the perimeter of the Metz defensive area was huge. It would take a vast force to secure it. So far, the German armies had won through weight of numbers and speed of manoeuvre. If they were forced to spread out and stay in one place these advantages would be lost. Then if the French organised a relief force, the besiegers would become trapped between those inside the city and those coming to rescue them. It made sense to me, but then I had no military experience at all.

I felt the first qualms of disquiet early the next morning, when we got reports that the Prussians were beginning to cross the Moselle River ten miles away, both north and south of the city. Perhaps, as Charlie predicted, they were trying to encircle Metz. I just hoped that Pascal had reached Thionville in time. Although as he was not a soldier, the Prussians might just let him pass.

Bazaine was clearly worried about his army on the eastern bank of the Moselle. Extra pontoon bridges had been built for his men, but these had just been swept away by the river, which had risen after the recent heavy rain. There were thousands of men, guns and equipment on the Prussian side of the river blocking the gap between the forts, but Bazaine now ordered them to use the few remaining crossings to retreat into the city as quickly as possible. I climbed up onto the walls to watch. From atop the ramparts, I saw lines of blue-coated men marching disconsolately towards me. Most I guessed had not fired a gun in anger, for only a few had engaged the enemy at Saarbrücken. Bazaine's men had not fought a battle since then – all they had done is retreat. Supply wagons and artillery all streamed with them over the narrow bridges. The forts southeast and southwest were keeping the Prussians at bay, but in the gap between them, due east, I could just make out columns of troops in black in the distance, moving in to take up ground conceded by the French.

Heaven knows how the battle started. Perhaps the Prussians resented seeing the French withdraw unmolested, or possibly the French simply tired of retreating. It cannot have been planned, for it started with just a few batteries of guns. Within minutes the booming artillery of the Queuleu fort had joined in. Then, when I looked down, instead of trudging into Metz, soldiers were turning around and charging back towards their enemies, ready to attack. Several gun batteries rushed back across bridges that they had just traversed, their men shouting in delight that they would finally be able to fight.

The battle centred on a village called Borny, a mile to the east of the city. I squinted into the morning sun and tried to make out what was happening through the plumes of smoke. More and more troops from both sides were pouring into the fray and soon the sound of rifle fire was near continuous. I could only just make out the more regular rattle of the Mitrailleuse above the general din. Hundreds of people from the city joined me on the walls, all anxious for a glimpse of the battle. While the bulk of the French army and the new reserves remained in Metz, most of Bazaine's original force was now engaged. Two weeks of bitter resentment spurred them into a ferocious attack. By noon citizens were pointing to where they thought the Prussians were pulling back. I thought it was wishful thinking at first, but by mid-afternoon it was clear that the blue-coated soldiers were advancing in triumph.

It was late afternoon when Marshal Bazaine himself arrived on the battlements. He had spent most of the day fighting with his men and had clearly been in the thick of the action. The shoulder of his tunic was torn where it had been struck by a spent shell fragment. There was no sign of any blood, but from the way he winced as he moved his arm, it was clear that his shoulder was badly bruised.

For a man winning his first genuine battle of this war, he was damned depressed about it. I had seen him before; he was not an impressive military figure with his stout sagging frame, and anxious eyes set into a flabby face. His downturned mouth was hidden behind a goatee beard and moustache like his emperor's, which seemed to be *de rigueur* for

French officers at that time. He shook off the congratulations of various civilians and went to stand on some steps that gave him a better view. I watched him staring through his telescope, first at the battle and then to the north and south. The longer he looked the angrier he got. He whispered furiously to a group of his staff officers and I edged closer to overhear his conversation. "I told them not to give battle," he growled before slamming a fist down on the parapet. "I absolutely forbade them from advancing a single yard!"

It was an astonishing reaction, for even if the territory gained was of little value, the effect of the victory on his army's morale was immeasurable. The trickle of wounded being helped back to the city were being cheered by the crowds watching from above on the walls. They looked up and despite their injuries, grinned in delight. It was the first time I had seen French soldiers smile in over a week.

Bazaine then sent a steady stream of messengers to his forward units. I pitied his poor commanders, who were probably being reprimanded for winning a battle. If they were perplexed now, then their confusion was set to increase. An hour later the emperor appeared on the city wall. Unlike his marshal, he was more than eager to accept the acclaim of the populace. Napoleon had no qualms at all about this being an excellent day for France. When he saw Bazaine, he embraced him warmly. Then, turning to the crowd, he announced that his marshal had broken the spell of recent bad luck with this triumph. He claimed that his victorious generals were receiving messages of congratulation from their emperor. Henceforth, he promised, the fortunes of war would change. As I noted this down, I looked up and saw Colonel Delafosse watching me and nodding approvingly. Unfortunately for him, it would take more than a royal decree to change the progress of the war.

A short while later as I turned to leave, I found the colonel at my side. "Again, Monsieur Harrison, I do not see you," he murmured. "But you are welcome to send a telegram on our great victory to the *Daily News*. Whether they choose to print it is another matter. I will of course need to approve it in advance, and I trust it will include the emperor's words. We would not want your readers to only hear of affairs from the German viewpoint after all."

"That is very kind of you, I am much obliged," I grinned, then added, "I look forward to you not seeing me again in the future."

"I very much doubt I will see you again, officially or otherwise, for you are leaving Metz tonight."

"But…but why?" I stammered. "I thought we had an understanding."

"This is nothing to do with your er…personal difficulties. You will be going with all the other correspondents still in the city and accompanying the emperor. It is a great honour. The details are still being arranged and I can tell you no more now. But get an early night, for a sentry will call for you at your hotel just after midnight."

Chapter 10

It was only as I met up with Charlie that evening that things became a little clearer. The day before, he had heard that the emperor had given Bazaine orders to leave a garrison in Metz and take the rest of the army all the way back to Chalon. There it would combine with the growing reserves and the remainder of MacMahon's army. A combined force of around four hundred thousand men would at last be able to take on the Prussian army in equal numbers. But this would come at a huge cost. I remembered all too well from my journey to reach Metz, that Chalon was around a hundred miles to the west.

"But that means giving up a huge swathe of French territory," I pointed out. "They are already close to revolt in Paris – that news is not going to go down well there."

"You are assuming that Bazaine can get his army out of Metz," Charlie cautioned. "That is why he was so annoyed today. He knows the Prussians will try and encircle him here. Ironically, winning a battle may lead to a greater defeat, for it has cost him a day's delay. On the other hand, to Napoleon a victory was priceless to assuage the mob in his capital. Now," he warned, topping up my glass with a very superior claret, "we have two more bottles to finish, for this will not travel well. At least we should be carried in style with the emperor. Every wine cellar between here and Chalon will be open to him and," he winked, "as his guests, to us too."

I did not get any sleep at all that night and had the beginnings of a sore head when a soldier knocked loudly on the door after midnight. Our luggage was loaded onto the top of a carriage. The clink of glass from my companion's trunk indicated that he was not relying solely on the emperor's hospitality. While we waited for another journalist at a nearby hotel, we found we were not the only ones moving at that ungodly hour. Under cover of darkness, the soldiers who had fought at Borny were ordered to give up their hard-won yards and return over the moat to the city. They were not smiling now as they trudged through the streets. Evidently, they had been told of the further retreat. I overheard two officers complaining bitterly about it. Instead of giving up more of France, they insisted, the army should be advancing. Then they could split the Prussian forces in two and turn on the weakest. "Give them a taste of their own medicine," the fellow suggested.

After congratulating Bazaine, Napoleon had left the city and spent the night in a farm at a place called Gravelotte, around seven miles west of Metz as the crow flies. The road was a winding affair, climbing up around hills that lined the river. It must have been closer to ten miles travelled when we reached our destination. We had been joined by a French journalist from *Le Figaro*, who had discovered that the entire army was to use this one road. Bazaine had refused to disperse his force over other routes in case they lost contact or were attacked before support could arrive. Charlie shook a tired head in dismay. "One hundred and sixty thousand men, artillery, cavalry and all the wagons needed for supply, not to mention the several thousand citizens of Metz who do not want to be besieged; all on this one track. It will take them a week to get to Verdun and I would be very surprised if the Prussians are not astride the road within the next two days."

"I do not understand why we are not using the train – it would be much quicker," I protested as the carriage wheel jolted over a particularly deep pothole.

"They think that the Prussians might cut the rail line, if they have not done so already," the French journalist said with weary resignation. "In the south they have sent forward cavalry patrols to cut telegraph wires and remove the bolts from railway lines so that the trains derail. I dare say that they will do the same here."

It was a grim reminder that, even travelling with an emperor, things might not be as safe as I first thought. My mind turned again to Pascal; a lot rested on his successful arrival. I comforted myself that the train line to neutral Luxembourg would not be a priority for sabotage.

Clearly a Prussian ambush was a concern among the emperor's retinue too. When we reached Gravelotte it was still dark, but burning torches revealed a veritable caravan of wagons and vehicles, not to mention three regiments of escort cavalry, including dragoons and lancers. Napoleon and his young son stepped out from the farmhouse, but instead of walking to their state carriage, they made for a light open-topped landau pulled by four powerful horses. It was built for speed. If enemy horsemen did appear then the emperor would not be easy to capture.

As soon as it was light enough to make out the road ahead, the coachman cracked his whip, and the landau sprang forward while other officials scurried about to find their place among other vehicles. One ran towards us and, checking we were journalists, handed us a sheaf of papers. They were a final gift from Colonel Delafosse: a copy of a proclamation the emperor had issued to the people of Metz. In it he insisted that he was "leaving to oppose the invading army," while his horses trotted swiftly in exactly the opposite direction. Then there was more guff about him relying on their patriotism to defend the city and hoping to see them again in happier times. I gave a snort of disgust as I screwed the nonsense into a ball and tossed it out of the window. "I am sure the people of Metz will be greatly comforted by their emperor's courage as they starve under siege," I scoffed.

"It will be a long time before they starve," insisted the man from *Le Figaro* defensively. The outer batteries will keep the Prussian guns at bay and there is enough food stored to keep the citizens and a garrison fed for several months."

By now our carriage was moving. We were around tenth in the column, with at least another half dozen vehicles behind us. The cavalry formed a cordon all around us, riding out in the fields on either side of the road. The dragoons were at the front, lancers at the rear and a regiment I was told were the *Chasseurs d'Afrique* flanked either side.

Gravelotte was on a crossroads, and we took the road heading northwest towards the town of Verdun. We had only gone a couple of miles when we came to the railway line leading to Metz. As the carriage rocked over the wooden planks between the rails on the crossing, we stared anxiously out of the window for any sign of Prussian sabotage. It was lighter now and as far as I could tell the track was sound, but I knew they left it looking that way to deceive the locomotive drivers.

On we went through the rolling countryside. The road kept to the shallow valleys and so often we could not see far into the surrounding fields and orchards. Squadrons of our north African escort cavalry strayed up to hilltops to survey the countryside around us. All was peaceful. Peasants came out of their houses to wave at the imperial coach, unaware that its occupants were court flunkeys and that they had missed their emperor in the less opulent carriage ahead.

After an hour we began to relax; surely we were beyond any threat from the Prussians now. My guts were rumbling, rebelling against the surfeit of wine the previous night and the lack of breakfast that morning. Yet my companion was not known as Champagne Charlie for nothing, for now he opened his bag and produced a veritable feast. We had left before the baker's opened, but there before us were biscuits, butter, slices of a local sausage, and plum tarts to follow. It was all washed down with a white wine, which he assured me would ease my hangover. It felt strangely decadent to be drinking wine as the sun slowly crept up higher over the eastern horizon, but Charlie was right, my head was clearing, and it was good to have something solid in my stomach again.

I watched idly out of the window as a squadron of cavalry rode towards us almost directly beneath the early morning sun. Something seemed odd about them, although squinting into the light I could barely make out any details. Then I noticed that the sun was glinting off their helmets and remembered that the African troopers wore cloth caps. "Christ, they are Prussians!" I shouted, pointing. Our escort must have identified them at the same time, for the intruders reigned up and reached for their rifles. Instinctively, we ducked down, although I doubt the flimsy wooden door would have stopped a bullet as they were only a hundred yards off. The coachman whipped up the horses and we lurched forward suddenly. I half fell off the seat as there was a fusillade of fire. There were two loud cracks as bullets slammed into our carriage, but we were still moving, faster now, even though we were swerving off the road. The man from *Le Figaro* produced a revolver from his pocket and leant out of the window to blaze away. Over his shoulder, as our carriage bounced wildly on its springs, I could just make out some of our escort wheeling in on our attackers

Crack, crack, crack went the revolver and then there was a curse as the carriage we were passing blocked his aim. "They are trying to capture the emperor," shouted *Le Figaro*. "Has he got away?"

Leaning out of the window on the opposite side, I was just in time to see the landau disappear around the next bend at the full gallop, a squadron of dragoons on either side. Two more carriages were racing after it and escaped unscathed, but the imperial state coach was not as fortunate. It must have been the focus of the fire; and one of its horses was down, the rest rearing in their traces as the vehicle slewed to a stop. In a moment we were alongside, our own horses now at the gallop, two on the carriageway and two on the verge. "Napoleon has got away," I called as we swayed wildly past. The royal coach had been peppered with bullets and I glimpsed a man inside clutching a bloodied shoulder. I stared around on the other side of the road for any sign of a further ambush, but it was clear. The Prussian troop was already galloping away, its work done. "Damn that was close," I said, breathing a sigh of relief.

"It was nothing," replied Charlie coolly. "Just an opportunistic attack I suspect. If they had known we were here, they would have sent far more cavalry." He turned to our companion and gestured at his still smoking revolver. "You know, you should not have used that. As journalists we are not treated as combatants. We are supposed to be calm and dispassionate reporters of the truth for our readers."

"That is easy for an Englishman to say, but I am French," the man replied stuffily. "I will defend my emperor with my life." Then his resolve suddenly crumbled as a look of horror crossed his face. "My God, I think I have been hit," he wailed. He reached up to the top of his head and gave a gasp. Yet as he brought his hand back down, while we could see it was wet, it was not blood.

I looked up to see liquid dripping down from a splinter of wood that now protruded through the carriage roof. Charlie leaned forward to smell the Frenchman's hand and then in an instant his demeanour changed too. Being 'calm and dispassionate' was forgotten and replaced with a sudden fury. "They've hit my fucking brandy!" he roared before leaping up to yell from the window at the distant retreating Prussians. "You bloody barbarians, that was over fifty years old!"

Finally, our own coachman having refused to stop so that Charlie could examine his luggage, we caught up with the emperor at a place called Étain, twenty miles from Metz. In the end the convoy had escaped lightly: one horse killed, three men wounded and two bottles of Napoleon vintage brandy smashed. Our escort claimed to have killed six of the Prussians to losses of two of their own.

While the emperor enjoyed a late breakfast, we carefully savoured a small cup each of an excellent spirit that was salvaged from the broken bottle pieces in the trunk. The horses were watered and given a brief rest from their recent exertions and then we were on our way again. We knew that the survivors of the Prussian attack would be reporting to their superiors that they had nearly caught the emperor. A much larger force would soon be on our trail. While the innkeeper at Étain had served the French emperor his breakfast, he was likely to be providing lunch to the Prussians.

That afternoon we rode on another twenty miles to the fortress town of Verdun. We alighted at the railway station where the emperor requested a train. There was nothing waiting on the platform and the stationmaster explained that all trains had been diverted to the stretch of track between Paris and Chalon to bring up reserves for the army. There was, however, a spare engine in a siding for a minor repair. He would see if it could be used and what carriages he could find. There was little Napoleon could do other than express his gratitude and sink down exhausted on a nearby bench. The railwayman fetched him a glass of wine for refreshment and then went off about his bidding. We all sat on the edge of the platform, our feet dangling over the empty tracks, and reflected on how the mighty had fallen.

Napoleon had arrived in Metz on the imperial train, with two more trains behind for his courtiers and equipage. Now he was sitting on a station bench and drinking wine from a chipped glass. His eyes were closed as he leaned his head back against the wall and I could only imagine what he was thinking. He had allowed a sense of national indignation to persuade him to declare war and now his empire was falling apart. His only hope of survival was to throw back the invader and even that might not be enough to placate those agitating in his capital.

A steam whistle presaged the arrival of the train and the emperor's humiliation was complete. The small locomotive was pulling four *third class* railway trucks, which was all the station master had available. Napoleon mustered a grateful smile and climbed inside the front carriage. I remembered thinking that he had appeared to be in pain sitting on his horse saddle and reviewing his troops. Hours sitting on the iron-hard wooden bench seats, would do little for his constitution. Two soldiers were detailed to stand on the front of the locomotive to look out for loose rails. A dozen dragoons boarded with their rifles, but the rest of the cavalry would continue by road, for there was no room on the train for their mounts. We were soon in the rear carriage, unpacking spare clothes to serve as cushions to make our own journey more bearable.

We still had fifty miles to go to reach Chalon, but the train made slow progress, and stopped again at dusk, I have no idea where. Possibly because the soldiers could no longer see that the tracks ahead were safe. That might have partly been the case, but the clanging coming from the locomotive indicated that repairs were still underway. It was more comfortable to climb down and stretch out on the ground beside the train than on those hard plank seats. I lay there under the stars wondering what was happening to the east. We had heard no sound of battle, although by now we were around seventy miles away. If the Prussians had managed to stretch around to the west of Metz, their lines would still be thin. Everything depended on Bazaine breaking through and marching towards us. There were bound to be skirmishes as he came on, but eventually he would meet the new army currently at Chalon coming the other way. I thought that the war would probably be decided at some climactic battle around Verdun.

We got steam up again at first light but had to stop later for fuel and water. Napoleon did not appear the least bit impatient to reach his destination. He sat chatting to his son and I had the distinct impression that for him the journey was an oasis of calm. At either end of it was one of his armies, who would demand decisions of him and present him with problems to solve. Yet sitting on a grass embankment waiting for a locomotive to build steam pressure, he was not expected to do anything. His idyll, though, was soon to end.

Chapter 11

We arrived at our destination on the evening of the sixteenth of August, a day and a half after leaving Metz. Chalon was now where the future of France rested. It was not a large town although its population had recently multiplied several times over, judging from the sea of tents and bivouacs in the fields surrounding it. There was just one platform at the station with a track on either side. As we pulled in, a longer train containing a mixture of carriages and even freight wagons was disgorging its passengers. We did not need to be told that they were some of the remnants of MacMahon's army. Some soldiers were missing their packs, left on the battlefield of Frœschwiller, while others were sporting wounds from the same place. They did at least all have their rifles, but they had been retreating through their own country, mostly on foot, for the last ten days and it showed. Shoulders were slumped; they looked tired and listless. They ignored us as we stepped down on the platform.

Looking along our train I saw that the door to the emperor's carriage was still shut. I wondered what he must be thinking as he stared out at his army. It had taken just two weeks to transform their high hopes of victory into humiliation and defeat. Did he blame his soldiers or feel responsible for their fate? Was he overwhelmed at the challenges that faced them? On the other hand, was he simply hoping they would clear off so that he could slip into the town unseen? If he was, disappointment beckoned, for they were in no rush. He could not risk being spotted hiding in a railway carriage, and so eventually his door opened, and he stepped down.

A coat covered his decorations and his hat was pulled down low; none of the soldiers paid him any attention at all. It was too much for the prince imperial in his pint-sized uniform. His father was the Emperor of France and he was being ignored. "Soldiers of France," his voice piped out, "your emperor is among you!" Napoleon looked as though he could have throttled the little brat. He looked up slowly, darting nervous glances along the platform.

Conversation quickly stilled. As the silence grew, men turned to stare at their monarch, who had clearly been trying to hide from them under a long coat on this warm summer evening. Their faces were hard, impassive, and for a moment I would not have wagered a centime on the emperor's chances. It would only have taken one of them to boo or shout an insult and he might have been strung up from the nearest lamp post. There was a moment of electricity in the air as everyone present sensed how finely balanced things were.

"Vive l'empereur!" The lone voice called out from the middle of the ranks, the shout echoing around the roof over the platform. *"Vive l'empereur!"* came a second yell and then a third and gradually the call was taken up down the ranks. Backs straightened, hats were waved in the air and smiles appeared on faces. They *were* soldiers of France; their emperor was with them and they were not beaten yet. Napoleon grinned, probably in relief, as he swept off his own hat and acknowledged their salute. I noticed that he too stood more erect, his chest and decorations now visible through his open coat.

Le Figaro was piping his eye and he was not alone. Others among the emperor's entourage were also blubbing at this restoration of national pride. Not everyone, however, was moved.

"Well, now we know he is not going to be shot by his own men," griped Charlie, "can we go and find somewhere to eat?"

"You are stone-hearted," I mocked although my stomach rumbled sympathetically. "Mind you, I thought the prince was due an arse-paddling there for calling out like that."

Charlie laughed, "That pampered pup has never been beaten in his life. Now come on, let's find some food."

Despite our best endeavours to leave, we were made to wait in the station. News of the emperor's arrival had quickly reached his military headquarters in the town. Officers pushed their way through the throng of soldiery on the platform to invite him to the town hall that had been requisitioned for their use. Napoleon's closest attendants went with him. These included the man from *Le Figaro*, who clearly had influential friends. The rest of us had to wait for the soldiers to march out. When we were finally able to emerge onto the street outside, we found it lined with guns of every description. They must have come by train from the south or from Paris; there were hundreds of them, together with crates of ammunition and other supplies. The whole town had been transformed into a vast regimental depot, with men in uniform marching in all directions. We had barely gone ten yards before we were intercepted by an officer dressed differently to the rest. He was all in blue – a marine. Now hundreds of miles from the sea, where they would have made little difference to the war, the marines had been ordered to join the forces gathering at Chalon.

He explained that no accommodation was to be had in town but that his unit had been detailed to provide us with lodgings. As we were led away, we soon saw for ourselves that every space was indeed full. Even the meanest shed already had two or three occupants crammed inside it. I imagined that we would be entering the newly erected suburbs of tents that surrounded Chalon, but the officer grinned and explained that tents were not part of a marine's equipment as they normally berthed on board ship. "Do not worry, gentlemen, you will not be sleeping under the stars, although that would be no great hardship on a warm evening like this." Instead, he led us to a large barn. I have never seen anything quite like it. Marines might not have tents, but they did have hammocks and so they had turned that barn into a vast cabin. Ropes were tied in all directions and from those and the rafters were slung hundreds of hammocks. They looked like cocoons in some human insect nest. We were given bowls of lamb stew and some fresh bread and then our own place to sleep in the hive. Mercifully, our beds were slung just two feet above the ground so there was little risk if we fell out. Finally installed, I looked up and counted at least six layers above me. After two days of travelling, it was not long before I was asleep.

So far, the army of Chalon had appeared a formidable force, but that impression was not sustained as we made our way back into town the following morning. There was a park on the outskirts where companies of young men were being drilled. Not one looked older than eighteen and none yet had uniforms or weapons. They must have been fresh off the trains from their towns and villages in the provinces. For many it was probably their first time away from home – and a very rude awakening. Many were still unable to march in step and when one was yelled at by a drill sergeant, the fellow burst into tears.

The situation was not helped by a crowd of onlookers, who jeered and mocked the proceedings. One man yelled his own orders at the recruits in a stentorian tone, causing chaos as they were obeyed. These spectators, a belligerent lot, were some of the Mobile Guard from Paris. The contrast between these louts and the three young members of the Mobile Guard we had travelled with from the capital could not have been greater. These fellows at least had uniforms and weapons, but also very firm ideas on what they would and would not do.

"We should never have been brought here," one told me when I asked how long they had been in Chalon. "We were raised to defend Paris and now instead they send us to this shithole. We're not going another metre east; we want to go home!"

"But aren't you the *Mobile* Guard?" queried Charlie. "You cannot expect to stay at home while others fight the enemy for you."

The man gestured furiously at the town hall. "Those bastards have not got a clue what they are doing," he asserted. "We will be wandering around in circles while the Prussians march on Paris. I am not having some bugger with a spiked helmet ravishing my missus."

"Don't worry," said his mate. "I've seen your wife, she'll be safe. My Mathilde on the other hand…"

We left them debating the relative appeal of their womenfolk to the enemy and made our way to the town hall. "It won't come to that, will it?" I asked Charlie. "Surely they will reach a peace treaty before the Prussians march through the streets of Paris." I had a sudden vision of Justine in her apartment staring out at black-uniformed Prussians marching past the bakery below. It seemed far-fetched, but then I remembered my grandfather telling me of joining foreign troops in Paris after Waterloo.

"I doubt it," replied my companion, dismissing the idea. "The French have built huge defences around Paris. It would take far more troops than the Prussians currently have in France to overcome them, especially as every Parisian able to hold a weapon would be on the ramparts." That was some comfort, at least. More reassurance came just a few minutes later.

Getting inside the headquarters was far easier than I had expected. At Charlie's suggestion, I just brandished the yellow card with all the ministerial stamps at the sentries and then we just kept walking in as though we owned the place. "Confident bluster works far more often than you would think," whispered my companion as we paused in the hallway. People were bustling about in all directions and to my surprise, more than a few were smiling. There was an air of celebration, and we did not have long to wait to discover why.

"Have you heard the news?" a familiar voice asked. We looked round to see the man from *Le Figaro* rushing towards us. "Bazaine has broken through the Prussian lines – he reports a great victory!" He shook our hands in delight, as though we'd had something to do with it. Then, lowering his voice, he confided, "Between us, when we were ambushed so far west, I did wonder if he would succeed."

"You were not the only one," grinned Charlie. "The Prussians must have been exhausted from the long looping marches to get around the city. It seems the tide of war is turning at last."

"Come share the office they have given me here," offered *Le Figaro* generously. "They keep bringing me fresh news and this triumph must be shared in London as well as Paris."

Life as a war correspondent was looking decidedly more comfortable. No more crouching in battlefields as shells whistled overhead as at Spicheren. Now there were desks to write at, good coffee and even pastries. Our French colleague was well connected with the staff and one of them would regularly put their head around the door to update him on the discussions underway.

A council of war was being held for the emperor, which we soon discovered had become a heated affair. Some swore it was vital he march west to Paris with the army at Chalon to quell the threat of revolution there. Others insisted he take the army east and join it with Bazaine's forces to beat the Prussians. Either way, they believed he could only protect his regime by a victory over his enemies, with him at the head of his army. Our spies told us that Napoleon took little part in these discussions. He just sat chain smoking, often with his head in his hands as the arguments washed over him. They spent hours quarrelling back and forth but could reach no conclusion. To delay matters, Napoleon dithered and ordered telegrams sent to Metz for news of Bazaine's progress. In the end, the only decision made was to send the Mobile Guard back to Paris. They refused to fight anywhere else and risked disrupting the rest of the army if they stayed.

By chance I had ended up with a ringside seat at one of the most critical decisions for France, if not the whole of Europe, for a decade. France would want to shout about Bazaine's victory to quell critics at home, as well as foreign powers that might be writing her off. The telegraph to London would probably be made available again soon, if only for censored reports, and so we set to work. Yet I struggled to concentrate as my mind kept straying to Pascal. Had he made it to Belgium and sent my despatch? How had my uncle received it? Would the need for business income outweigh his personal animosity? I had no idea if I still had a job, but if Uncle Frank was wavering in his decision, a telegram with more critical news might tip the balance. I began by writing an account of the battle east of Metz I had witnessed from the ramparts of the city, as well as the emperor's dramatic journey to Chalon. Then I added what little we had of the latest French triumph. Charlie did the same, but by late afternoon we discovered that we had all been wasting our time.

An officer put his head round the door. Before now he had happily brought us good news, but now he was pale, his features etched with worry. He spoke in hushed tones to *Le Figaro*. "We have had more messages from Bazaine." He licked his lips nervously. "He writes that he is marching his army back towards Metz for more supplies – they will form up again near Gravelotte. His supply column became disordered in the battle, and he needs artillery ammunition. He will set out for Verdun again tomorrow."

We all stared at him dumbfounded, for that made no sense at all. "But the battle was yesterday," I started, "which will give the Prussians two days to regroup and bring up more reinforcements of their own. He is bound to be outnumbered when he sets off again."

"Not if the Prussians have already been thoroughly beaten," insisted *Le Figaro*. "They would not dare try to stop him again. At least, they would think twice about it..." His voice trailed off as even such a fervent French patriot realised the improbability of what he was saying.

Bazaine's forces had numbered around one hundred and sixty thousand when we had left Metz, but he would need to leave some of them to garrison the town itself. Both sides would have lost men in the recent battle, but according to Forbes there were some two hundred thousand Prussians in the area. Depending on what garrison he left, he might be outnumbered by nearly two to one.

"If he had won his battle as he claimed," concluded Charlie, "he would not have needed to go back with his whole army. He could have ordered the supplies to come to him and continued to clear the road ahead."

"What does the emperor think?" asked *Le Figaro*.

With a weary sigh the officer conceded, "He does not know what to think or what to do. His council are more divided by this news than ever, both groups insisting they are right. He is most likely waiting for advice from the empress in Paris."

The next day was one of heightened tension in the town hall headquarters. We sat around in our little office trying to imagine what was happening a hundred miles to the east. Had Bazaine marched as planned? And if he had, what opposition had he encountered? The telegraph clattered incessantly. There was a constant gathering of around a dozen men loitering outside the telegraphist's office trying to glean news before anyone else. Most of the messages were to and from Paris, as ministers made their reports to the emperor or sought instruction. It was mid-afternoon before we heard anything from the east: the Prussians were attacking the French positions near Gravelotte but were being repulsed.

Replies were sent back to Metz eagerly demanding more news. I could picture couriers riding full tilt along that winding road to Gravelotte to catch up with the army, and then galloping back. If they did then their efforts were in vain, for by late afternoon the telegraphist reported that the line to Metz had been cut. It could have been damaged in the fighting, but it felt like an ominous development. Modern inventions can be a frustration, for now we knew that a battle was underway, but we had no way of knowing the outcome. More messages were sent to Verdun, Thionville and other nearby towns asking them to report news as soon as they had it, but the lines remained suspiciously silent.

No one wanted to speculate on what would happen if Bazaine and his men were beaten back; the consequences were almost unthinkable. The largest French army would be trapped, its only hope of rescue lying in the forces at Chalon, a good number of whom were untrained. That afternoon I went for a walk in the park where teenage soldiers were drilling. This group had been given uniforms, still freshly creased from their packing cases. Their Chassepots were just as new, and it was evidently the first time they had fired them. I watched as a dozen were instructed on how to load and aim. Then they lined up on targets in front of a wall of sandbags. At the order to fire, one boy panicked and did not discharge his weapon at all, while two others dropped their guns in surprise at the recoil into their shoulders. As far as I could see, the targets remained unscathed. I looked back at the town hall to see a figure watching them from the central window on the first floor. I could not be certain at that distance, but from the slumped shoulders and cigarette in hand, I suspected it was Napoleon. What, I wondered, would he make of this scene. The boys were little older than his own son. Was he imagining these poor devils pitched against the now battle-hardened veterans of the Prussian army?

By evening there was still no news. We dined at the headquarters, a quiet and subdued affair with everyone lost in their own thoughts, and then made our way back to our barn of hammocks for the night. As we strolled through the park enjoying the twilight, we saw that some of the wretched raw recruits were still being put through their paces. They all looked thoroughly miserable as they repeatedly fixed bayonets and charged sacks of straw.

"What a bloody mess," I concluded. "If Bazaine had broken through, surely a courier would have made it to the telegraph at Verdun by now."

"Do you care what happens to the French?" asked Charlie curiously.

"Yes, of course." I gestured to the men in front of us. "Knowing what we do, how could you not feel sorry for those poor sods. Half of them will probably be dead by the end of the month."

"Well, you shouldn't," insisted Charlie firmly. "They are just stories and articles to us. Do you think Forbes cares about the Prussians?"

"Since you ask, he seemed pretty smug about them when I last saw him."

Charlie grinned. "Make the most of this, lad, for it is the best war I have ever seen." He held up his cigar. "All the luxuries we could want to hand, and no freezing mud, murderous savages or scorpions that hide in your boots. You don't know how lucky you are, Harrison. And," he held up a finger to stop me interrupting, "we are right at the heart of what will be the story of the decade. The complete collapse of a major European power."

"That is all very well if you still have a job," I admitted, "but after my treatment of Chalmers, I fear that mine hangs by a thread. Frank has already sacked me, but Pascal has taken the Spicheren story to try to get me reinstated."

"I did wonder if you would get away with that. Your editor is a very sober fellow. I had an interview with him once and I don't think he approved of me."

"You don't know the half of it. He is my uncle, and the bastard hates my father and by association, me. Do you know anyone else who might want a correspondent?"

Charlie laughed, "You are not lost yet, young Thomas. Frank and his shareholders have taken a big risk with their pricing strategy. If he speaks to his owners about you, I dare say they will steer him in the right direction. The fact that we are here and our rivals aren't is worth a fortune to our employers. He cannot afford to let you go."

"I hope you are right."

"Chin up," chided Charlie. "If the worst happens, being fired is not the end of the world. Unless you are Napoleon, anyway. He could face the real prospect of a firing squad like Emperor Maximilian in Mexico."

"Do you think there will be another revolution, then?"

Charlie gestured back to the town hall. "Napoleon must drive the Prussians back out of the country to keep his throne. I don't see that happening, do you? No, the only way he will see Paris again is for a trial that would end in his exile or execution. I think the poor bloody fool knows it too."

"But what is the point of being at the heart of a story, as you put it, if we cannot report it? We still can't use the telegraph, our letters are censored and the Belgian border is now too far away."

"Don't worry about that, things will soon be changing," Charlie assured me confidently. "The British reader loves an underdog. When France declared war on Prussia, sympathies were mostly with the Prussians, who were expected to lose. But if a German army roundly thrashes the French one and marches on Paris, our subscribers will start to feel sorry for the French. The new government here will also see the value of having the British public's support. They will let us send anything we want, especially if it gets Londoners writing to their members of parliament and demanding that they intervene to save poor France."

"You are a cynical devil, but you may well be right," I laughed. "Do you never feel any sympathies for the people you write about?

"Of course, especially the redcoats in the Crimea. I think the correspondents cared about them more than their own generals. But you cannot let it get in the way of the work."

I thought about what Charlie said as I lay in my hammock that night. The snoring of five hundred men packed closely together, not to mention the creak of the hammock ropes on the timbers of the barn, made it hard to sleep. I could not find a flaw in my companion's logic, but then he had not slept with Justine. Once you had enjoyed that pleasure, it was hard to be entirely dispassionate. I smiled as I considered that she might get her precious republic back at the end of all this.

Chapter 12

There was no firm news of Bazaine the next day either. MacMahon, with his drooping moustache, had always had the demeanour of a chief mourner, but now he resembled a grief-stricken bloodhound. No one could make any decisions until they knew the fate of his fellow marshal. More telegrams were sent, but this only revealed that now all lines to the area had been cut. Eventually, we received word from Paris that someone from Thionville had made it to Luxembourg and sent a cable from there. They reported that they had heard a huge battle, which had lasted the whole of the previous day. Yet ominously, when they rode to investigate, they were intercepted by Prussian cavalry.

We sat about, watching regiments of the Mobile Guard being marched back to the station for trains to Paris. 'Marched' might be the wrong word as it gives the impression of a soldierly appearance. 'Shambled' might be more accurate, for these soldiers took a perverse pride in their own independence. Tunics were unbuttoned, caps tilted back and they sang many a coarse song as they went. You would think that they would show some gratitude seeing as they had got precisely what they wanted: whatever mess the army of Chalon was going to find itself in, it would not involve them. Certainly, one officer thought so, for as they passed in front of the town hall he called out a salute of loyalty to the emperor, expecting them to follow suit. As his *"Vive l'empereur!"* rang out, however, the soldiers simply looked at each other and grinned. *"Un, deux, trois, merde!"* they chorused in reply. As the obscenity rang around the central square, the officer nervously looked up at the town hall windows, but the emperor was not to be seen. Perhaps he knew his citizens better than the officer.

By nightfall even the most optimistic Frenchman was reluctantly concluding that the lack of news from the east could not portend anything good. Another council of war was held but all the old arguments were simply repeated. Once again Napoleon used the lack of any hard facts to postpone any decision. We were soon to learn that his time for prevarication was coming to an end.

I slept poorly that night and as absolutely nothing seemed to be happening the following day, I slipped back to the barn for an afternoon doze. I awoke to find Charlie vigorously shaking my shoulder. "Wake up, a Prussian cavalry patrol has been spotted twenty-five miles to the south."

"The south?" I repeated. "But I thought all the Prussians are to the east."

"The ones fighting Bazaine are," he confirmed. "This is probably the army that beat MacMahon before. While his French soldiers sped here by train, the Prussians have been marching by road."

In the town centre we found people running around in all directions. A single squadron of Prussian cavalry had thrown the French headquarters into pandemonium. All were convinced that an army was on the heels of the Prussian horsemen and MacMahon was clearly not keen on facing his former nemesis again any time soon.

No one had expected Chalon to be attacked. It was where the French army intended to begin a journey from, not one they would have to defend. Consequently, there were no fortifications around the town; it had been chosen as a rallying point for its rail connections and because it was between Metz and Paris. Unfortunately, the army had still not yet decided where it wanted to go, but it certainly could not stay where it was. Before long a hurried decision was announced: the army would travel thirty miles north to Rheims. As far as I could tell, this destination was chosen because it still lay in easy reach of the rail connections to Metz and Paris. The decision on our ultimate destination could be postponed, but not for long. Having marched so far to find us, the Prussians were bound to follow.

Telegrams were sent to Paris to update them on the latest developments. Then efforts began to organise a steady flow of trains between Chalon and Rheims to carry the vast amount of men, equipment and stores that had been stockpiled. Most of the infantry were to set off on foot first thing in the morning for what was hoped would be a two-day march. Meanwhile horses were fed and their shoes checked, wheels greased and countless other preparations made for the journey. We watched as the new recruits stood in queues for boots, packs,

110

ammunition, blankets, tents and all the other stores then available. Some of them looked terrified and I did not blame them. They had been in the army for less than a week and already they were on the run from the enemy.

We did not have to worry about walking as once again the man from *Le Figaro* had come up trumps. He had organised seats for us on the royal train, which had been sent from Paris and was waiting in a siding ready for use. We would be sitting in the rear carriage with some of his entourage, but no one complained about that.

As the human hive emptied for the final time, the marines set off on their journey with a look of grim determination. They were at least skilled and professional soldiers who were confident of giving a good account of themselves. Many were even determined to outfight their army colleagues. They sang naval songs as they marched off, all in step in a tight column of blue uniforms. The regular troops had a more resigned air: they had marched before and been beaten before. The expression on many of their faces indicated that they saw no reason to expect a different outcome this time.

The new recruits did not march in step. As they left the town many were already limping from the effect of fresh, poorly fitting boots. I did not dare think about what state their feet would be in at their destination. There had not been enough packs for all and so many had used their blankets to carry rations, ammunition and kit, holding the corners over their shoulder. They hurried down either side of the road to Rheims, which was soon filled with carts and guns slowly heading in the same direction. Behind them a division of cavalry remained to provide cover for stragglers and to set fire to stores left behind. For some reason piles of winter greatcoats had been sent to the army in August and these burned fiercely, sending up dark columns of smoke that would be seen for miles around. An old stone barn was used to destroy huge quantities of Chassepot ammunition. The roar of thousands of explosions in the confined space was deafening and blew out a wall of the barn, causing it to collapse in flames.

By the time we boarded the train there were a dozen blazes around the town, covering it with a pall of smoke that made it hard to breathe.

I was glad to hear the steam whistle and feel the jolt as the carriages started their journey. Charlie passed round a well-filled hip flask – we were certainly travelling in more comfort than most. The road was often in view and filled with a long line of men and animals sweating in the morning heat. We passed a large forest on our left and I noticed various abandoned bundles at its edge, including brand new rifles, which meant that some of the new recruits had already taken the opportunity to desert. I grinned as we passed half a dozen trying to march in step beside the trees. They must have seen the train coming and were giving their best soldierly appearance. I looked out of the back window of the train to confirm my suspicions. Sure enough, once we were past, they ran straight into the woodland.

We had to wait for a Paris train to move before we could pull into Rheims station. The platform was still packed with its passengers as word must have got out that the royal train was the next to arrive. As we finally stepped out of the carriage, all attention was directed to the coach with the imperial cypher on the door. It was not a particularly celebratory welcome for the emperor. There were a few cheers, but many were just there out of curiosity rather than admiration. How was their monarch holding up as his world was falling apart? He was alone now, his son had been sent back to Paris, but he still managed a wave as he was introduced to a line of dignitaries.

"Thomas!" I looked up in surprise as I heard a familiar voice calling my name. To my delight, here was Pascal pushing his way through the crowd towards me.

"What news do you have?" I called out impatiently, although I could see he was grinning. Already my hope for ongoing employment was soaring. By way of an answer, Pascal pulled out and unfolded a newspaper from his jacket. "You are a bloody good artist," I laughed embracing him and passed the copy to Charlie. It was a two-day old edition of the *Daily News*, with a very familiar drawing on the front cover and some damn fine words beneath.

"Well done the pair of you," said Charlie, patting me on the shoulder. "I told you Frank could not afford to turn down such material." Then, ever the reporter, he turned to Pascal. "Have you heard what is happening at Metz?"

"There was a battle near Gravelotte," he told us. "Bazaine had his men dig in near the town and the Prussians marched against them. There was a terrible slaughter of the enemy by our rifles and batteries of Mitrailleuse. The line stood firm the whole day." His words indicated that the French might have won, but the mournful tone with which he imparted them told us that they had not.

"What happened then?" I urged.

"In the evening the enemy outflanked the line at a place called Saint-Privat. Bazaine could have stopped them if he had reinforced the line with his reserve, but he did nothing. Our best men, the Imperial Guard, sat uselessly idle for the whole battle. Then when men saw the Guard retreating, the rest of the line collapsed. They have all withdrawn back into Metz."

"How do you know all this?" asked Charlie.

"That man was there." Pascal pointed to a wounded soldier who was now talking to the emperor. "He was in Saint-Privat but escaped through Prussian lines during the night. We shared a train from Belgium to Paris together and then to here. He tells me that many more Prussians were killed than the French and so it must be a French victory."

"Not if Bazaine is trapped again in Metz," I told him. "That leaves the French army divided and vulnerable." I was going to say more, but then another voice called out my name. Pascal had not been the only familiar face on the Paris train. The crowd was now thinning as the emperor had left and then I saw him: staring at me through a gap in the throng was Chalmers.

"You!" he bellowed, his face reddening with rage as he pointed a finger in my direction. His mouth was working like a gaffed codfish, yet for a man who made his living from words, he was strangely unable to find any. Then the dam in his lexicon broke, "You contemptible backstabbing traitor," he roared at me, causing various heads to turn in my direction. "You despicable wretch, you…you vile, double-dealing swine!"

"I don't think he likes you," murmured Charlie, suppressing a smile, but Chalmers was not finished yet.

An army officer was among those who had stopped to stare at me and my accuser grabbed at his arm. "Arrest that man," he demanded. "He is an imposter who has no right to be here."

Summoning a level of condescension that only a Frenchman can achieve, the officer shook Chalmers' hand away. "I do not take orders from you, monsieur," he sneered before turning on his heel.

The man from *The Times* now turned to face me, shaking with rage. "You should not be here," he insisted. "You have been sacked and your career is ruined…I have already seen to that."

"Apparently not," I replied, grinning. "Pascal, show Mr Chalmers our latest front-page story in the *Daily News*. Now, if there is nothing else, you will have to excuse us as we have work to do."

"The hell you have," Chalmers fumed. "I will have you sent home in disgrace if it is the last thing I do." With that he stormed from the station.

"The bloody fool," I scoffed. "The French have far more important things to worry about."

"I am not so sure," cautioned Charlie. "Even in all this chaos he will find someone to listen to him. They will worry he will complain about them to Paris. Then you will have a problem, for most French officers have heard of the famous *Times* newspaper of London, but none will have heard of the *Daily News*, or the *Pall Mall Gazette* for that matter. They are likely to take his word over yours."

"Then we need to find some way to discredit him," I concluded. I wracked my brain for something we could use and, after a moment, had an idea. "Have you ever been to Prussia?" I asked Charlie.

"Yes, twice," he answered. "Once in sixty-four for their Danish war and again in sixty-six when they fought the Austrians. Why do you ask?"

"Can I see your passport?" Charlie handed over the well-used document. Unfolding it, I looked on its reverse where various rubber stamps marked his entry into a myriad of countries. I found the Prussian ones and grinned in delight. "I don't think Chalmers is going to cause us any problems at all," I told them.

Pascal and I were busy all afternoon, but after Charlie's warning we were not surprised when, later that evening, we were tracked down by a young lieutenant. He informed us that we had been summoned to appear before the military governor of Rheims at nine-thirty the next morning. As the day had progressed, my confidence in the scheme underway had begun to wane. There were all sorts of things that could go wrong, especially if the governor had been exchanging messages about me with Paris. Yet surely in this time of national crisis, the line would be far too busy for such trivial traffic. That at least was my hope as we made our way to the governor's office the following morning. We arrived early and two minutes before the appointed time, Chalmers joined us. I knew that he would not be able to resist witnessing his moment of triumph.

"If there is any justice here, you will be sent home in irons," he sneered. "Then, when you are of no use to him, we will see if your editor will still defend you." I did not bother to reply, for at that moment the door opened and a harassed elderly officer gestured for us to enter.

"Today of all days, I do not have time to deal with squabbles between British journalists, so make this quick," he snapped.

"Certainly, sir," said Chalmers, and swiftly followed him into his office, leaving us trailing behind. "I am the chief correspondent in France of the London *Times* newspaper and this fellow is an imposter, who has been masquerading as me to get attached to the army."

"Is this true?" The governor glared in my direction.

"I took his place with the army after he was arrested for espionage in Paris. I was concerned that he might be a spy," I replied calmly.

"Espionage!" exploded Chalmers, "you arranged it all. You sent the information on the Mitrailleuse to *The Times*."

"But is *The Times* not your paper? Does Mr Harrison work for *The Times* too?" The governor was struggling to understand.

"No, he works for a tawdry rag called the *Daily News*, or at least he did. By now he should have been dismissed for his underhand behaviour."

"I still work for the *Daily News*, sir. This is one of my recent articles – the illustration was done by my French artist here." I handed over the copy Pascal had brought with him. I was not sure that the governor could read English, but he looked impressed with the picture of French soldiers fighting heroically on the cliff top of the Spicheren.

"So, if Mr Harrison works for this paper," he held up the *Daily News* as he looked at Chalmers, "why should he send confidential information to your employer?"

"He must have guessed that your government would read it," Chalmers replied irritably. "But that is beside the point. This man is an imposter and must be sent back to Paris in disgrace."

"The Ministry of War saw fit to arrest Chalmers for espionage and hold him for several days," I cut in. "I have no idea what he said to get released, but as further evidence I submit this." I leaned forward and placed a document on the governor's desk.

"Hey, that is my passport," Chalmers exclaimed. He reached forward to try to take it, but the governor snatched it away.

"You recognise this?" he enquired, studying it closely.

"Yes, as I say it is my passport. This wretch must have stolen it to support his deception.

"Have you been to Prussia, Monsieur Chalmers?" There was a warning tone in the governor's voice now, but Chalmers did not notice.

"No, I was with the Austrians in sixty-six when they fought the Prussians."

"How convenient, as you are with us now," muttered the governor reaching forward to ring a bell on his desk. The door behind us opened and two soldiers stepped into the room. "Perhaps, he continued, "you did not think I would notice these stamps amongst the others." He laid the back of the passport across his desk and pointed to two faded ink marks. "I see you disembarked from a ship in Hamburg on the tenth of June this year and then arrived in Berlin a week later. Less than a month after that you are in Paris, possibly gathering confidential information. How do you explain yourself?"

"But...but that is impossible, I have never been to Berlin." Chalmers leaned forward to inspect the marks, barely able to believe the evidence with his own eyes. Then his gaze whipped around to me. "You! You have done this." His anger overtook him and he lunged towards me, his fist raised. I stepped back just as one of the soldiers managed to grab his arm and haul him back to face the governor. "They have forged those stamps," he gasped as he struggled in vain to be released. "I swear I have never been to Berlin."

I laughed, making him even wilder as I countered, "Are you going to blame me for all your dark deeds, Chalmers? How would I get hold of a Prussian passport stamp? I have no idea what one even looks like and besides, that eagle mark looks impossible to forge." Turning to the governor, I added innocently, "Do they look genuine, sir?"

"They do indeed," he growled. "Mr Chalmers, you will be returned to Paris and the custody of the Ministry of War. This passport will be going with you as evidence."

"What? No! I am an Englishman, dammit. You can't send me back there; I work for *The Times*." Chalmers did not know whether to threaten or plead and in the end tried both, but to no avail. "You bloody fool, he has tricked you," he roared, gesturing at me. I struggled to maintain my look of shocked concern, while Pascal gloated openly in triumph. "I'll ruin you for this," he shrieked at the governor as he was dragged out of the door. "I will make your name a laughing stock all over Paris. I know the British foreign minister; he will have your head… My cousin is a lady in waiting to the queen. You wait, my editor will demand an apology from the emperor…"

The threats continued as he was dragged away down the corridor. By then he must have been virtually frothing at the mouth in his fury, shrieking accusations in English that his guards did not understand.

I turned to the governor. "I do apologise for my countryman," I said, trying to sound sincere, while inside I was bursting with delight at the success of our scheme. "Not all correspondents are like Chalmers, even at *The Times*."

We thanked the governor and hastily took our leave, professing not to want to waste any more of his time. The truth was I was more worried about him noticing the ink stain on Pascal's hand that I had just spotted myself. It bore a striking resemblance to the colour of ink used for one of the stamps. The marks on the passport *had* been near impossible to forge; it had taken an artist to do it. Pascal had practised them in pencil and then used a knife to shave down the point of a pencil rubber.

Dipping it in ink and then stamping it on some spare paper until the marks looked genuinely faded, he set to work. The result was a masterpiece of forgery that matched perfectly the stamps on Charlie's passport. All I had to do then was scribble in the incriminating dates beside them.

Chapter 13

"Tell me again about his editor demanding an apology from the emperor," laughed Charlie when we regaled him with the story. "Oh, how I wish I could have been there – it must have been priceless." Naturally, he had found some champagne to celebrate our success.

We were sitting on a balcony enjoying the evening sun as we watched MacMahon's army arrive from Chalon. They had taken two days to cover thirty miles, which was a good distance with pack and rifle. Even the regular soldiers were covered in sweat as their columns trooped into the square. The new recruits had long since lost any marching formation. They arrived alone or in twos and threes. Some of them had also lost their packs to lighten their load and at least one his rifle too. Most were limping. I saw several in bare bloodied feet with boots hanging from laces around their necks. They just slumped down in the shade of trees or against the rows of guns that now lined the centre of the city, while its concerned citizens rushed about with tankards and jugs of water to help revive them.

You could not help but pity the poor devils. Still no one knew where they were going next, but wherever it was, they were due for another long march. Paris was a hundred miles from Rheims due west, or Metz the same distance due east. *Le Figaro* had told us that MacMahon favoured taking his army to Paris. He had seen the state of the men on the march and thought them in no state to fight a larger Prussian force. There had been huge numbers of desertions into the forest among the raw recruits. Those that were left would not stand for long. If they turned west for the capital, they might just be able to keep their pursuers at bay long enough for some of the Paris defenders to come out to deter a Prussian attack. It seemed the obvious course of action to me, but there were other factors at play.

Chalmers had not been the only journalist on the Paris train; there was a French correspondent from a paper called *Le Temps*. I took an instant dislike to the fellow. If I am honest, it was partly because his paper's name was a direct translation of *The Times*, although they had different owners. He brought with him news from the capital, which gave us some idea of the pressure that the marshal was under. The prime minister of France was all too aware that if the army at Metz was captured, his regime would fall. MacMahon's army alone was not enough to liberate France and they would be forced to terms. To avoid another republic, their only hope was for MacMahon to march east and, as he drew away some of the besiegers, for Bazaine to break out and join him. It sounded so simple when you were sitting safely in some Paris office.

The prime minister was clearly determined to save his own political skin at any cost. He resolutely refused to believe that the situation was as dire as his generals reported. *Le Temps* showed us newspaper coverage from Paris in which the minister had insisted that all was not lost. Morale in the German army was low, he informed Parisians. Some of the Prussian reservists were close to mutiny after long, punishing marches day after day. The enemy army had been ravaged by dysentery and typhus and he was convinced that there was still a chance of Austria intervening in their favour.

It all sounded wishful thinking to me, but *Le Temps* insisted that the prime minister believed it to be true. Ignoring the state of the weary soldiers filling the town, this correspondent, who had only walked from the railway station, insisted that the exhausted troops march again without delay. "They are at least a day, possibly two ahead of the Prussian army behind them, who have travelled much further. The French army must stay ahead so that it is intact to fall on the forces besieging Metz."

I was scornful of this demand, but it turned out that the man from *Le Temps* was more in tune with what was going on than the rest of us. That evening, after days of prevarication and delay, the prime minister gave MacMahon a direct order on behalf of the government: he was to march to the relief of Bazaine without delay.

Le Figaro brought us the news early the following morning. "Napoleon has refused to intervene," he told us. "He does not seem to have the energy to countermand his own government and so will march with his army instead."

"But will they stand a chance?" I queried. "They have to keep ahead of the Prussians behind them and then fight their way through a larger army ahead, who are bound to patrol the main road to Paris."

"But the pursuers must be exhausted by now," insisted *Le Temps*. "They will surely fall further behind each day."

"And MacMahon does not plan to go down the main Paris road," Le Figaro informed us. "Surprise will be essential to their success. He believes that Bazaine's best chance of breaking out of Metz will be to the north; he plans to march northeast, so that he can also come down on Metz from the north. There are few towns in that direction and with hills and stretches of forest, he might be able to keep his army hidden from enemy scouting parties."

Looking at the map, this made a lot of sense. It would be a longer march for his tired men, but if they could catch the enemy by surprise, it would be worth it. The only obstacle was the River Meuse, which they would need to cross to reach Metz.

"Well, it looks like bloody madness to me," concluded Charlie. He glared at *Le Temps* and added, "I very much doubt the Prussians are as exhausted as you say, and this army will not be hard to track. It will probably have a long trail of stragglers behind it – for goodness' sake some are still arriving this morning from Chalon. No, it is time for me to return to Paris. If the government falls, I need to be there to report on it." The other two French journalists nodded in agreement.

"In that case, I will go on with MacMahon," I decided.

"Why on earth would you do that when the big political stories will be in Paris?" queried Charlie, puzzled. "You must know that MacMahon has little chance of success."

"Because when Chalmers gets released by the ministry a second time, he will raise merry hell with Frank about me. If I am in Paris, I will just be reporting the same news at the same time as everyone else. I need to have something new to report to keep my job a second time. Because MacMahon looks doomed, I might be the only correspondent with him." I turned to Pascal, "You do not have to come; I will quite understand if you want to return home."

"Do you know how many unemployed artists there are in Paris?" Pascal grinned. "No, I will stick with you. This Frank pays well for very few drawings."

Charlie clearly thought we were being reckless. "That job is not worth getting killed over," he chided.

"Don't worry," I told him. "I have no intention of getting killed. At the first sign of a battle, I will be diving out of the way waving a white flag high over my head, but I don't think it will come to that." I pointed at a map on the table, "You have seen how strung out this army became over thirty miles. With little time to rest, it will never manage another hundred. I suspect it will disintegrate or be overhauled long before it gets to Metz."

I turned to Pascal, "Not that we are going to be walking," I reassured him. "We will buy some horses to stay in the vanguard, well away from our pursuers." I grinned at Charlie, feeling a completely unjustified confidence, "I will wager you ten guineas that in a week's time MacMahon will have led what little he has left of his army into Belgium, to avoid having to surrender to the Prussians."

We set off on the twenty-third of August. The following nine days were amongst the most disastrous in the annals of military history – a gold-plated balls-up of mismanagement right from the very beginning. MacMahon's army was still a substantial force, the bulk of which consisted of professionally trained soldiers. There were a hundred and thirty thousand men including a sizeable cavalry contingent and more than four hundred guns, including Mitrailleuses. Further fresh reservists from Paris had replaced many of the new recruits who had deserted. Normally a force that size would give any enemy pause for thought. The raw numbers, though, did not tell the whole story, for it was an army that had suffered defeats and retreats without a single taste of victory. We were not the only ones assessing its chances, for even the lowliest private had heard by now of the battles around Metz. Most of them would have agreed with Charlie about their odds of success. Consequently, the morale of this huge host was near rock bottom.

It had been impossible to *buy* horses, but a substantial bribe to a cavalry officer in charge of remounts secured us the loan of two sturdy mares. I was damned if I was going to walk a hundred miles, especially if a fast withdrawal might be required. The animals had the army stamp on them, but when we were challenged, I merely had to show my yellow card to be waved on. Our saddlebags were packed with food and supplies as it was immediately obvious that we would need to look after ourselves.

The French army commissary had repeatedly demonstrated a staggering lack of preparation. While there were plenty of rations and supplies at Rheims station, the commissary troops had no idea where they were. It was akin to a blind man trying to find the tits on a sow, and they soon gave up any pretence at a search. When soldiers came for their rations, they were left to fend for themselves. Hundreds of crates were smashed open and pillaged, but often there was no food to be found within. Many were sent away empty handed. So, from day one soldiers were breaking ranks and raiding farms. What they found, however, was not nearly enough to sustain an army, so on just the second day of its march, the army of Chalon changed direction away from its objective. Instead of going east or northeast towards Metz, it now had to travel eighteen miles north. Its new interim destination was a town called Rethel, where the much-needed supplies could be brought by train.

Hunger increased the pace of march considerably and most reached the rail depot the next day. I was amazed that we did not already have Prussian scouts on our tail, but there was no sign of our pursuers. They must have been blind, I thought, to miss us. While the paved roads might have hidden the multitude of wheels that passed down it, at least until the paving ran out in the countryside, thousands of boots and hooves had flattened the fields in great swathes on either side of the highway. A partial explanation was waiting for us at Rethel.

"What the hell are you doing here?" I asked Charlie when I saw him standing outside the railway station. "I thought you were going back to Paris."

"I did," he replied and only now did I detect a grimness to his features. "I came back to make sure you, and more importantly the marshal, is aware of this." He held up a newspaper, a copy of *Le Temps*.

123

As he handed it over, he added, "You were right about that weasel, he sold out his country for a story."

I looked down at the front page and could barely believe my eyes. The paper had printed in detail MacMahon's plan to take a northerly route to Metz in the expectation that Bazaine would also break out in that direction. "How on earth did this get published after they have censored everything we write?" I demanded.

"The authorities tried to stop it, but it was too late," sighed Charlie wearily. "In the time it has taken me to get here, other copies will have made their way to Belgium and will now be in the hands of the Prussians. They now know exactly what the army of Chalon is trying to do."

In the circumstances, the marshal took the news reasonably well. When we brought the paper to the attention of his aide, the man was so furious he nearly had us shot. Only with some difficulty did we convince him that we were not the journalists responsible for its production. Then like any sensible fellow, he realised that giving such bad news to his superiors was not the job for him. A few minutes later we found ourselves being shown into the stationmaster's office that MacMahon had taken over. I watched his grey eyes as he scanned the lines. His lips moved behind his soup-strainer moustache as he muttered to himself. Then to my bewilderment, his shoulders started to shake, and he began to laugh, to my mind, slightly hysterically. It would not have been surprising if he lost his mind under the pressures he was dealing with. Eventually, he looked up, saw our expressions and brought himself together. "Thank you, gentlemen, for letting me know. I agree with you that the Prussians are bound to have read this now too, but I regret it changes nothing."

"But can the emperor not give you new orders?" I queried. "If you were to march back towards Rheims," I suggested, "you might catch your pursuers by surprise and win a victory."

The marshal shook his head sadly. "The government in Paris," he held up the paper, "who allowed this to be published, gives me my orders now. It has been made clear that we must relieve Metz at all costs. The emperor is resigned to remaining with his army until the end."

We took our leave from his office then. "He has given up," I said to Charlie as we walked back along the platform. "The emperor too from the sound of things. They don't have a hope of fighting their way to Metz. It is simply a matter of when and where they will be defeated."

"You should see how things are in Paris," he replied. "They refuse to accept that their armies can be beaten. There is much talk of treachery and betrayal by its commanders. Many think Bazaine should be able to break out unaided and cannot understand why he does not. To them it is inconceivable that he should be trapped. Now they believe that all effort must go into joining the army of Chalon with the army at Metz. If this can be achieved, then victory might still belong to France. No one will listen to MacMahon or even the emperor, if they claim this cannot be done." He grinned and then added, "This has disaster written all over it. I would be tempted to stay myself, but I am due to interview the war minister tomorrow."

"Anybody in their right mind would be running for the hills now," I agreed, while knowing I would do no such thing. I had already learned that bad news sells papers far more effectively than good. Subscribers might hail a hero they read about, but the armchair generals will get far more worked up over incompetence and misfortune. They will argue for hours over who made mistakes and when, while utterly convinced that if only they had happened to be there to sort things out, all would now be to the good. While a few of the officers might be writing for French papers, I was the only foreign correspondent still with the army. All I had to do was stay alive and find a working telegraph. Then my miserable bastard of an editor would have another big story on his hands. More importantly, my job would still be safe whatever Chalmers might whine to him about.

It rained the next day, and the greyness and gloom matched the mood of the army. Gnawing disconsolately on hard tack biscuits, they splashed through puddles as they finally turned back east towards Metz. While I have just claimed that catastrophe is good material for a correspondent, there are times when a man must look after himself. For that reason, I am damn glad that we travelled at the head of the army with the emperor and for most of the time with MacMahon too. The rear-guard was commanded by a general called Failly, who, as it turned out, was 'fail' by name and 'fail' by nature. Rarely had there been such a consistent display of ineptitude in command.

The morning after we set off, the Prussian cavalry that had been searching for us finally tracked us down. Enemy horsemen were spotted watching the army from a hill. Somehow commanders, including Failly, became convinced that the entire Prussian army was waiting just beyond them. For hours tens of thousands of men reorganised themselves into full battle order, awaiting attack. When no assault materialised, French scouts discovered that they faced just a single squadron of bemused cavalry. Nearly an entire day was wasted with these needless manoeuvres and a large gap left in the marching line.

On we went and when the weather improved, more Prussian scouts were spotted shadowing us to the south. All hope of surprise was now gone; the enemy generals were probably getting hourly reports of our slow progress. The main obstacle between our army and Metz was the River Meuse. MacMahon had been planning to cross this at a place called Stenay, but of course a Saxon division of the German army were already there in strength, waiting for us. Reluctantly the army turned north again, away from Metz and towards another crossing at a place called Mouzon. Well not quite all the army, for by now it was so broken up that Prussian cavalry amassed in vast numbers between the scattered corps. French horsemen could not be roused to chase them off and as a result, the messenger carrying news of the change in direction to Failly's corps was captured. Failly's men blithely continued on to Stenay, unaware that they were now on their own. Having prepared to defend themselves against one army that did not exist, they now blundered into a very real one, waiting to ambush them by the crossing. They were badly mauled as they made their escape.

Marching through a thick forest at night they got away and by dawn the next day had reached a place called Beaumont, where the exhausted men threw themselves to the ground to sleep. No one thought to organise guns into defensive batteries or even to post any sentries. By noon the next day Failly was still refusing to put out any scouts or pickets, despite warnings from locals that the enemy was in the vicinity. Much to his annoyance a woman running the local orphanage interrupted his lunch to show him on a map where German troops had been seen. He dismissed her concerns, claiming that "women do not understand war", before having her ejected. He had barely taken a spoonful of soup before the first artillery shell struck the village. It was a Bavarian force that found the still resting Frenchmen. One said that it was almost unfair to open fire on such an unsuspecting target, but open fire they did.

We heard the shooting from Mouzon, four miles to the north on the other side of the Meuse. Some wanted to cross back over to help, but MacMahon would not allow it. He could not afford to fight with his back to the river. It took the rest of the day for Failly's men to fight their way clear of Beaumont, aided by the rest of the army providing artillery support from our side of the Meuse. It was a chaotic mess that cost Failly over a third of his command, many of his cannon and left the survivors disordered and exhausted. We watched them stagger across the bridge, shaken from their recent exploits. Many were wounded and a few sodden figures had abandoned their weapons and swum across. Slowly and disconsolately, the vanquished men made their way to Mouzon.

It was obvious now to all but a complete imbecile, that the relief of Bazaine's army at Metz was not going to happen. There were German forces now to the south of us on both sides of the Meuse, cutting off that approach. It was no surprise when the army began to march north again. I did not know it then, but one such imbecile had just joined us. His name was General de Wimpffen and he had travelled by train straight from Paris. There, desperate politicians had filled his head with nonsense about the poor morale of the German army, along with the imperative for victory and the relief of Bazaine. What no one knew then, was that they had also put in his pocket orders giving him command if something happened to MacMahon.

We knew or cared nothing of this as we proceeded. I thanked my stars for the horses, as the infantry had now been marching for days. They were staggering with fatigue and spread out over miles of countryside. The army desperately needed to find a safe place to rest and regroup. It also needed to resupply itself with food and in the case of Failly's corps, ammunition. Word spread down the line that we would do so at a place called Sedan. There was a fortress there we were told, but more importantly it was only six miles from the Belgian border.

"That is where we will end up," I confidently predicted to Pascal. "This army has no more fight left in it. It is cornered and rather than surrender it will slide out beyond the reach of the Prussians." As it turned out, I was wrong on every point.

Chapter 14

The fortress at Sedan was a huge structure, its tall walls vulnerable to explosive shells. It was surrounded by great earthworks originally designed to impede attackers from storming it, but these had been neglected over the years. A few of these ramparts had collapsed and bushes, even trees, grew from between the stones of many of the others. It had been designed for the wars of old and would not stop a modern army. The valley of the Meuse, broad and marshy, protected the town from the south. Looking at a map, Sedan lay in the middle of the base of a triangle. About a mile on either side of the town there were valleys that ended at the river, but both began at a single point around two miles north of the town. The ground rose up away from the river and so the valleys became steep obstacles as they progressed towards this point. This larger space would be much easier to defend than the castle; for all its disasters and losses on the way, MacMahon's army was still too big to fit inside the ramparts. The river served as a moat for the triangle to the south, while any attacker would have to run down the slope on their side of the valley and then assault the French positions uphill.

We had arrived on the thirty-first of August 1870. MacMahon was convinced that this natural redoubt would provide protection for his army while it gathered its strength and restocked from supplies at the railway station. Having been on a march for over a week, he issued an order to the army that the next day it would rest. Following his own advice, he and the emperor retired to the castle to consider their options. His hospitality was restricted to a small group of aides that did not include foreign correspondents, so Pascal and I followed the rest of the army up the slope behind the town.

It was a peaceful scene late that afternoon. In the centre of the triangle was a forest and men were soon dragging wood from it to make cooking fires. I never ceased to be amazed by the tasty stews French soldiers could produce from a few scavenged ingredients. We had bread, cheese and wine in our saddlebags and tucked into this feast while we left the horses to graze.

Sated, I turned my attention to the goings on around us. Back down the hill across the river, I could just make out the blue uniforms of the Bavarian soldiers that had ambushed Failly's corps. They were moving up on the opposite bank, I guessed in case the army tried to retreat towards Paris. I was just finishing the last of the cheese when Pascal called for me to look over my shoulder. "There," he said pointing to the southeast, over the valley. "They must be the Prussians that stopped us crossing the river at Stenay. They have followed us up on this side of the Meuse."

I peered across the valley that formed part of the triangle. More soldiers were indeed appearing on the far hilltop. "They will be making sure that we do not try to double back to Metz," I concluded, swigging from my bottle. "I tell you, we will be in Belgium by this time tomorrow, or the day after at the latest. MacMahon and the emperor do not have a choice. This army will not fight its way back to Paris now and the Prussians will not let it anywhere near Metz."

"That is easy for an Englishman to say," grumbled Pascal. "But if we are driven out of the country, where does that leave France?" I did not need to reply, for we both knew the answer; without an army France was stuffed. It would be humiliated and with no alternative but to sue for peace. It was astonishing how things had changed in little over a month. Back then everyone was expecting the French to march on Berlin. Now there was little to stop the Prussians reaching Paris. I had to admit that Forbes had been right, that Bismarck was a wily bastard. He had provoked the French into a conflict that his forces had prepared meticulously for. Warfare had changed from the era of the emperor's uncle, in this conflict newly laid train tracks and railway timetables were as important as cannon.

I lay back to enjoy the early evening sunshine, running through in my mind how I would describe the abject surrender of France. I chuckled as I imagined how furious Chalmers would be on missing out. Even sweeter would be the conflict on my uncle's features as he was forced to congratulate me for helping to save the paper's finances. Another big story on the end of the war and the shareholders would never let him sack me. Things, I thought, were finally breaking my way. Pascal shook my shoulder. "You had better see this," he muttered. Something about his tone warned me that when I opened my eyes, it would not be good news.

He was staring to the eastern side of the triangle. Where we had just seen soldiers, now we saw guns– hundreds of them. They stretched in an unbroken line from the banks of the Meuse, up as far as we could see around the trees. "That is a hell of a lot more guns than Failly reported at Stenay," I said. My guts twinged as I had a nasty premonition that the following day would not be as restful as MacMahon had expected. French gunners were starting to move their pieces now to face these batteries, but they were at a disadvantage. Not only did the Prussian guns have a longer range, but the hills the enemy were on were, in many places, higher.

Pascal and I mounted up and rode further up the hill around the central forest, only for our worst fears to be confirmed. The line of guns extended to the pinnacle of the triangle, with the first ones just appearing on the western side. There too the guns were higher than our own. To my horror, I saw that the Prussian generals had built a trap and we had blundered right into it. The force now wrapping itself around us was far larger than the army that had followed MacMahon from the south. The only explanation was that they had seen the course of our army and detached some of the besiegers of Metz to join the attack. As far as I could see, the enemy now had double the number of cannon and, possibly hidden beyond the hilltops, double the number of men too. Retreat to Belgium was now out of the question, which raised a nasty predicament for your trusty correspondent. I had always assumed that I would witness any battle from the rear. As I stared about me with some alarm, I realised that in this case there was no 'rear'; we would be attacked from all sides.

A general I did not know sat on his horse nearby, studying the enemy with a glass. Once satisfied he'd fully grasped what he saw, he delivered the most succinct summary of the situation. "Gentlemen," he announced to the group of officers around him. "We are in a chamber pot; tomorrow we will be shat upon."

There was silence for a moment and then one of his aides commented, "Well, it is time we stopped retreating anyway." The rest nodded in agreement.

I had despaired of the French army over the previous week, for every day its morale and level of organisation sank ever lower. As discipline had broken down and they had fled from much smaller groups of the enemy, it was hard to imagine their forbears conquering the whole of Europe under the emperor's uncle. You would not have put money on most of them fighting their way out of a wet sack. Yet now, when the odds were stacked massively against them, they suddenly found some backbone.

"You English would not understand," explained Pascal. "You are cold and logical; you do not understand *la gloire*. It is pride and spirit. It is unthinkable to surrender now when the future of our country is at stake. Every Frenchman must fight tomorrow or hang their head in shame."

"But you are an artist, not a soldier," I protested. "Neither of us has guns. We are supposed to be impartial observers."

"You can be impartial if you want," he snapped back. "But I shall fight." He could not be dissuaded and went off to help those digging trenches on the eastern side of the triangle. For nothing better to do, I went with him.

I encountered raw recruits digging alongside veterans. They cast nervous glances across the valley at the line of muzzles facing them, but they took their turn with the spades. They had grown up a lot in the last week. Their uniforms had lost the packing case creases and were covered in mud like the rest. None looked like they would burst into tears if they fired their gun now. But they still had a lot to learn. Two of them struggled over with a log they planned to use for cover at the front of the trench.

"Get that away," ordered one of the old hands. "If an artillery shell hit that, the splinters would kill half of us." Pale-faced at the thought, the youngsters hauled their burden away. It was a grim reminder of the dangers ahead. It was a warning for me too, as I had been considering hiding in the forest for the battle. I would need to look elsewhere. My next thought was the castle and town of Sedan, but walking down the hill in that direction, I saw that the Bavarians had already set up their own batteries on the other side of the river.

The occasional shell was fired into the town to disturb the eerie peace of the early evening. They were landing around the bridges, which I guessed the French were now destroying. In the morning the town and fortress would be the obvious targets. Two-hundred-year-old walls would not last long against modern artillery. The prospect of being buried alive or crushed under falling masonry did not appeal. It was growing dark now, and so I made my way back to where I had last seen Pascal.

I weaved my way through campfires. Over the surrounding hills a glow from German fires reflected off the clouds. There had to be at least a hundred thousand men packed into the triangle and judging from the cannon, perhaps double that number on the far slopes around us. Every man there knew that there would be a big battle the following day; it was only natural to wonder if this would be one's last evening on earth. Christ, this was not what I had expected when I had talked with Forbes of being a war correspondent. With the range of the German artillery, nowhere would be truly safe. My stomach churned in fear as I realised that I would have to take my chances with the rest. This would be no Spicheren, where there was very little real risk on that hilltop. Any fool could see from looking around that the general was right: tomorrow we would be pelted with real explosive metal 'shit'.

Men face the prospect of death in different ways. I passed an army padre holding an impromptu service. Some quietly sang hymns, while others queued up to give what they hoped would not be their final confession. One group were playing dice, a pile of rings, watches and coin on the blanket they sat on – as though the risks of the following day were not chance enough. More than a few found solace in a bottle.

"Thomas, over here." Pascal's voice called out in the darkness. I found myself nearly falling into the trench that he and the others had dug. "Take this," he said, pressing a flask into my hand, "I saved you some."

"This is bloody good stuff," I gasped as the warming cognac eased the anxiety in my guts.

"Monsieur Charlie gave it to me. He said to save it until we had something to celebrate, but I thought it better we share it today." There was a moment's silence as we both acknowledged the words unsaid…

"Are you really going to fight?" I asked him.

He gave a bitter laugh, "Are you really going to tell Justine that you sat on your arse when the future of France was at stake?"

"Right now, I would be happy to be alive to tell her anything," I admitted. By then it was so dark that we could not see the opposite hill, but I gestured to it anyway. "You know France cannot possibly win, don't you? You heard what that general said."

"Yes," he admitted, "but we can keep some pride in the manner of our defeat. Men can hold up their heads and say with dignity that they fought at Sedan. We did what we could for the honour of our country." He could see that I was far from convinced and so he tried another tack. "As you are back, I take it you have not found a safe place to hide?" When I nodded, he grinned, "So if you are going to be shot at anyway, you might as well shoot back."

"Maybe," I replied. Perhaps because I was British or more likely because I was fearful of the consequences, fighting still seemed wrong. I was a civilian, a certified war correspondent and should I survive the morrow, I had expectations that the enemy would treat me well. All hope of that would be lost if they found me blazing away at them. We settled down to try to sleep, but I would venture that very few on that hillside got much rest that night. Our minds were too busy ruminating on what the next day would bring and whether we would see another sunset.

Chapter 15

The battle started in the early hours of the following morning. I could not say precisely where, as it was still black as pitch, but the sound of gunfire came from the southeast corner of the triangle. "The Bavarians must have tried to cross the river," I predicted. We listened as the crackle of rifle fire grew, occasionally enhanced by cannon, which created flickers of light in that direction. I looked apprehensively into the void opposite, where we knew hundreds of muzzles were pointing in our direction, but they stayed silent, as did the French gunners near us. Those artillerymen did not want to waste shot firing blind.

I stirred up the embers in a fire and in the dim glow could make out from my watch that it was just after half past four. We sat on the hillside for another two hours listening. The fighting was not getting any closer, but nor was it dying away. I remembered that there was a small village in that corner and thanked my stars I had not chosen it for sanctuary. As well as the gunfire, we also heard shouting and, several times, a woman's high-pitched scream. They must have been fighting house to house. Hooves thudded the ground nearby as a handful of officers galloped down the hill to investigate and report back, but beyond that everyone stayed where they were and waited for the dawn.

As the morning light began to spread across the sky, we could once again make out the line of muzzles opposite. It felt only a matter of time before they joined the battle still ongoing in the southeast. At the sight of them the men around me set to with their shovels again to widen and deepen the trench. This time I joined in, for it was as safe a place as any for me to cower. The prophetic general rode past, offering encouragement to his men. I gathered his name was Ducrot. He was the second in command of the army and had made his headquarters in a broad trench behind a nearby shepherd's hut. There was still no sign of MacMahon.

"They're loading their guns!" As the shout went up we all looked across to confirm. There was movement of men around the canon breeches, then, as one, all the men I could see scattered into their burrows with the speed of a mouse at the sight of a cat. If there were any stragglers, I missed them, for I was gratefully pressing myself into the earth too. The trench was only waist deep, but it was broad enough for us all to sit with our knees drawn up against our chests. Pascal was crouched on one side of me and a raw recruit on the other. The mud on the boy's face contrived to make him look even younger. He was quietly whispering a prayer to himself, but his heavenly appeal was soon drowned out by an ungodly roar. The ground literally shook as shells exploded all around us. Piles of earth that we had piled in front of the trench for more cover began to fall back in.

The lad beside me panicked. "We are going to be buried alive!" he gasped as he struggled to get to his feet.

I grabbed his arm and pulled him back. "Sit down, you bloody fool," I told him. "You will be killed for certain if you go up there." The French artillery returned fire and we sat and listened to a battle raging over our heads. With the hillside around us we were relatively safe, for the Prussian gunners were not aiming at the trenches. Their targets were the opposing artillery. Soon we were hearing clangs and screams as guns and those who served them were hit. The French must have had four hundred guns of their own on that hillside, but it was still a horribly unfair duel. There was a battery twenty yards from us. After a while, when we had got used to the barrage, we risked a glance over the parapet in their direction. While they had dug an earthwork in front of the guns, the loaders still had to go around it to push fresh charges down the muzzle. Three bodies lying in a crater just in front of one muzzle was testament to how horribly exposed they were. Another gun had already been thrown on its back. Through a gap in the embankment, I could see several injured men being bandaged. There was a palpable reluctance by the gunners to step forward again, for the rate of fire amongst the French guns was already falling. Meanwhile the breechloading Prussian artillery was firing as quickly as ever, concentrating on their rapidly reducing number of targets.

"Get ready!" a voice called above my head. I looked up to see a corporal crouching down over our trench. "The general says we are pulling back to the northwest. Wait for the order, then move quickly." With that he was gone, running on to the next burrow in the line.

"Thank God someone has some sense," I breathed.

"Another retreat," Pascal muttered glumly.

"Once they have finished with the artillery, those Prussian gunners will be turning their attention to us," I warned him. Nodding to the boy on my other side, I whispered, "I don't want the lad's premonition to be proved right." The thought made me shudder and suddenly the wet earth about us felt more oppressive. I risked another look over the parapet. Half of the nearby battery had now been destroyed, but to their credit, men were still loading and firing the remaining guns. Beyond them I could see the stone hut that protected General Ducrot's headquarters. I had a sudden memory of Forbes' suggestion for the best place to be in a battle and knew that was where I needed to get. "I am going over there," I told Pascal, pointing. "Are you coming with me?"

"You must be mad!" he exclaimed shaking his head. "You will be killed."

I was sure I was right but knew if I stopped too long to think about it, I would probably die of indecision. I did not allow myself to hesitate; I wedged a foot in the earth and pushed myself up over the top. A second later I was up and running. There were explosions to the left and the right around our batteries and then the roar and plume of smoke as a French gun returned fire nearby. I locked my gaze on that stone hut as a shell whistled low over my head and kept my legs pumping as fast as I could. I half stumbled and fell into the trench and, to the surprise of both of us, nearly landed in the general's lap.

"Who the hell are you?" he demanded, shifting away to give me room.

The others stared at me with curiosity; I was the only one not in uniform and suddenly the situation seemed absurdly formal. I reached up to doff my hat before remembering I had lost it. "Thomas Harrison, sir," I introduced myself, "from the London *Daily News*."

To my surprise the general laughed. "I have an army to command. I do not have time for interviews at the moment."

"But what about Marshal MacMahon?" I asked, puzzled.

"He was shot in the leg during the attack in the south," came the curt reply. Impatiently, he turned to a lieutenant. "Continue your report."

"They already have guns along two-thirds of the western side, sir. We can see more coming and ammunition carts too. But they have not yet opened fire – perhaps they do not have enough shells yet to maintain a barrage."

"Then there is not a moment to lose." Ducrot was energetic and decisive. "If we give them the chance, they will surround us. We must break out now. We will have to abandon a lot of the guns, but it cannot be helped." He turned to another officer. "As soon as word has been passed along the line, give the order. I don't want anyone left..." He paused as another general reined up next to the trench. I had not seen him before and judging from his immaculate uniform he had not shared the marches of the last two weeks. "De Wimpffen," Ducrot gasped in surprise. "What on earth are you doing here? I thought you were in North Africa."

"I was until a week ago," the newcomer advised sternly. "Paris summoned me back and sent me here as they are alarmed at how this campaign is being conducted."

"Well, there is no time to brief you now," Ducrot snapped irritably, evidently wishing this new visitor had stayed in Africa. "We are withdrawing to the southwest."

"No, we are not," said the newcomer. "There will be no more retreats. The government demands victories and—"

He was interrupted by an explosion in a nearby battery. I looked round to see a bronze cannon barrel tumbling through the air as the surviving gunners screamed in agony.

"Have you seen our gun line?" Ducrot demanded. "I am now in command here and I say we will withdraw."

"Ah, but you are not in charge," de Wimpffen countered, unable to hide his delight. He flourished a paper from his jacket like a card sharp producing an ace. "I have here authorisation from the prime minister that I should take command if MacMahon is unable to lead the army. We will drive the enemy attacking in the south back. Then we will push on and outflank these guns," he gestured across the valley. "The emperor will lead the attack and it will end in triumph for France."

"Triumph?" repeated Ducrot ashen-faced. "If we do not withdraw now, we will be lucky to have a retreat."

I stood and watched aghast as this Johnny-come-lately, who had no more idea about attacking Prussians than my Aunt Agatha, started to give orders to plan a new assault. Ducrot did his best to deter him, pointing out that the tactics he was used to employing against North African tribesmen would not work here. Attacking from a corner would also mean that the men would be under fire from two lines of Prussian guns, not just one. But de Wimpffen would not listen. "You are defeatist," he insisted. "France demands victory." With that our new commander rode off to summon the emperor to join him in his new venture.

"Should we send our reserves to join this new attack?" a major asked of Ducrot.

The general looked out at the line of trenches that contained his men and then gave that expressive shrug of the shoulders that only the French can do well. "We are ordered to defend the line here. We will need our reserves before this day is done."

I stayed hunched down behind that shepherd's hut for much of the morning, listening to regular reports of de Wimpffen's attack. You will not be surprised to learn that it did not go well. Many of his requested reinforcements managed to 'get lost' in the triangle on their way to joining the assault, which I presumed meant 'hid in the forest', for soldiers are not fools. Anyone with a spark of sense could see that such folly could only end in disaster. The absentees included the emperor, who flatly refused to appear.

By then Ducrot had ridden off to see what was happening on the other side of the triangle. We could hear that a new artillery duel had started there, but the Prussian fire on our area had diminished. Most French guns had been disabled and the surviving gunners remained behind their emplacements. They had discovered that any attempt to approach the muzzle of their pieces with a shell, would bring a score of Prussian guns firing in their direction. I have since learnt that there is often a lull in battles as armies regroup. So there was in this one. With nothing better to do, I wandered back to join Pascal and his comrades, who were now sitting on the grass near their trench. Someone produce apples and we munched on them quietly and somewhat dejectedly, wondering what would happen next.

A crackle of musketry further up the line signalled that our peaceful sojourn was coming to an end. "Look there!" the corporal with us called, pointing. We followed his gaze and saw lines of men in black coming down the opposite slope. "Now we have them," the man crowed, "for there is damn all cover down there." He snatched up his Chassepot, took aim and fired. The bullet, less than half an inch in diameter and just under an ounce of lead sped towards the Prussian soldiers. It was extreme range even for the French rifle, yet it did not go unanswered. There was a dull roar as the first of the Prussian artillery opened fire again, which turned into rumbling thunder as the rest of the line of guns were obscured behind a bank of smoke. In exchange for the single bullet, a six-pound explosive shell whistled low over our heads. Fortunately, the aim had not been adjusted since the earlier bombardment and it slammed into a destroyed French battery behind us. We did not wait to give them a second chance, and, like rabbits, jumped quickly into our burrow.

For the next hour the Prussians slowly made their way across the valley between us, while their gunners did their best to keep our heads down. My comrades would periodically leap up like some demented jack-in-the-box, snatch a quickly aimed shot and then duck back, shouting directions to the others. "You know that rock that looks like a lion's head?" called Pascal breathlessly. "There are two to the right of that." At one point he turned to me as I sat crouched in a corner of the trench trying to keep out of the way, "Are you going to sit there all day?"

"I don't have a gun," I replied, holding up my empty hands to show that I could not fight even if I wanted to. Although right at that moment I was quite glad I was not expected to stick my head over the parapet, for the Prussian gunners were most certainly getting their aim in. Just moments before, an exploding shell had slammed into the mud bank in front of us, showering us with earth. I was beginning to fear that we might have dug our own grave. To give myself something to do, I reached into my jacket for my notebook and pencil. I had barely written a line when the wall of the trench slammed into my back and another cascade of earth tumbled over my head and neck. My ears were ringing from an explosion and the trench filled with smoke.

"Who is hit?" shouted the corporal, but we all replied that we were unhurt.

"My God, look at that," called Pascal and even I pushed the clods off my shoulders to peer over the end of our slot in the earth. It was lower than it had been before; next to us was now a shell hole at least two yards across and a yard deep.

"I am going in there to fight," declared the new recruit, who earlier had been praying. Instinctively, he touched a small metal crucifix that hung around his neck and declared, "They say that a shell never lands in the same place twice." None of us tried to stop him, for the hole was almost as deep as the trench it joined, and this gave us all more room. A minute later and it looked to be the right decision as there was another thud into the earth nearby. I braced myself for the explosion but there was nothing. I looked up and to my horror found a pointed steel cone poking out of the mud just above my head.

I was frozen with terror and could only stare at it. There was a fuse device on the tip, and I imagined a clockwork mechanism inside down ticking my final seconds to oblivion.

"Keep still, man," barked the corporal, in the mistaken belief that I was capable of movement at that moment. "It has an impact fuse," he explained calmly. "If it falls into the trench we are done for." With that he reached forward and picked up the shell, cradling it in his arms like a precious infant. I gasped as another shell exploded nearby, rocking us both with the blast, but the corporal was steady. He calmly reached up and laid his charge beyond the parapet of the trench while Pascal used his rifle butt to roll it further away down the slope.

"I am really going off those bloody Prussians," I muttered. I was trying to sound calm, but I could feel my face tingling with the aftermath of the shock. I was probably as white as the ghost I thought I was about to become.

For the next few minutes, the bombardment was intense. Shells rained down all about us and several times we were covered in showers of falling dirt. Still Pascal and the others would dart up to snatch a shot at the approaching Prussians. "The first ranks are down in the valley," he explained. "It would be madness now to try to go forward and shoot them, but they are sending more down the far slope."

"What are we going to do when those front ranks climb up to the top of our hill?" I asked. "They will be right in front of our trench and we will be trapped here like fish in a barrel." I was already speculating on my chances of making a run for it during a break in the shelling, when the corporal gave what he thought was good news.

"We will know when they get near the top," he explained, "because their artillery will stop firing in case they hit their own men."

"So we can shoot them as they climb the final few yards," Pascal grinned.

"Yes," shouted the corporal over a nearby explosion, "But even their rifles are accurate at that distance."

"Well at least we will not be shot and blown up at the same time," I added sarcastically. "That is a great comfort." We at least knew that the Prussians were not near the hilltop yet, for suddenly there was another shell blast very nearby. It sprayed us with earth and what we later realised was gore. It was only when the Chassepot rifle fell at my feet that I realised what had happened. There were scorch marks on the polished wood of the butt, yet it was otherwise intact. A quick glance along the trench showed we were all present. Then I remembered the young lad in the hole alongside.

His theory that shells do not land in the same place twice had been violently disproved. The crater was now even deeper and at first we could not find a single trace of its former occupant. "Look there," Pascal pointed, and I saw a boot in the mud. Then to my horror, I realised that there was still a foot inside it. Suddenly, I was angry. Perhaps it was a reaction to several hours hunkered down in fear; or maybe it was the lad, barely out of the schoolroom, now blown to oblivion, but right then I wanted to hurt someone in return. I bent down and picked up the rifle. "Show me how this thing works," I demanded.

The corporal demonstrated how to load the Chassepot and then told me how to fire it. "Rest the barrel on the mud in front of the trench to keep it steady and keep your head low against the sights. Squeeze the trigger and don't hang about to see what you hit."

I pulled back the bolt on the gun and slid in the paper cartridge. Closing the chamber, I pushed myself forward over the mud covering the front of the trench. Even though my head was only inches above the level of the earth, I felt precariously exposed. Forbes would be appalled at what I was about to do. It was against the 'rules' of being a correspondent, but I did not care. The bastards had been doing their best to kill me for hours, not to mention blowing that boy to kingdom come. It was about time I got some revenge.

I stared across the valley and could easily see the lines of figures in black coming down the hill. The helmets gleamed in the sunlight. They looked like lines of big black ants emerging from a nest. I took aim at one in the middle of the line and squeezed the trigger. The gun slammed into my shoulder, but not as badly as I had feared. Despite what the corporal had said, I squinted through the muzzle smoke to see if I had been successful. A man was down, with another Prussian soldier bending over him, but already the corporal behind me was pulling on my trouser leg and ordering me back into the trench. "I told you not to do that," he grumbled.

"I had to see if my aim was right," I muttered as I ducked down into the trench, reaching for another cartridge. I defy anyone firing their first shot in battle not to see where it went. The corporal did not argue as he slid up in my place.

"Did you get one?" asked Pascal as he readied to go up too.

"I think so."

"Good," he replied. "Now you can write to your readers about defending France." Pascal was still shouting, as had been necessary over the sound of artillery fire, but just then his voice seemed unnaturally loud. We all realised why at the same moment.

"The guns have stopped…"

A cold fear fell over me as I recalled the corporal's earlier comment: "We will know when they get near the top because their artillery will stop firing in case they hit their own men."

The words were barely out of Pascal's mouth when there was an increased crackle of musketry to our left: the first Prussians were charging over the edge of our hill. They had bayonets fixed and were shooting down into the trenches, before stabbing into them with the blades. I was up and out of our dugout in a moment, glancing over my shoulder for the first spiked helmet to appear opposite us. The corporal, though, was made of sterner stuff. He leapt up and grabbed the six-pound shell that had lain in the mud a yard away and hurled it down the hill towards any approaching enemy. There was a distant shout of alarm, but no explosion. The thing must have been a dud, but I was past caring. I was running down and across the triangle towards the only other sizeable number of French troops I could see. There were thousands of them and horsemen milling about at the edge of the forest, facing the Prussians that were stopping the army's escape west. Looking over my shoulder, I saw Pascal and hundreds of French soldiers in my wake. The eastern line of our defences was being abandoned. The only option now was to break out to the west.

This was the move that Ducrot had wanted to make since daybreak, and I did not doubt that he would be trying to marshal the mass of men we were approaching. His scheme might have worked earlier in the morning, but since then the enemy had been closing the neck of the trap we were in. I ran past rows of French guns that had been dismounted by enemy fire, like the ones on the eastern side. Now, the only resource left to punch a way through the Prussian ranks was cavalry. Dozens of riderless horses were testament to the fact that this had already been attempted once, to no avail, but as we got closer, we saw that, incredibly, another attempt was being made. Even though they were under continuous shell fire, the animals with riders were brought back into order and lined up for another charge. Bugles rang out when we were still some five hundred yards away and we watched as the troopers disappeared down the far slope. Even though we could not see what was happening, we could certainly hear it. The roar of enemy artillery was almost drowned out by an even louder and continuous noise of rifle fire. The German needle gun might not be as accurate as the Chassepot, but it could still fire at least three times while the cavalry charged down the slope. A man on a horse makes a big target and whole rows of horsemen would be almost impossible for the Prussians to miss.

The reaction of the watching French soldiers told us what was happening. Instead of preparing to charge in the wake of the horsemen, they were turning away. Some were running to our right to take shelter in the forest, while others were hurtling down the slope towards the town and castle. I could see the men milling about in the embankments around the fort, and guessed that the gates had already been locked against a panicked rout. Those packed earthworks would soon make a tempting target for enemy gunners. I turned to Pascal, "Where the hell do we go now?"

We were surrounded by Prussian forces on every side. There was hardly any French artillery left, most of France's cavalry was probably lying dead on the western slopes of the triangle and nowhere could I see any infantry making a stand. Men were fleeing in all directions, like hens before a fox. The woods seemed the best option for us, and I was just about to suggest it when a salvo of half a dozen artillery shells exploded just behind us. The nearest one had been twenty yards off and we had both dropped to the ground at the first detonation.

"Christ that was close. Come on, we had better get into those trees." I had got up, shaking the mud out of my hair, and had taken a couple of steps before I realised that Pascal had not moved. I turned back to see him still lying on the ground and staring at a dark stain in the middle of his shirt. He raised his head and our eyes met in a look that spoke a thousand words. "Bloody hell," was all I could whisper, for there was no doubt it was bad; he gave a slight cough and blood dribbled down his chin. Another shell exploded nearby and two more men went down screaming. If we stayed where we were, it was only a matter of time before we would both be hit. "Come on, grab me around the neck and I will carry you into the trees."

Pascal shook his head. "No, drag me over there into that shell hole, it will be quicker." He even managed a sad smile as he added, "Remember, they cannot hit the same place twice."

There was no time to argue so I did as he suggested. As I manoeuvred myself behind him and hooked my arms under his, I noticed a matching stain on the back of his shirt. Whatever had hit him had passed right through. He gave a gasp of pain as I lifted him up, but then panted for me to go on. A moment later I was laying him gently at the bottom of the crater. You did not have to be a surgeon to know that it would be a miracle if he survived. Suddenly, I felt a crushing sense of responsibility. "This is all my fault," I wailed. "You would not be here if it were not for me. You would be safely in Paris drawing some topless beauty."

"*I* found *you*, remember?" He reached out and gripped my hand with surprising strength. "I asked for the job." Then, as though he felt a need to comfort *me*, he smiled and added, "There are only so many tits a man can draw… I wanted something different."

I laughed and lay down low beside him as another shell whistled overhead. "You cannot be a real Frenchman to say such a thing," I chided. "Too many tits indeed."

"I have never drawn you, have I?" His voice was getting weaker.

"There will be plenty of time later for that," I told him, although I could not look him in the eye as I said it.

"At least…I will not live to … see the defeat of France." As he uttered the last word another gout of blood came from his mouth, and he lay back. His grip around my hand was still so tight, I did not notice immediately that he had stopped breathing. The noise, or lack of it, was drowned out by the sound of battle, but when I looked at his face, I saw that he had gone. The eyes that had seen such beauty, now stared lifelessly at the sky; the hand that had so skilfully recreated it, was covered in blood within mine. It may seem a strange thing to do in the heat of battle, but I lay in the cover of that shell hole and talked beside him for several minutes even though I knew he could not hear me. Dead men keep your secrets and he had been a good friend, even though I had only known him for just over a month. Apart from his trip to Belgium, we had been together for all of that time. He had introduced me to Justine and helped me keep my job twice.

It was only as another shell exploded nearby, covering us both with mud, that I finally sat up and blinked the tears away from my eyes. Every Prussian gun around the triangle must have been firing. They had to be driving the French into the forest, but I knew they were not safe even there, for I could hear the smash of wood and branches falling to the ground. When I was covered in mud a second time by a shell, I realised that Pascal would likely be buried by the Prussians as well as killed by them and I would share his fate if I did not move.

There was nothing for it but to risk the flying splinters of the forest, for even that would be safer than staying in the open. Taking a deep breath, I jumped up and started to run straight towards the nearest trees. Another French soldier ran across in front of me. Christ knows where he was going, but he did not get there. The shell must have landed on top of him, for he was obliterated in the explosion. I felt wetness spatter my face, which must have been his blood. A life, an existence gone in an instant. Yet at that moment I did not care, for I had just noticed that another Prussian gun might have provided sanctuary. The shell must have landed against the base of the tree and the explosion had partly torn it from its roots. The trunk stayed up at an angle, but far more importantly there was now a gap on one side between the roots and the earth. It was the perfect place to hide. Unfortunately, I was not the only one to see it. Another soldier started to wriggle his way into the gap when I was still ten yards off.

"Go away, there is no room," the man called as my boots slid in beside him.

"There bloody is, move over," I said, kicking at the fellow to make him shift. This was my best chance of surviving the day and I was not giving it up. Eventually, I slithered my way in, but he was right, it was a damn tight fit, with barely room to move. My companion was another of the raw recruit soldiers. Like me, he had been crying– there were tear streaks in the mud on his face and he was still trembling with fear.

"What if the tree falls back on us?" he whispered.

"It won't," I told him. "But we need to dig out some of this mud to give us more room." We both began to scrabble in the earth beneath us and clumped in the roots over our head. We pushed it all out at the entrance to our little refuge to hide it from anyone else planning to join us. We barely spoke. The noise of gunfire was now a continuous rumble. Every so often a shell would land nearby, causing everything around to shake and mud to fall from the tree above us. Each time, the lad would whimper and look fearfully up as though the trunk would fall back into place and bury us beneath it.

We spent over an hour excavating that hole. It gave us something to do as the barrage continued, which was good for both of our nerves. We had a reasonable amount of space when we finished, enough room to roll over and move about. It was as I was pushing one of the final clods of earth out that I saw a sight I will never forget. Chalmers later insisted that I was lying, but other soldiers and officers reported seeing it too. There, alone on the open ground beyond the trees, was Napoleon. He was standing with his arms outstretched, staring into the heavens like a young boy enjoying a shower of rain. I sensed it was an entirely different downpour the emperor was seeking. His eyes were closed and he was wandering around as though in a trance. This monarch had now lost two armies and a war he himself had declared. He must have known that his rule of France was over. There was nothing left for him but pain and dishonour. He was seeking oblivion in the form of a Prussian shell, so that he could at least die with his men. Even that dignity was spared him, though, for as he wandered amongst the shell explosions, he did not even suffer a scratch. I last glimpsed him, between explosions of mud, staggering back down the hill towards the town.

Chapter 16

At least another hour passed before that hell finally ended. The gunfire stopped gradually, battery by battery, as the ceasefire order spread along the lines of guns that surrounded the triangle. As the shelling died away, a new noise took its place: the pitiable cries of the wounded. We stayed in our lair for a full five minutes after the last explosion nearby in case this was a trick to lure us out of cover. Then, as we saw men staggering out from the trees, we emerged to join them.

The barrage had gone on for so long that I had begun to believe that their intention was to bombard us to extinction. I imagined that we would be among just a handful of survivors, yet as I looked on, hundreds began to emerge from the forest. Many were sporting wounds, a few were in tears of relief at having survived so far, but most wore haunted expressions of fatigue and shock. The first into the clearing were pointing at the fortress. Following their gaze, I saw that a white flag was now flapping from the castle's flagstaff.

The sun was already going down for the evening and it seemed it was setting on the French empire too. With the surrender of this army, the final hope for the breakout at Metz was dashed. Beyond its disorderly militia guarding Paris, France had no forces left to defend itself. The war was over. The great nation had been utterly humiliated; now the German forces could demand what they liked. Pascal would have been sickened at the thought, yet I would have rather had him disgusted beside me than where he was. I took a glimpse into his shell hole, perhaps hoping he had miraculously come back to life. Instead, I found him half buried with earth. I remember feeling absurdly relieved that I had closed his eyes before I had left him, before bitterly mocking myself, for he was long past caring about mud in the eyes now.

I walked on, past the top of the slope that the French cavalry had repeatedly charged down to break the Prussian line. I stared in horror; I had never seen so many dead men in one place. It was made worse by the bigger animal corpses amongst them. Even then the odd voice called out and a hoof twitched where life lingered. In many places they were

149

piled two or three deep. French and Prussian soldiers moved slowly through the throng, helping to untangle the survivors and carry them to safety. The odd rifle shot rang out, presumably to despatch the horses, although for all I know they could also have served the wounded who were beyond hope.

Most soldiers were heading down the hill towards the town and I followed in their wake. My mind was becoming numb to the horror, for the town of Sedan was worse than the hillside I had just left. With thousands having fled there during the battle, and the castle gates locked against them, the shelling had been devastating. Some stretches of the earthworks around the fort were full of bodies, while the main road was littered with the dead and wounded. People casually stepped over them as they would dung in the roadway. I passed three headless corpses within twenty yards, their noggins removed by shells as cleanly as a guillotine. The town itself was a vision of hell, buildings partly destroyed but still packed with wounded. More dead were piled in the streets, some stacked into piles to make room for the living. Citizens of the town mixed with the soldiers and some of those were now trying to cross over the Meuse. To my astonishment I found that the French had failed to blow the bridges at the start of the battle. These were secured now by Prussians. The sentries let civilians pass across, but the French soldiers were turned away. I had no thought other than simply to get away from this charnel house of horror. I headed now to the nearest bridge, looking apprehensively at the men in black uniforms who guarded it.

They were calm and sympathetic to those about them. One helped a woman with two children carry a sack of possessions across the river, yet only an hour before they were shelling her home. It was hard to believe that the kindly old sergeant puffing on his pipe was part of an army that had not just beaten, but utterly destroyed the force that had stood against him. The fellow looked less amenable as I approached the bridge, his eyes narrowed in suspicion. Under his piercing glare I felt a tremor of guilt; could he somehow detect that just hours before I had been shooting at and had perhaps killed one of his comrades? He certainly could see that I was not dressed as a peasant farmer from

Sedan. Perhaps he thought I was a soldier who had raided the wardrobe of someone in the town with a penchant for brown suits and was trying to escape in disguise. "*Nein*," he barked when I tried to step onto the crossing. He said some more, but I did not understand a word of it.

"I am an English journalist with the *Daily News* in London," I tried in English. "From London. British," I added, pointing at my chest. He still was far from convinced and so I reached into my pocket and pulled out my French press accreditation document. I doubt he recognised half of the stamps on it, I did not know what most of them meant myself, but he could see that it was an official document. He summoned one of his squad and gave the paper to him, while he pointed over at the Prussian side of the river and muttered instructions. The soldier made off in that direction, while a point of the finger indicated that I was to wait where I was.

I sat down against a wall and watched a stream of refugees getting away. One old woman with bandages around her head and legs was being carried on a stretcher. Her daughter berated the soldiers, complaining that they had demolished the old lady's house on top of her, but I doubt they understood. It was dusk and I was just wondering if I would get across before nightfall, when I heard a familiar voice calling my name. "Harrison, are you here?"

"Forbes!" I shouted back and felt a wave of relief that I was not alone. He was standing at the end of the bridge and beside him was a Prussian officer, the sergeant now standing to attention behind him. "My God, it is good to see you," I grinned. Of course, I should have guessed that if there was a big story to report in this war, and Sedan was certainly that, then my colleague would be on hand.

As we shook hands and embraced, the officer came up and stood awkwardly stiff beside us. "Mister Harrison," he said in English, snapping his heels together and giving a little bow from the neck. "I am required to demand your parole, that you will not re-join the French army for at least seven days and then you can go free."

I stared at him dumbfounded. "But there is no French army left to re-join, even if I wanted to."

"That is correct." The man could not resist a Teutonic smile of satisfaction. "I take your parole as given," he continued more formally, "and so now I give you this pass. It will allow you to travel wherever you like, without being taken prisoner by any German troops." He handed back my French paper, on top of which was a new document written in German. The only thing I recognised on it was the Prussian eagle at the top. With more heel snapping and nodding, he was suddenly heading back across the bridge.

I stood bemused at my sudden and complete release, "Are they always like that?" I asked Forbes, nodding to the now retreating ruler-straight back of the officer.

"They are very, er…efficient," he smiled. "Now come on, we have not got a second to lose. You only just caught me before I left."

"What? Where are we going then?" I asked, realising that my hopes for some rest and a comfortable night's sleep were diminishing.

"Harrison, have you forgotten what the hell we are doing here?" Forbes looked puzzled. "Don't you realise what this means? The emperor is now a prisoner of the Prussian king. The war is over and France will have to sue for peace. This is the biggest story of the decade and we need to get it to London first…" He frowned suddenly and looked around. "Where is your artist? Will he have pictures to send back, or has he returned to Paris?"

"He is lying dead in a shell hole up the hill," I told him wearily. "I only survived because I burrowed under a tree like some demented badger." Suddenly I felt angry; there he stood perfectly clean and unscathed, while I was covered in mud and gore. "You have no bloody idea what I have just been through, have you?" I demanded. "I am sure it was fine for you to watch the battle safely behind the guns. Did they serve a good wine with your lunch as you had the spectacle of us being blown to pieces? I can tell you that it was certainly no flaming picnic on the receiving end of that bombardment."

Forbes had the grace to look somewhat shamefaced as he apologised. "I am sorry, Harrison, I should have realised." Then, incapable of keeping straight-faced, he added, "It was a Riesling, but it wasn't chilled." We both laughed then. This was the lot of the war correspondent, to sit, watch and report. He was not to know that I had done rather more than that.

My colleague, I discovered, travelled in style. I had no idea what had happened to my horse, but Forbes did not suffer the saddle; he had a carriage and driver. This man was now instructed to ride for the Belgian border and a town with a telegraph. We soon needed the lanterns to show the edges of the road and another inside that we could both work from. I pulled out my notebook and somehow found the energy to plan an article. Then I tore out some pages and began to write. I have often found that when I am tired or half asleep, I produce better content than when I am wide awake, and so it was then. While Forbes described the Prussian encirclement from the German perspective, I gave an account of the doomed French army. I concluded with the description of the emperor seeking his own destruction before what seemed the inevitable subjugation of a once proud nation. It was stirring stuff, even if I do say so myself.

And so we come to where I started this tale: the Belgian telegraph office in the dead of night and the clicking of the telegraphist's key. We sat and waited for an acknowledgement from London and joked that on the morrow, the paper boys would be bow-legged from the weight of copies they would sell. I was the only foreign journalist with the French. Any army officer commissioned by a paper was still trapped in the triangle. On the German side there was a small number of British correspondents, including Russell, but Forbes was certain he would get nothing out that night. "He will probably be amongst those dining with King Wilhelm and all the German princelings, congratulating them on their victory." The man scoffed. "Anyway, this is the nearest telegraph and we are the only ones here." His eyes glinted as he stared at the operator, then he held up a gold sovereign. "You can have this if you give me your word not to send any more messages until midday tomorrow."

Of course, the man agreed and was even happier when Forbes produced some strong schnapps, which burned the night chill from your innards. I virtually had to help the Belgian to bed before we finally staggered back to the carriage. "Do you think he can be trusted?" I asked

Forbes as we settled back into our seats. "There will probably be a queue of hacks waiting at his door in the morning."

"Oh, I think so," Forbes grinned. He held up an item I only just recognised in the moonlight before it was casually tossed out of the window. "He will struggle to send anything without his telegraphist's key."

I was exhausted, but my mind was too active to sleep. "What do you think will happen now?" I asked.

My colleague shrugged, as though the answer was obvious. "Napoleon has no choice but to surrender his army and sue for peace. The terms are not likely to be easy for him to swallow. The Berlin papers are demanding that France be punished so that it can never again be a threat to the German states."

"What does that mean?" I probed.

"They will want millions of francs in reparations to pay for the war, but they will want territory too. I have heard talk of seizing the eastern regions below Belgium, including the border forts such as Strasbourg, and Metz when it surrenders. They would then become bastions to protect German territory."

"But Napoleon could never agree to that," I gasped, astonished. I had anticipated a financial penalty for the war, but to lose a whole swathe of the country would never be accepted. "And it would not matter even if he did," I continued, "for he is bound to be overthrown now and a new republic declared in Paris."

"Then the new republic will have to accept these terms," insisted Forbes, "or they will find Prussian troops marching down the Champs d'Élysées to insist upon them."

"They couldn't," I retorted. "Not unless they wanted to be the briefest government in history. Paris still does not understand why they are not winning the war. They sent some fool of a general to replace MacMahon, who was trying to order an attack while we were surrounded. Hell, even *I* don't understand why Bazaine has not managed to break out. From what we heard about Gravelotte, his army had the better of the battle, yet still fell back. There is no way on earth that Paris would agree to giving up their eastern provinces; they would be lynched by the mob for suggesting it."

"I was at Gravelotte," Forbes admitted. "The Prussian Guard regiments tried to attack the French line over open ground. The Mitrailleuse and Chassepot combined to slaughter eight thousand of them, including most of the officers in that elite division. The Prussian generals told me that if Bazaine had used his reserves they would have been beaten. Instead, he was timid and almost anticipated his own defeat. But if the army of France cannot stop the Prussians, a Parisian mob certainly will not. They need to face the reality of the situation: this war is over, and they have lost it."

There was a simple logic to his statement that was hard to argue against. Yet if he was right, this account would be nearly finished, when in fact the more extraordinary parts are still to come. But back then I could not have imagined what would follow, and if I had, they would have been dismissed as the ravings of a fool.

We woke a Belgian innkeeper and spent the night there, before returning to France in the morning. We passed at least one carriage of correspondents heading in the opposite direction. Forbes wanted to visit Sedan and explore the triangle, but I had no wish to see that bloody patch of ground again. I stayed on the western bank of the Meuse, where I ascertained that negotiations for the French capitulation were underway. They had begun the previous evening at a nearby château called Bellevue. It might have had a 'beautiful view' when it was built, but now the vista was rather grim. De Wimpffen was conducting the negotiations and had initially refused to even consider the terms the Prussians were offering. In response the Prussian commander had pointed out the lines of German guns still surrounding Sedan. He warned that if they had not signed by the following morning, the artillery would open fire again. Even someone as dim as de Wimpffen could see that he had no alternative, but before ink was put to paper the emperor had one final attempt at improving terms. He summoned his carriage with a view to appealing personally to his fellow monarch. Bismarck, however, was too canny for that. He intercepted the emperor by some weavers' cottages and made it clear that King Wilhelm would not receive him until the terms were agreed. Forbes spotted the pair of them talking together as he returned to meet me.

At noon that day the treaty was signed and around a hundred thousand French soldiers and one emperor were now prisoners of war. They were required to hand over all weapons, with the Germans also capturing a thousand wagons, six thousand horses and over four hundred guns. German dead and injured were fewer than ten thousand, most from the fighting at the south-eastern corner of the triangle early the previous morning. Only then were the French allowed to leave Sedan, but they did not go far. They were taken two miles north, where a finger of land was surrounded on three sides by the Meuse. The emperor spent the night at Bellevue. The next morning he left in his carriage to go into captivity. His only request was not to be driven past his army. He did not want them to see his humiliation, but I doubt they cared any more.

That afternoon I finally went back up onto the triangle. Large work parties of prisoners were digging mass graves. I searched for him but realised Pascal's body was missing – I did not think he would mind being buried as a soldier. It was pouring with rain and the wet, miserable men toiling with spades and carrying bodies to the trenches muttered mutinously. They glared not at the Prussians, but at the few French officers overseeing proceedings. Unlike the enlisted men who were confined to camps, many of the officers had been allowed to give their parole not to fight again and go home. More men were at work butchering the dead horses; there was certainly no shortage of supply. Cartloads of meat were being taken back to the hungry prisoners in their camp.

By the time we returned over the Meuse it was getting dark and we needed a place to dry out and spend the night. Driving past the Bellevue château, we noticed it was dark and empty. I was amazed some German officers had not taken the place over, but it was too good an opportunity to miss. Our carriage went up the drive and we persuaded a gardener to let us in.

We quickly lit candles as a deterrent to other visitors and then toured the rooms where the negotiations had taken place just the previous day.

The place was as its owners had left it, beautiful clocks still ticked on every mantle and some half-completed embroidery lay on a workbox. Beyond an abandoned sword, there was little sign of the capitulation of a nation that had taken place there. We soon had fires lit and a cook summoned. She apologised that she had little to offer, but we had brought a ration of horsemeat with us, enough to feed the household. She went off, delighted that we would all eat well that night, and provided us with wine in return. Forbes slept in the bed that Napoleon had occupied the night before. He told me, and indeed included in his published memoirs, that Napoleon had been reading a translation of Lord Lytton's *The Last of the Barons*, which lay open on the bedside table. It was a novel of a weak monarch and a scheming courtier. I wondered if the emperor saw any similarities between himself and Bismarck.

Chapter 17

In most countries when there is a national reverse, the government of the day will throw their shoulders to the wheel to sort things out. In France the nature of government is such that ministers slide out of the back door and leave the mess to someone else. So it was this time. At first the imperial ministers in Paris refused to believe that such a defeat at Sedan was even possible. It was only the emperor's telegram to his wife admitting he was now in captivity with the entire army that convinced them. A mob gathered at the traditional place, outside city hall. Fiery speeches were given and new ministers were appointed. I confess that I had not heard of any of them, but a Belgian correspondent we met the next day had spent far longer in Paris than I had. "They are left and right wingers," he told us dismissively. "A general, politicians, intellectuals and writers, they will never agree about anything." He may have been right, but the one thing that did unite them was a determination to protect the borders of France. They called themselves the Government of National Defence and in their first proclamations insisted that not an inch of soil or a stone from a fortress would be yielded to the invader.

The success of their army had given the Prussians a diplomatic problem. The head of the only recognised government of France was now their prisoner. The leaders of the mob in Paris had not been elected and, according to our Belgian friend, would not be approved in a national ballot. "The people in the countryside do not care about politics," he insisted. "They want peace to be able to get on with their harvest, and low taxes. They will vote for the local people they know, not any hothead from the capital." The one remaining French army in the field, that commanded by Bazaine, also remained loyal to its emperor. Messages had been sent to Metz advising the besieged army that Napoleon had surrendered, but they refused to follow suit. Surrounded, they were also unable to communicate with the new national government, which was busy sweeping away all imperial appointees. Bismarck, the arch schemer, found he had no one to negotiate with.

The head of the Prussian army, a man called von Moltke, had no time for diplomacy. On the seventh of September, less than a week after the battle of Sedan, he gave his own orders to resolve the situation. With the Prussian king's approval, a German army of a hundred and fifty thousand men began a march on Paris. They were not intending to capture the city, which was ringed by strong defences. Instead, they would encircle it and if necessary, starve its inhabitants until they accepted the reality of their position. They were a conquered people and would be forced to accept Prussian terms. With nothing better to do, we went with them.

France in September 1870 was a strange place to be. No one really knew who was in charge, how the government would work or what would happen next. The countryside we travelled through had largely been untouched by the war and the villagers did their best to ignore it. Farmers would stare curiously at the men in strange uniforms who marched down their roads, while often their wives would appear with baskets of fruit and cheese to sell. Forbes would generally wax lyrical on all things Prussian, and even I had to admit that the invaders behaved in a far more orderly manner than the French soldiers I had seen. There was no hint of looting, and the Germans were polite and paid for everything they needed. The village cobblers would soon have an orderly queue of Germans waiting outside their shop, boots in hand for repairs. The owner of one hotel we stayed at freely admitted that she preferred her new guests to the regulars. "They cause no trouble, and they have a taste for expensive wine."

German soldiers bought enthusiastically at town markets and the traders warily accepted German coin. Given the volatility of their own country, perhaps they thought it might have a more stable value. Most of the purchases were for food; anything, one corporal told me in halting English, was better than pea sausage. When I looked puzzled, he handed me something that looked like a cartridge for a very large rifle. I showed it to Forbes, who explained that millions of these 'sausages' had been produced in Germany in readiness for the war. They were paper tubes that, according to the label, were supposed to contain pea flour and pieces of dried pork, although most soldiers insisted that they were full of grit and gristle. They could be mixed into a gruel with water or added to a stew pot to thicken the contents. It just highlighted how prepared the Prussians had been for this conflict. While the ubiquitous *Erbswurst* was not popular that summer when other food was plentiful, it was to come into its own during the winter.

I was surprised that the new French government did not do more to stop the advance of the invader. If they had been issuing instructions to citizens, then these were largely ignored. Only once did we encounter any obstacle in the road: a trench had been dug across it, but within an hour, the Germans had simply refilled and paved it. Perhaps the scouts riding ahead of the army saw more than we did travelling with the main columns. There were rumours of bandit gangs, called *franc-tireurs*, forming among deserters and other disaffected Frenchmen. They had shot at the odd lone sentry but had no means to take on a regiment. We found a French newspaper in which the new government described the war as a "folly of the old imperial regime". Perhaps they thought that by disassociating themselves from Napoleon, the Prussians would deal with them more benevolently. If they did, though, they were in for disappointment. Bismarck finally agreed to meet a representative from the new regime on the eighteenth of September. I have no idea what leniency this fellow called Favre expected from a man known as the 'iron chancellor', but when the Frenchman heard that German demands included most of the provinces of Alsace and Lorraine, he left the meeting in tears.

Rumours of the event had spread quickly throughout the army and one Prussian officer I spoke to chuckled as he told me of the encounter. As far as they were concerned, these punishing terms were what France richly deserved. "Never again will they disturb the peace of Europe," he insisted, echoing the Berlin papers. "They are soft, they think victory is theirs by birth right, but we have shown them. Their armies are destroyed or trapped. They have no choice now but to capitulate."

Forbes readily agreed and even I could see little alternative, but the new Paris government had other ideas. Pascal had once told me that the

French are more creative than other nations. He thought that was the reason that so many artists and philosophers were French; they could imagine solutions and concepts that would not occur to others. He may have been right, yet I think the truth is that those freshly minted politicians simply could not conceive of a defeated and diminished France. They had perhaps been part of the mob that had marched just weeks before, demanding that their own army advance on Berlin. Now that enemy was approaching Paris and this reversal of fortune was far too much for them to accept.

When minister Favre returned and reported back on the German terms, there was wild indignation. Their armies might have been defeated, but the French people had not. Calls went up for the populace to be armed, and for 'total war'. These politicians, sitting safely behind their desks, insisted that the whole nation would fight the invader to the last man. In the days ahead the French newspapers we came across urged readers to remember the glorious days after the first French Revolution, when this approach of total war had worked for the French. Using the simple expedient of shooting generals if they were not victorious, France had managed to hold back the combined European powers determined to snuff out their infant republic. This volatile time had also allowed military leaders of talent to rise to the top, including the first Napoleon and most of his marshals. But that was then; things were very different now.

Back then the French peasants had very little to lose. Now, as we had seen on our march through France, the people were more prosperous. They had not voted for these rabble-rousers in Paris, who demanded they risk everything, and many did not trust them. Several I spoke to told me that peace was something for Paris to sort out, as though it was nothing to do with them. Perhaps they also appreciated that the nature of war had changed since the eighteenth century. With the random nature of smoothbore muskets and cannon, a well-led, armed mob might have stood a chance against a foreign army. Now, with rifles, accurate artillery and explosive shells, it would be little more than a mass execution. However, the biggest issue the French politicians now faced was that the day after they announced their 'total war', the Prussian encirclement of Paris was completed.

The entire government was trapped in the capital. They could rant and rave all they liked but only Parisians could hear them. The Prussians had enough men to stop people and food supplies from entering or leaving the city. Paris was surrounded by a ring of strong forts and to assault it would be a bloody business. But neither Bismarck nor the army commander von Moltke had any intention of attacking. They would sit back and let Paris stew until it eventually realised the war was lost. That was likely to take some time and we were in no hurry to join the besiegers.

Forbes and I were staying in the town of Meaux, twenty miles east of Paris. We had been sending the *Daily News* regular reports on the march, but my uncle clearly did not feel he was getting value for money. As we sat drinking wine together one evening a telegraph boy arrived. Our employer caustically pointed out that he was not paying two correspondents for the output of one. The sympathies of British readers, he told us, were now swinging behind the French. He wanted stories on their suffering and what they were doing to fight the invader. Forbes was to return to Metz to witness the siege and the state of the French army when it finally surrendered. I was to travel south to report on the 'total war'.

I could understand the change of mood at home. The empress and the prince imperial had fled across the Channel to England and were staying at a hotel in the town of Hastings on the south coast. The Queen had sent a letter of sympathy – the least the empress deserved staying in that tedious place. The newspapers would follow her every move, reporting her grief for the loss of her country and her imprisoned husband. Gallant Germany defending its territory from Gallic invasion, was now 'the beastly Hun', trying to starve the poor people of Paris. Still, it did not seem to matter much, for no one expected a city the size of Paris to survive a siege for more than a week or two.

As the Germans had approached the capital, the new French government got word out that it would set up a centre to administer their policies at a city called Tours, a hundred and fifty miles southeast of

Paris. It seemed a good place to aim for, although I half hoped that the war would be over before I arrived. Then I could get back to Paris and into the welcoming arms of Justine.

Chapter 18

I had learned a little from travelling with Forbes. Instead of getting another mount, having lost mine at Sedan, I followed his example and hired a carriage and driver. Turning south off the main Paris road, I was not sure who I would encounter. I decided to keep my German pass in one pocket and my old French papers in the other. We drove through a couple of small villages where I was watched suspiciously by those in the streets. I certainly felt more vulnerable without an army around me – of either nationality. Progress was slow on these little country lanes, and twice we had to crawl along behind carts gathering in the harvest. The second time the farmer had seen us coming, but impudently pulled out onto the track in front of us. I saw him send a boy running on ahead to warn of our approach, while we were forced to follow at a snail's pace.

Eventually, we came up to a small town and as evening was drawing in, I thought we would stop there for the night. The place must have been home to over a hundred people, but only two old men sat in the central square. They both glared at me with undisguised hostility, one hawking and spitting in my shadow as I went past. I strolled to the only inn, which was as empty as a pauper's purse. I could smell tobacco in the air though, indicating that people had been there recently. Beyond a loudly ticking clock, the place was now as quiet as a grave. Two shouts for service brought no response. To hell with this, I thought. I have seen invading armies given a better welcome. If you want a landlord to appear, just reach over his counter and help yourself to his booze. There was a bottle of cognac within reach. I was just pouring myself a glass when, sure enough, an old woman stepped out from behind a door with an expression so sour it could have curdled milk.

"We are shut," she announced, pulling the bottle to her scrawny bosom.

"I need a room for the night," I told her. "I am not a Prussian if that is what you are worried about."

"We are shut," she repeated, "I want you to leave."

There was little scope for debate and so I downed the glass, left a coin on the counter and stepped back outside. A tall man was talking to my coach driver. He looked worried until something the driver said made him laugh. Then the stranger turned to me as I approached them. "Welcome to Rozay, monsieur."

"I have had warmer welcomes in an ice-house," I told him. "What is the matter with people around here? Do they think I am some Prussian spy?"

"No monsieur, they think you are from Paris."

"Paris!" I repeated, surprised. "Why the hell would they think that? And why are Parisians so unwelcome here?"

"Because officials of the new republic are trying to raise new armies. All unmarried men under the age of thirty-five have been called up. But there are not enough guns or men, and no time to train them. Those fools will just march them up against the Germans to be slaughtered. I am not losing my son like that and neither is anyone else."

There must have been a score of people watching our conversation, but now I noticed that they were all women and older men. Potential recruits had clearly been told to hide from the stranger in their midst. The coach driver had told them that I was a journalist, who had recently been marching with the Germans. That made me a far more acceptable visitor than a man from their new government. Suddenly, rooms at the inn were available, as was food and wine. Several wanted to hear what had really happened at Sedan, as the army had been decried in some papers as traitors to France. They told me that the local magistrate as well as the military commander were both from the old imperial regime. Neither trusted the new government. The new prefect was a young lawyer nobody knew and now he was demanding their sons.

"They can go to hell," one farmer insisted. "My boy stays here. I need him for the land he will inherit. They call themselves a republic, but we are not getting a vote. Paris started this war and Paris can finish it themselves." There were nods of agreement at this and, listening to them speak, I was even more convinced that the war would be over quickly.

The coach driver and I set off the next morning after a hearty breakfast. At a leisurely pace it would take us at least five days to reach

Tours and I was in no rush. If an isolated Paris imagined a country rising up in arms to save them, then they were set to be disappointed if that village was typical. The administration that had been set up at our destination would soon be urging peace negotiations. I wrote some notes on my evening's discussions and was having an afternoon doze when I felt the jolt of the brake on the carriage wheels and shouting outside. A man was rudely barking at my driver to haul up unless he wished to be shot there and then. I looked out of the window to find a dozen men and a similar number of teenage boys now surrounding us. They had a few rifles between them and all were pointing in my direction. "What the devil is going on?" I demanded. They clearly were not Prussians and so I added, "I am a British journalist on my way to Tours."

There was not a shred of uniform among the lot of them. A man swaggered forward wearing a red, white and blue tricolour sash over one shoulder. He had his thumbs stuffed into the tops of his trousers and sneered at me contemptuously, "Get out of there, you scum, or I will have you dragged out.

"Are you mad?" I blustered. "I am an Englishman; you have no authority over me." By way of response, I heard a rifle being cocked and hurriedly stepped down. "Look, there has clearly been some confusion. Where is your officer? I have papers that prove who I am."

"We don't need an officer," the man with the sash retorted, before adding, to my astonishment, "to deal with Prussian spies."

"Prussian spy! But that is absurd. Look, I have a passport here proving that I am British." I showed him the document, but he barely looked at it and I suspected he could not read. I reached into my other pocket to pull out my French accreditation papers. "I have been attached to the French army for weeks," I continued. "I was at Spicheren and at the battle at Sedan. Here is my accreditation by your government confirming that I am a journalist."

My accuser looked more closely at this, especially the stamps on the yellow card. "Those are imperialist stamps," he shouted as though that was evidence of my guilt.

"Well of course they are. The imperial government was in charge of France when the war started." I was beginning to wonder if I was dealing with some kind of village idiot, a thought that was largely confirmed by his next claims.

"Everyone knows that the emperor was in league with the Prussians to bring France to ruin. That is why he surrendered the army at Sedan. And if you were there in the French army, you would be a prisoner now."

"I was paroled and allowed to leave. They also paroled many of the French officers too."

"You lie," the man snapped. "They would have kept a loyal Frenchman prisoner. The only ones they would have allowed to escape are their agents and spies." He looked round at the rest of his little band and announced, "We will hold a court martial to determine his guilt." My arms were roughly grabbed by a couple of his ruffians, and I was hauled into the garden of a nearby cottage. They made me sit on a barrel while arrangements were made to convene what was possibly the most bizarre proceeding in legal history. A bench was set opposite for my three judges, naturally chaired by the fellow in the sash, while the rest of his band formed a circle around us.

"Look," I started, "I have papers to prove who I am. If you bring me before the magistrate or any lawyer, he can confirm them for you."

"We don't need magistrates," sneered my 'judge'. "This is a military court. Bring forward the coach driver." The coachman was reluctantly pushed into the circle, darting an apologetic glance at me. "When did you first see the Prussian spy?" demanded the judge, who also seemed to be acting as prosecuting council.

The driver explained that he lived in Meaux and had been hired by me there. He was then grilled about the area to prove that he was a local man. Finally, when asked how many Prussians he had seen me talking to, he insisted there were none. I was grateful as this was a lie. There had been several Prussians with Forbes when he had seen me off. Meaux had been full of Prussians at the time and we both knew I had arrived with them.

The judge looked disappointed, but he was far from done yet. He dismissed the witness and then looked around at his followers, picking out a man with dribble on his chin and a wide squint. This unpromising character was called forward. "Calvet," the judge instructed, "speak to the spy in English."

The fellow shambled towards me, one eye staring over my right shoulder and the other over my left. "Ala ba al kazoot,"

"Do you actually speak English?" I asked in that language.

"Ala ba al kazoot," the man repeated, gazing expectantly for a response.

I turned to the judge, "This man is speaking gibberish…"

"Silence," shouted the man with the sash before enquiring in French of Calvet, "What did he say to you?"

Calvet furrowed his brow as though the response took all his concentration. Then he announced, "He did not understand me. He does not speak English. He is a Prussian."

"This is a ridiculous charade—" I began, then went to get up but two men behind me pushed me back down on my barrel. As they did so, I heard the judge announce his verdict.

"You have been proven a Prussian spy and I sentence you to be shot." He pointed at the wall of the cottage and only now did I notice that a body already lay at the foot of it.

"My God…you have killed someone already," I stammered. Until then I had believed that this farcical situation would be resolved with some common sense. Now, with a shock, I realised that it could realise a fatal conclusion.

"It is Reynard," whispered one of my young guards. "This is his cottage." Then with a slight sob he added, "They made us do it."

"Quiet!" roared the judge, pointing at him. "You youngsters must be blooded in the enemies of the republic. If you don't like it, you can stand against the wall with the spy."

Reason was not working with this fellow and I searched my mind for a new approach. "Look, I am not worth much to you dead," I announced. "I have perhaps a hundred francs on me. But if you were to get me to a bank, I have a letter of credit in my pocket that will enable me to pay you a thousand francs."

There were murmurs of interest from some of the gang around me and for a moment I saw greed glitter in the eyes of my judge.

Unfortunately, he was not a complete fool, for he must have realised that once I was safely inside a bank, he would never get me out again nor see a centime of my money. "You cannot buy your way out of this, spy," he reluctantly concluded. "You have fifteen minutes to live so make your peace." With that he turned and began to organise my firing squad. Some of the youngsters were chosen and handed rifles, with two detailed to give me the *coup de grâce* if the volley did not do its job.

It is impossible to give you my thoughts as these grim arrangements were being made. My mind was numb as it refused to comprehend that this was happening at all. It was like a bad dream that I could not wake up from. Surely I could not end my days like this. I had not even thought to look at my watch when my final moments were announced and so I had no idea of the limited existence left to me.

Any hope of a peaceful period of divine reflection was dashed when one of the gang decided to give my novice firing squad a rehearsal. With fascinated horror I watched as they lined up and took aim at a hat hanging from a nail on the wall. I flinched at the volley and nearly brought up my breakfast in fear. The spread of stone chips from the wall indicated that a *coup de grâce* would almost certainly be necessary to end my suffering. I stood up, feeling the need to pace about as I always thought better on my feet.

"Tie his hands behind his back," shouted the man with the sash. "You might as well start getting him ready."

"No, please!" I shouted. I was starting to panic now as my end drew steadily closer. My arms were grabbed and dragged behind me and I struggled wildly, but then I heard a voice in my ear.

It was the young boy who had told me about the man called Reynard. "Ask to see a priest," he whispered.

Hope is a strange thing that shines brightest when fate seems as black as pitch. One moment I was gibbering in terror and the next my mind had locked onto an idea that might at least give me a few more minutes; and suddenly I was envisioning salvation. "I want to see a priest," I shouted at the man with the sash. "Even in your republic a condemned man is entitled to the last rites."

"You Prussians are all Lutherans," he shot back. "Everyone knows Luther was a German."

"Not all of us are," I replied. "Do you want to spend time in hell because you denied a final blessing and absolution to a fellow catholic?"

"I will fetch Father Jacques," called out the boy at my shoulder as he saw doubt spread across his leader's face.

"No," shouted his chief. "You will stay here. I swear by God, that if the prisoner escapes, you will replace him." The man paused, thinking hard, but ultimately decided not to put his eternal soul in jeopardy. He turned to the idiot Calvet. "Fetch the priest but tell him to hurry. I want the spy shot before dinner."

I could have wept with relief even though my fate still hung by a thread. My firing squad was stood down and I began to pace around the little garden, my legs still trembling with fear. I found myself wondering at the intricacy of a leaf, and the delicate existence of a butterfly. When you understand that life is limited, you suddenly appreciate the smallest signs of creation around you. There were rows of flowers and vegetables; in different circumstances it would have been a jolly place. I could not help but glance at the corpse of its former owner. The hands that had tended this garden were still bound behind his back as he lay sprawled over his own cabbages. A look of surprise was still frozen on his features, as though he could not quite believe what was happening to him. I knew all too well how he felt.

With my hands bound, I had no idea of the passage of time. It felt like I had been pacing for an hour, but it was probably much less. The leader was beginning to twitch with impatience. I wondered if he would decide to forgo the priest after all. Would they leave my corpse abandoned to feed the garden worms too?

With relief I heard a shout and saw Calvet running back, a man in a priest's cassock hurrying in his wake. As he reached the gate, the cleric stood for a moment surveying the scene. Then he paused to give my coach driver a blessing, which I thought was a damned cheek considering he was not the one facing a firing squad. Finally, he walked over to me.

"Can you help me?" I gabbled impatiently. "They think I am a Prussian spy and are going to have me shot, but I am a British journalist. You will find my passport and accreditation in my coat pocket. You must tell them that they are wrong." He made no attempt to look at my papers, but he had a kindly face, which darkened when he noticed the body of the man lying against the wall.

The priest looked at the man in the sash and then pointed at the corpse, "Did you do that?" he asked quietly.

My judge was unrepentant. "Yes, he refused to tell us where his son was. The boy must be enlisted in the new army to defend France, you know that. And don't try to interfere here. That man is a Prussian spy – he does not even speak English. He will be dealt with as soon as you have heard his confession."

"I do bloody speak English," I exploded. I pointed at the man with the squint, "That fool was just talking gibberish."

"Please stop," the priest held up a hand to forestall my tirade. "The captain is quite right; I cannot interfere in military justice. You have been tried and sentenced in his court—"

"This isn't a court, it is a vegetable patch!" I was nearly shrieking in desperation. "He was acting as judge and prosecution. I did not stand a chance." Panic rose in me again as the ship containing all my hopes was steering itself deliberately into the rocks. The man with the sash could not help but beam with delight at the compliance of the priest.

"Please be quiet," snapped the cleric. "This is French justice now and you must accept it. Now, I imagine that a Prussian spy will have a lot to confess." He gazed around the little clearing and then turned to my judge. "Perhaps we could have a little privacy? I could hear the confession in the spy's carriage, and these two men," he gestured at my guards," can stand nearby to ensure he does not try to escape."

"Very well, Father," the man with the sash grudgingly conceded. "Keep it to five minutes if you can, I am getting hungry."

The priest led the way to the coach, my guards pushing me on from behind. Even though I had not eaten for hours, I felt as though I could easily be sick. My guts were churning as was my mind at the shear injustice of it all. As we got close to the vehicle the priest turned to my captors. "Please stay out of earshot if you can. His words should be heard only by me and God." He then addressed the boy who had suggested that I summon him, "Marcel, you wait on the other side so that both sides of the carriage are watched."

As soon as we were both inside I felt the dam burst as tears of despair began to roll down my cheeks. "You have got to believe me," I wailed. "I am British, I have never even been to Prussia."

"Of course I believe you," said the priest quietly. Then he opened the far door of the carriage and gestured for the boy to get in.

"What is going on?" I asked as the lad settled beside me on the seat. By way of an answer the priest knocked on the side of the carriage and a second later we were moving.

"Keep your heads down," warned the cleric as we picked up speed. I heard the crack of the coachman's whip as he sent the horses into a gallop and then a very different crack as the top of the doorframe shattered. There were several more rifle shots from the men we had left behind, but as far as I could tell, they had all missed. We were barrelling along down the road now and were soon out of sight around a bend. I found that I was still crying, but this time with joy and not a little relief.

"I knew we could not reason with that fool Foche," the priest explained as the horses settled into a steady canter. "He used to be the village butcher. He was a bully then and now he is drunk with his power. He leads the local *franc-tireurs* and thinks the republican government has given him *carte blanche* to do what he likes. I warned your driver to prepare for a fast escape as I pretended to give him a blessing."

"Well, you deceived me," I laughed. "I thought I was going to end up lying in the dirt like that poor bloody villager." I was lightheaded with relief. My hands, after the priest untied them, were still shaking from shock. I could almost have choked with the joy of having an open-ended life span again. Trust me, you can never really appreciate the prospect of unknown days ahead of you until your future is measured in minutes.

My first thought was just to get out of France and go home; I never wanted to go through an experience like that again. Yet as I calmed down, I began to think more clearly. I had just been unlucky – there could not be that many Foche characters in France in league with an imbecile who pretended to speak English. Anyway, I had no prospects at home and was just starting to make a name for myself as a war correspondent. This is what they did, and I was still in the middle of the biggest story for at least a decade. The climax was coming and I would be on hand to report it. That was one reason, but there was another argument for staying in France that had an even greater pull: Justine.

Forbes and I had discussed what would happen next on our journey. He was convinced that the Prussians had spread themselves too thin, and for a Prussophile like him to admit that, I knew it must be true. They had been forced to leave some two hundred thousand men around Metz to guard against a breakout from the force trapped there. They also had to guard all of their supply lines from the German border to the French capital, which meant that they only had around a hundred and fifty thousand men to besiege Paris. That might sound a lot, but with the outer forts the city perimeter was vast, spanning some thirty miles. Not only that, but inside Paris were some four hundred thousand French troops. Most of them were from the belligerent and undisciplined Mobile Guard, but surely, I thought, they would be able to break out through the thin cordon and drive the enemy back. With Paris liberated and the German army on the back foot, more sensible peace negotiations were likely to begin. I smiled at the thought of ending my assignment back in the capital. I could report on all the diplomatic tussles while spending my evenings enjoying the delights of a small apartment above a certain baker's shop.

Before I could be reunited with Justine, however, I first had to reach Tours, which had to be safer than these countryside villages. The priest would accompany me to the nearest town where we could report on the death of Reynard to the magistrate.

"I doubt he will be able to do anything," the old man said. "Like the church, magistrates appointed by the imperial regime are distrusted by the new Republicans. The whole of France has gone mad. There are bands of men roaming the country more interested in settling old scores than fighting the Prussians."

His tale was only confirmed by the magistrate when we reported to him what had happened. "The local military commander has been ordered to give these villains weapons from his armoury, which will only make the problems worse." The man gave a heavy sigh. "If you are going to Tours, sir, I pray you tell them there what you have experienced. If there is no order in French governed territory, then we will sink back to a time of brigandage. Our nation as it was, will be lost."

It was a gloomy assessment of the state of the country, and I did not relish the next stage of my journey. The magistrate had given me a pass confirming that I was a British journalist and allowed to travel where I pleased, but my confidence in documents for protection was knocked. The *franc-tireurs* had not wanted to examine the papers I had before. I doubted this one would make much difference. Then, far more usefully, he passed on information from the local colonel. The officer was sending a report on garrison strength and readiness to Tours. Even the army did not think it safe for a courier to travel alone and so there would be an escort of half a dozen troopers. I was invited to accompany them; I have rarely accepted an invitation so eagerly.

Chapter 19

I arrived in Tours on the twenty-ninth of September. I know the date, for news of the surrender of Strasbourg the previous day had just reached the city. While Metz still held out and guarded the northern end of the border region with the German states, Strasbourg had guarded the south. A hundred years ago it was a formidable bastion, but unlike Metz it did not have outer forts to keep enemy gunners at bay. Advances in the range and power of modern artillery meant that it was now hopelessly vulnerable. When the garrison had refused to surrender, the Germans had shelled the city. They had flattened whole suburbs to break the morale of the citizenry. When that failed, they destroyed the French gun emplacements, smashed down walls and dug trenches until they had a breach to storm the city. Only then, when there was no hope of a successful defence, had Strasbourg capitulated.

I thought there would be dismay at this latest catastrophe amongst the officials of the new regime, which after all called itself the Government of National Defence. Instead, they merely shrugged their shoulders as though they had written the city off weeks ago. "It was an imperial army," a clerk told me dismissively as he stamped my new press accreditation. At least getting my press papers had been quicker than under Napoleon's government. The harassed official told me that most journalists had stayed in Paris. The expectation had been that the Germans would only be able to maintain the siege for a week, but a fortnight later it showed no sign of lifting. What had been raised though, was their last link to the city. A telegraph cable ran from the capital under the Seine, but as soon as the Prussians had learned of it, they had dredged the river and hauled it up so they could cut it.

While Tours now had no way to reach ministers in Paris, fortunately the lines to other places, including London, remained intact. On my first day I sent a message to the *Daily News* to report my arrival and give an account of my capture by the *franc-tireurs*. I knew my uncle well enough now not to expect any sympathy. His reply was short and direct: 'Report what France will do now.'

That would be much easier said than done. The city was crowded with a growing band of officials, soldiers and politicians, who all had very different ideas about what was happening and what the government and army should do next. I managed to find lodgings in a garret and then set about trying to discover what was really going on.

The war felt a long way off; Paris was a hundred and forty miles to the northeast. Tours was on the southern bank of the mighty River Loire, which also passed through Orléans sixty miles northeast. That city too was in French hands, as was the broad expanse of forest to its north. The woodland to the north of Orléans marked the 'front line' in this war, although there were not many soldiers there. The Prussians could only spare cavalry patrols from their siege to keep an eye on the French positions, while the French had hardly any army left at all. Before the cable from Paris had been cut, the few thousand soldiers gathered at Tours had been ordered to march on Paris to help break the siege. The general had been appalled, for his command was utterly inadequate for the task. He probably thought that the large garrison in the city could break out for themselves. But then contact with the ministry of war was lost and no one was willing to countermand the order. So now a reluctant army lurked among the trees, but no one expected victory. Instead, if you listened very carefully, you would hear whispered as though it were a great blasphemy, the word 'peace'.

The obvious place to get news was the great City Hall, which was now surprised to find itself the seat of a national government. These officials were never meant to be running the country. They were just administrators who had expected to carry out instructions from Paris. Now they flailed around like a headless dog, limbs working independently, but with no one in overall control. It would have been easier for them if the country was of one mind, but it was riven with factions. Large cities like Marseilles, well away from the fighting, had formed revolutionary councils, tearing down any vestige of their imperial past and persecuting the church that had supported it. They were determined that the fight should go on and that the new republic should be defended at all costs. In contrast the more rural areas nearer the Prussians were already pressing for peace. They were getting caught between the attacks of *franc-tireurs* on small German patrols and punitive reprisals from the invader.

All parties had their own representatives in Tours and I often overheard furious arguments as I strolled the corridors of power. France was a rudderless ship heading towards the Prussian reef, unsure whether to turn to the radical left or the Conservative right for salvation. Few wanted to talk to a British journalist about the situation. That would be like showing your dirty linen to an old enemy, but one sage counsellor did spare me some time, on the insistence he would not be quoted in the paper.

"A government raised by the mob in Paris does not represent France," he told me. "Only a properly elected government can commit us to peace or war. Otherwise, the decision could be repudiated and declared invalid. Bismarck knows this and he will want to negotiate with someone who can give a lasting decision. We need an election. To get that we need an armistice so all can vote."

"So why have you not asked for an armistice already?" I pressed.

He grinned, "Because those radicals raised up in Paris know that they would lose. People vote for what they know. They do not care about principles of liberty; they worry about how to feed their family, farm their land and live in peace. Mark my words, there will be an armistice, a vote and then the war will be over."

It sounded logical to me, the most sense I had heard since I had arrived in Tours. That evening I sat in my attic room and confidently penned an article on the future of France. But as my nib scratched at the paper, a coal gas balloon was rising high over the streets of Paris. The wind blew it south. In the basket beneath the great cloth bag was a man who would change everything.

I confess that I had not heard of Leon Gambetta before then. He was a lawyer by trade and an agitator and troublemaker by inclination. A minor politician who, through a mix of chance and ambition, now found himself centre stage, and he was certainly relishing the limelight. He had arrived in Tours by carriage that morning and shouted to the crowd in the central square. "All the army of Loire to Paris!" A guard was about to have him removed for disturbing the peace when it was

177

discovered that he was the minister of the interior. When I first glimpsed him at City Hall, he certainly resembled no minister I had ever seen. In his early thirties, he was full of energy as he boomed out greetings to those he recognised and clapped his hands on strangers' shoulders as though they were instant comrades. He had a dark shaggy beard and his long hair was still dishevelled, perhaps from his flight. Everyone wanted to congratulate him on his escape, flying over the Prussian lines, but he brushed the achievement aside. Confidence oozed from every pore of his being as he expounded to them about what must be done to save France. It was obvious that for this administration he provided something that they desperately needed: direction.

One of his first acts was to issue a proclamation, which began as follows:

We must set our resources to work – and they are immense. We must shake the countryside from its torpor, guard against stupid panic, increase partisan warfare, and, against an enemy so skilled in ambush and surprise, ourselves employ ruses, harass his flanks, surprise his rear – in short, inaugurate a national war.

It was immediately apparent that there would be no more talk of armistices and elections. To drive that point home even further, Gambetta next announced that as well as being minister of the interior, he was also assuming the responsibilities of the minister of war. While there were other ministerial briefs, they were all in Paris. To all intents the government of France was now concentrated in just one man. He stated that his aims were to galvanise the defence of France and to lift the siege of Paris. It was an extraordinary brief for any individual, especially one with no military or ministerial experience, yet Gambetta spoke as though success was inevitable.

Men who had lacked the confidence to make decisions, were now propelled into action by his arrival. The first step was to build a new army. The call had already gone out for unmarried men under thirty-five to come forward, but many had been hesitant, and the response had been poor. Now mayors and other civic leaders were being made accountable for raising regiments in their regions. No excuses would be tolerated, and they would be responsible for arming and equipping the men too.

There was to be not a moment's delay, he declared, for the siege of Paris must be lifted before the people starved. Deadlines for the delivery of the new regiments were set, as I am sure were consequences for failure.

The day after Gambetta's arrival he gave a talk to local dignitaries and members of the press were invited. He was introduced to those present and was delighted to learn that I was an English journalist. "We already have British volunteers joining the bands of *franc-tireurs* in northern France," he informed me. "I read that the London papers are now in support of our efforts to throw back the enemy. We will also need the cooperation of your arms manufacturers if we are to succeed. I trust I can rely on you to portray our energies fairly?"

I assured him that my editor was all too aware of the support for France among our readership and that I looked forward to reporting on their progress. Then for the next half hour I sat and listened to him talk. I confess I was transfixed. If Gambetta had not gone into politics, he would have made an excellent preacher. There was a near fanatical glint in his eye as he paced the room like a barely restrained wild animal. He was full of energy, sharing jokes with his audience one minute and then suddenly stern and forbidding, jabbing a finger to insist that his goals would be achieved. When he invited questions from the floor, not only was he never lost for words, he made the solutions seem so simple.

When asked how the new armies would be different from the imperial ones that had suffered catastrophic defeats, he explained that the Prussians had a clear superiority in artillery. They used impact fuses on their shells, while the French had used timing fuses. Henceforth, he declared, all French artillery shells would use impact fuses.

Another man enquired where experienced officers would come from to form the new regiments. Gambetta announced that previous restrictions for army promotions, such as serving for a set time in a subordinate rank, were cancelled. Enlisted men who showed the right skills and drive for success could quickly be promoted to sergeant or even officer if they had experience. "Men learn leadership when they are well led themselves, as well as from a staff college," he insisted. Furthermore, he had decided to double the size of infantry companies, which would halve the number of company officers required.

He strode up and down the room, warming to his own theme. During the first revolution in 1792, he reminded us, France had faced a similar existential threat. Then, audacity and courage were valued over form and procedure. As a result the cream of French officers was allowed to rise to the top. Men like Ney, Murat, Davout and many others. He insisted that there must be similar great leaders in the army today and he was determined to give them a chance to prove themselves. I noticed that the obvious example he had failed to mention was the first emperor Bonaparte, but that, I imagined, would be too unpalatable for the Republican.

France, he assured us, would rise up from the ashes of defeat. Foundries across the country were already working around the clock to replace lost cannon. While Chassepots could not be made in time for all, a way had been found to convert stocks of muzzle loader guns into breech loaders and officials were buying more guns from abroad. He smiled at me before adding, "Especially from Britain and America, who have surplus stock after their civil war." Modestly, he admitted that this was not his doing. These steps had all been put in place since the republican government took over a month before.

I confess that I went away from that meeting greatly impressed. I was half convinced that despite the huge obstacles it faced, France could push the Germans out of their country. The dilatory and hesitant leadership of Napoleon had been replaced by someone with drive and vision. Surely this was a turning point in French fortune. I went back to my lodgings and tore up my old draft piece about armistices and peace, then set to work on a new article about war and possible victory. Thank God I did not send that one either.

As I had been writing that evening, the French general instructed by Paris to march to relieve the capital was reluctantly following his orders. There was no military logic to the advance. He was hopelessly outnumbered and as he emerged out of the forest, the size of his single corps was clear to the enemy. Initially, the Prussian cavalry outposts were pushed back, but the French force only got to within thirty miles of Paris before a well-prepared enemy attack was launched against them. Empire or republic, the result to French arms was the same:

another defeat. The French force was broken and fled in disorder back towards the forest. An army of Bavarians pursued them and a day later marched into the nearby undefended city of Orléans, capturing a vast stockpile of supplies.

When news of this latest disaster reached Tours, Gambetta was said to be incandescent with rage. In another echo of the motivation techniques used in 1792, he wanted the unfortunate general court martialled and shot for incompetence. Instead, he had to satisfy himself with replacing the man with a new commander, a man called Aurelle. Almost as angry as Gambetta was Uncle Frank. He had been waiting days for incisive commentary on the new French government and where it might lead. I was the only London correspondent in Tours at that time and he wanted some advantage before I was joined by others. But what could I say? If I had transmitted either of my earlier draft articles, I would now look a fool. It was safer to risk his wrath a while longer and say nothing. I needed to get away from politicians and see things for myself. I resolved to visit a nearby army camp to witness the transformation of French forces first hand.

The following morning I rode thirty miles along the river to Blois. A large camp was being constructed there to train the new recruits that towns and cities were already sending to strengthen the army of the Loire. Gambetta had not yet visited the place, but I suspect he pictured it full of shiny-faced recruits leaping over vaulting horses or doing marching drills; soldiers, eager to earn glory for their new republic and for France. I had seen French army camps before and tried to keep my expectations more realistic, but even so what I found was a shock.

The long lines of tents made the camp easy to find. It was French military tradition to keep all soldiers in tents when on campaign, regardless of what sounder buildings may be available. I gather it was a practice that they had acquired in the warmer and dryer climes of North Africa. It had been fine in August, but now it was mid-October. There was frost on the ground when I had set off and for much of the previous day, torrential rain. The fields of the camp must once have been meadows, yet there was precious little sign of grass now. Thousands of boots and hundreds of hooves and cartwheels had churned it into a muddy ooze. The tents in the bottom corner of the camp were in the middle of a vast puddle. They must have been uninhabitable, but had not been moved, I guessed to keep the lines of canvas mounds symmetrical. I was surprised no sentry challenged me as I rode through the gate that evening. Perhaps they had been drilling earlier in the day, but a fine rain had just begun to fall and there were few people about. A handful hunched around campfires and I spotted a few muddy, resentful faces glaring at me through tent flaps. Over their shoulders I could see that they had straw to sleep on, but it must have been a miserable existence with the rain soaking up from underneath.

I made my way to the largest tents at the top of the field, rightly guessing that these would be the officers' quarters. Here at least there was a sentry to take my horse and as I stepped into the largest tent, I saw a portable stove giving out some warmth. I stood beside it for a moment to take the chill out of my bones. I had planned to find the officer in command to introduce myself, but instead someone found me.

"Monsieur Harrison, what are you doing here?"

I turned to see Duval, the officer who had shown me the Mitrailleuse back in Paris. That had been just two months ago although it felt so much longer, given all that had happened. "Lieutenant Duval," I grinned, "I am delighted to see that you have escaped capture or worse during the recent battles."

"It is *Captain* Duval now," he corrected, pointing to the fresh marks of rank on his shoulders. "Although I rather think I got promoted simply for staying at liberty."

"Well, if your luck holds and you say the right things to Gambetta, you could be a general by the end of the year. Have you heard he has dropped the restrictions on promotion?"

To my surprise he greeted the new minister's name with scorn. "That fool is ruining the army. He has no idea what he is doing."

I was intrigued by his reaction as Gambetta's improvements had sounded sensible to me, but then I had never served in uniform. "Let us talk, for that is why I am here. The minister makes daily announcements to strengthen the country against the Prussians. He says he will transform the old army and ensure victory. But Orléans has been lost and I wanted to see the truth for myself."

"Well Gambetta is transforming the army all right; he is making it much worse. Has he told you that he has made us burn all of our regimental eagles as they are symbols of the old regime? He has no idea that the eagles were the reliquary of our regimental spirit, our pride. It is what we fought for. What makes us proud now? He has also dismissed all of the regimental padres as he sees no place for religion in the army. Who will hear our confession now or help us bury our dead?"

"But surely he has had some good ideas? The change of artillery fuses seems sensible. And what about increasing company sizes to match the men to the numbers of officers available?"

"The fuses needed to change," Duval admitted. "But there was a reason army companies were around a hundred men. That is the largest number that a captain can manage, especially in battle. How can I lead two hundred when I would not even be able to see or hear half of them when guns are roaring and belching smoke all around? And the officers he is now promoting, some of them are barbarians."

"He said men would learn from the good leaders they have served under," I told him.

"But many remember the bad leaders they have served under too." Duval pointed to a grizzled lieutenant drinking in the corner. "He was a corporal in the summer. I had to stop him beating a recruit unconscious yesterday. He said he was clubbed and hit when he was a recruit and so he was entitled to beat his men now it was his turn."

"That is hardly likely to build morale," I agreed. "The few soldiers I have seen here look thoroughly miserable and I was surprised that there was no sentry on the gate."

Duval cursed quietly and then admitted, "The man has probably deserted. We try to use the most reliable for sentries, but often the opportunity to get away is too great a temptation."

"Do you have many desertions, then?" I asked.

My friend laughed. "Of course. Half of the men were rounded up reluctantly to meet town quotas by their mayors. They do not want to fight at all. They do not believe that they can win when our well-trained army has failed. They are often supplied with the cheapest boots and thinnest coats. Some of the guns they have been given are worse than useless. We had a company arrive last week with rifles of one calibre and ammunition of another. Either local officials did not care, or they did not realise that cartridges come in different sizes. Many of those that run away, hide in the countryside or join the *franc-tireurs* instead. There they are safe from arrest and often get a solid roof over their heads rather than canvas. Those who try to return to towns and cities are often informed on. We have a company of deserters returned to us every week. You know some of them will only run again."

"So, what you are telling me," I concluded, "is that instead of a new army burning to avenge previous defeats, as Gambetta describes, what we actually have is a demoralised and poorly equipped rabble that will likely run at the first opportunity."

Duval grimaced. "That is a harsh description. Every Frenchman wants to see France victorious, but they need to be convinced that we *can* win. They are not throwing their lives away for nothing. Gambetta is obsessed with raising the siege on Paris, but the Prussians will see us coming and be well dug in to defeat any army we send. You can guess how badly I want to see my Madeleine again, but we would be better placed attacking their long supply lines to turn the besiegers into the besieged."

"Can Paris afford to wait that long?" I asked

He shrugged. "In the last letter she got out, Madeleine wrote that they still have large grain stores in Paris. Herds of cattle were driven into the fields between the outer forts and the city walls. They might last out to the end of the year."

It was a grim and depressing picture that my friend painted. It was no better the following morning when I managed to speak to some of the recruits. They were unanimous in their wish to leave that wretched camp. They complained about the living conditions, appalling food, brutal officers and most of all that little they were being taught would help them beat the enemy. "Who cares if we can march in a straight line?" demanded one. "That would just make it easier for the Prussians to shoot us." That fellow insisted that if he was just given a Chassepot and some ammunition, he would soon open his account against the Germans on his own. Others were less belligerent. They just wanted to go home or to relatives in the country, who could hide them until the war was over. All were convinced that the Prussian army could not be beaten in open battle – the failures of their professional army had proved that. Yet they did not lack patriotism; many declared a willingness to die for France, it was just that they did not want a futile death. One bookish recruit insisted that they would do better joining the *franc-tireurs*. "We should fight a guerrilla war," he told me. "Like the one the Spanish fought against our armies in the old days. They forced us out of Spain then. We could drive the German armies out of France."

Chapter 20

I rode back to Tours with, I thought, a clearer idea of the prospects for French military success. I reflected on the battles I had seen: this motley band of recruits did not have the discipline to put up a robust defence as I had seen the French do at Spicheren. Nor did they have the spirit that turned a retreat into an attack at Borny during the withdrawal into Metz. They were poorly equipped and poorly led. I was confident that they would probably break and run at the first opportunity. I put pen to paper once more and finally gave my uncle what he had been demanding. I wrote that many Frenchmen were keen to defend their country, but you cannot impart the traditions and discipline of an army in a fortnight. Especially when you have abolished some of those traditions that soldiers valued, such as their eagles. I told the readers of the *Daily News* that they should not expect any great victories from French arms until the spring, if indeed the war lasted that long. Of course, once my article was printed, the French army set about to prove me wrong.

To be fair, the new French general, Aurelle, agreed with me that the army needed time to regroup and reorganise. He gathered the remnants of the corps that had been defeated south of Paris and took them away from danger. These were the surviving units of the professional army, and they would form the backbone of any new force. Ignoring Gambetta, he gave them back their priests and calmly made a start on giving them back confidence and pride too. He had wanted a month to do this, but his new chiefs insisted this miracle be achieved in a fortnight; Paris could not wait for ever. Gambetta was frustrated at the apathy of those around him who did not share his sense of urgency, or the need to prosecute the war at all. In particular, he resented how those communities living near the Prussians did little to impede their progress.

In mid-October he announced that all departments within a hundred kilometres of the enemy were now in a state of war. Bridges were to be destroyed and roadblocks put in place. Then he ordered a scorched earth programme. Areas threatened by invasion were to be stripped of crops and livestock. Where possible these were to be transferred to safe areas or otherwise destroyed, with the owners indemnified by the state. Citizens of these areas were to be evacuated and the remainder would fight at the barricades. He appointed local notables such as mayors and schoolmasters to carry out these orders and threatened them with military court if they failed. I read the proclamations with astonishment. Did they really expect whole villages to give up their homes and livelihoods in the middle of winter and just march off into the unknown? The promise of an unspecified indemnity, from an unelected government that might not last out the year, would hardly reassure many.

Gambetta's fury over the following weeks must have boiled over, for his proclamations were widely ignored. Farmers stayed in their homes and kept their herds in their fields. No villages were abandoned. Regiments were, however, being raised around the country. While the Army of the Loire was only around seventy thousand men then, including the recruits I had seen, many more were expected to arrive by the end of the year. The minister must have realised that as a one-man government, he was spreading himself too thinly. He could not manage the army in detail, but he did not trust the military to manage themselves. The solution was to appoint his own man to oversee them. In the increasingly deluded world of the government of Tours, it almost goes without saying that the candidate did not have a shred of military experience. Gambetta selected a former mining engineer, primarily because he shared his master's radical views. Citizen Freycinet was in his early forties, older than Gambetta, but, as it turned out, wisdom had certainly not come with age.

It was around the time of his appointment that my uncle responded to my article. Having harassed me to give him an opinion, he now claimed that I had given him the wrong one. The British public, he told me, now viewed France as a boy knocked down by the school bully. They wanted to read that the lad would get up again to punch his oppressor, not run squealing down the street. Thousands of pounds were being raised to support the starving people of Paris for when the siege was lifted. The *Daily News* was running its own appeal. I was to focus

187

on efforts to relieve the city and, even if I did not believe it, give the impression that they stood the ghost of a chance.

Gambetta's decrees had been reported in London. The generally law-abiding British had assumed that the French were following them to the letter. They imagined a whole country mobilised for war, every man fighting bravely and every woman a budding Joan of Arc. The government did all it could to support this illusion to keep the arms and supplies flowing. The minister had a messianic zeal now as he insisted that vast armies would be raised, victories won and Paris liberated. No objection to this view was tolerated, certainly in Tours, and it now seemed, in the London press too. I ground my teeth in frustration. Time would prove who was right.

The French army was due to go on the offensive again at the end of October, less than three weeks after its most recent defeat. Citizen Freycinet invited all correspondents to a briefing. He was far more interested in extolling the martial ambitions of his nation than in warning the enemy. He explained that the army under Aurelle would use trains to travel the eighty miles to Tours, which, he had calculated would take no more than a day and a half with civilian trains still running on the line. Then they would join up with other recruits camping nearby and march on Orléans. He insisted that a combined French force of seventy thousand should be more than sufficient to vanquish the garrison of twenty thousand Bavarians. Once Orléans was back in French hands, then all efforts would turn to the march on Paris, with more reinforcements on the way.

He made it sound ridiculously straightforward. It was obvious that he had never heard of the problems on the Paris to Metz line. In the end it took three days for Aurelle's force to reach Tours. Then it had to march forty miles in heavy rain along the river to Blois to join the more recent recruits. By then Aurelle declared it was in no shape to start an attack and insisted on a few days to reorganise his forces. He was probably also dismayed at the state of the recruits he found. Freycinet, furious that his timetable was being ruined, had no choice but to agree. The attack that had been scheduled for the twenty-ninth of October was eventually started a week later. That might sound insignificant, but on the twenty-ninth of October the French garrison at Metz finally surrendered. This released two hundred thousand battle-hardened Prussians to support the siege of Paris and the suppression of French armies.

Even for a war correspondent, there are times when it seems sensible to witness a war from afar. Why ride forty miles in foul weather to reach Blois and then on another forty miles to Orléans, only to get tangled in a routed army running the other way? If I described a defeat, I thought, no one in London would want to believe me anyway, so I stayed in my comfortable lodgings while the French army slogged miserably through the rain and mud. Not that I did not suffer for my profession; every day after finding a café for lunch, I would make my way to City Hall for any news. Each time there would be excuses or evasions to explain the lack of progress, or simply no information at all. I was beginning to wonder if Aurelle had simply cancelled the attack, when suddenly the telegraph sprang into life. The news, when it finally came, left us all astonished, for it was good.

As the French approached, the Bavarians had decided not to try to defend Orléans and risk getting trapped against the river. They fell back to a better defensive position, the village of Coulmiers. It just so happened that Aurelle had designated that same spot as the rallying point of his army for the attack on Orléans. The outnumbered Bavarians found French forces converging on them from all directions. It was a foggy day and their artillery struggled to pick out the attackers from any distance. There was no great appetite for heroic charges amongst the French, but they could use their Chassepots to snipe at the enemy. The battle dragged on inconclusively all day, but the following morning it was discovered that the Bavarians had withdrawn during the night. The French had finally had their first victory of the war.

The news of this long-awaited triumph of arms was greeted in Tours with unbound delight and not a little relief. Freycinet basked in the glory as though he had led the men personally and ordered every bell in the city to be rung in acclaim. They were still clanging away as I wrote an article that would finally please Uncle Frank. I informed London readers that the Republicans saw this victory as a turning point in the war and proof that their radical approach was working. That was true as far as it went, but it was not a view I shared. Beating twenty thousand Bavarians, when you had accidentally caught them by surprise and had three times their number was one thing. Defeating a much larger, recently reinforced Prussian army in well-prepared defensive positions was entirely another. But the politicians were not interested in this reality; Gambetta issued a proclamation to the army reminding them that their task had only just begun: *Never forget that Paris is waiting for us. Honour demands that we wrest it from the grasp of barbarians that are threatening it with pillage and fire.* Then, to counter any claim from Aurelle that he did not have enough men, the entire male population of France between twenty-one and forty was called up, with exceptions only for infirmity. Local civic leaders were exhorted to send any men they had to the army as soon as possible.

Every week in November Freycinet would hold a briefing for journalists to report on progress. He would start by announcing increases to the size of the army of the Loire, which was growing by around fifty thousand men a week. They were coming in from all over the south of the country in varying degrees of readiness. Some had received no training at all. They were just given uniforms and weapons and sent straight to the front on the newly restored trainline to Orléans.

It was soon apparent that Freycinet had fallen out with Aurelle; in fact the two men loathed and detested each other, but the politician could not afford to dismiss the only victorious French general. I had written to Duval for news. He told me that Aurelle wanted to use the army to defend Orléans against the inevitable Prussian counterattack. With well-prepared defences and the new artillery that was also arriving, he thought they stood a chance of defending the city.

Freycinet was furious at the proposal; his goal was to relieve Paris and nothing else mattered. He tried to persuade Aurelle to move north, but the general delivered a string of excuses and refused. He insisted that any advance on the capital must be coordinated with the defenders, which he knew was impossible. Eventually, the politician lost patience. He called a press briefing to announce that he had ordered Aurelle to send a force of fifty thousand men, under a capable general, to destroy an isolated Prussian outpost of just nine thousand soldiers. Given those odds, even I was expecting news of another victory. When the follow-up briefing was unexpectedly cancelled, however, I began to fear the worst and so cabled Duval for news. The attack had been a disaster: three thousand French had been killed, wounded or captured and the rest had fled in disarray. The exercise had merely shown that numbers and enthusiasm were not enough to beat well-placed, disciplined soldiers with artillery.

Aurelle must have thought his case was proven, and so it would have been had it not been for an appalling misunderstanding that would soon become apparent. Late November another balloon rose above Paris, but this one was blown north, all the way to Norway. By the time the message was transmitted to Tours on the thirtieth, we had learned that the Paris garrison had launched a breakout the day before.

Freycinet immediately rushed to Orléans to ensure that the army was ready to advance as soon as more information had come in. This time there was no alternative but for me to follow in his wake. At least the train was more comfortable than eighty miles on cold wet roads.

Tours station was packed with more fresh soldiers. When I tried to get in one carriage, I was told that it was reserved for the *mains rouges* or 'red hands' regiment. I thought it was some bloodthirsty nickname and stayed where I was to find out. When the soldiers boarded, I discovered that their hands were actually red. Well, orange might be more accurate, as they were all stained by rust from their guns. They had been equipped with muzzle-loading Springfield rifles left over from the American Civil War. Recent recruitment had evidently far outweighed the decent weapons available; men were now being issued with guns that had previously been rejected. These had been many years in storage and all of the metal, including the firing mechanism, was rusty. To make matters worse they did not have any cartridges as the Springfield used a bigger calibre than the Chassepot. They were told that there might be some in Orléans, although few were hopeful. Some had an equally rusty bayonet, but by no means all. In effect, they had been sent into a modern war armed with weapons that could only be lethally used as spears or clubs. They knew it too and were quiet and

191

apprehensive about what the future might hold. One said optimistically that they might be able to pick up some Prussian weapons to use instead, but from the silence of those around him, it was obvious few thought this likely.

"We are lambs to the slaughter," announced another man gloomily, and I struggled to disagree. They asked me if I had seen Prussian soldiers fight and if they were as brutally efficient as people said. I could not think of anything to say that would give them hope and so pretended that I had only just arrived in Tours from England.

The train rolled into Orléans and the *mains rouges* were immediately marched out of the city to another camp on the outskirts. That miserable existence could not have done much for their morale given that the December weather was freezing. There was already a couple of inches of snow on the ground and, looking at the sky, there was more on the way. I hurried on to City Hall to find out what I had missed while I had been entrained, for there was an air of excitement about the place. Everyone was rushing about; something was certainly afoot. I was just in time for another of Freycinet's briefings. This time his audience was not just a few journalists; dozens of city officials were there, even army officers. He clearly wanted to spread this news far and wide.

Freycinet stepped up to a lectern in the middle of the hall clutching a handful of notes. Next to him was an easel covered with a blanket. The crowd quietened and he welcomed us in his clipped tones like a schoolmaster with a recalcitrant class. Then he announced that, "Republican France has given General Aurelle an army that now totals a quarter of a million men. This is the biggest army a French general has commanded since the days of the first emperor. It is now high time he used them." He glared pointedly at the army officers present as he said this, clearly intending this rebuke to carry to their leader. "We have known that the forces in Paris have been planning a breakout through the Prussian lines," he continued. "I am delighted to announce that it has been a success. Today another balloon has escaped the city with news that the Paris army has captured the town of Épinay." With this he stepped over to the easel and removed the blanket to reveal a map of

192

central France. Orléans was ringed as was another town further north, which I guessed was Épinay.

"We must now advance just fifty miles from our forward positions to join our Parisian colleagues. All we will face is a light enemy screen as the Prussian force concentrates on Épinay. We will crush the invader between our two great armies and break the siege on our capital." He glared at his audience and particularly at the army officers before adding, "This time there will be no excuses; Paris is hungry and demands our help." I suspected that Aurelle had been invited to this gathering. His headquarters was now in a village ten miles to the north, but he had wisely stayed away, sending officers in his place. Freycinet was making it crystal clear that he would tolerate no more delays; the general would advance, or he would be replaced.

When Freycinet had finished speaking, I stepped up to the map. Épinay was Épinay-sur-Orge. I had never heard of the River Orge but saw that the town was fifteen miles south of Paris. To get there the Paris forces must have smashed through Prussian lines. Now all available German forces would be converging on them to contain the breakout. If the army at Orléans could come up behind them, then there was the chance of victory.

I looked at the snow out of the window and wondered what state the army would be in to fight after a fifty-mile forced march in winter weather. Freycinet's claim of an *army* of a quarter of a million men was a wild exaggeration. Even if there were actually that number of bodies, which was doubtful, many if not most of them were far from being fully trained and equipped as effective soldiers. Yet in all probability, the future of France really did rest on their shivering, threadbare shoulders.

We were handed yet another of Gambetta's proclamations, which was already taking victory for granted. It included phrases like: *The Prussians can now judge the difference between a despot who fights to satisfy his whims and a People in Arms determined not to perish.* As most of his officers had been loyal supporters of said 'despot', it hardly made them feel appreciated. But there was no time for such sensitivities as the army was immediately ordered forward. The most advanced position was around twenty miles to the northwest, where the flank of the army guarded against the Bavarians who had withdrawn from Orléans. They were to attack to drive them off, while the rest of the army was to advance. With Freycinet's insistence that we would only face a light opposition, the army would move on a broad front of some thirty miles. The aim was to wrap around any enemy forces encountered, as the Prussians had done to defeat earlier French armies.

This, it seemed, would be the climax of the war: a battle south of the walls of Paris as Prussians fought to keep two French armies apart. If they failed, the siege would be broken, and the German army would be forced to retreat and regroup. On the other hand, if the Prussians won, the siege was likely to be maintained and the army of the Loire would be crushed. All was likely to come to a head in the next few days and I had a nasty feeling I knew where my uncle would expect me to be. I had observed enough of this conflict from a comfortable distance in Tours. It was time for this correspondent to go back to war.

Chapter 21

Anticipating troubles to come when I arrived in Tours, I had already purchased the thickest woollen winter coat and the stoutest boots I could find. I was wearing two shirts and two pairs of trousers underneath the coat when I finally set off, with leather gloves and a fur hat. Over my shoulder was a satchel with my notebook. Assuming supplies would break down, the bag also contained a large garlic sausage, some bread and a bottle of brandy. At least the first part of my journey was not too onerous. I could travel the ten miles north to Aurelle's headquarters by train. While the general had not endeared himself to his political masters, he had impressed me with his cautious approach. Here was a man who would not lead me recklessly into danger, which is a quality I can admire.

Two other French journalists joined me in the carriage. They both talked excitedly about meeting up with old friends in Paris. To them there was no doubt about the outcome.

"Have you visited any of the army camps?" I asked, suspecting I knew the answer.

"No, but Citizen Freycinet knows what he is doing," one answered. "With such a vast army coming up behind them, the Prussians will not stand a chance." The train was packed with soldiers, but more trudged along beside the tracks. I was pretty sure I recognised a straggling column of the *mains rouges*, with their heads bowed down against the sleet. Further away from the rails, the land was largely covered by forest. Twice I glimpsed small groups of men amongst the trees moving in the opposite direction to the rest. I wondered if they were deserters who had already given up on the advance. I could hardly blame them. An icy wind whistled through gaps in the window frame, and it was damn cold in the unheated railway carriage. Those outside did not have the layers I did. Their feet were probably sodden with poorly made boots and they would have been chilled to the bone. Yet as the train rattled into the little village station of our destination, it was not the cold that we noticed first. When the little locomotive finished hissing steam, we picked up another sound: the dull thud of artillery. Surrounded by trees, it was not easy to make out the direction, but it seemed to be coming from the northwest.

"That will be our flank forces pushing back those Bavarians," said one of my new colleagues confidently. The French guns with their new shell fuses were now much more effective, but even so, it sounded like the Bavarians were putting up stiff resistance.

I had not met General Aurelle, but one of the journalists knew him and led us to his headquarters. We had to walk through a vast expanse of tents to reach it. More fields on either side were similarly occupied. There were acres and acres of misery as far as the eye could see, surrounded by dark forbidding forest. Several tents had their flaps open and through the gaps I glimpsed shivering and miserable soldiers. I really did not understand the French preoccupation with the use of canvas. Few things could have been designed better to sap the men's morale in winter. There was a village around the station and a few barns visible in fields cleared from the forest, all of which could have provided better shelter for thousands of men. Patches of straw in the snow showed where other tents had been dismantled. I guessed that the occupants were already marching north. Hundreds of the canvas shelters remained, though, and I could easily imagine Freycinet being furious at the lack of movement had he been there himself.

The journalist led us to the centre of the camp, where several tents much larger than the others indicated the presence of senior officers. Just one glance at the long, worried faces told me that something was amiss, but my companion missed the mood entirely, "Has the advance on Paris begun?" he asked brightly.

A grey-haired general with the obligatory imperial moustache and goatee looked up from a map table. "I know you," he barked. "You are that fool who keeps parroting Freycinet's nonsense in your paper. Have you published that we will only face a light screen of troops now that the Prussians have pulled back?"

"But...but Citizen Freycinet was certain..." the man stammered in surprise, admitting what I was guessing was a grievous error.

"Then explain to me how fifteen thousand Prussians with plenty of artillery are now supporting the Bavarians and blocking our advance," he growled. He nodded to one of the nearby officers and added, "Get them out of here."

"But I'm from a London paper," I interjected, "I have not published that nonsense." It made no difference, I was pushed out with the rest. A moment later we were all standing back in the cold. I pulled my fur cap back on and stared around. It was clear we would learn nothing from Aurelle and I was damned if I was spending the night in a tent. I would go into the village and pay whatever it took to get a solid roof over my head for the night. The French would not advance until the force on its flank had been pushed back; the rumble of artillery indicated that that fight was continuing. Aurelle had suggested that the combined Bavarian and Prussian force was around thirty-five thousand men to the northwest, but the French had well over two hundred thousand. The general must have already sent men to outflank his enemy.

As I turned to go into town, a movement through the distant trees caught my eye. Cavalry were coming towards us at the gallop. I could just make out the red breeches; they were French, although it made no sense exhausting their mounts this close to the camp. The leader was waving frantically, and I could hear distant shouting. I felt that first qualm of disquiet. Then there was a 'sput' sound over my shoulder. I spun round but could see nothing, just a deep drift of snow built by the wind in the forest clearing. I was about to turn back to the horsemen, when some instinct made me search the ground again. This time I spotted what looked like a metal tin protruding from the snow. Steam was rising off it as it settled deeper into the drift.

"Christ, that is a shell!" My words were lost in several explosions, as more artillery rounds found harder landings that triggered their impact fuses. One must have hit a tent, for I remember seeing men and scraps of canvas flying through the air. Then everything was confusion.

My first thought was to get back to the train. Without waiting for the others, I set off at a run in that direction. At first I was alone in having a direction of travel, but then others also abandoned all thought of fight and concentrated on flight; there would be precious little space in the carriages for the thousands wanting to get away. The whole camp had erupted. Some men were running towards the stands of rifles, others were yelling orders and a few were screaming in pain, The barrage was growing, the Prussians had got several batteries within range of the camp. Although they were firing through the edge of the forest it was a target too big to miss.

Another shell landed nearby and something wet struck my face. I glanced about me while I cleaned a smear of blood off my cheek. The next moment I was knocked by someone from behind, then I was sprawling over a guy rope. Two more soldiers stumbled over my prone form before I was able to stagger back up onto my feet. Getting my bearings, I ran south again, but now I found that most of those around me were heading in the same direction. It felt like fifty thousand men were running for a train where there was at most space for five hundred. Rows of tents and ropes created bottlenecks across the field as men pushed and jostled others out of their way. A man stumbled just in front of me, and I sprawled to the ground again, this time with three of four others falling on top. One fellow bounded over the lot of us – I felt his boot land in the small of my back. Then we were writhing around untangling limbs, desperate to get up and running.

As I finally reached the edge of the field, I could see that I would never make the train now. There were at least a thousand men already in it and around it and some, who could not get inside, even climbing up onto the roof. The driver was gesticulating at men crowded around the engine. It would take a while to get steam up and by then the chaos on the little platform would be even worse.

Another shell exploded near the train, causing a few to run back. Then two more burst near the tracks. The gunnery was surprisingly accurate. When I looked over my shoulder, I could see a new German horse artillery battery setting themselves up at the edge of the forest with a clear view of the camp and village. Their next shot hit the iron rails just beyond the train. As the snow and dirt settled, one of the two girders could be seen, now twisted, and pointing to the sky. There was a collective groan from those about me, even though we had stood little chance of getting aboard. It was clear that no one would be getting to

Orléans by train. Like a flock of sheep at the appearance of a dog, our herd changed direction from the train to the trees. There was a growing crackle of small arms fire behind me now too. Aurelle, or some other officers, were belatedly organising a rear-guard with those that remained. I saw one of the French batteries open fire on the enemy artillery they could see at the edge of the forest. Yet beyond those guns there was now more movement. Freycinet had clearly been talking out of his arse, for the Prussian army was not all gathered around Paris. A good part of it was emerging from the trees behind me.

I paused to get my breath as we entered the forest to the south of the village. I had run, slipped and stumbled for over a mile and was puffing more than the impotent train. French and German gunners had settled into a duel between themselves. This left the poor bloody infantry alone, but Prussian troops were slowly fighting their way across the abandoned campsite. It was obvious that yet another military disaster had befallen the French, but what was I to do? I was not a combatant. I had been treated well by the Prussians when I had surrendered to them in the past. I still had the pass they had given me to prove my identity. Yet to change sides in the middle of a battle was a bloody risky business. I was not wearing a uniform, but, I noted, neither were those men running alongside me, who were adorned with a diverse range of coats, scarfs, waistcoats and hats. In the rush to raise the army, most civic authorities had not bothered supplying greatcoats and so men had either bought, looted or been given items to keep them warm. From what I could see, the German army was kitted out in a similar manner, with only their spiked helmets marking out their nationality, although many wore knitted scarfs or balaclavas underneath. On top of that, everyone's clothes had a light covering of snow, more where we had sprawled in it. Soldiers and civilians were virtually indistinguishable. It would be madness to walk towards the Germans with the noise of battle all around us. They would shoot first and possibly find my papers later, as they rolled my frozen corpse into a ditch. I turned and continued into the forest.

Men began to run parallel to the railway tracks, using them as a guide to reach Orléans. I thought that the sheer number of them would attract the attention of German cavalry sooner or later and so I moved deeper into the trees. The ground was bare of bracken and ferns in winter. There was not much cover, just tree trunks, fallen logs and the odd holly bush. However, the attack had started in late afternoon, so it would soon be dark. If I managed to keep a straight course, by walking through the night I should be at least close to Orléans if not in its streets by morning.

I concentrated on keeping my bearings, fixing a point such as a strangely shaped tree that I thought was due south and then walking towards it. Then picking a new target on the same bearing. This worked at dusk but got harder by night. Twice, straining my eyes on a distant mark, I sprawled over a fallen log. Both times when I got up, I was not certain I had found my target again. Men around me became mere shadows flitting through the snow between the trees. I could still hear the distant rumble of artillery and nearer still the odd crackle of rifle fire. Muzzle flashes would flicker briefly through the trees, often accompanied by shouting, although I could barely make out the words.

Then, suddenly, I realised that I was alone. I tried to convince myself that I was safer that way and pressed on in what I hoped was a southerly direction. Sounds became confused, bouncing off tree trunks, and it became harder to make progress at all. It gradually became quieter until I could hear nothing but the odd owl and wild creatures snuffling about. I began to wonder where I was. The forest north of Orléans was a vast tract. If I got lost in the middle of it, I could easily freeze to death before I found help. I decided to turn to my right in the hope I would be heading west. If I did not encounter anyone who could confirm my course, I should eventually hit the railway line, which would do the same. I moved cautiously. I was probably the only man in the forest who was not armed and did not want to take anyone by surprise. Twice I tensed as I thought I saw shadows darting between the trees, but neither time was I certain they were human, nor did they approach me.

I heard the Prussians before I saw them, a guttural curse to my right. I ducked down instinctively behind a bush and peered around its edge. A dozen dark shapes were moving through the forest in a line. Faces were obscured by the vapour of their breath in the night chill. Uniforms were similarly lost under a covering of knitwear and overcoats, but the

200

steel points on their crowns, glistening in the moonlight, gave away their identity. They looked exhausted; rifles rested on slings over shoulders and hands were plunged deep in pockets. One man stumbled and they seemed half asleep as they cursed and got in each other's way. For a moment I considered calling out and surrendering to them, but I did not speak a word of German. I might startle them and be shot, or at best be forced to march before them as a prisoner. French soldiers had to be nearby and I did not want to get caught in the crossfire. I decided to stay still, breathing into my own coat in an effort to stop my breath betraying my position.

They went past no more than a hundred yards away from where I was crouching. I sighed in relief and decided to wait five minutes before moving on. If German patrols were overhauling the French rear-guard, the forest was an even more dangerous place than it had been before. As I sat hunched behind my bush it began to snow again. Fat flakes polka'ed before my eyes, whipped up and carried on the wind. It fell more thickly, hampering visibility and perhaps making it easier for me to escape…or to stumble into some hostile force. Five minutes passed and I decided to give it five more, counting the seconds in my head as I did not want to take my hands out of my pockets and burrow in clothing for my watch. Thank God I did, for it was at around eight minutes that the shooting started. The sharp crack of guns sounded duller in the snow, or perhaps it was the trees that deadened the sound. I could see the occasional flicker of light in the direction that the German patrol had marched. A bullet hit a tree nearby and I darted behind a stout trunk awaiting developments.

I stared carefully about in case the sound of fighting attracted others of either side, but the rest of the forest remained still for as far as I could see. Gradually, the shooting stuttered to a stop and an eery silence resumed. I was just considering a cautious recommencement of my journey when I saw movement. It was the German patrol coming back. There were fewer of them now, eyes and rifles scanning the trees about them. One man was limping, his arm flung over the shoulder of a comrade. I ducked back down out of sight. This time they passed by even closer. I could hear the wounded one whimpering in pain, but then a shroud of snow swallowed them up into the night.

Cautiously, I got up and began to move forward; I needed to press on to Orléans. Yet the last thing I needed to do was stumble into a French ambush like the Prussians before me. As I got closer to where I had seen the flashes of gun muzzles, I took a deep breath and called out into the night. "I am an English journalist. I am unarmed and attached to the French army." I shouted the words in English and French. Then to my relief I got a reply.

"*Ici*," shouted a voice, "Here." I advanced slowly, keeping my arms out from my sides to show I had no weapons. I was staring into the snow ahead and almost stumbled over the first body. I had taken it for a fallen snow-covered log until I saw the dark stain. A trail of vapour rose from it into the cold night air, the blood inside the body still warm. He had his back to me, the snow was settling all over his clothes, which were now white, but there was another smaller dark spot on his front, near his heart. His face was wet with melted ice and in the moonlight, I could see that the eyes were wide open, with the fixed stare of someone now looking at eternity.

I continued on my way and ten yards further on, found myself in a clearing. Even then there was the smell of gun smoke in the air. The French must have heard their enemy and used this space to ambush them. Another of the Prussians lay on his back nearby, his spiked helmet upturned in the snow beside him. This one was still alive; his legs twitched, but I could see that he would not live for long. A huge amount of blood had seeped from a wound into the snow around him. In day light it must have been crimson, but now it looked black as pitch against the whiteness. When he looked up and saw me standing over him, he spoke. It was German, but I could tell he was angry. He jabbed a finger at me as he ranted and raved. Perhaps he was furious at his comrades for leaving him, the French for shooting him, or the fact he was dying in this frozen forest; all would have been entirely reasonable.

"*Ici*," the voice came again from the other side of the clearing. Leaving the Prussian to his tirade, I made my way across.

"Where are you?" I called in French and then I spotted him amongst the trees. His leg lay at an odd angle. From the dark marks on his clothes, I guessed he had been shot in the hip.

"They have gone to get help," he gasped. "I can't walk like this." He looked little older than a boy, seventeen or eighteen at most I guessed. His pale features looked almost ethereal as he lay in the snow. Then he shattered this angelic image by shouting something across the clearing in German, which resulted in more curses from the other side. The lad managed a smile, "I told him that there are wolves in this forest, and he will end his existence as wolf shit."

"There aren't really wolves are there?" I asked, glancing around.

"No, but that will teach him to march on France." He pulled a thin coat tighter around his shoulders. He was shivering.

I rummaged in my bag and pulled out the brandy. "Here, take a drink of this, it will warm you up." He took the bottle hesitantly and swallowed a gulp before starting to cough. He was clearly not used to strong spirits. The wound looked bad; from the position of the ragged hole and the position of his leg, I guessed that his hip was shattered. In a hospital he would lose the leg, but they might save his life. Out here in a frozen forest at night, his prospects were bleak.

"Do you think they will be much longer?" he asked, gesturing over his shoulder to where his comrades had disappeared. He offered me the bottle back.

"They might be a while yet," I replied. I was sure they were not coming back at all. They had seen he was beyond help, but the promise of a return had made it easier for them to depart and gave the lad some hope. I felt a wave of pity for the poor sod and wondered when the realisation would hit him too. "Keep the bottle and take a swig when the cold or pain gets too bad."

A random bullet in a dark, frozen forest had shown the fragility of life. I offered a silent prayer that I would not suffer a similar fate. There was still a night of travelling ahead, through poor visibility and a lot of trigger-happy soldiers from two armies. I got to my feet, "I will go and look for your friends," I told him. I had to get back on my way or risk another Prussian patrol finding me. I reached down and squeezed the boy's shoulder, offering a last "Good luck". Then I paused and looked back across the clearing to where the German lay, still muttering to himself, perhaps some kind of prayer. Two men dying slowly yards apart, yet instead of giving each other comfort, one was tormenting the other. I looked back down at the boy at my feet. "I'm sure you will be away on a stretcher soon," I said, "but let that Prussian die in peace. It is the least he deserves."

An hour later and I had made it back to the railway line and turned south to walk beside it. Hundreds of French men trudged in front and behind me and none showed the slightest interest when I emerged from the trees. Many had run from the camp without collecting their weapons and others were sporting minor wounds. Without exception, heads were down and shoulders hunched against the cold. A few walked in small groups, but most were on their own, lost in their thoughts. You did not have to be an expert to see that the morale of this force was at rock bottom. They had been drafted into an ill-equipped army, given precious little training and left to freeze their balls off in snow-covered tents. They had been poorly led and were now defeated by an army they were told did not exist. It would take a hell of a lot more than one of Gambetta's proclamations to make them soldiers again.

Just after dawn we turned a bend in the track to see Orléans ahead of us, but by then we did not even have the strength to muster a cheer. The pace only quickened when we noticed a reception committee of local citizens, welcoming us with much needed sustenance. At the city gates long tables had been set up with an offering of bread and jugs of weak but hot coffee. We supped greedily, grateful for food in our bellies again. All we had thought about for the last few hours was putting one frozen foot in front of the other to reach safety. Now we were there, minds turned to what to do next. The man beside me muttered that he was going to get drunk, while his mates insisted that they should make for the train station. They wanted to get out of the city before the Prussians arrived – they were sure they were close on our heels. I had been promising myself a different reward for reaching sanctuary. There was a large public bath house near the centre of the city. I had used it once before on my way to Tours and now I wanted a hot tub to myself to soak in again. Everything else could wait.

Half an hour later I was luxuriating in warmth. The attendant had brought me cognac and a cigar. I lay back, half asleep, watching the smoke drift in the morning light coming through the window. It felt the height of decadence, soured only slightly when I remembered that poor lad I had left back in the forest. I wondered if he was dead. I hoped he had died peacefully in a brandy-fuelled sleep. Unfortunately, I suspected that he was still alive, the realisation that he had been abandoned finally hitting him. I comforted myself with the fact that there was nothing I could do. With a wound that severe he would die anyway, and even if I tried, there was no way I could find him again in that vast forest.

I was ruminating on whether the war had made me more callous, when splashing in the next cubical heralded the arrival of another survivor of the march. There were several gasps as cold body parts met hot water and then a long, satisfied sigh as warm immersion was achieved. To enjoy the pleasure of a hot bath, you really must first endure the hardship of a freezing night's march. The contrast between the two experiences is positively exquisite. I left the man in peace to enjoy the bliss of the moment, though unfortunately not everyone was as considerate.

"General, are you in here?" The voice from the corridor outside was hesitant. There was silence from all of the cubicles on the floor, at least half of which were occupied. "General, they said you had just come up here. Are you all right?"

There was a weary sigh from the cubicle next door. "Jean, if you do not fuck off right now, I will have you shot."

"Apologies, General, but I thought you should know that no soldiers are staying in the city to form the rear-guard. The few regiments that have arrived intact have refused to stop and are marching on to Tours."

"I don't care," my bathing companion responded brusquely. "Tell the poor sod who is to command the rear-guard. Now, please leave me in peace."

A boot scraped awkwardly on the stone outside and I had a premonition of what would be said next. "But my general, I thought you knew; Aurelle has put *you* in command of the rear-guard."

I managed to stifle a snort of derision at this latest example of incompetence. Organisation in the old professional French army had been poor, but this cobbled together replacement was beyond a joke. The general stayed silent too. I could picture the man peering over the top of the bath at the cold, damp clothes he had just discarded, torn between a sense of duty and a minute or two more enjoying the pleasure of being warm.

Finally, I spoke up. "You might as well stay where you are. The army will never stand here, Orléans is lost."

"Who the devil are you, sir?" came the voice from over the partition wall.

"Just someone who marched south with the army last night." I had already realised that telling people I was a journalist did not always encourage honesty, especially when there had just been a foul up in the chain of command. "The shock of that attack has broken what little spirit they had. The only good news is that the Germans are spread across miles of forest. It will probably take them a day to regroup before they march in."

The general stayed silent, but his aide spoke up. "Aurelle was planning to abandon the city, yet now he wonders if it can be held with a rear-guard. But..." he hesitated, perhaps wondering who the unseen stranger was.

"But what?" demanded his general impatiently.

"Well, we have heard that the government is abandoning Tours," the aide said quietly. "They are anticipating more defeats and moving to Bordeaux."

"If you have heard that, then so has the rest of the army," concluded the general. "You are right," he told me, "we will never get them to stand here now." He sniffed the air, "Is that cigar smoke?"

"Yes, they do cigars here," I replied, puffing on mine, "and a good cognac."

"Jean," commanded the general, "fetch me a cigar and cognac and then pass the word that we will leave in two hours."

The general and I chatted for a while over the partition wall. He admitted that he thought the army had lost around twenty thousand men in the recent encounter, the vast majority as prisoners. "We will probably lose at least another ten thousand through desertions over the next week or so too," he admitted. "Those bloody Prussians are everywhere, here and fighting the Paris breakout. I doubt we will ever beat the bastards."

That less than ringing endorsement of his army's abilities helped me make up my mind. He was right; the new recruits could not fight their way through a line of Chelsea pensioners. They would never stand a chance against a trained and battle-hardened force. Following them was too damned risky – I did not want to die alone in some frozen forest. On top of that I was fed up with being cold and wet. If I kept retreating with their 'Government of National Defence', I would probably end up being driven out of the country entirely and into Spain.

On the other hand, the Prussians had treated me well as a prisoner before, so I decided it was time to throw in my lot with them again. Uncle Frank would be furious, which reminded me that I had one more job to do before the telegraph wire to Tours, and hence London, was cut. I would send him a final article on recent events, though it would not do much for the paper's portrayal of the French cause: the bullied schoolboy, instead of turning on his tormenters, had blindfolded himself, tied one arm behind his back and then presented himself for an arse-kicking outside the bullies' den.

Chapter 22

The German army marched into Orléans unopposed that night. There were still several thousand French soldiers in the city, but hardly any now in uniform and even fewer sober or awake. I slept through its change of hands again myself, having secured lodgings in the city. The locals too seemed unperturbed by developments; this was the third time that the French army had marched away and abandoned them to the enemy. I dug out my Prussian papers and made my way into the centre of the city, but there were hardly any German soldiers to be seen. They had commandeered a theatre and several other buildings in the night, and most were still sleeping off the exhaustion of the march. A weary sentry at City Hall told me to come back later.

I wandered around Orléans to discover that, perhaps deliberately, they were not guarding the southern gate. A steady stream of young men in civilian clothes, having sobered up from the day before, were now slipping away. I doubted that they would be in any great rush to fight again. Meanwhile a handful of old men, well beyond the age of recruitment even in this desperate time, were sporting the distinctive red trousers of the army.

I returned to the City Hall that afternoon, displayed the papers from my previous capture and was once again given a pass to travel where I pleased. The Prussian officer I dealt with could not have been more helpful. When I told him I was interested in travelling to the Prussian lines around Paris, he advised that the train tracks in that direction would be repaired in a day or two.

"Have you managed to contain the breakout from Paris?" I asked. "We heard the French had captured the town of Épinay, some ten miles south of the city."

The officer just laughed at me. "There has been no breakout from Paris. They tried a diversionary attack to the north and then a breakout to the south, but neither broke through our lines of defences."

I frowned, puzzled. Had Gambetta lied to get the army to march? No, there was no advantage in that, for the truth would come out. "But the

French had telegrams from somewhere confirming that Épinay had definitely been captured," I countered. "Are you certain that none of their forces reached the town?"

Instead of dismissing me, the officer called for a map, and we studied it together. He showed me where the breakout had been attempted; it was nowhere near Épinay. Then he gave a grunt of satisfaction. "I think I have solved your puzzle, sir. If you look here, near the northern diversionary attack, there is another village called Épinay, Épinay -sur-Seine."

I could not help but laugh. The French attack and the destruction of the Army of the Loire was all based on a misunderstanding. Instead of capturing a town ten miles south of the city, all the French had done was occupy one in the northern suburbs.

I thought again of the waste of life as I travelled north by train, passing countryside I had trudged past on foot just days before. The ground was still covered in snow. We passed a work party collecting bodies from the forest and laying them by the tracks, a tangle of limbs frozen solid in the positions they had died. I pictured the boy; he had to be dead by then. I wondered if he and his angry German companion were lying in the pile. I sincerely wished that Freycinet had been with me to witness that scene. He never got any closer to actual fighting than counting regimental musters and studying maps, and, as I had discovered, he had not done the latter well. He and his chief, Gambetta, lived in a fantasy world where all regiments were fully equipped, trained and motivated, and shared their fanaticism for an unelected republic raised by a mob. In fact, the more I considered it, I thought France would be better served if the pair of them were gut shot and left to die alone in the forest themselves.

As I headed towards her, even though I knew it would be impossible to enter the city, my thoughts turned to Justine. Paris had been under siege now for three months; it was hard to imagine the modern, beautiful city surviving such a medieval attack. Freycinet had claimed Paris had food for eighty days, yet I knew he had a tendency to exaggerate. There had been a desperation to his efforts to relieve the city, as though its fall could be imminent. Given all other mismanaged French endeavours, I was surprised that it still stood defiant. I had not paid much attention to the city walls around Paris when I had arrived there as we had expected the war to take place in Prussia. I had since learned that they were over thirty feet high and, if Duval was to be believed, there were nearly a hundred bastions and a moat ten feet wide. More importantly, given the fate of Strasbourg, there were also fifteen detached outer forts to keep the German gunners at a distance.

Yet despite these defences, even by Freycinet's estimate, the grain was running out and the meat too. I wondered how Justine would survive in a city on the edge of starvation. Had the rule of law broken down? Were feral gangs roaming the streets, taking what they wanted and leaving the rest to starve? As I scraped ice off the train window, I speculated on what coal and other fuel might be left. My imagination ran amok with the likely horror of the siege. I pictured Justine's beautiful features now pinched and drawn, her splendid curves now emaciated and huddled under blankets. With luck I would arrive just in time for the capitulation. I pictured myself riding up to that bakery and rushing up the stairs loaded with bread and meat, not to mention the grateful coupling that would result.

It was, by then, mid-December. The locomotive had been forced to stop twice while snow drifts were dug off the tracks. After a long day on the train we finally arrived at Versailles, the great palace complex built by Louis XIV a few miles south of his capital. Now it was home to a German king instead of a French one and served as headquarters to a vast army. The town that had built up beyond the palace gates was occupied by a massive entourage of hangers on, such as minor German princelings, their politicians and, in one of the rougher cafés, members of the international press. It was there I was reunited with Forbes. While I had been risking bullets in freezing forests and dealing with rampant incompetence, he had been sitting comfortably witnessing Prussian efficiency. I had expected him to be rather smug, but to my surprise he was jealous of me.

"The British public have turned against the German army now. Everything I write gets twisted," he pulled the latest edition of the *Daily News* from his pocket and dropped it on the table, "while your articles get front-page treatment." I looked down and there was my account of the latest French defeat. Well, it was not exactly my account, for it had been heavily re-written. Uncle Frank had known before I did that the French were not at Épinay. The article managed to portray the disaster as France being tricked by a devious Prussian spy, rather than their own misunderstanding.

"If it makes you feel better, this has been more than a little twisted too," I told him. "But tell me what is happening in Paris. Is the city close to surrendering?"

"No, they are still holding out. A balloon leaves the city once or twice a week and according to the reports they carry, things are getting desperate. They are eating cats and dogs now. Even the animals in the zoo have been slaughtered and served in restaurants. Yet still they insist they will not give up a yard of France, even though they know now that a rescue from the provincial armies is near impossible."

"So are they just to be starved out?" I asked, picturing Justine again, her beautiful eyes dull in a sunken face.

"No, the Prussians are bringing new siege guns here by train. They fire vast shells six inches across that will blow buildings apart and they have the range to reach inside the city. Bismarck wants them to start the bombardment now, but the army is reluctant. They do not have enough shells yet and such a barrage did not break the spirit of the defenders at Strasbourg. You can imagine how news of these giant artillery batteries was received in London; I think the French are hoping that Britain or another European power will intervene."

I had not seen Strasbourg after the shelling, but gathered it was left a ruin. It was unthinkable that a city as magnificent as Paris could be destroyed by guns they could not even see; its people cowering, waiting for the random blast of oblivion. I could not stop my imagination picturing a certain French street, with a crater and pile of scorched rubble where a bakery had once stood. "Can you see Paris from here?" I asked, suddenly needing reassurance that the city still stood.

"No, but there is a hill nearby that has a good view," replied Forbes. "I will take you." A short while later we stood on a bluff. There was the capital of France spread out before us, as yet untouched by shelling.

Forbes pointed to the outer forts still flying the tricolour of France and the place where a recent breakout attempt had been made. With a glass I could make out the tops of churches including the twin towers of Notre Dame and what I thought was the Arc de Triomphe. Around us were the Prussian positions, firing trenches and gun batteries, although there did not seem to be many Germans about.

"Why have they not managed to break out?" I asked, puzzled. "Freycinet said there were four hundred thousand troops in the city and there are hardly any in the lines here."

"There are half that number in the lines," Forbes admitted. "In total there are around eight hundred thousand Germans in France, spread across various armies and guarding supply lines. Nearly all males of military age have been called up now. There had been hopes that the war would be over by Christmas, and they could go home, but that is impossible now."

"Yes, but I still don't understand why the French have not broken out," I repeated.

"It is simple," he replied. "From here you can see when they are planning something, the build up of soldiers and guns. The Prussians have plenty of time to strengthen the line where the attack will come. Often they change their minds, but when they do sally out it is in a disorderly mob. A few explosive shells in their midst sends most running back. Perhaps they are weak from hunger now, but they are more of an armed rabble than an army."

While we were on the ridge we went over to look at one of the new siege guns being installed in a new emplacement. It was a monster, vastly bigger than any gun I had seen before. Its captain proudly assured us that it had the range to fire right into the centre of the city. "Surely they will have to surrender then," I suggested. "They must be on their last legs already."

Forbes laughed, "We can tell you are a new arrival here. People have been predicting the capitulation of the city for weeks now, but they are as stubborn as mules. They cannot possibly win, but they refuse to lose. The Germans want their menfolk home. Some of the press there is calling for the city to be levelled in a bombardment to bring things to a close."

"It won't come to that, surely?" I protested, appalled.

"No," Forbes pointed at the big gun, "I think just a few shells from that will force them to come to their senses."

We returned to Versailles, where I discovered that the destruction of the Army of the Loire had barely been noticed. No one there had expected it to present any kind of threat. Instead, attention was focused on political affairs. Now it was becoming clear what had really prompted this war. Bismarck was not just interested in humiliating France, that was just a side benefit. What he was, in fact, intent on doing was unifying the various German states into a single country under Prussia's leadership. The wily devil must have been planning this for years, although surely even he had not expected the war to go quite so well for his countrymen. He had needed France to declare war to provoke the German states to unite. Now that their leaders were in Versailles and the military might of 'Germany' had been revealed, intense negotiations were underway. The 'Iron Chancellor' was busy bribing, bullying and cajoling the hapless princelings into giving up their independence. Word in the cafés was that most had already succumbed. Bavaria, which was holding out for better terms, would submit within the next few days. Speculation was now turning to what King Wilhelm of Prussia would be called, with most expecting emperor or *kaiser* of Germany.

As we celebrated Christmas the following week, it was a reminder to everyone of the time that had passed since the summer start to the war. Men thought longingly of the family celebrations that they were missing. Church services were held and carols sung. And as the mournful tones of *Silent Night* rang out, I sensed the soldiers were remembering fallen comrades. But there was an undercurrent to the mood of the place now; a collective determination that one way or another, this war was coming to an end, and they were going home. Suddenly, there were no more arguments; the bombardment of Paris would begin.

213

The intention was to start the attack on one of the outer forts, to demonstrate the awesome power of the new artillery to the people of Paris. On the twenty-seventh of December seventy-six of the great German guns lined up on the French fort at Mont Avron. The forty-five guns in the fort were quickly silenced and then buried under piles of rubble. The bastion was completely destroyed, and the following day the French had little choice but to abandon the position. If the Germans had been impressed with the power of their huge shells, however, the people of Paris remained to be convinced. With no peaceful recourse left to force surrender, eventually the order was given to attack the city.

Fog delayed the start of the bombardment, but on the fifth of January the barrage began. Most of the siege guns were still aimed at the defending forts; once those had been destroyed the guns would be moved closer to the city. However, a few targeted the city itself, where with an extra-large charge, they could fire shells right into the centre. I stood close to one of the batteries for a while – the noise of their discharge was beyond deafening. I had cloth stuffed in my ears, but it was so loud I could feel it in my chest too. We watched expectantly for some sight of an explosion in the city or a great building collapsing, but there was nothing. A plume of dust here and there, and once smoke from a fire, but from such a distance away, it was impossible to see the effects of such destructive power. Things had to be different at the receiving end, of course. A single shell would demolish a house, perhaps two, and surely the random nature would put already frayed, hungry nerves on edge. I cursed the stubbornness of the Parisians. Why would they not see sense and give up? Being so near to Justine and yet unable to see her, or help her if she was suffering, was intensely frustrating.

I found out later what was happening in the city. Food supplies were now desperately low, and the people were demanding action against the bombardment. Throughout the siege they had fed and equipped an army of four hundred thousand men but had very little to show for their sacrifices. Some of the soldiers too felt that they had been mismanaged and demanded to be let loose at the Prussians. The politicians, who must have known that capitulation was their only option, realised that a bloodletting would be necessary before such a proposal would be palatable to the populace. Little did we know it at the time, but the end of the siege was finally in sight.

King Wilhelm of Prussia finally became Kaiser Wilhelm of Germany on the eighteenth of January 1871. Ironically, he was acclaimed in the grand hall at Versailles, the palace of his nation's bitter rival. All of the kings, princes and ministers were present, while the gentlemen of the press were forced to wait outside. As we shuffled around waiting for news, we received word that guns had been seen moving on the streets of Paris, presaging an imminent attack. Forbes, who had witnessed such forays in the past, cautioned against spending a freezing night out in the trenches to witness the assault.

"Best stay in a warm bed tonight and see how things are in daylight. But we should not delay after breakfast," he advised confidently, "for the attack is likely to be over by lunchtime."

We did as he suggested, but he was wrong; they were still fighting at midday. We were awoken at daybreak by the thunder of distant cannon. For all my colleague's caution, I was anxious to get underway. I wanted to see first-hand why the French had been unable to break out of their capital. The sound of fighting came from the west of the city. We set off in Forbes' carriage, but I was not disappointed when a Prussian officer stopped us getting too close. The countryside was covered in frost and fog. The last thing I wanted was to blunder accidentally into the fighting. The officer told us that some hundred thousand of the Paris National Guard had swarmed out of the city. Some of the Prussians had even been driven out of their forward trenches. But there the attack had stalled, as well-prepared German artillery rained down on them. "They will not get any further," he predicted, before directing us to a vantage point where we could see some of the fighting. From that distance with a glass, I could make out dark shadows of men gathered in hollows and other sheltered spaces. Only once did I see a group try to advance. Several hundred launched themselves forward, but after half a dozen shells had landed in their midst, most ran back the way they had come. The few valiant souls left advancing, soon found themselves with little cover, under withering rifle fire from the Prussian trenches. Even I could see that the position was hopeless. I could already see small groups of men

215

running back towards the city. I guessed that the rest would wait for nightfall and then withdraw under the cover of darkness.

The bombardment continued over the next few days. We discovered from prisoners taken in the battle, how desperate things were in the city. Even the rich were struggling to find food and fuel, while the poor had not been able to heat their homes for weeks. Prices had risen so that now most Parisians could not even afford the cuts of meat that came from cats, dogs and even rats, while bread too was a luxury. Most subsisted on watery vegetable soups as the cold January weather had begun to cull the weak and infirm. One man told me that the dead had been left on the streets where they fell, as no one had the strength to move them. Surely, we argued, they could not hold out much longer. Starvation beckoned while their recent attacks proved that no military option remained. All they had left was their pride, and you could not eat that.

Then, at long last, the whispers began: French officials had been rowed across the river and taken to see Bismarck. The chancellor must have hoped his negotiations would stay secret, but it was the news that every German had been anticipating for weeks. Negotiations meant peace and then they could go home. By the end of the day the news had spread far and wide and there were wild speculations on what the outcome would be. While there was plenty of rumour, hard facts were impossible to find. Forbes had good contacts among the Prussians, but he was told that Bismarck had met the French officials alone and was saying nothing. The French were represented by the minister called Favre, who the chancellor had reduced to tears when he first made his demands about seizing the provinces of Alsace and Lorraine. I doubted the new negotiations gave him any more comfort, but we knew progress was being made when orders were given to cease the bombardment and the French guns fell silent too. Finally, late on the evening of the twenty-eighth of January 1871, it was announced that an armistice had been agreed.

The peace would last initially for twenty-one days to allow a new assembly to be freely elected and its representatives to meet at Bordeaux. The new government would then decide whether to accept Bismarck's terms or continue the war. To buy even this respite the

French had agreed to pay an indemnity of two hundred million francs, surrender the outer forts around the capital and dismount the guns from their city walls. It was agreed that no German troops would enter Paris during the armistice, but to our delight there was no restriction on civilians. Forbes got us included in a party led by the Prussian crown prince who was going to inspect and takeover some of the outer forts. I was in a fever to get on into the city, but we swiftly realised that things would not be that straightforward. The negotiations had been conducted in such secrecy, that when emissaries approached the forts, they found the commandants unaware of the terms. We had to wait while enquiries were made. Further clarification was needed before soldiers were willing to give up positions that their comrades had fought and died to protect for months. It was soon obvious that we would not enter the city that day. The French soldiers and sailors who had manned the guns of the fort glared at us angrily until they received orders to withdraw. Their battlements might have been half smashed to ruin, but it was clear that these men at least still had some fight in them. We returned to our lodgings and waited for news that Paris was open.

It was another day before the city gates were unlocked to visitors. Even then a local Prussian commander advised against it. One of his patrols had been pelted with stones for getting too close. He thought there was a good chance we would be lynched. We both had our passports and, as usual, I had my French press accreditations in one pocket and my Prussian ones in another. The roads were too broken up for my colleague's usual carriage and so we both borrowed horses, stuffing the saddlebags with food. I thought I would fit in rather better than Forbes; my winter clothes were all French made, whereas his wardrobe had a distinctly Germanic cut to it. Perhaps it was his military bearing or the fact that he had not had to grovel in the dirt, but there was something of a triumphant air about him.

"Try and slouch a bit," I suggested. "If they think we are Prussians things could get ugly." A German cavalry patrol was detailed to see us up to the neutral zone. The young officer tried to talk us out of proceeding. When Forbes wished him *au revoir*, the German shook his head sadly as though he did not expect to see us again. That did nothing

217

to settle my nerves. If it were not for Justine, I would have turned around myself.

We joined a group of French farmers who were driving a flock of scrawny sheep up towards one of the city gates. The flock was mostly skin and bone, but I did not doubt they could sell for a king's ransom inside. The gate was shut and sentries shouted at us to wait. A crowd of others with vegetables and other goods to sell gradually built up around us. I was uncomfortably aware that we were the focus of their attention. Well, not us so much as our horses. I heard muttering that we had to be Prussians to have such plump mounts. One fellow ran an appraising hand over the haunch of Forbes' mare, as though sizing up the time it would take to cook.

"We are English journalists," I announced loudly in French. "I was with the French army at Spicheren and Sedan and later with Aurelle near Orléans."

"Well, your horse wasn't," growled an old man standing near the head of the animal. "That is a German horse all day long." I wondered if it had some German army marking I had missed. Then, to my horror, the fellow reached into his coat and pulled out a huge knife. I feared he would butcher the creature while I was still astride, or possibly me too. But before he could do anything, we were interrupted by the creak of the gate opening. Several soldiers stood in the opening, greedily eyeing up the meat on hooves before them. "You had better see these two first," called out the old-timer, before adding hopefully, "and confiscate their horses."

We spurred our mounts through the gate and handed down our passports and my French accreditations for inspection.

"Did I hear you say that you were at Sedan?" asked the officer.

"Yes, we both were," I confirmed, neglecting to mention that Forbes had been on the other side of the valley.

Our interrogator looked highly dubious. "Perhaps I should send you to General Ducrot, to see if he remembers you."

"Please do," I invited him. "I was in his headquarters for much of the morning, in fact I nearly fell on top of him. He will certainly remember me."

218

The man looked somewhat mollified by this and turned to Forbes. "And you, sir, do you not have any French papers?"

"I have this," replied Forbes reaching into his pocket. He pulled out a thick packet wrapped in waxed paper. The officer cautiously opened one end of the package and then stuffed it quickly inside his own uniform.

"You are free to proceed, gentlemen," he announced before turning his attention to the farmers.

"What on earth was in that packet?" I asked as we rode away.

"Several thick slices of ham," Forbes laughed. "Now, are you sure you do not want to ride with me to the embassy? We can leave our horses safely there."

"No thank you, I have some errands to run first," I replied. I watched him ride off with a sense of relief; he was already getting more hostile glares from soldiers standing nearby. I turned my mount in the direction of a bakery I had been dreaming about for the last six months.

As my horse trotted along, attracting hungry glances as it went, I studied the streets about me. There was surprisingly little evidence of the bombardment. While hundreds of shells had been fired, Paris was a huge city and had been left mostly unscathed. The corner of a street had been damaged by one shell and there was a large crater in a park, but that was the only damage to the buildings I passed. The impact of the war on the people, however, was much greater.

The most obvious thing was that virtually every male above the age of twelve was in uniform, or at least bits of uniform worn under coats. With perverse logic, I discovered that the Paris militia I had met in Chalon, called the Mobile Guard, which refused to be mobile, was now known as the National Guard. Despite the name, they were only present in the capital. Few had weapons with them as they went about their business, but it was easy to believe that there were four hundred thousand of them in the city. Most had a beaten look about them and few held my gaze when I looked in their direction. Given the claims of the prisoners we had spoken to before, I had half expected the streets to be littered with the dead, but they were only occupied by the living. That said, in the mile or so of my journey, I passed no less than five funeral processions.

Everyone looked gaunt and thin, despite being wrapped in several layers of clothing. The great treelined boulevards I had seen before were treelined no more. They were bare and stark, and some of the stumps had even been dug out in a desperate effort to get wood for fuel. I passed by abandoned houses that had been stripped bare of timber, including floorboards, stairs and window frames and that were now just stone shells. As I was forced to wait for yet another funeral cortege to pass, I began to fear for what I would find at Justine's home.

The bakeries and butchers' were all shut, display windows empty with a look of dust and neglect about them. Other shops were still open, but no one was buying. As I got closer, I had to pass Pascal's apartment. I felt a pang of sadness when I looked up at the window I had knocked on back in the summer to get him to come with me. Then at last I was standing in front of the bakery and the door to the apartment above. There was no smiling face in the window as I had imagined. The panes of glass were still covered in the morning frost and the space beyond was dark. I had a chill then, imagining the worst or if she had just moved away. The bakery beneath, like others I had seen, was shut, a thick layer of dust coating the shelves in the window.

With a feeling of trepidation, I unbuckled the saddlebags and threw them over my shoulder before dismounting. A group of skeletally thin children had crowded around nearby. They were eight or nine, and I beckoned one forward and offered him a silver franc if he would hold my horse. The boy stared wide-eyed at the coin, which was far more than the task was worth. I hoped it would result in a full belly. Then again, as I looked up the street, and noticed for the first time the heads appearing in doorways, to look at the stranger who had stopped among them, I wondered if I had underpaid the lad. He was now guarding a fortune in horseflesh. I did not care, it was not my mount, I just wanted to see inside that apartment.

I knocked at the door, but as I feared there was no answer. Trying the door handle, I found to my surprise that it was unlocked. I stepped into the dark hallway and saw the staircase before me. There were no piles of books on it now and screw holes in the wall showed where a banister rail had been removed. Gingerly I climbed up, fearing what I might find. To my relief, much of Justine's furniture was still there and the bed I remembered so fondly did not contain her frozen corpse. Her clothes still hung in the wardrobe and I found some of the last of her books by the hearth. Staples among the ashes showed that they were now fuel for the body rather than the mind.

Relieved that she was still in residence, I found some plates and began to lay out my gifts on the table to surprise her when she returned. There was a large leg of mutton in one of the saddlebags, while the other contained some dark bread the Germans are fond of, three eggs, a small bag of coffee and some potatoes. I had just finished the display when I heard boots coming up the stairs. It was a slow, plodding step that sounded far too heavy for Justine. Sure enough a man walked in, I recognised the baker from my earlier visits.

"Ah, you are Justine's friend," he smiled in greeting. "They told me a stranger was in the apartment and…" His voice tailed off as he noticed the table behind me. "*Mon Dieu*," he gasped staring at the bounty as though it were the crown jewels.

"Do you know where Justine is?" I asked, but I had lost his attention.

"Look at that mutton," he gasped, "Oh and eggs too, I cannot remember when I last saw an egg."

"I am sure that there will be enough to share," I offered, "but do you know where Justine is?"

Collecting himself the man looked back at me. "She is at her school in Belleville. You will never find it. I will send a boy to get her and don't worry, I will light the oven for your mutton." With that he disappeared, descending the stairs much faster than he had come up. I thought he was being rather presumptive about the oven, until I realised that the joint was far bigger than the little range in Justine's hearth would accommodate. I could hear him shouting outside as he sent boys to find my missing host. I looked down from the window and was pleasantly surprised to see my horse still there. The baker was now beside it, talking excitedly to his neighbours, holding out his hands like a fisherman to describe the joint of meat he had just seen, and like them, exaggerating considerably.

The little room was freezing. I cursed myself for not thinking to bring some coal. In a few minutes I had a two-volume treatise on the rights of the working man, serving a more useful purpose in providing heat from the hearth. It was then I heard women's voices and more footsteps coming up the stairs. It was the baker's wife and a neighbour. They had come, they explained, just to look at the meat. They stood there gazing, cooing over it as though it were a new-born baby, while I stood protectively nearby as the anxious father. To my relief I then heard more footsteps running up the stairs and even, before I saw her, I knew it was Justine.

Chapter 23

She was in my arms in a moment. As I swung her around in delight, I could feel she was lighter. My fingers could now detect her ribs under her dress, but as she stood back to look at me, she was just as beautiful. Those sparkling eyes were just the same. If her features were more angular and her cheek bones pronounced, the vulnerability made me want her even more. I could have taken her to bed there and then, but her eyes had strayed to the table. She gasped in delight before hugging me even tighter. Soon we were making a procession down the stairs, the baker's wife at the fore. She held the meat for inspection by the street as though it were a religious relic. The mutton and potatoes were placed into the oven with due reverence. Then, as more neighbours crowded into the tiny shop, I was plied with questions.

First, they wanted to know about the armistice and how long it would last. Then if I knew anything about food coming to Paris. When I told them of the vast funds and piles of supplies raised in Britain to feed the city, some of them wept with relief. "Within a week," I promised, "the first shipments should arrive and then there will be food for all."

"And what about the relief armies?" asked an old man. "When will they arrive to drive those Prussian swine away?"

I was shocked that they knew so little of what was happening in the rest of the country. I knew Gambetta and others had been sending news via carrier pigeons brought out of the city by balloons. "There are no relief armies," I told him gently. "Last month I was with an army of two hundred thousand men when we thought the National Guard here had broken through the siege lines. But that army was beaten and scattered by the Prussians. Then we heard your forces had not broken out at all." I looked around the little shop to find them all staring at me in amazement at this revelation. "All attempts to relieve Paris were beaten back," I announced. "There will be no more relief forces. The armistice is to allow for elections so that the country can vote on peace terms, which are the same as those offered after the battle at Sedan."

There was a stunned silence in the bakery for a moment and then the old man croaked, "That can't be true. It means we have suffered for nothing. It has all been for nothing…" Tears started to stream down his face as he turned and hurried from the shop.

"Did they really try to relieve Paris, or did they betray us?" demanded another and there were murmurs of agreement from the others at this suggestion of treachery.

I thought back to the boy dying in the forest and felt a flush of anger. "I can assure you that thousands of young French men and boys have died trying to liberate Paris. But the biggest army France had was the four hundred thousand right here. Many wondered why you could not break out yourselves."

"There are half a million Prussians surrounding the city," insisted my interrogator. "Our army tried to break out just last week, but it was impossible."

There was no point telling him that the besiegers were less than half that number, nor that I had seen their paltry attempt at a breakout. I did not want an argument to spoil my reunion and so I took Justine by the arm and led her into a corner where we could talk in private. By now a delicious roasting smell was filling the shop, which was attracting even more of the neighbours.

"Does Madeleine live nearby?" I asked. "Should we invite her to share…" As I started to ask my question, I saw a look of sadness cross her features and could guess what was coming next.

"Madeleine died last month." Justine gave a heavy sigh, "I tried to help her, but prices kept going up and she could no longer afford fuel or food. I told her to sell her ring, Henri would not have wanted her to suffer, but she refused."

"But wasn't there help available for the starving in the city?" I asked.

"If you are a man you can join the National Guard. They will pay you one and a half francs a day, two and a quarter if you are married, but of more value is the food rations they give you as well. There are soup kitchens for the very poor, but Madeleine was too proud to go to those. She tried to stretch out her allowance, but a pound of potatoes is now two francs. A fowl or a rabbit, if you can find one, are now over forty francs. The rabbit will almost certainly be a cat, which has much less meat on it. Many of those who have died are middle-class women, who could not face the shame of queuing at the soup kitchens. I only got by with scraps from the bakery when they had flour and with food rations given out at the school. Madeleine got weaker until she just gave up trying to survive. I did not realise what state she was in until it was too late."

We sat in silence for a while considering such a miserable end. I doubted poor Henri Duval knew the fate of his fiancée. He was probably eagerly planning his return to the city to see her, much as I had done with Justine. "Pascal is dead too," I confessed at last. When I told her how he had died, her eyes brimmed with tears before she dashed them away with her cuff.

"They cannot be allowed to die in vain," she insisted. "They would not have wanted to see France so humiliated. We must fight on and drive the Prussians out."

"They are Germans now," I told her. All of the German states have formed a new nation under Prussian leadership, and they are just too strong for France. There are no French armies left that can defeat them, not here in Paris or elsewhere. If you tried to fight on, they would probably raze Paris to the ground with their guns. They might even make the whole country a province of the new Germany."

At that she fell silent. Any further conversation was interrupted by the distribution of the lamb and potatoes. The baker performed some kind of miracle, on a par with our saviour with the five loaves and fishes. Everyone in that shop got to taste something and many of those outside the bakery too. As the provider, they insisted I had a portion, but I took it outside to the lad still holding my horse. I was amazed the animal had not been taken – it would have comfortably fed the street. Yet there was a pride in these people; they might be close to starvation, but they looked after their own. I was now a welcome guest. Someone offered me stabling and I was delighted when, a week later, the animal was still alive just as food began flooding into the city.

As soon as I decently could, I persuaded Justine to return with me to the apartment. She was still asking questions such as were the German

225

troops also starving, had not the *franc-tireurs* cut their supply lines and was their morale not low at the constant attack from French citizens. Disappointment showed in her face at all of my answers, as the reality of the situation began to sink in. Some warmth had come up from the bakery below, but the rooms were still bitterly cold. We were soon hugging each other for warmth under the covers. The lovemaking was strangely disappointing, but perhaps it could never have lived up to the months of anticipation, at least on my part. After her interrogation, Justine had gone quiet and just wanted me to hold her. I think we were both still coming to terms with the change in circumstances.

The following morning she brightened up after a breakfast of eggs and black bread and then took me into the heart of the city. Plenty of other horses had clearly survived the siege, for the omnibuses were still running and the trees lining the Champs d'Élysées had also been spared. Despite the armistice, though, there was no air of celebration; people were guarded, fearful of what the future might bring. The only common topic of conversation was when more food supplies might reach the city. It was the Germans who were to provide the first extra food rations to the Parisians. Most if it was pea sausage, which the gastronomic French viewed as a culinary obscenity. Only the desperately hungry would even try it, for by then word was coming of the food on the way from England. Ships had sailed full of supplies from London on the day of the armistice and trains and barges were being laid on to bring the haul to the city. Not everyone was staying put to wait for it, though. Wealthier citizens trapped in Paris for so long, were using their new-found freedom to travel to friends and family out in the country. There was an exodus at all of the railway stations as those who could, abandoned the cold dour city for a life of comfort and plenty elsewhere.

Justine did not want to leave. She still went daily to her school, while I rode from the city and came back with coal and other luxuries for her comfort. In just a week she was putting weight back on and a blazing hearth made the apartment more habitable. We sat more easily in the evenings and talked. I told her why the armies of France had been beaten. She explained how Paris had expected the siege to fail from *franc-tireurs* ambushes on the supply lines and attacks from the armies of new recruits. The only thing we argued about was Gambetta. She had cheered his appointment at City Hall when the old empire was overthrown, as she thought he was the right man to help create the new republic. They had received copies of his proclamations in Paris. Many in the city felt that the rest of the country had failed him in not rising up as he instructed. Those with family outside of the city disagreed, but as most of them had left to visit that family, their voices were few.

Over the next week life began to return to something resembling the new normal. Supplies were pouring into the city by train and later by barges along the Seine. While there had been riots around the first arrivals, now food was being fairly dispersed among the citizens. We would awake to the delicious smell of baking from the shop below. I wrote a couple of articles on life in Paris for the *Daily News*, although I had to ride to Versailles to send them as the telegraph in the city was still not working. I would come back with a fowl or some other luxury item, such as soap, which was in short supply in the city. Then we would eat and make love. For a few days life was perfect.

Of course, I should have known it could not last. The first cloud on the horizon was the election of the new government, which took place on the eighth of February. Given the febrile political atmosphere during the siege, I had been expecting riotous hustings outside City Hall with candidates yelling promises and shouting down their opponents. That is what would happen in a British election, with the crowd pelting rubbish at the disfavoured. In Paris it was hard to believe there was an election at all. Hustings were not a French tradition; no candidates made speeches. There were just written statements published, which few bothered to read. Given all the sacrifices made and the importance of the vote, such apathy was beyond my comprehension. When I mentioned this to Justine, she took me again to the Belleville area of the city, this time to one of their republican clubs. There I found the fearsome speeches I had been expecting, but they were being delivered to an audience of only a hundred or so packed into a small hall. I discovered that there were various left-wing factions, known collectively as 'reds', I think due to the red woollen hats worn by the largest group, the Jacobins.

One orator was all for returning to the days of the terror in the first revolution. He wanted all those who had agreed to the armistice guillotined. To this, the crowd cheered their approval. His supporters encouraged him more as if he were an entertainer, than the potential leader of a lynch mob. The speaker might have been more imposing if he had not been covered in fluff. He looked as though he had been tarred and feathered, whereas in fact he was a journeyman flock bed maker. Like a fluffy chicken, he capered about the stage, his next goal to encourage the audience to retake the vast Fort Valerian, which guarded the eastern approach to the city. He pledged to lead the audience to retake it then and there from the Prussians, to whom it had been surrendered. Yet as he reached the door, he realised that he was alone and sheepishly returned after being offered a drink from someone in the crowd. There were other speakers, but most were similarly deluded from the reality of their situation. Nearly all declared that the war should continue until French victory was achieved, but were vague about how such a miraculous triumph would come to pass.

The election results were not a surprise to me but came as a shock to many in Paris, who viewed their city as the heart of the country. Parisians who had stayed to vote had overwhelmingly supported the red candidates, yet the situation in the rest of the country was very different. In the views of the wider electorate the Bonapartists were blamed for starting the war, while the Republicans carried responsibility for continuing and losing it. Voters wanted peace and stability and so they turned to politicians from the past. Over half of those elected were former monarchists, although none suggested the return of a king. They were old-school Conservatives, who would sign whatever it took for peace and had little interest in radical politics. Of the seven hundred and sixty-eight seats, only one hundred and fifty were gained by Republicans and many of those were of the moderate variety, such as Minister Favre, who had negotiated with Bismarck before. Of the radicals there were only twenty, most elected from Paris.

The new prime minister was Adolphe Thiers, who had previously served in the same role for the last French king. His first job was to agree peace terms with Bismarck. While the amnesty was extended by a few days, he found the iron chancellor almost as inflexible as Favre had done. France was to lose all of Alsace and most of Lorraine. Thiers managed to save the city of Belfort, which had never surrendered, but only at the cost of allowing the Germans a triumphal march through Paris. Germany also demanded a war indemnity of five billion francs, an almost unimaginably vast sum, around two hundred million in pounds. The new assembly was appalled at these demands, and several made speeches promising revenge on the new Germany, but at the end of the day they knew they had little choice. The peace treaty was ratified by over seventy percent of the assembly. Gambetta was so disgusted with the result that he soon resigned and fled to Spain.

On the first and second of March the people of Paris were forced to suffer their first indignity: the triumphal parade of the Germans. The victors of the war gathered at the racecourse at Longchamp. Then thirty thousand of them marched down the Champs d'Élysées. Great long columns of immaculately dressed infantry, cavalry and rows of their lethally effective artillery. They were not supposed to go under the Arc de Triomphe, which had been damaged in the bombardment, but half a dozen of their hussars could not resist the temptation. They jumped their horses over the protective chains to insolently ride through what Parisians considered a sacred space. There were gasps of indignation, boos and catcalls from those watching near me, but nothing worse. With so much anger and so many weapons inside the city, it felt to me that the Germans were sparking a light on a gunpowder barrel. It would only take one shot to trigger a conflagration. Most of the reds had barricaded themselves in Belleville, swearing they would kill any enemy that entered their territory. They need not have worried, though, for the Germans were not interested in the crowded slums. They promenaded around the grander parts of town, before withdrawing to the well-to-do western suburbs and outer forts. There they would maintain a presence until the reparations were fully paid. The only violence during those days was dished out to fellow French. Cafes seen serving the Germans had their windows smashed. Other civilians, such as Forbes, who was seen raising his hat amiably to a German princeling, were chased by the mob and badly beaten.

I felt a sense of relief when the third day of victory marches was unexpectedly cancelled, and the Germans withdrew from the city. Parisians claimed a triumph, insisting that their intimidating demeanour had frightened their enemy away. A more likely explanation was that ratification of the treaty by the assembly had happened quicker than expected, which specified the German withdrawal. Citizens set about washing the streets that had been 'defiled' by the enemy with Cindy's Disinfecting Fluid and chloride of lime. They even went as far as to replace the chain around the Arc de Triumph that had been crossed. Disaster had been averted. I dared to hope that life in Paris would begin to settle back to how it had been before the war. However, that ambition proved hopelessly naïve, for I had no idea of the political, military and literal inferno that was to sweep through Paris over the following weeks.

Chapter 24

It all started at the assembly, which was still meeting at Bordeaux. Perhaps they resented that historically Paris had ruled France and thought that now the provinces should show they were in charge. Whatever the cause, the decisions they took in early March seemed designed to provoke further outrage in the capital.

First, they passed legislation that cancelled the moratorium on debts that had protected citizens from their creditors during the war, making all sums due within two days. Even the better off middle class would struggle to pay rents at such short notice when many had earned little for months. Then, to exacerbate financial pressures, they voted to cancel the one and a half francs' daily allowance for the National Guard. Finally, they appointed Aurelle as the new commander of the guard. As I well knew, the general detested Freycinet and the other radicals, while to Parisians he was the man who had failed to march from Orléans to rescue them.

As each new announcement was made the tension in the city rose a notch higher, until there was almost an electrical charge in the streets. Even the moderates were outraged by the cancellation of the debt moratorium, while the reds were positively incandescent with fury. If any rent collector had tried his hand in the Belleville suburbs, he would have been beaten to death with his own ledgers within minutes. Justine had wept when she learned of the debt legislation. "This is a republic in name only," she protested. "They don't care about government for the people; it is a monarchy without the king."

"I doubt any landlord would be foolish enough to enforce the new laws in Paris at the moment," I reassured her. "You must remember that in the rest of the country, many people have continued to work, and those surviving conscripts are going back to their homes. Things will settle down when the government returns to Paris."

But the government did not return to the capital. The new assembly must have been aware of the antagonism they had stirred up, for instead of returning to their usual building in the city, they instead decided to base themselves at Versailles. "They are little better for Paris than the Germans they replaced there," grumbled the baker. Some of the newly appointed ministers did nervously return to their ministries in the city, but they kept a very low profile. There was talk of tunnels under ministry buildings and City Hall, so that they did not have to mix with the populace. One person who did not hide was General Aurelle. He announced that he would take swift action to quell any disturbance of the peace. Then he summoned the battalion commanders of the National Guard to a meeting in order to stamp down his authority. Perhaps I should have gone to see what happened, but to me the war was over. I was a war correspondent and so my duties were complete. I was half expecting Frank to summon me home and in two minds whether to return to continue my career, or stay to enjoy the not inconsiderable delights of Paris – and Justine.

Instead of listening to Aurelle shouting at his new command, I took Justine for a walk in the park to cheer her up, then afterwards, while my letter of credit still carried sway, to one of the better restaurants for lunch. They no longer served elephant or giraffe steaks as they had during the siege, but they still managed to put on a fine spread while food was still only trickling into the poorer suburbs.

"Why don't you come back with me to London?" I suggested. "A break from Paris will do us both good."

"I can't do that," she insisted. "My school needs me and if there is any hope of retaining even a vestige of the republic, then I want to be here to help it survive."

"But what *is* the republic?" I asked. "The elected assembly would say they govern as a republic, but their ideas are very different to those of the reds." I regretted asking, for she started to talk of political theories and philosophies, and I confess my thoughts turned to how delightfully her breasts moved when she was animated, which was rather distracting.

When we got back to her apartment, we found a note sent to me from Forbes. He had returned to London briefly after his beating but was now back and wanted to meet me in the suburb of Saint-Denis the next morning. I was not surprised he was reluctant to re-enter the city.

I met him at a café outside the cathedral. The bruises from his encounter with the mob were still showing. I noted how he sat down gingerly, clearly still in some pain.

"So, has my uncle ordered me home?" I asked cutting to the chase. I knew he must have visited the *Daily News* offices while he was away. I doubted Frank would continue to pay for two war correspondents when there was no war.

"That was his plan," Forbes admitted. "But I have persuaded him to stay his hand a while longer."

"How on earth did you manage that?" I asked gratefully.

"I told him that the verminous scum in Paris were likely to start a civil war." His sympathies had always been with the Prussian cause, but since being attacked, his hatred of Parisians was almost visceral.

"Don't be ridiculous," I rebuked him. "There is some anger in the city certainly, but no one is talking about war. Give it a few weeks and things will settle down…although I suppose there is no need to tell Frank that yet."

"Have you not heard what happened at Aurelle's meeting?" he demanded. When I shrugged – I was already adopting gallic gestures – he went on. "Of the two hundred and sixty National Guard commanders ordered to attend, only thirty obeyed. Most of those were from the battalions raised in the middle-class areas, many of whose members had already left the city."

"What about the rest?" I asked, feeling a twinge of unease.

"They have announced that they no longer recognise Aurelle's command. They have set up a Central Committee of the National Guard to rule themselves."

I was surprised, but still not alarmed. "That does not mean that they want to start a civil war," I insisted. "They must know that they do not have much support outside Paris. When I saw them at Chalon, all they wanted to do was return to the capital. They are probably going to negotiate to try and get their allowances back."

"You don't understand, do you?" pressed Forbes as though speaking to a dim-witted child. "The National Guard is now the biggest military force in France. There are four hundred thousand of them, while the

233

army is restricted to forty thousand by the treaty agreed with Bismarck. The Germans also seized most of the army's artillery, while the Guard has a huge park of some two hundred cannon on top of the hill at Montmartre. Members of the assembly are terrified that the National Guard will march against them at Versailles, for with odds of ten to one over the army, there is little they could do to stop them."

I considered this for a moment and then shook my head. "No, they won't do that. I have spent time in Belleville and been to some meetings of the reds. The one thing I have learned is that they never agree about anything. There are so many factions and they all have contrasting ideas on how the country should be run, most completely insane. You give them too much credit; they would never organise to march on Versailles and even if they did, they certainly would not agree on what to do when they got there. The best thing that the assembly can do is leave them alone, and sooner or later they will turn on each other." Then I uttered the prophetic words, "It would take an act of incredible stupidity from the government to get them all working together." Forbes looked doubtful, but I was sure I was right, indeed I still am. All the horrors to come could have been avoided but for a staggeringly dim-witted piece of incompetence.

At first it seemed that the government was taking my advice. The army sent a detachment of men to try to recover the artillery from Montmartre, but when a belligerent contingent of the National Guard blocked the one road into the area, the soldiers timidly backed down and retreated. Buoyed by their success, the Guard burned down a vacant army barracks in the city, but beyond that took no action. As I had predicted, they fell to bickering amongst themselves. All would have been well but ten days after their first effort, Adolphe Thiers, the new prime minister, decided to make a second attempt to seize the cannon. Early in the morning of the eighteenth of March, some fifteen thousand soldiers marched. Some went to cover the hotbed of Belleville, others to the Bastille area, but the critical contingent marched up the hill at Montmartre to seize the guns. In all but one respect it was a perfect operation. A cold rain kept everyone off the streets in the early hours and by four in the morning the few National Guard sentries had been chased off. Beyond one wounded sentry, no blood had been shed and the guns were under the army's control. Teams of horses harnessed to the guns could have whisked them away long before the National Guard had time to react. By dawn the removal would have been complete, leaving the reds impotent in their fury.

Unfortunately, the incursion had been planned by a complete dunderhead. No teams of horses had accompanied the soldiers. How the general in charge had not noticed this omission, was beyond me. He could hardly have expected his men to haul two hundred guns away, especially down some steep hills. Incredibly, it was only as he took possession of the weapons that he seemed to notice this shortcoming. Messengers were hurriedly sent back to barracks for the required animals, but they would never arrive in time. Instead, the apprehensive soldiers were left standing in the heart of 'enemy territory', as the city slowly woke up around them.

The first we knew of this mismanaged foray was the dull ring of church bells. We were lying in bed together and it was barely dawn. I remember thinking it was too early to be ringing for Sunday Mass, and then I realised that it was Saturday. I got up and looked out of the window to see two National Guardsmen running down the street, one still pulling on his coat. "Wake up," I urged, shaking Justine's shoulder. "Something is afoot." It may sound like hindsight, but I had a nasty sense of foreboding as I hunted around the floor in the morning gloom for my clothes. We were out in the street in just a few minutes, joining a tide of people all running in one direction.

"The government are trying to steal our guns," an indignant guardsman told us as we joined the throng. "We paid for them, they have no right to them," he insisted. Justine explained that many of the cannon had been paid for by public subscription. Then we heard that there were more soldiers guarding the approaches to Belleville and I began to wonder if the government was launching a broader attack. By then we could not change direction even if we wanted to.

The streets were packed with National Guards and civilians, all pressing up the hill to Montmartre. Justine shared the outrage of the crowd and eagerly joined in a chant to save the guns as we closed in.

"We will show them the power of the people," she told me excitedly as we got to the top of the hill.

There was hardly any room to move now, and we could see little of what was happening. As a correspondent I had to report on events, but more importantly it was highly likely that this day would end in violence. I did not want to be penned up in a crowd when soldiers opened fire on it. I looked around and saw two houses with first floor balconies. The first was packed with spectators, but the second was empty. I guessed the occupants had joined the mob.

"Let's get up there," I pointed and led the way through the throng. The door to the house was unlocked and we quickly slipped up the stairs and into the front bedroom. As we stepped outside, we could see that fifty yards along the street several ranks of soldiers were trying to maintain a cordon between a surging crowd and the rows of cannon. A general was on horseback behind them, pointing with his sword, but it was impossible to hear him over the din. The soldiers were hopelessly outnumbered and were being pushed and jostled. The faces I could see were all young and terrified. They kept glancing over their shoulders for orders that would get them out of this mess. The soldiers were armed as were many of the National Guard in the crowd, with women and even children mixed in amongst them. It seemed only a matter of time before someone fired the first shot. Then there would be a massacre, with the soldiers hunted down through the streets.

Suddenly, to my surprise, there was fresh cheering at one end of the cordon. I could see some of the soldiers raising their rifles, butt upwards, as they stood back and let the crowd towards the guns. They had come to the sensible solution that it was time to throw in their lot with the National Guard. Faced with the alternative, the rest of the soldiers quickly reached the same decision as they were soon surrounded. The line did not just melt away; to show its new loyalty to the people, two of the young soldiers helped pull their general from his saddle. He was hoisted up into the air in front of the baying mob and for a moment I thought he would be killed. Just in time, some officers of the National Guard pushed their way through and under their protection, the general was taken to a dance hall that served as one of their guard posts.

I breathed a sigh of relief at a disaster averted, while Justine celebrated the people's triumph in saving their artillery. Yet to most in the crowd their victory had been just too easy. Their anger at the government's attempt to steal from them had not been sated...a bloodlust had been raised that now had to be satisfied. A large crowd stood outside the hall still baying for the general's death, while others began to search for targets elsewhere. Safely above the throng, you could see that no one was in charge. It was a feral mob. I could understand now why Forbes was reluctant to re-enter Paris, for it was evident that it could not be reasoned with. A shout would go up for the destruction of a ministry or the death of a minister and they would roar their acclaim at the thought. Slowly but surely the crowd began to disperse, but not to go home. Some with weapons and others without, they would run on to cause destruction elsewhere.

Only an idiot would follow them, especially one who was foreign. It would only take someone who knew me to shout they had been betrayed by the British, for them to turn in my direction. Instead, I waited until most had gone and then Justine and I left the house. She had wanted to follow the gangs and talked about my duty as a journalist to report what was happening, but to hell with that. My duty to keep our precious skins intact was far greater. We turned to go a different way, our route passing close by the dance hall. As we drew near, I saw that another group had arrived there just before us. They were all wearing red sashes and one man, brandishing a paper, was talking about a release document. There was booing from the crowd, who thought that the general was to be set free. Then one of the sash wearers said something I did not catch, which elicited another cheer. The general was brought out in front of the mob. The poor bastard looked terrified and who could blame him, for he must have known that his life hung by a thread. He was dragged away down the street, collecting a few more blows along the way. Justine and I followed at a distance, curious to see what would happen.

We ended in a pleasant avenue on the edge of the city called the Street of the Roses. It was named for the gardens that surrounded the few cottages along it. In the summer it would be a riot of blooms, but then in March only a few bulbs gave any colour. The general was taken into house number six. A few minutes later another older gentleman was dragged up the street by a new crowd to join him. We found out that he was another general. He had not been in charge of soldiers, he was retired, but had foolishly left his house to see what was happening and had been recognised.

The crowd was chanting for their deaths, beating on the windows and doors of the cottage to intimidate those inside. The chilly garden reminded me of the cottage vegetable patch I had nearly been shot in months before. On this occasion, though, the poor devils inside the little house were beyond the help of a priest.

"Oh no, they are bringing them out" gasped Justine as the door opened and the old man was dragged through it. To a chorus of yells and jeers, he was pushed into the garden. My mind flashed back to my own terror when I thought I was to be shot, but even though he must have known what was coming, the older general showed not the slightest fear. He stood against the wall and yelled insults at those calling for his death. There was no orderly firing party, anyone with a gun just opened fire, yet after a dozen wild shots the old man still stood, just as belligerent. Then, as Justine turned away and buried her face in my shoulder, a bullet hit him in the eye and must have killed him instantly. The younger general was then dragged out of the cottage, now struggling against his captors. He had only just reached the garden when someone stepped up behind him and shot him in the back. Even then the generals' torment was not over. The bodies were left in the middle of the flower beds while various men, even some of the younger general's soldiers, blazed away at them with their rifles long after they were dead. With their corpses now a bloody ruin, still the crowd were not satisfied. Some women lifted their skirts and urinated on them, to cheers from those watching.

I turned away in disgust and led us away down the Street of Roses. Justine had fallen quiet. She might have read all the books on revolutionary politics, but the bloody reality of it had left her shocked. "What have they done?" she asked at last. "What will happen now?"

"I think the people of Paris have just declared war on the government of France," I told her. I remembered the warning Forbes had given me just days before and how then it had seemed unlikely. It had just taken one poorly planned spark to trigger the revolt, but now the generals were dead, the Rubicon had been crossed. There would be no going back now. The government could not forgive such an act and the people were certainly in no mood to back down. Heaven knew what atrocities were being committed around the ministries.

As we walked back towards the centre of the city, I listened for more sounds of gunfire. I imagined running battles between the army and the mob, but it was eerily silent. Curious, we pressed on, until eventually we came across a ministry building with a crowd of people celebrating in front of it. When I looked up at the flagpole at the top, to my astonishment instead of the tricolour of France, a plain red banner flapped in the wind.

Chapter 25

The events of the eighteenth of March had taken everyone by surprise, including the government. Prime Minister Thiers took the decision to abandon his capital for Versailles. He took his remaining soldiers with him; he could not afford any more of his army coming under pressure to join the reds.

Yet if the government had been caught on the back foot, so had the people of Paris. The following morning when the excitement of the day before had died down, people wondered the streets in something of a daze. We joined them and stared up at the red flag flying over City Hall with very different expectations. "This is our chance to build a true republic," Justine enthused. "A government of the people, by the people. No kings, emperors or bishops telling us what to do, just logic and fairness. When the rest of France sees how successful we are, they will want to follow our example. Thiers will have no choice but to adopt our policies."

I will admit that I was more than a little in love with Justine. At that moment her eyes shone brightly as she imagined this paradise and I don't think she ever looked more beautiful. Yet her looks were matched by an extraordinary naivety. "You have spent too much time studying your books," I cautioned. "Have you forgotten the things we saw yesterday? That mob, wild and unpredictable is governing Paris. It will turn on any decisions it does not like. Its leaders know to keep it happy, or they will suffer the same fate."

"You are wrong," she insisted. "We will be ruled by reason and logic."

To prove my point, I led the way to City Hall. Thousands of National Guard were gathering in the square outside, but the sentries by the door let us in when I showed them my press papers. I led the way up to the gallery that overlooked the debating chamber. We stared down on a scene that reminded me of tales of the Tower of Babel. There were dozens of men in the room below all arguing or shouting at each other. It was immediately apparent that there was no one in charge. Some had red sashes, others wore the tricolour, still more had no sash at all. They had broken into groups rather than having one debate and few were making any progress. I spotted an old French journalist on the balcony who was somehow taking notes. I asked him if he knew what was happening.

"Those there are the central committee of the National Guard," he said, then he pointed to a second group. "Some of them are mayors of areas of the city, while those," he pointed to others wearing red sashes, "are members of the vigilance committees."

"What on earth are vigilance committees?" I asked. I was sure I recognised one of them as among the group that had taken the general from the dance hall.

"They preserve the principles of this revolution," he said, before adding with a grin, "which, of course, have yet to be agreed."

We could only discern what they were arguing about when voices were raised. A row developed over the death of the generals. Some insisted that this must be condemned or there would be no hope of negotiating with Versailles. One of the vigilance men shouted in reply, "Beware of disavowing the people, in case they disavow you!" Naturally, no conclusion was reached. Then a young National Guard officer passionately put forward the case for marching on Versailles…exactly as Forbes had predicted.

"You will never get a better chance," he implored. "We hugely outnumber the army and many of the troops they do have, are likely to change sides and join our ranks." He had some support, particularly from the reds, but others saw negotiation with Versailles as the only way forward. After the death of the generals, they did not want to antagonise the national government any further. In exasperation the young man begged them to at least occupy the mighty Fort Valerian, one of the outer fortresses that guarded the western approach to Paris and the route to Versailles. He had discovered that it had been abandoned by the government the day before, but they would not even do that. Just about the only decision they did make was to replace themselves with a newly elected body to govern the city. That at least gave Justine hope of better things to come, for she had watched proceedings with mounting alarm.

"You cannot expect perfect government from the first day," she insisted. I got the distinct impression that she was reassuring herself rather than me.

To my surprise, over the next few days life in the city began to return to normal. Some barricades that had been hastily thrown up, were taken down, the omnibuses began to run again and food was still getting into the city and into the shops. In cafés people began to talk about compromise and reconciliation. They wanted to elect their own municipal council to run the city, but some were happy to recognise the ascendancy of the national government. They would even accept some legislation around debt arrears, as long as it gave them longer to pay. It was beginning to appear that matters could be resolved peacefully after all, but then, before long, things began to unravel. First, Thiers made a speech in Versailles calling out the rebels as criminals. This antagonised the vigilance committees against any form of compromise.

Sensing the accord falling apart, a group of moderates in the city calling themselves the 'friends of order', marched on City Hall to encourage further discussions. I watched what must have been over a thousand of them go past. They were unarmed and carried banners such as *'Vive la République!'* They chanted slogans for peace and compromise as they turned into the ironically named Rue de la Paix, or Peace Street. At the other end a cordon of the National Guard waited to block their access to the centre of the city and City Hall. As so often on these occasions, there are varying accounts of what happened next and who fired first. I had been planning to follow them to hear any speeches made when they reached their destination. Instead of reasoned argument, however, I heard a sudden volley of shots and what was quite possibly the discharge of a small cannon. There were screams then and more firing as people turned to run back out of the street. The first few hundred fled around the corner in panic. Then came others who had been wounded, staggering alone or held up by their fellows. Once the firing had stopped, I cautiously moved to the end of Rue de la Paix. At least a score of bodies lay scattered across the roadway, some moving but others still, blood pooling around them.

Officially, only a dozen were killed, but many more were wounded. The National Guard claimed that one of their men had been shot too. More importantly, it was the end of all talk about conciliation. The city of Paris was now on track for a head-on collision with its national government. The death of the generals had been a big enough obstacle to peace. These poor souls, shot for supporting the French republic in its capital, would never be forgiven.

Slowly, realisation dawned across the city. The next morning the train stations were packed with those who had places outside the city to shelter from the coming storm. The British ambassador had left, and other diplomats followed him to Versailles. It looked highly likely that I was about to become a war correspondent again. I had already written a story on the Peace Street massacre, yet when I went to send it to London, I found that men with red sashes were now in occupation of the telegraph office, and that all transmissions to and from foreign countries were banned. Even messages to people in France were carefully inspected, as there was a growing paranoia about finding spies and traitors. I hurried away before they discovered that I was a journalist, for that would only have placed me under more suspicion.

Fortunately, I still had my horse. While an Englishman riding back and forth would have been apprehended, the baker knew of a farmer's lad who regularly travelled in and out of the city with crops and animals. With a loan of my mount, he would happily ride to and from Versailles, taking my articles to Forbes for transmission to London. I already knew that nobody was stopping travellers at Versailles. One of Justine's red friends, a mad harridan called Louise, had made the offer to the reds to go and shoot Thiers. They had turned her down, but to prove it could be done she walked there and back, claiming she got close enough to kill him with a revolver.

The farmer's boy brought back with him a bundle of British newspapers given to him by Forbes, which were now banned in Paris. In fact, given that the Republicans had been vociferous in their criticism of Napoleon and his press censorship, the reds were not slow to follow suit. Le Figaro and various other papers that had supported the old regime were shut down, while others were taken over. Still, I could easily understand why the British papers had been prohibited. Their readers had been horrified by recent events in Paris. The last thing they wanted was the poor of Whitechapel in London or poverty-stricken northern mill towns rising up, killing generals and seizing power. Just weeks before the English press had been full of sympathy for Paris, raising thousands of pounds to feed her. Now they felt this generosity had been thrown in their faces. Publishers were quick to seize on this sense of betrayal and were scathingly critical of the barbaric reds and their mob justice. Thiers' speeches of harsh condemnation were printed in full, while Parisians were described as suffering from some "collective madness". Slowly but surely, Paris was becoming as isolated as it had been when under siege by the Prussians.

Some of that siege spirit returned over the next few days when elections were held for the new municipal authority to govern Paris. As most of those against such a government had already left the city, there were few objections. Others might have been deterred from protesting by hundreds of, often drunk, National Guardsmen, who stood, menacingly, around the voting offices. Neither Justine nor I got a ballot, but the result was a foregone conclusion. The reds won eighty percent of the vote and promptly declared a Commune of Paris. The people of Paris would henceforth govern themselves, although how long this arrangement would last was anyone's guess.

It started well; I will admit that. The National Guard might have been shambolic in any form of fighting, but they certainly knew how to throw a parade. At least two hundred thousand of them must have marched during the inauguration. They went past a gaudily decorated stage in front of City Hall where the new elected Commune representatives sat, adorned in their red sashes. Massed bands thundered out the *Marseillaise*, while guns regularly boomed in salute. A few people tried to make speeches, but they were lost in the din, which was enhanced by vast cheering crowds. We stood among them, watching as many pointed out their menfolk in the massed ranks. Their joy was genuine; they must have realised that they had now crossed the point of no return. Many of the poorer members perhaps thinking that their lives could not get any worse, threw in their lot with this new regime. Justine had adopted a similar fatalistic approach to affairs. "We are where we are," she said. "If the assembly will not let us exist in peace, we will have to fight them. But if we make the Commune a success, then they will have to fight the people to stop them joining us."

Over the next few days a stream of decrees came from this new legislature. Predictably, the debt law was overturned. All tenants were exempted from rent over the previous nine months. The Bank of France was seized and the daily allowance for the National Guard restored, but they could not gamble with it, for gambling was now illegal. There were new laws banning relieving yourself in the street elsewhere than public urinals, looting was punishable by death, and the display of announcements from Versailles was prohibited. Conscription into the army was abolished, but before potential recruits could celebrate, they found that there was now compulsory enlistment into the National Guard.

Most of this new legislation the citizens of Paris accepted with ease. But on the second of April the Commune also disestablished the church. That did cause murmurs of disquiet. Many Parisians were Catholic and did not want to be cut off from their faith. The church had been disestablished before under the first revolution, but Napoleon I had seen sense and restored it. But after the support the Pope had given Napoleon III, Catholicism was too closely associated with the more recent imperial regime and the Communards did not trust it.

The Commune was settling into the running of Paris as though it had all the time in the world. Their spies might have told them, as Forbes messaged me, that Thiers had now amassed an army of some sixty thousand men at Versailles, but this was still far less than the forces of Paris. The National Guard had regarrisoned some of the forts beyond the southern wall, but they had been too slow to seize the mighty Fort Valerian. Thiers' soldiers had got there first and they now guarded approaches towards Versailles.

No one expected the forces of the assembly to attack with their paltry numbers when the much larger Prussian force had been kept at bay for months. Yet on the day the church was abolished, we heard gunfire out to the west. Some of the National Guard ran through the streets declaring

245

that the forces from Versailles were being defeated, but soon more of their number arrived with a different story. They had been betrayed, they claimed, although did not explain how. The nub of their tale was that they had been beaten and the Versailles forces had captured a key bridge over the Seine at Neuilly to the west.

There was palpable shock in the streets. Many had still hoped for a peaceful resolution despite the massacre in Rue de la Paix. The announcements from the Commune had been about internal Paris affairs; they had not challenged the national government. Nobody wanted a civil war, they just wanted to be left to manage themselves.

"I cannot believe it has come to this," admitted Justine. "But I think they have made a mistake. Their soldiers in Paris saw the benefits of the Commune. Most of those that changed sides are still in the city, while they could have left if they wished. Perhaps more of their soldiers will come over and join us."

"Possibly," I admitted. She was right, a good number of the soldiers had stayed, but they would have heard lots of promises about the future of the Commune. Regiments outside the city would be getting Thiers' version of what their enemy stood for. "Yet those who fought at the bridge were happy to drive the National Guard off it. I don't think we can rely on their soldiers changing sides."

After the shock came a sense of indignation among the reds. How dare the assembly try to attack the city, when they had held off marching on Versailles. By the end of the day it was widely known that the National Guard would stay its hand no longer. The call went out for regiments to gather at the eastern gates the next morning. I was a war correspondent again.

Chapter 26

It was one of the strangest battles I ever saw. There was certainly no element of surprise involved. Parisians had all but blocked the streets with carriages, carts and commandeered omnibuses to view the coming spectacle. The main players, the soldiers, struggled to reach the stage at all. Their precious artillery was at Montmartre and they had none with them as they began to march through the city gates to cheering from the crowd. Wives rushed forward to kiss husbands and friends pass them bottles, although despite the early hour a number were drunk already.

They were to advance, we were told, in three columns, although this gives the impression of neat ranks of orderly men, when the reality was nothing of the sort. There was not a straight line amongst the lot of them. Former soldiers and National Guard were marched side by side. Given the amount of patching and individual adornments, I doubt two uniforms were identical. Their commanding officers set the tone. One, a fellow called Bergeret, a former bookseller's clerk, arrived adorned with sashes and pistols, wearing great boots that went halfway up his thighs. He looked like a cavalier from the English Civil War. Another commander, a man called Flourens, was equally extravagant in his dress, with blue pantaloons and an immense executioner's scimitar that dragged the ground from his belt. They strutted around like peacocks before their men and made speeches to the crowd. They assured all who listened that there was no doubt of victory. Their vast host easily outnumbered the enemy, they claimed, and the forces of the assembly would soon learn not to tangle with the people of Paris. I could not help but wonder if they had made similar orations before their futile attacks on the Prussians. Yet most of the watching crowd allowed hope to outweigh experience. Many spread out blankets and began to prepare a picnic lunch to enjoy while they watched proceedings. Justine and I had brought bread and ham with us too. We followed the army out of the gate and joined others gathered on a nearby hilltop to get a good view of the day's events.

Seeing the great host coming towards them, the Versailles troops holding the recently captured bridge at Neuilly had swiftly retreated. This news was promptly reported back, which increased confidence further. Most were sure now that the National Assembly's forces would crumble before their might. The great army marched confidently over the Neuilly bridge and other bridges across the Seine. Marching bands had gone with them and the *Marseillaise* rang out once more. There was no sign of the enemy as they pressed on up onto the Bergère plateau and I began to wonder if Thiers had pulled his forces back. The army divided into three or four parts, two going close to the brooding ramparts of the Mount Valerian fortress, passing by on either side. I looked up at its walls and could make out heads watching proceedings from the battlements. Some of their larger guns had been taken by the Prussians to Berlin, but surely, I thought, they must have some working artillery there.

My speculation was answered by the boom of cannon from the side of the fort facing Bergeret's men. The shots were not accurate. They exploded on either side of the vast horde, showering some with mud, but nothing more. Some in the crowd around us took them for warning shots, while others were convinced that a fort designed to protect Paris would not dare fire on its people. Through my glass I could see some of the soldiers waving and perhaps jeering at the fort. If they were, it was a mistake. The next salvo landed right in the middle of the tightly packed mass of soldiers. Bodies must have been blown apart, others tossed high in the air. Above all, there was panic. Those at the front ran on to get away from the fire and to find cover at the far end of the plateau. Those at the rear turned around and ran pell-mell back towards the city. Some of the spectators around us yelled in dismay. There were angry curses at the fort and even more at those retreating, urging them to turn around and help their braver colleagues who were pressing on.

The men on the other side of the fort, under Flourens, had not yet been fired on. He must have urged them to advance, for many broke into a run now, heading for cover in the village of Rueil that lay some distance ahead. Not all followed their flamboyant leader; a good number took the example of the rear of the first column and headed back to the city. More gunfire from the fort encouraged them on, while through the smoke I could now see distant lines of regular army cavalry appearing to charge those who remained.

It took just a few minutes for members of the National Guard, who had boasted and promised so much, to start to stream back across the bridges over the Seine. A family near us who had brought camp tables and chairs, along with more silver cutlery and crystal glasses than I had seen in a while, saw no need to abandon their lunch. As a footman served them slices of pie, they muttered in disgust as the fearful soldiers ran by. The head of the household even went as far as to put down his fork to order those nearest to him to go back and help their comrades. He was wasting his time. By now there was the distant crackle of rifle fire, indicating that a battle of sorts was underway on the other side of the plateau.

Justine and I stayed to eat too. Apart from Fort Valerian, which had not fired in our direction, none of the French army was now visible. From the sound of things those that had gone forward were putting up a fight. There was at least one more column of the National Guard to our left who might still be advancing. In any event the city gates were far too congested. The few ambulances available were struggling to get out towards the wounded, obstructed by a stream of retreating soldiers and countless spectators' vehicles.

The attack of the National Guard had been similar to the one I had seen from the Prussian lines, except back then they had all retreated. This time some had continued forward. "Do the National Guard fight better when they are defending?" I asked Justine.

"They did not really have to defend the city walls much," she admitted. "The outer forts kept the Germans at bay; they were manned by gunners from the army and navy." Then she brightened, "But I am certain they will fight to defend Paris if it is attacked. After all, their families and homes are in the city."

"And there is nowhere to retreat to," I added, straining my eyes to see what was happening on the horizon. At the time I was not convinced that the National Guard would ever acquire a backbone when it came to fighting, but the later events of that day did more to stiffen their resolve than I could have imagined.

The rumours began to spread around the city the following morning. Then bloodthirsty accounts appeared in the red newspapers. While Bergeret had made it back to the city, his fellow commanders had not. Flourens had spent the day with his remaining men fighting hard to defend his position in the village of Rueil. During the night the village was surrounded, and he was denounced by the locals. As Flourens was being led forward as a prisoner, his head was cleft in two by a sabre strike. All the National Guard leaders were then summarily executed, as were any found wearing the vestiges of uniform from the national army. They were deemed as deserters, which was clearly a deterrent to stop any other soldiers thinking of changing sides. The same brutal treatment was dished out to the column making up the left flank of the attack, where fifteen hundred men had been captured. The message was clear, at least to leaders of the Commune; this was a fight to the death and no quarter could be expected.

Impressive state funerals were held for the dead of that encounter, who had been carried back by their comrades. There were muffled drums and many more weeping widows. The hearses bore red flags and Commune leaders led the procession before making speeches that honoured all those executed as well as those buried. As we made our way back to Justine's apartment, we heard that the city gates had been shut and the trains out of the city had now stopped running. Paris was besieged again. Fortunately, like many Parisians we had been stocking up with food for just this eventuality. The bakery beneath had sacks of flour and warehouses were still stocked with the largesse from the people of Britain.

Five years before the Commune was created, a book had been published in London called *Alice's Adventures in Wonderland.* You may have read it as it was very popular. Over the following weeks reality began to mock art as the situation in Paris became every bit as fanciful as the worlds Alice encountered. Firstly, an explanation had to be found as to why the forces of the Commune had been defeated by a vastly smaller force. The real reason, that they were an undisciplined

250

rabble, could not be admitted to, and so instead the head of the National Guard was arrested for treason. He was charged with failing to capture Fort Valerian. Yet several of his accusers had been in the City Hall debating chamber the day after the murder of the generals, when that proposal to seize Valerian had been overruled. Then Bergeret, the surviving commander, was also seized and imprisoned. By all accounts he had fought bravely. His sin was merely surviving his encounter with the enemy, while his fellow commanders had been executed. Finally, they abandoned all idea of the Commune being a benign government for all its citizens and passed something called the Hostages Act.

The idea was simple: while the French army continued to kill prisoners, they would hold as hostage anyone accused of complicity with the Versailles-based government. Then every time a Communard was shot, they would select three hostages and in the words of the Queen of Hearts, it would be "Off with their heads!" A frisson of fear ran through the city – who would the hostages be? As the Commune leaders often referenced the first revolution, it was perhaps inevitable that the Reign of Terror and rule of Robespierre came to mind. Back then people would inform on their neighbours to protect themselves, or pre-empt an accusation from someone with whom they had a grudge. Many innocents ended up under the guillotine. Foreign journalists would certainly be under suspicion. For the first time I was grateful for Justine's support of the reds. She was so beyond suspicion that she had been invited to join one of the women's vigilance committees. She had declined as she wanted no part in accusing people, but I hoped she still held some sway in case a finger was ever pointed in my direction.

The Hostages Act was the final straw for many, especially the wealthier citizens of Paris. A few days later when taking a walk, I found that half of the shops were shut, their windows empty of stock as their owners had fled the city. Even some of the National Guard, having seen how easily they had been beaten by a professional army, were now lying low or had slipped away in civilian clothes. I thought of leaving myself, but several reasons persuaded me to stay. The first was Justine; she would never leave Paris now and would probably never forgive me if I ran out on the city. There was bloodshed coming, that was obvious, and

I was determined to keep us both safe. Secondly, you did not need to be a journalist of long experience to know that this was a big story. There had never been anything like the Commune: a capital now at war with its own country. The surrounding nations were all monarchies, and none had any interest in it succeeding and giving their own working classes ideas. Most readers of newspapers were middle or upper class, supporting law and order and elected governments. The Commune was an anathema to them. But while they certainly did not support it, they would still want to read about it and understand how this strange body rose and fell. I was perfectly placed to tell them. My final reason to stay was Colonel Stanley.

He was the last person you would expect to have any sympathy with the reds; an aristocratic lieutenant colonel, on leave of absence from the Grenadier Guards. Even he admitted that he could not fully explain it. "They are fighting to run their own city," he insisted, "which is what most of our towns and cities have always enjoyed." There was far more to it than that, though, as we both knew. Some aspects, such as the Hostages Act, he certainly did not approve of. We had met when I had visited one of the hospitals treating the wounded from the disastrous attack on Versailles. He was working as a volunteer for the American Red Cross and had showed me around. At first he was haughty and dismissive, clearly having little time for the press. Then we met one of Justine's friends who was working as a nurse. As soon as he knew that I was living with a red, his demeanour changed. He clearly thought that I was another sympathiser.

He spent some time talking with me and painted a grim picture of the hospital. He admitted that virtually all patients who underwent amputations died of their wounds, mostly from infections or gangrene. There were none of Nurse Nightingale's standards of cleanliness there. I saw two doctors in stained aprons smoking in a corner of the ward. One stirred his coffee with an instrument he was probably to use on his next 'victim'. Stanley pointed out how thin and emaciated some of the patients were, with the after-effects of the siege on top of years of subsistence living. They had few if any reserves of strength to call on for their recovery. One patient we passed was clearly dying and begged for a priest to hear his last confession. An orderly harshly told him that the church no longer existed. The fellow could certainly have worked on his bedside manner. What's more, as he passed us, I noted the distinctive smell of drink about him. Stanley must have smelt it too for he shrugged and confessed, "We have had to add carbolic acid to the medical alcohol, as too much of it was disappearing down the throats of the orderlies."

As I left, he asked where I was living. I told him that Justine's apartment was halfway between the centre of the city and Belleville. "What will you do when the Versailles forces attack?" he asked, then added, "You do know that an attack is now inevitable, don't you?"

"I do." I was relieved that despite his inexplicable support for the Commune, he was realistic about the likely outcome. "I am not sure what I will do," I admitted. "The area is not that prosperous; there is likely to be fighting in the streets and I want to protect Justine. I would leave the city if I thought I could persuade her to come with me."

"When the fighting starts come to me," Stanley offered. "Bring Justine as well – you will both be very welcome. I have rooms at a hotel in the centre of the city and a large Union Jack to hang over my balcony. There are plenty of other foreign diplomats and officials there. Neither side is likely to shell that building, so you will be safe." I accepted his invitation with relief, for it seemed the perfect solution.

In early April a new commander of the National Guard, a man called Cluseret, was appointed. He tried valiantly to introduce some of the improvements necessary to turn them into a more effective fighting force, but was only partly successful. He did manage to separate the guardsmen, so those under forty became active battalions, while those over that age formed a more sedentary reserve. He also tried to cut down on the number of generals and streamline the chain of command, only to discover that it was a hopeless task. The central committee of the National Guard and the elected Commune both thought that they commanded the Guard and tended to block any initiative agreed by the other. Then local leaders, vigilance committees and various other officials thought that they could issue commands to units raised in their own areas. In the end, having upset too many people, Cluseret was

253

arrested for treason and thrown into jail. His replacement fared little better, but did at least manage to construct a ring of barricades around the city as a second line of defence if the city walls were breached.

By then it was early May and Thiers, presiding over the national government had not been idle. Stanley had heard from his American friends at the consulate that the French government had appealed to Bismarck for help. The Iron Chancellor had no love for insurrectionists who could disturb his recently hard-won peace. He did not want to involve Germany in another conflict, but he was prepared to help his former enemy sort out their own mess. The release of France's professional army from their prisoner of war camps was accelerated and the number of French soldiers permitted around Paris was increased. Soon Marshal MacMahon was back in command of a French army, this time planning an attack on his own capital.

Thiers knew the defences well; he had been responsible for signing off the construction of many of them. The weak point was where the Seine passed out on the southwest boundary, an area already under the guns of Fort Valerian. During April and May the nearest large fort occupied by the National Guard was shelled until it was a pile of rubble. The nearby suburb of Neuilly was also flattened and like the Prussians before them, the army then began a bombardment of the wider city. The Arc de Triomphe was hit several times, in fact Stanley showed me an elbow that he'd picked up from one of the relief sculptures as a souvenir. Yet the random nature of the shelling did as much to demoralise the more prosperous supporters of the republic as it did the reds. More than one wealthy merchant saw their house or business destroyed while they waited for the army to deliver them from the threat of being taken as a hostage. Before long it was obvious to any sane individual that one side in this conflict was preparing to bring things to a conclusion.

That sane reasoning obviously did not apply to the Commune, which in its *Wonderland* way largely ignored any threat from Versailles. A mass of legislation continued to pour out of City Hall. All government employee salaries were capped at six thousand francs a year, roughly equivalent to a skilled workman's wages. The Commune said it would also 'adopt' the wives and children of all those who had died defending

Paris, but those unfortunates only got a pension of six hundred francs a year. Then they proudly announced an end to night baking in the city. This pleased the bakers, but in the view of many reduced all of Paris to eating stale bread. A raft of edicts was issued to schools, some of which had been run by the church, to remove all religion from their activities. There were efforts to clamp down on prostitution, but legislation was not aligned across the city. In one suburb these women could not ply their trade in houses, while in another they were banned from soliciting on the streets.

A rather sinister tone to the Commune developed as more and more hostages were gathered. They started with the archbishop of Paris and other leading clerics, before they moved on to rounding up parish priests. They were all accused of being anti-Commune, although it would probably be fairer to say that the Commune was anti-church. A few were also accused of smuggling away or hiding relics, church funds or plate, which was now considered property of the Commune. Some churches were converted into 'red clubs' where the Communards would gather and invariably get drunk and argue with each other. I went to one with Justine in which the statue of the Virgin looked as though it had been used for target practice. What was left was wrapped in a red scarf and hat.

Yet not all the hostages were clerics; a few came from the *bourgeoisie*. By mid-May there were over three thousand incarcerated. Many were former reds or members of factions within the Commune. The new chief of police occupied himself with settling political scores on his own account and for friends. That suited me, for if they were busy watching their own backs and scheming against each other, then they were not bothering with foreign correspondents. Not that I had managed to get anything out for publication for several weeks, although even if I had, they would not know, for foreign papers were not getting into the city either.

As the net closed ever tighter around the city, astonishingly, its leaders made few military preparations. They still argued over who controlled the National Guard and what the priorities should be. The men could still appoint their own officers, which meant that little discipline was imposed in their companies. That is not to say that some did not fight well. I remember seeing what was left of a battalion marching back through the city having been relieved from the front line. The cheery marching band sent to herald their approach contrasted starkly with the gaunt, exhausted figures who staggered on behind. Following them were two carts laden with rifles, which I was told were the recovered weapons of their dead.

Yet while these men showed courage, others in the Guard took the opportunity to 'disappear'. Sensing disaster, they had gone into hiding rather than attend their battalion roll calls. Others too had shown a marked reluctance to fight. The new commander of the National Guard, a man called Rossell, tried to instil courage and pride in his men. He held a parade at which he singled out soldiers, including officers, and ripped the right sleeves off their uniforms as a mark of cowardice. By all accounts this created greater resentment than if he had had them shot.

Fearing adjustments to their tailoring as much as the enemy, the next day even more battalions failed to appear. The now familiar cries of "treason" and "betrayal" rang out across the Commune. Rossell knew what was coming and got ahead of the inevitable by sending in his resignation, which included a request for a cell in the prison. He probably thought he had done as well as he could in the circumstances. It had been a miracle that they had held the outer perimeter in the southwest at all as the lines there had been under heavy bombardment. While they had done what they could to disrupt them, the trenches dug by the professional army were creeping ever closer. The inner line of barricades and some central redoubts had also been completed. Great stacks of paving slabs now filled some of the streets, overlapping to make gaps for pedestrians and vehicles to pass by. Where the stones had been removed, trenches were dug to create further obstacles, the earth and sand used to fill bags and they too were piled up upon the barricade.

Of course, in this crazy world of the Paris Commune, at this critical juncture, the obvious thing to do was to appoint a new commander for the National Guard with no military experience at all! His name was Louis Charles Delescluze and if ever there was a 'father of the Commune' it was him. He was sixty-one then but looked at least ten years older as he had spent much of his life in prison, including the notorious Devil's Island. His health was not good. His frequent incarcerations had left him weak and consumptive. He spoke rarely, and in a rasping wheeze, but his written declarations were full of energy and passion. He was a fervent Jacobin and revolutionary and had been all his life. As a radical he was beyond reproach, which was why he was voted to the post. No longer would committees or the Commune challenge or undermine military decisions…it was just unfortunate that the new 'general' had no idea what military orders to give. I am not sure the old man even visited the front line. The reports from his commanders must have been full of excuses and pleas for reinforcement, for slowly but surely the line was now giving way. But instead of marshalling his reserves for some tactical counterstrike, Delescluze concentrated his time on more important matters.

He could have looked at food supplies, which were once again getting dangerously low, especially for the poor. There were also the appalling conditions in hospitals to address and growing numbers of homeless after the bombardment. He did none of that, or at least nothing that made a difference. Instead, he decided that now was obviously the time to reintroduce the old republican calendar, with its ten-day week and twelve months of thirty days. We now found ourselves in the year 78 in the month of Floréal, with most of us thoroughly perplexed as to the day of the week. This was just the extra layer of confusion an already chaotic situation demanded. Orders were issued in the new calendar and brows would furrow as people worked out when things were supposed to happen. The poor devils at the front line must have been pulling their hair out when told supplies would arrive on the eighth day of the second week of the new month.

As parts of the city remained under heavy bombardment, the Commune now decided to do some demolition of their own. Nothing to impede MacMahon's men, of course, no; their target was a column in the Place Vendôme. With a statue of the first Napoleon at the top, it was found to symbolise imperialism and so had to come down. There had already been several attempts, which the stone slabs had resisted. It had been partly sawn through like a tree, with ropes and capstans installed to pull it over. The date set for its destruction was the sixteenth of May, or the twenty-sixth of the month of Floréal, if you prefer. It was to be a grand event, with tickets sold for grandstands.

On the day ten thousand people crowded into the square and the surrounding streets. I did not need a ticket, for Colonel Stanley's hotel balcony overlooked the square. He invited us to join him to watch the spectacle. Justine could not go as she was on a new revolutionary committee distributing food, but it was a sight I did not want to miss.

This was vandalism on a grand scale, with a decent chance that some poor fool or two would be crushed by falling masonry. Stanley was an excellent host, laying on an opulent spread of food for his guests. Joining us were an English vicar and an American called Wickham Hoffman, from their consulate. We even had a bottle of champagne on ice for the moment of success. At three a band struck up the *Marseillaise* and the crowd surged forward in anticipation. A huge pile of sand and wood faggots had been laid down and spread out across the square where the column was expected to fall. At the end of it was the windlass and now the ropes were pulled taught. We watched the statue of the emperor for the first sign of movement. Instead, there was a loud crack as one of the blocks gave way and a scream as several men were whipped by a flaying rope. At once the crowd began to yell treason. The engineers looked nervously about, as though fearing arrest.

It was another three hours before they could make another attempt. The band distracted the crowd with patriotic tunes, while more wedges were bashed into the sawn side of the column. A brave engineer scaled the edifice to attach yet more ropes and once again these were wound round the capstans. One benefit of the delay was that Justine had time to come over and join us. By then we had already drunk the champagne, but Stanley insisted on providing more, and food for his newest guest. He was most attentive and with her radiant beauty in the room, interest in the column dropped considerably. Justine did not mind the attention and was happy to discuss revolutionary principles with Stanley, while I caught Hoffman glancing from her to me and back again in naked envy.

The repeat of the national anthem heralded the second attempt and we all returned to the balcony. This time the column did fall, breaking up into segments on its way down. It sent up such a cloud of dust, we could not see across the square. We retreated inside again until it had settled. When we opened the balcony doors once more, thousands of people were pouring over the ruins. Many had brought saws or chisels and were hacking away at the bronze relief panels to secure a souvenir. They must have developed a zest for destruction that night, for later they marched to the mansion owned by Thiers. It had already been ransacked on orders from the Commune, but now they set fire to what was left.

As Nero fiddled while Rome burned, so the Commune spent its final days debating their rights. They tried to clarify where its responsibilities would end and those of the national government would begin. Many were still under the impression that, ultimately, they would reach some compromise with the National Assembly. They congratulated themselves on completing this work with grandiose announcements of a new political era.

Even Justine still harboured this hope of cooperation. Despite everything that had happened, she still struggled to believe that many of the same politicians who had led the city through the siege against Germany, would now turn and attack Paris. "It is like a child killing a parent," she insisted. "All families have arguments, sometimes fights, but sooner or later they see sense. We all have French blood in our veins. You wait and see, there will be threats and ultimatums, but in the end we will work together. We have to."

I did not argue, for I had seen so much in the last few months that I would have thought impossible. Defeat at Spicheren, the entire French army bottled up and captured within a month, a city as great as Paris suffering the torment of a medieval-style siege and now a capital at war with the rest of the nation. Over the coming days, despite the continued shelling in the east, life in the city went on as normal. Perhaps the earlier siege made its citizens more fatalistic, but children still played in the streets and old men tended their vegetable plots. The Sunday after the Vendôme column fell there was a vast open-air concert in the Tuileries gardens. Fifteen hundred musicians took part and much of Paris was there to listen, including Justine and me. The music even drowned out the sound of the guns, or perhaps the gunners too had stopped to listen.

In many ways it was a perfect day, with my sweetheart on my arm. In the evening we made our way back to the bakery and an excellent meal of roast chicken. All of the restaurants had been shut for weeks, but the baker had acquired the bird in exchange for clearing a customer's bread account. Now that he was baking during the day, the ovens were still hot in the evening. He and his wife had cooked the fowl with potatoes, onions and herbs, while I had bought some good bottles of red wine. The four of us sat down together for what was a rare feast. I think we all sensed that this was the calm before the storm. There was an unspoken agreement between us that we would not talk of what was to come. Instead, we laughed and chatted about times past, before the war. The baker regaled us with tales of the old days in the bakery, Justine talked of Pascal and Madeleine, while I recalled my earlier visit to Paris with my grandfather. We raised our glasses and drank to our good health during that little oasis of carefree happiness. It was a good job we did, for little did we know that the storm was just about to break.

Paris street map around Place de la Concorde

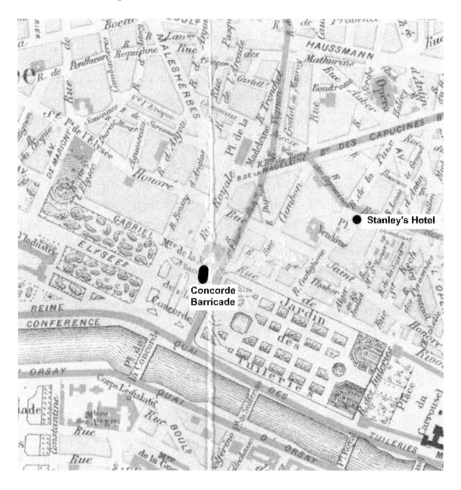

Chapter 27

When the end came, it was due to a typical act of mismanagement by the National Guard. As our chicken was roasting late that afternoon, one of the perimeter fortresses had come under intense bombardment. The garrison had been under heavy fire for several days from a huge battery nearby. Many of their positions had been demolished and they had taken fearful casualties. They had sent back requests for reinforcements and ammunition, but the couriers had either been killed or ignored. On the twenty-first of May as evening fell, exhausted and demoralised, the surviving garrison simply slipped away back to their homes. They had endured enough. I don't know if any of their officers survived, but certainly no one thought to warn surrounding positions that the entry point was now unguarded.

The southwestern part of Paris had been full of attractive treelined suburbs that housed its wealthier citizens. They had never been supporters of the Commune and now that most of their homes had been damaged or demolished in the fighting, this was even more the case. The majority had long since left the city, but a few remained to guard their property. One, an engineer called Ducatel, had seen the garrison slipping away and not noticed any replacements. Curious, and prepared to risk the shellfire, he set out up the street and to his dismay, found the fortress empty. He fashioned a white flag from his handkerchief and a pole and waved it above the battlements. A soldier was sent forward to parley, but the tale he came back with sounded so incredible that he was not believed. Many were sure it had to be a trap. A major went forward with a group of soldiers to check carefully around the fort and the ground beyond, but not a single National Guardsman was to be found. Before long the forces from Versailles, the *Versaillais*, were pouring into the city.

The soldiers quickly spread out on both the north and south banks of the Seine. By three in the morning there were some seventy thousand *Versaillais* in the western suburbs. They formed fighting columns that moved around the edge of the city, attacking other perimeter forts from the rear. Caught by surprise, the National Guard forces were routed. Fifteen hundred were captured and the few survivors fled back into the city. Despite the barricades, the street layouts invariably allowed them to be outflanked. Furthermore, residents in that part of the city readily welcomed the *Versaillais* and showed them shortcuts through gardens to get behind the defenders.

Justine's apartment was in the northeast of the city. We knew nothing of the night's events when we awoke the following morning as we had got used to sleeping through distant gunfire. It was as I was cutting some bread for breakfast that I first heard the new sound. It was a bugle call, strident and urgent, repeating over and over again. Our eyes met on the second call. Not a word was said, but we both knew what it signified. I took her in my arms and held her tight. In many ways I had never felt closer to another human being, yet in some respects we were miles apart. Privately, I welcomed an end to the Commune. To me it had always been doomed; it had become darker recently with so many arrests and accusations. I wanted a return to the old Paris I had enjoyed before the war. But to Justine the Commune was a living experiment straight from her books on political theory. She admitted that it made mistakes, but was convinced that, given time, it could show the world a better way to live.

"I must go to my committee," she insisted, "they will need me."

"But I thought we agreed that when the attack came, we would shelter with Colonel Stanley."

"We don't know what is happening yet," she argued. "It may just be an incursion that is being pushed back." I don't think either of us believed that. There was a note of panic to those bugle calls, but as Justine could not be budged, I decided to go with her. I wanted to get the news first hand too.

The committee met in a requisitioned church. The chaotic scene that greeted us was everything I had feared. Firstly, the chairwoman of the committee was missing. As it turned out, like a number of Commune leaders, she had anticipated the worst and had gone into hiding. Those that had gathered were ashen-faced with fear and unsure what to do. Most stood around a map of the city spread out on a table, where pins

263

had been placed to show reports of where the enemy were and the Commune's barricades. However, even on that first morning it was clear that the western quarter of the city on both riverbanks was lost. Also evident was the fact that there was no plan to defend the city, even though it had been obvious for weeks where they were likely to break through. A second line of barricades, planned by Rossell to slow the advance, had never been built. The Communards were falling back to strong bastions around the Place de la Concorde and opposite, on the south of the river. These protected the centre of the city against an attack from the west, although I was alarmed to note that Colonel Stanley's hotel was just a couple of streets away. We would be taking shelter in an area that was likely to be heavily fought over. I just hoped his Union Jack would provide the protection he promised.

There was a shout as a messenger arrived with a paper from Delescluze. Any expectation that this was a plan for the defence of the city was quickly dashed. It was a proclamation calling the people to action, although offering scant detail on where they should go. It was a powerful piece, I will give him that. They were soon being posted all over the city. I kept one, which I have copied below:

To the People of Paris, to the National Guard, Citizens,

Enough of militarism; no more general staff with braid and gilding on their uniforms. Make way for the people, for fighters with bare arms! The hour of revolutionary war has sounded. The people don't know anything about clever manoeuvres, but when they have a rifle in their hands and pavement under their feet, they have nothing to fear from all the strategists of the royal military school.

To arms, citizens, to arms! It is a question, as you know, of conquering or falling into the merciless hands of the reactionaries and the clerics of Versailles, of those miserable ones who have, by their actions, delivered France to the Prussians and who want to make us pay the ransom for their treason!

If you desire that the generous amount of blood which has flowed like water for the last six weeks shall not have been in vain; if you want to live in a France that is free and where all are equal; if you want to spare your children from your pain and misery, you will rise up like one man and because of your formidable resistance, the enemy, who proudly imagines he will put you back into your yoke, will find himself shamed for his useless crimes by which he has been stained.

Citizens, your representatives will fight and die with you if needed, but, in the name of this glorious France, the mother of all popular revolutions, permanent home of the ideas of justice and solidarity which must be and will be the laws of the world, march at the enemy, and let your revolutionary energy show him that traitors can try to sell Paris, but no one can surrender it or conquer it.

The Commune is counting on you – count on the Commune!

When I asked if more precise orders were coming, I was told that the great man had burned his papers and gone to the barricades to fight himself. Given his proclamation, perhaps I should not have been surprised that he had left the people to marshal themselves. Those still in the women's committee were ably doing just that, organising supplies of food and spare ammunition for those on the barricades. They had handcarts to pull through the streets and alleys. Several were destined for the large bastion at the Place de la Concorde. Justine caught my imploring eye and volunteered to take one. I just hoped we got there before the *Versaillais*, as since we had arrived at the committee, the sound of fighting from the west had grown considerably.

We soon realised that getting any wheeled vehicle across Paris now would be no easy task. New barricades were springing up everywhere. Omnibuses and carts had been overturned in the streets rendering them impassable. Anyone using the road was ordered to help to make sandbags by lifting a paving slab or filling a sack with earth from beneath it before they were allowed to move on. Justine's red sash of a committee member excused us this work, although several times she did it voluntarily and I was obliged to help too. We were able to get the cart through several unfinished obstacles, but first it had to be emptied. We all formed a human chain to carry the contents and lift the handcart over the top. We were told about nearby alleys that circumvented other barricades; the attackers would not have the same local knowledge, but

265

I doubted it would take them long to find ways round to outflank the defenders.

We heard that the *Versaillais* were at the Arc de Triomphe. That was a worry, for the Arc was at one end of the Champs d'Élysées. That broad boulevard ran straight to the Place de la Concorde, meaning the enemy had a line of sight on the Commune stronghold for their artillery. As we got closer, I realised that the reverse was also true, for there was the sound of a heavy barrage coming from Concorde, supplemented by the familiar regular rattle of Mitrailleuses. I cautiously peered around a corner to discover that the Communards were putting up stiff resistance and here at least they were well organised. A huge barricade had been built west of us on the corner of the square where it met the Rue Saint-Florentin. It was a virtual fortress in itself; twenty feet high and almost as thick, made up of paving stones and sandbags. There were gun emplacements and embrasures for cannon and Mitrailleuses, which could easily reach the Arc, as well as riflemen. Behind was a trench several feet deep, where earth had been excavated to store ammunition.

"We must get over there," Justine shouted as a shell whistled low over our heads to crash into a building across the street behind us. I glanced over my shoulder to see masonry and timber falling to the ground. Turning to look north, where the dubious sanctuary of Colonel Stanley's hotel beckoned, I would happily have abandoned the cart and made a run for it, but that was not an option with my red-sashed committee member at my side. I knew further hesitation could be fatal and so we grabbed hold of the handles and pushed the cart towards the barricade as fast as we could go.

A minute later and puffing for breath, we hauled up in the shelter of the barricade. Bullets had whizzed overhead as we had sprinted along the road – it seemed a miracle that neither of us were hit. More bullets were cracking off the stonework of the barricade and some buildings around us, but the bastion was reassuringly solid. As I got my breath back, I passed down the boxes from the cart to a fellow stacking them in the trench, while Justine went off to talk to the man in charge. They had plenty of ammunition, which was just as well as they were keeping up a heavy rate of fire. I could hear the rattle of Mitrailleuses just to one side and an almost identical reply from the other end of the boulevard. I ducked as a shell exploded against the rampart, showering us with dust. Their quartermaster did not even flinch; he was far more interested in the loaves of bread I was passing down.

Justine ran back with news: the reds thought that they had stopped the *Versaillais*' advance. I recognised the man in charge as the one who had suggested capturing Fort Valerian on the first day of the Commune. His name was Brunel and if they had listened to him that first attack on Versailles might have succeeded. Now he was skilfully marshalling his forces. I risked a quick glance through a gun portal. The square in front of us and some open space beyond was well covered. Anyone who tried to cross it would be cut to pieces.

"Come on, let's go," I shouted before she had any ideas about going back for a second cargo. I grabbed her arm and pulled her north. Still in the shelter from the barricade, we entered a side street that led on to the Place Vendôme. The stone stump was still in the centre alongside the remains of the column. Compared to Concorde the space was strangely quiet. More barricades in the corners meant we were not in view of any government forces, but we kept our heads down anyway as we ran. I looked over to Stanley's hotel, it was on the corner of the square and the now infamous Rue de la Paix. From a balcony on the third floor a large Union Jack flapped reassuringly in the light breeze.

Justine stopped suddenly when we reached the great lumps of bronze-covered stone that had so recently pointed up at the sky. "Wait," she called, glancing over her shoulder in the direction we had come. The gunfire was muffled now by the surrounding buildings, but you could still make out the staccato rattle of fire. "I think I should go back. My place is at the barricades."

"No," I said firmly. This was exactly what I had feared. "We have talked about this; you promised to come with me." Her jaw began to set in a determined expression and so I tried a different approach. "Brunel's men know what they are doing, while you have never even fired a gun before. You will not be any use to them now and worse, you could get one of them killed as they try to help you. You will be far more valuable to the people as a teacher when the fighting has stopped." She could reluctantly see the sense in what I was saying and so we went on across the square. There was a concierge in the hallway, but he remembered us from our previous visit and let us through. Once seen, Justine's beauty was rarely forgotten.

A minute later and Stanley was welcoming us into his suite of rooms. I had expected him to have other guests, but there was just the three of us. "Keep well back from the windows," the colonel warned. "The Chassepot has a long range and either side might just shoot at any movement they see."

"I know, I shot one at Sedan," I told him. "Is your American friend Hoffman not here as well?"

"No, he has found a place to watch from the north side of Concorde. He is overlooking the barricades and will hopefully escape the shelling."

"This is not entertainment for tourists," snapped Justine. "People are out there fighting and dying for what they believe in."

"I apologise," Stanley said and looked chastened before adding, "and as a military man, mademoiselle, I can tell you that they are fighting well. Here, let me show you on the map." He led us to a table where he had spread out a map of the city. "The bastion at Concorde is their key position," he said, pointing at it. "The left flank is guarded by another strong point south over the Seine, while they also have more fortifications around the La Madeleine church a few hundred yards to the north. They have held there all morning and stopped government forces advancing into the centre of the city."

Given the loss of territory on the first night, this was far better than I had been expecting. Yet we knew that forces were also advancing around the outskirts of the city, and I wondered what progress they were making. The sound of fighting rose and fell, but did not seem to change direction. Occasionally, we would see groups of National Guard marching to and from the fighting around La Madeleine church to the north. We also saw men carrying their wounded.

For the rest of that day, though, we saw little of the fighting that raged about us. Stanley had corner rooms with windows facing both Vendôme and Rue de la Paix. The colonel was a generous host and had recently received a hamper of food from London. God knows how that was smuggled into the now starving city. We enjoyed tinned ham and biscuits, along with an excellent port. As the crackle of gunfire began to die away in the evening, Justine turned to Stanley and asked, "Tell me honestly, do you think the reds can win?"

The colonel paused before replying and put down his glass. "I know what you would like to hear, but I will not patronise you. No, I do not think that the reds can win. Their men do not have the discipline for a long campaign or sufficient food and ammunition. But if they can hold out for the next few days, then they might be able to negotiate favourable terms for a truce and perhaps some concessions on how the city is run. The national government must know that they will lose a lot of men if they have to fight street to street. Yesterday was easy for them, but today they will already have suffered considerable casualties." He gestured to his map at the other end of the table. "The barricades at Concorde are the keystone to your defences. They link defenders north and south of the river and keep the *Versaillais* out of the centre of the city. If your men can hold there for a few days then they have a chance, but if they lose that position, then I fear all will be lost."

It was a grim assessment, but Justine thanked him for his honesty. As night fell, Stanley insisted that we use his bedroom, while he slept on a chaise-longue in his living room. As we settled down for the night Justine was lost in her own thoughts. There was an urgency to her lovemaking, as if she worried that our time together was limited. Afterwards, as she cuddled in my arms, she asked if I knew she loved me.

"Of course I do, you silly goose, especially after what we have just done. Don't worry, we will be safe here. There are enough diplomats staying in this hotel that no one would risk shelling it. We will just sit tight here and deal with whatever comes next."

I hoped I was right about the diplomats. Most ambassadors had moved to Versailles months before, but a few kept officials in the city to protect their citizens still there. Both sides knew where they were. Even if they didn't, a Russian flag had been unfurled that afternoon on the balcony above the one with Stanley's Union Jack. None of the combatants would want to offend powers such as Austria, Russia and

Britain. Still, accidents happen in war. It would only take a stray shell to put us in danger.

The noise of gunfire woke me early the next morning. Most was coming from the north, around La Madeleine church, the right flank of the defensive line at Place de la Concorde. Cautiously, I pulled back a curtain to see a score of Communards heading towards the sound of fighting. They were all ages, from grey-haired old men to young boys barely into their teens, little taller than the rifles they carried. I turned back to the room. The break in the drapes had illuminated Justine, still asleep. She looked angelically peaceful lying there, her dark hair spread across the pillow. She would never leave Paris, I knew that now, but I was more than prepared to stay with her. Despite the hardships and the madness of the Commune, the last few weeks had been among the happiest of my life. I had already decided that if Frank would not let me stay and be a Paris correspondent, I would resign and work freelance, perhaps doubling as a baker's assistant. I gently kissed her cheek and quietly got dressed.

Stanley was already up and watching affairs from his window. "I tried to go out on the balcony," he complained, "but one of their officers ordered me back inside. He said the government have snipers picking off people around the city."

"The Chassepot is certainly accurate," I replied, "but that bloody great flag should give a bit of a clue as to your identity." We laughed and set about organising breakfast as Justine joined us. It was frustrating, as while we could hear the fighting to the west, we could see very little of it. Stanley paced impatiently from one window to the next. Nothing was happening in the Place Vendôme and other buildings blocked our view of La Madeleine area. Twice he risked another reprimand by calling out to passers-by, but they knew little more than us. Then, just before midday, we had our first clue as to how things were going.

"That is not a good sign," said the colonel gesturing out of the window. I followed his gaze to see a man with a wounded leg being helped down Rue de la Paix by two of his comrades, one arm round each of their shoulders.

I frowned, puzzled. "We have seen wounded men pass by here before."

"When an army is fighting well," Stanley explained, "soldiers are reluctant to miss the moment of triumph. Sometimes it is hard to get anyone to carry the wounded away. But when things are going badly, the reverse is true. Many use the wounded as an excuse to slip away. That fellow has one good leg; it only needs one other man to help him. He could even have managed on his own with his rifle as a crutch. Look there," he pointed to another group coming around the corner. This time I saw a man borne on a stretcher carried by two comrades, while a third walked alongside holding all their rifles. "They clearly are not planning on coming back. That is a sure sign that the defence at La Madeleine is under pressure. If it falls, then it will make it even harder for those at Concorde." He pressed his face against the window to try and squint up the street to see more but gave up in exasperation. "This is ridiculous. Let's try and get up on the roof of the hotel – we might be able to see more from there."

"The roof?" I repeated, astonished. "Surely we would be sitting ducks for any snipers, and besides, how on earth would we get up there?"

"The central section is flat. I know where the trap door is and there are chimneys for cover. The buildings around here are all the same height as part of the redesign of the city, so we should be able to see much further."

Justine had no wish to join us and so, somewhat reluctantly, I found myself following Stanley up an iron ladder that had been bolted to a wall near the back stairway. We emerged onto a flat, windy roof covered in slate and lead. It was dotted with short chimneys like a stunted forest that could not be seen from the street below. I followed my companion until we were crouched behind one on the northwest corner of the building. Cautiously, I peered around the brick stack to find that we were not alone on the rooftops. In the distance I could see groups of soldiers shooting down on enemies below. "They are government troops," the colonel explained, staring through some field glasses. "They are shooting down on the reds."

271

I could picture the scene; the barricades would offer no protection from shots fired from above and possibly behind the defenders. "It is like shooting fish in a barrel," I said grimly. "The reds have no chance unless they get up on the roofs too." The soldiers must have thought that they were doing just that, for a moment later there was a sharp crack as a bullet chipped a brick just above my head. We both ducked back behind the stack. "We are trapped up here now," I grumbled. "We will be shot if we try to make it back to the hatch and we cannot see what is happening on the ground." I was annoyed with myself for following Stanley, as the streets were now narrow canyons four storeys below us.

"Don't worry, they will soon lose interest in us," he assured me. "Anyway, I have brought this."

He held up a polished silver hip flask. "I don't need a drink right now," I said, still irritated.

"Very wise," the colonel replied cheerily before tipping the contents away. "Now, reach out with your foot and bring that big stick over here, there's a good chap." In a moment he had given the silver a final polish on his coat and jammed the stick into the neck of the flask. Impressed, I realised that he had just created a mirror that he could hold out beyond the bricks. "It should be safe to look again, he announced, "their snipers are moving away."

Cautiously, I craned my head around once more and saw that he was right. Less than five hundred yards away a score of soldiers were running along the rooftops and descending through the hatches they had used to come up. "The Madeleine barricades must have fallen," Stanley announced, now striding to the corner of the roof. The floor below us had sloping sides but he held out his stick, angled at the ground, and added, "Yes I can see reds in the street below."

"They are streaming across the Place Vendôme," I confirmed, for I could see that open space without a mirror. I noticed that instead of running to support the Concorde barricades, which would now be under more pressure, most were retreating east into the centre of the city. I thought that the red positions were doomed then, even more so when we saw snipers emerge back onto the rooftops closer to Concorde.

"They are on the Rue Royale buildings," the colonel reported. I remembered the wide boulevard that ran directly from La Madeleine to Concorde. Soon the defenders there would have men shooting down on them from above. I doubted that they would hold out for long. The sound of shooting was getting closer and there was gunfire now in Rue de la Paix beneath us. I could see a number of reds taking cover amongst the fallen stones of the column in Place Vendôme and shooting back up our street.

"Perhaps we should go back down," I suggested. It was likely that government snipers could come up to our rooftops and then we would be sitting ducks.

"Yes, you are right," agreed Stanley before stopping again and pointing. "Hang on, it looks like that Brunel fellow has found his own way of dealing with snipers." I turned to see smoke pouring out of the buildings at the Concorde end of Rue Royale and flames licking out of the attic windows. This was no ordinary fire; Brunel must have sent men with accelerant such as petrol bombs to fire every floor starting at the top. The snipers had already retreated behind plumes of smoke. Then we saw some running back the way they had come before the roofs collapsed underneath them. We watched, fascinated, as sheets of flame leapt from the windows. The weather had been dry for days and the fresh breeze at roof level was spreading the fire along the street.

"They will burn the city down if they are not careful," I cautioned, as I watched burning cinders spiralling high into the hot air. I had one final look around the city before we retreated. There was another building burning up by Montmartre, where the rebellion had started. I could see a flag flying there now, but it was not the red banner that had flapped there for the last few weeks. The tricolour showed that while the attack of the national forces might have stalled in the centre of the city, it was still making progress in the suburbs.

We broke away from the chimneys and ran half crouched across the roof until we reached the hatch. I had feared a sniper's bullet as we ran and was glad to get back inside. We hurried down the stairs and I rushed into Stanley's apartment, keen to give Justine our news. I called out her name as I entered, but she was not in the living room and nor did she

273

emerge from the bedroom. It was only a two-room suite and I hardly thought she would be hiding in the wardrobe, but I checked the bedroom anyway in case she had gone back to sleep. "Where the devil is she?" I muttered, before I noticed the colonel standing by the table. He wore a look of shock as he read a note that had been left there.

Chapter 28

"I am sorry, Harrison, you had better read this," he said quietly. I took the paper from him and while my rational brain had already guessed the contents, my heart refused to believe it.

Dear Thomas,

I know I promised to stay, but I cannot sit here doing nothing. I must fight for what I believe in. I will try to find you when it is over. Please forgive me,

Your loving Justine.

"Oh God, what the hell has she done," I muttered. The thought of that beautiful spirit running about in the violent maelstrom made me feel physically sick, or perhaps it was my next thought. "I have got to go after her and get her back." As the words left my lips there was an increased crackle of rifle fire nearby. Stanley stepped up to the window facing the square to see what was happening, only to give a shout of alarm and fall back as a windowpane shattered just above his head. "Are you all right?" I called as he rolled away into a corner.

"I am fine," he replied, but you cannot go out there now. *Versaillais* forces must have entered the far end of Rue de la Paix. The reds are shooting at them from the square." A small, guilty part of me felt relief, for it was obvious that to emerge into the middle of a running street battle would be suicidal. I had an excuse to stay in cover a while longer.

"I think she will have gone to Concorde," I predicted. "She was listening to you last night when you said it was their key position. With luck that Brunel fellow will hold out a bit longer and I can get her back."

But I did not just need Brunel to hold, I also needed those in Vendôme to push the *Versaillais* back, so that I could get out of the hotel. Yet as we moved into the afternoon, the reds made no advances. In contrast, the government forces had got some artillery at their end of the street, which could fire into the square. Fortunately for the reds, the shells made little impact on the vast lumps of bronze-covered stone from the column. We lost several more broken windows as time passed, and Stanley counted three bullet holes in his flag. We took turns using a shaving mirror balanced on a washstand to watch the square without being shot. Slowly but surely the reds began to pull back. Stanley was right about those helping the wounded. Not only that, when they did run down the street at the back of the square, they did not turn right towards Concorde, but left towards City Hall.

As the last of them disappeared, we heard boots running up the stairs of the hotel, swiftly followed by a sharp knock at the door. The army sergeant did not wait for a reply before pushing on into the room. "Are you the only ones here?" he demanded, gesturing for one of his soldiers to go into the bedroom to check. Despite our assurances, the wardrobe was opened and a soldier glanced under the bed.

"What the devil is going on?" demanded Stanley. "We are both British citizens and we have passports, as well as that flag," he gestured out of the window, "to prove it."

We proffered our documents, but the sergeant was just as interested in our hands, and made me turn mine over. On seeing my puzzled expression, he explained, "Lots of the reds are now going into hiding. Most do not have Chassepots so are using old rifles that have been converted to breech loaders. When fired and reloaded they leave soot on the hand."

"And what do you do if you find someone with a dirty hand?" I asked.

"We bloody shoot them," grunted the sergeant, before he was corrected by a new voice.

"No we don't, we take them prisoner." The lieutenant walking into the room gave his sergeant a warning glare before adding, "I have just learned from the hotel clerk that one of these men is a British journalist. Now I regret I must ask, do you have any weapons in your rooms?"

Stanley had a pistol, which was produced and smelt to confirm it had not recently been fired. The lieutenant ordered his men on into the next suite before turning to give us a salute. "I apologise for disturbing you, gentleman. You must understand that the reds have been melting away into the streets when they are cornered. Sometimes they re-emerge when our backs are turned. We have lost several comrades that way. My men are understandably cautious. For your own protection I would urge you to stay in your rooms; I cannot guarantee your safety if you leave. Good day, gentlemen." He was turning to leave when there was a dull thud from outside. It made the floorboards vibrate under our feet and pieces of loose glass fall from the window frame.

"What the hell was that!" I exclaimed, rushing to the window that overlooked the square. I saw debris flying high in the air from an explosion to the southeast. Most buildings in Paris were the same height, but some rose above the rest and as flames started to lick through new holes in a massive cupola dome, it was not hard to guess which building was now ablaze.

"They have set fire to the Tuileries Palace," gasped the lieutenant. "We have heard that women, *pétroleuses*, are going through the streets with petrol bombs. They are throwing them into basements to burn the parts of the city they are forced to abandon."

"Well, that was not a petrol bomb," said Stanley, watching over my shoulder. "That was gunpowder. I would guess a heck of a lot of it, which must have been stored at the palace ready for its destruction." He had barely finished speaking when the dome began to collapse onto the inferno beneath, sending up more sparks and flame.

"If they burn down the city, we will make them pay, by God we will," muttered the lieutenant. Then he strode out of the room, shouting for his men to hurry their searches.

Stanley waited until he was well out of earshot before he murmured, "I would wait until dusk before you make your move if I were you. Both sides will try to reorganise their forces during the night and keep them in areas that are easy to defend. You will stand a better chance of getting through the lines then. If they are burning the Tuileries, I suspect that means that the Concorde barricade has fallen. If Justine has survived that, where would she go?"

If she had survived... I felt sick at the thought she hadn't. Yet if she was still alive when the barricade fell, she would have soon discovered that she could not make her way back to the hotel with government troops in the street outside. If she was alone and frightened, there was a good chance she would make her way back to her apartment above the bakery. That was where I would go. Surely, she had to return there sooner or later.

277

As shadows lengthened in the city, I began to make my preparations to leave. Stanley had offered me his pistol, but warned me it might be my death warrant if I was captured with it. I decided to go unarmed. By then dozens of fires had sprung up from those at Rue Royale and the Concorde barricade, all the way into the centre of the city and the government quarter. Records were being burned somewhere too, and bits of blackened paper were falling from the smoke onto the balcony like dark confetti.

There was no one in the Place Vendôme when I slipped out of the hotel and made my way south. I had planned to go east on the Rue Saint-Honoré, which ran roughly parallel to the much wider Rue de Rivoli, which joined Concorde and City Hall. Honoré was eerily quiet when I reached it. I could see a barricade to the east, but it was unmanned. The short side street towards Rivoli was also empty and I could not resist the temptation to look up and down the wide boulevard to see what was happening. Nervously, I crouched low and peered around the corner. I saw what was left of the barricades at Concorde. They must have been battered by artillery all that day, but now they were being dismantled, no doubt so that guns could fire further along the street. Men walked along the top of them, silhouetted against the flames behind like devilish imps, throwing down sandbags.

When I looked in the other direction, towards the city centre, I could see little more than orange glows of various fires through smoke that was drifting towards me. There had to be more barricades down there, perhaps one with Justine behind it, but it would be madness to go there to find out. If a red did not shoot at a murky figure emerging towards them in the smoke, a government soldier could easily pick me off against the flames from the other direction. I made my way back to Rue Saint-Honoré and hesitantly turned towards the barricade. I stayed in the middle of the street with my arms raised, unsure if there was anyone there at all, or whose side they were on. I was only twenty yards away when a voice whispered out from a nearby house, "They have gone, there is no one there."

With a sense of relief, I ran forward and struggled to find a way to climb it. This was no easy task in the gloom of the evening, but eventually I was over the top and dropping down on the other side. As I brushed soot and ash from my jacket, I looked ahead. The road was long and straight and there was another barricade in the distance. This one had two lanterns fifty yards in front of it to illuminate anyone approaching. Again, I walked down the middle of the street with my arms up in the air to show they were empty. Despite the chill of the evening, I could feel sweat running down my back as I imagined hard, angry faces squinting down rifle sights aimed in my direction.

"I am alone and unarmed," I called out, my voice echoing off the surrounding walls. There was no reply and I was forced to go closer until I was standing directly between the two lanterns. I took a deep breath and shouted out Justine's full name. "I am searching for her; she is my friend. She was probably helping at Concorde this morning. We both took supplies there yesterday."

"Stand still," came a voice from behind me. I had a sudden horror that this was a government trap and I had just confessed to helping the reds. Was I living my last minute before I was put against a wall and shot?

"I am a British journalist," I added weakly as I felt a hand move around my waistband, searching for hidden weapons.

"Push over the ladder, Jacques, he is clean," called the man behind me and I could almost have wept with relief. "I don't know where your woman is," the man added as he guided me to the descending rungs, "but most of those still fighting are gathered around City Hall. I would go there."

I scrambled up the ladder and looked down in surprise at the other side of the barrier. I had expected there to be twenty or thirty men defending this key street, which would allow the *Versaillais* to outflank any defenders on Rivoli. Instead, there were only half a dozen, including the one by the lanterns. Two of them were boys, armed with pistols, who stared at me in wide-eyed fear. I doubted they would stand for long if the *Versaillais* arrived with artillery to blow the barricade of two carts and some furniture apart. I hurried away, anxious to be long gone before their defences were put to the test.

279

There were more people on the streets here, taking advantage of the respite in the day's fighting. Most were moving in the same direction as me, to the east. The glow of orange from buildings on fire lit the night sky. To this day, the smell of smoke reminds me of that night, for it was so thick in the air. The roads, pavements and even windowsills were coated in a layer of ash and cinders, much of which was burnt paper.

It was only a short walk to City Hall, with its grand statues mounted on the walls that had looked down on the city for centuries. I had stood in the square in front on several occasions, watching soldiers of both an emperor and a Commune march past to cheering crowds. There was no celebration now, though. The square was filled with huddles of men and women speaking in urgent voices about what was happening and what they would do next. As I wandered between them, I heard tales of massacres and atrocities. It was said fifty men, women and even children were shot in Montmartre, at the spot the two generals were killed all those weeks before. There was word of courageous fighting south of the river, where the reds were holding the might of the army at bay. But above all, there was a sense of stoic acceptance of their fate. People whispered in hushed tones of the areas that had already fallen. While some of the place names were unfamiliar to me, it was clear the net was closing in.

Delescluze, they said, was still there in his office at City Hall, but there were rumours that other leaders had slipped away. I heard men openly discussing whether they would go into hiding and if they could trust people not to turn them in. Others were resigned to the inevitable; perhaps they had nowhere to hide, or they were determined not to go down without a fight. Such stubbornness reminded me of Justine. I climbed up on the base of a lamp post and yelled out her name. Curious faces turned in my direction, but there was no answer. I called her name again, asking if anyone knew where she was, but all I got in reply were sympathetic glances and the odd shake of a head.

I scrambled down and remembered my first thought that she had gone to her apartment. Hope soared again as I hurried away in that direction. In no time at all I was strolling up to that familiar battered door and reaching into my pocket for the key. I called her name as I raced up the stairs but there was no reply. By the time I burst into those cosy rooms I half knew what I would find. The plates and glasses from our last meal together were still on the drying rack and the bed was untouched. I sank down on the coverlet, still refusing to accept what was an increasingly obvious possibility. No, she had to be out there somewhere. She had said she would try to find me; perhaps she was working her way around the backstreets to get to Stanley. We would find each other in the morning.

It must have been gone midnight when I finally fell asleep. A rumble of gunfire woke me the next morning. As I squinted against the light coming in through the undrawn curtains, I realised that it was quite close, a few streets away to the north. My stomach rumbled, as much through hunger as apprehension. I hurriedly dressed and went downstairs to the bakery. The old couple welcomed me, and we swiftly discovered that neither of us had any news of Justine. As the baker's wife dabbed tears from her eyes, I explained how we had parted and that I thought she had gone to join those fighting at Concorde.

"Find her for us and keep her safe," urged her husband, passing me some breakfast. He was old enough to be her father and had taken a paternal interest since the first siege, always ensuring she had something to eat. He was a pragmatic man, however, and not sold on her politics. Like most businesspeople, he had little sympathy for the reds, despite them passing laws to give him a good night's sleep.

"What will you do?" I asked. "It sounds like the fighting is coming this way."

The baker gave a wry chuckle. "I will make bread as always. The government men will not bother shopkeepers and the people around here will soon be hungry. Now, go and find our girl."

"We shall pray for your success," his wife added, crossing herself. She was still tearful as though, like me, she worried I might already be too late. Putting some more bread in my pocket, I hurried away. I had no wish to run the gauntlet of crossing the battle lines again and so made my way straight back to City Hall. Surely this time, in the bright light of day, I would find someone who knew where she was or, God willing, she would be there herself.

The crowd in front of that imposing building was even larger. I must have spent an hour walking through it, calling her name and asking if anyone had seen her. But apart from a couple of men who had known Justine as a teacher in Belleville, no one had heard of her. The noise of battle was getting louder, with a steady 'crump' of artillery fire echoing through the streets, accompanied by the more staccato rattle of the Mitrailleuse and the random cracks of rifles. Government forces were fighting their way towards us down the Rue de Rivoli from the west. I could hear fighting to the north too. While across the river a red flag still flew over some buildings, gunfire there indicated that the defenders were also hard pressed. Glancing over the top of one of the barricades, I could see that part of the Tuileries was now a smoking ruin, as were several government buildings, although the Louvre, mercifully, had been saved.

There was an uglier mood to the crowd now compared to the previous night. Shock at their defeat had passed and I guessed that those planning to slip away had already done so. These men knew they were cornered, with little chance of escape. They talked angrily about the massacre of captured comrades and a number were shouting for the execution of the hostages in retaliation. I was just deciding what to do next when there was a disturbance in the gathering. An old man in long leather boots and a top hat was trying to make himself heard to give a speech. Those near him were cheering, but I could not hear a word he said. I discovered that this was the elusive Delescluze. Men came running out of City Hall behind him to yet more acclaim. At first I did not realise why, but then I saw the flicker of flames at the windows and understood that another historic Paris landmark was being put to the torch. There were more cheers as the blaze spread up to the next floor. Those who were resigned to losing the coming battles, and perhaps their lives, took comfort that no *Versaillais* official would be able to sit in their old seat of government.

As excitement died down, men returned to the barricades on the surrounding streets, their backs now warmed by the flames behind them. Others, led by Delescluze, began to move off to the east, but I had no wish to follow them. The *Versaillais* would soon see this latest column of smoke rising into the air and would work out the source. Then they would be in an even more murderous mood. With no wish to be caught in a crossfire, I decided that I would go back to Justine's apartment. There were no barricades nearby and I could wait at the bakery for the area to be retaken. There was still a chance Justine could appear and if not, I would go to Stanley. He might have news, and then although the thought sent a shiver through me, there would be the prisoner camps to search. I wondered if MacMahon would remember me from my warning to him at Rethel. Perhaps I could call in a favour to get a prisoner released.

I was lost in these thoughts as I made my way back. Crossing the front line in a moving street battle was no easy business. The crackle of gunfire echoed between buildings, making it hard to gauge its precise origin. Soon it seemed to be coming from left, right and ahead. At each corner I would carefully ease my head around to check the coast was clear. At one junction I saw soldiers with their familiar red trousers crossing the road in the opposite direction a hundred yards away. I waited for them to pass before I cautiously emerged. I was near the apartment by then. While I had been living there, Justine had shown me various side alleys and paths between buildings as shortcuts and these felt safer to me now. I darted down one alley, crossed a small, empty garden square and then moved down another narrow passageway that emerged a few doors along the street from the bakery. I heard the scene before I saw it; a woman was wailing hysterically. As I looked around the last corner, I saw her sobbing over a body sprawled in the street. Two more corpses lay against a wall opposite the bakery and another man's body lay further down in the middle of the road. I glimpsed the frightened face of one of the baker's neighbours staring at me from a window, but what really drew my attention was the door of Justine's apartment. It was half hanging off its hinges and the bakery door beside it was wide open too. The army had clearly got there before me, but why had they attacked those rooms? I had a vision of Justine blazing away at the soldiers with a revolver. Without thinking further, I ran across and charged up the stairs, half expecting to find blood-spattered walls and a corpse. There was no body, yet evidently someone had been hunting for one, for the bed was upturned and the wardrobe doors wide open.

Puzzled, I went down into the bakery, but beyond some half-proved dough, that was empty too. Surely the couple had not been arrested? I went back out into the road, intending to ask the fearful neighbour where they had gone, but then I happened to glance across the street. The blouse was torn and covered in blood, but the pattern still showing on the shoulder looked familiar. Apprehensively, I walked towards the bodies. The wall above where they lay had freshly cracked bricks from bullets. Smears of blood on the wall at chest height confirmed that they must have been shot against the side of the house and left to lie where they fell. The lifeless eyes of the baker's wife stared up at the sky. They were eyes that had looked kindly on me just hours before, as she gave me breakfast and wished me well in my quest. I felt a bitter anger grow in me. Why on earth had the soldiers shot her in this peaceful street? I looked at the other body, a middle-aged woman I vaguely recognised as another local. Neither gave the slightest hint of being a budding revolutionary. Then I noticed the broken glass. A bottle had been smashed against the wall near where they had been shot. Nearby was a large glass jar that I knew the baker's wife used to collect milk from the nearby dairy. Could they have been mistaken for those *pétroleuses* that the army officer had told Stanley and I about? I was not even sure they really existed, for it had been *men* running out of City Hall when it had been set ablaze. Certainly, the reds had been burning civic buildings, but even a cursory sniff of the jar would have proved that it had never contained petrol. Instead, the mere presence of the glass container had evidently been enough to have these poor women shot.

"Hey, you are Justine's friend, are you not?" The voice that broke my thoughts came from an old man who was leaning out of the alley that went behind the bakery.

"Yes, do you know where she is?" I asked eagerly, feeling hope rise in my breast again.

"Quickly, my friend, this way before they come back." With that he disappeared. By the time I got to the alley he was already halfway along it to the next street. A cursory glance in each direction and he was off again, heading east.

"Where is Justine?" I puffed as I ran after this spritely fellow, but for an answer he merely pointed around a corner. There I found the street blocked by another barricade, this one facing north. I shouted her name, more in hope than expectation as I was sure she would have gone to the bakery if she had been this close. There was no reply, but I did see a face I recognised. Sitting on a doorstep the baker, still in his apron, was staring down at a rifle resting across his knees. I sank down beside him, noticing that one side of his face was now swollen and purple with bruising. He looked as though he had been smashed in the face with a rifle butt. I put my hand on his shoulder and whispered, "I am so sorry."

He looked at me then. He was not crying; I think he was still in shock. "I have baked my last bread," he said firmly. He gestured at the barricade, "That will not stand long, the soldiers who came up our street had a cannon with them, but I want to make at least one of them pay for what they have done." Then he took my hand off his shoulder and gripped it. "This is not your fight, lad. Get out of here and write in your paper about what they did to us."

It was advice that struck home. I sat back to think rationally, perhaps for the first time in a couple of days. Justine was either dead or a prisoner, I had to accept that now. Running around the city would not find her and could easily get me killed. I had to get out of there. I could see plumes of smoke rising above the surrounding streets to north, south and to the west, with heavy gunfire in the same directions. But where to go? As if on cue, that question was answered by a volley of shots from the northern end of the street.

"Go, lad," the baker urged again as he got up, hefting his rifle and heading towards the sound. Thank God I did not dally in taking his advice. I shouted good luck to him and took to my heels in the opposite direction. I had gone twenty yards and had just found another alley heading east when it started. There was the crackle of rifle fire from both sides, but then came the awful regular rattle of a Mitrailleuse. I never actually saw the soldiers at the far end of the street as my view was blocked by the barricade. In places like Concorde, where they had time to prepare defences, the paving slabs and sandbags could absorb shot and shell. Here, this hurried defence was built around two overturned carts and furniture dragged from nearby houses. There were beds and mattresses, tables and chairs, even the benches and blackboards from a local school. They needn't have bothered, for the big Mitrailleuse bullets punched through them all as though they were made of butter. There was the sound of smashing, crashing and screaming, with splinters adding to the lethal hail. The reds were falling back, their bodies jerking like marionettes dancing at the end of their plucked strings. I watched in horror as the baker was hit in the chest with such force that his back exploded out of him. I am sure I glimpsed his spine as he fell. Then I saw no more, for I was off and running for my own life.

Chapter 29

I spent all of that day avoiding ambush and battles. If there was an unguarded street that would let me slip west again, I did not find it. I strayed south as far as the Austerlitz bridge over the Seine, only to find that the defenders from south of the river were retreating over it with the *Versaillais* hot on their heels. They carried their own tales of summary executions of suspected or captured reds. Even some doctors helping the wounded had been shot. I somehow doubted that they would be more sympathetic to a foreign journalist, who had witnessed and could report what had been going on. I shrank back into the city. Isolated pockets of resistance, such as those around City Hall, were being steadily extinguished. The reds were now concentrating in the northeastern quarter of the city. To them, this was 'home turf'. They knew its streets and alleyways well and had their own families and hearths to defend. By nightfall I was in a busy square, then called the Château d'Eau, now called the Place de la République. Several streets converged there and those to the north and west had barricades that were being hard fought over.

I found an abandoned apartment to spend the night, hoping it would not be shelled or stormed before I woke up. The Communards remained in control of the area for much of the following day. It was Thursday the twenty-fourth of May. Government forces had slipped unopposed into the city on the Sunday night, so this was the fourth day of fighting and it was now taking its toll. Nearby houses were packed with the wounded, but there were few doctors to tend their injuries. It perhaps did not matter, for most of the injuries from Chassepot and Mitrailleuse were far too severe to survive. The leaders of the Commune were diminishing too. One by one, those who had not already gone into hiding, were getting killed. All day I watched Delescluze bustle from one barricade to another. By evening it was obvious that the stand they had made that day could not last much longer. Various positions had already been abandoned and those left were all but battered into submission.

Word had got out that many of the hostages taken during the previous weeks had now been executed. The dead included the Archbishop of Paris, the confessor of the former empress, various priests and policemen. They had been shot in retaliation for the execution of red prisoners. The news dashed my hopes that there might be a peaceful surrender, giving me the chance to explain that I was a journalist. When the army found out about the hostages, they were even more likely to shoot first and ask questions later.

Any hope that Delescluze had a plan to get us out of this mess were in vain. Well, he had a plan for himself, but it was not one I envied. At around seven that evening I watched him limp out from his headquarters, still immaculately dressed in his top hat and polished boots, his red sash around his waist. He headed towards the barricade across the Boulevard Voltaire, which was being abandoned. At first I thought he was consoling the former commander of the position, who was coming the other way on a stretcher. They shook hands and then Delescluze continued, until he was standing at the foot of the barrier. Men were pointing and shouting at him now, even more so when he started to slowly climb. He stood for a few seconds right on the very top, a frail figure, still leaning on his cane, silhouetted by the setting sun beyond. Then shots rang out and he crumpled and fell. For a revolutionary, it was a brave and noble end, the type that had eluded his former emperor.

The last red leader was dead, and soon four more were killed trying to recover the body, for they would not abandon it. The Commune might have been defeated, but it still had its pride. Men rushed forward once more to defend the position. It was getting dark now and the army clearly did not relish the prospect of a night assault in streets that the enemy knew far better than them. Slowly the crackle of fire died away and I slipped back to spend another night in that abandoned apartment.

I awoke early the following morning to find that the reds were pulling back. Most planned to withdraw to the Belleville quarter. It would be near impossible for the army to get cannon or Mitrailleuse down those twisting narrow streets, while the criss-cross of alleys was ideally suited to ambush. I had no wish to follow them to their suicidal last stand. The government forces would take many casualties and be even more brutal in their reprisals. Yet equally, I could not see a way out of the current pocket the reds were defending. The *Versaillais* were closing in on all sides. I doubted my press accreditation would give me much protection from bullets in some wild charge. How I envied Gambetta being able to escape the city in a balloon, although the army was so close now that I was certain the basket would be riddled by bullets before it was out of range. As it turned out I was looking in entirely the wrong direction for my escape.

The barricade Delescluze died on was now under heavy fire. Perhaps the army guessed it had been abandoned, for it was a matter of minutes before the first heads appeared on the other side. Then Chassepot bullets began to pick off anyone in sight. I quickly ducked back down an alley, but not before I saw two reds caught out in the open and shot down. The army would storm the Château d'Eau area at any moment now they knew it was not being defended. I had no idea what to do next. I pushed at a door to a tobacconist's shop, which had long since been looted and abandoned. A forlorn bell rang above my head as the portal swung open and I looked for somewhere to hide. Boxes and jars were strewn over the floor, but they would not cover a dog, never mind a man. I pushed on out of the back into the alley beyond and saw something that attracted my attention. It was the fond farewell of a family.

The father was staying to fight, that much was obvious, and his comrades further up the passage were calling for him to hurry up. His wife and three children were going elsewhere, along with an old man I took to be the grandfather. If they were not going to Belleville, then where were they going to hide? More importantly, would there be room for me?

"Please could I come with you?" I shamelessly begged the grandfather. More gunfire was coming from the square behind, and it felt we only had seconds to spare. "I am a British journalist reporting on the Commune for my paper in London." I looked down at the youngsters; they were poor, grubby urchins, but perhaps they would deter a soldier from opening fire. "I can help carry one of the children," I offered, with thoughts entirely of self-preservation.

"You will not want to go where we are going," the old man replied curtly. He muttered something about trusting strangers to the woman as he turned his back on me, but she pulled on his arm.

"Wait, he will be useful for the children if it takes too long," she countered. She turned back to me, "Did I not see you asking about a missing girl?"

"Yes," I admitted. "A friend. She was probably at the Concorde barricade, but no one has seen her since."

"A close friend?" the woman probed. I heard what sounded like a bullet slam through the shop front behind me. It did not seem the time to discuss in detail my personal life and so I just nodded. She turned to the old man, "Let him come with us. If his lover is still alive, it is the least we can do."

The grandfather was still not happy about me coming along, but reluctantly nodded his agreement. I bent down to pick up a slightly startled child before he could change his mind. "Should we not be going?" I asked hopefully to the accompaniment of more shop glass breaking behind us. With ponderous slowness he moved off, a walking stick held over one shoulder and a child holding his other hand. I seethed with impatience, for we would never outrun the *Versaillais* at this rate. As I cast nervous glances over my shoulder, we walked along one alley and then another, before emerging on a small street.

"It is here," the old man announced. An elderly crone watched us anxiously from a nearby house, but staring around, I was damned if I could see any sign of the promised sanctuary. Then the old man hefted his stick and inserted it into a manhole cover in the road. I saw now that it was an iron crowbar.

"Are we going into the sewers?" I asked incredulously.

"I told you that you would not want to come with us," he reminded me. "They forget that it was us poor labourers that built this city; we know its secrets."

"Where does it lead?" I asked apprehensively, as a sickening stink wafted around us. As I listened to the sound of more gunfire and screams behind us, I knew I did not really have a choice but to follow.

"To the west of the city, but we must not delay," said the man who had dawdled along the last hundred meters. "If you are coming, get down there and take the children."

I dropped down so that my legs dangled into the hole, peered inside and nearly changed my mind about coming at all. Below us was a brick-lined vault, not tall enough to stand in, with a brown sludge washing along the bottom.

"Hurry up," the man urged, before striking the necessary note. "The soldiers will be here shooting us in a minute." I dropped down, reaching out to steady myself and finding that the walls were covered with an unspeakable slime. Before I knew it, the first child was being lowered down followed closely by the woman, forcing me to crouch and back down the passage. I had to get further away from the entrance as the rest of the family came down and I did not like it one bit. It was not the stink or the ooze seeping in through the lace holes of my shoes, but the constricted space. I had to fight back a burst of panic as the old man dragged the manhole cover back into place, leaving just the tiniest chink of light from the space for a crowbar.

"Should we not stay here until the soldiers have gone?" I whispered, suddenly reluctant to leave that glimmer of the outside world.

There was a swift scratch of a match and then the light of a candle lit the tunnel. I retched when I saw a turd floating against my shoe and heard the old man chuckle at my reaction. "Welcome to the world of the workers," he grunted. "Don't worry, we will have more space and cleaner water in a minute, follow me." Slowly, to the sound of splashing and squelching, we moved forward. The children could at least walk upright, while I was bent nearly double, not wanting my head to touch the ceiling. It was darker at the back of our little band, with the old man and the light at the front. This may have been a good thing, as I heard a creature splashing in the water nearby. It was either one rat or several, I did not want to know for sure. I just locked my eyes on the glow from that candle and tried not to think what I would do if a breeze in the tunnel blew it out.

We must have gone at least a hundred yards when he stopped. By then my back was aching, yet that was nothing compared to the growing terror in my mind as we inched deeper into that hell. A good part of me wanted to splash back the way I had come until I found that manhole cover. Suddenly, taking my chances with the soldiers above ground was much more appealing. I was on the verge of doing just that when the old man called out that we were "at the junction". I had no idea what that meant, but reasoning that it could hardly be worse, I pressed on. I found him standing by an archway in the vaulting, the candle illuminating an iron ladder on the wall beyond and the head of a descending child.

"It leads down into a storm drain," he told me. Then, seeing a lack of comprehension on my face, he added with a grin, "More headroom and less shit." I hurried down the rungs after the small boy and then slid through a gap in the wall. The space beyond was as black as pitch, but gingerly I eased myself upright. Even stretching my arms above my head, I could feel no ceiling. The man with his light followed and I saw that we were all in a much larger brick tunnel, though still with several inches of water underfoot. It smelt dank, but much better than what we had been wading through before. But just when I thought our situation had improved, the old man spoke again. "We must hurry now before the tide comes in."

"The tide?" I repeated, puzzled.

The woman and her brood were already splashing on when he turned back and patiently explained as though to one of the children. "This tunnel drains into the Seine, but when the tide comes in the river flushes through these tunnels, that is why it is much cleaner."

"How far up will the tide come?" I asked, not sure I wanted to know the answer.

"Several meters," he warned. "We will all drown if we are still in here then, so we need to make our way to the west side of the city quickly."

I was fully with him then and hurried after the others. Twice we passed large channels to the left that I guessed led down to the river as I could hear water gurgling at the far end. Then as we progressed water started to flow into the vault from smaller channels on the right and once through a large drain overhead. "It is raining," our guide announced. I cursed the Almighty for his timing – it had been bone dry for over a week. At first I was not too alarmed, a shower would surely not fill a drain this size. Yet above my head water would be running off roofs and down streets and all of it flowed into the street gutters and hence to the drains, like a massive funnel. Soon water was gushing into the vault like small streams. I had to grab one of the children before they were knocked off their feet; the old man did the same and in doing so he lost the candle. A dim light in the distance from a drain above us was now our only illumination. It acted like a navigation star as we pressed on, the freezing water now close to my knees. Each child was now being carried by an adult, but even we struggled to maintain our footing when we crossed one of the increasingly strong inlets. Then we were forced to walk under the drain providing our light and were soaked from head to foot.

The children were cold and frightened. The mite I was holding was wailing loud enough to wake the dead, but there was no time to stop and comfort her. "Keep going!" shouted the old man and if there was any doubt as to the urgency, I noted that the gurgling from the channels leading down to the river was getting louder. Water from the streets was meeting and swirling with the tide from the Seine rising towards us.

"How much farther?" I gasped. My legs were burning with the effort of pushing on. Twice I had barked my shins against unseen obstacles in the water, and I had grazed my head when I had stumbled into the side of the vaulted ceiling. He did not answer, which gave me little comfort, but now I could see another drain ahead, providing some light at least, if promising another drenching. I saw that the woman had hauled up her skirt to make easier progress through the current, but she looked exhausted and called out for a moment's rest.

"We can't," the old man called, "look." He pointed at the channel from the river near the next drain. From the dim illumination we could all clearly see water now gushing in from the river side of the tunnel. "There is another ladder in about a hundred meters," he encouraged. It did not sound far, but now every step was an effort.

How we survived the next few minutes I will never know. By then I had my child on my shoulders to keep her out of the water, her body crouched low over my head as we had already brushed against the ceiling more than once. The roar of the water in that narrow tunnel sounded like a waterfall. In the darkness, it seemed that a vast wave could wash you away at any moment. I remember a rat swam against me and tried to climb up my body before I knocked it away. We had to negotiate other flotsam too – bits of wood and a length of fishing net that wrapped itself around my legs. I really thought I would drown then as I struggled to get free, nearly toppling over into the current as I did so. After another drenching from an open drain above, at last I could make out the rungs of the ladder ahead. The water was now up to my chest and there was not a moment to lose. With every last ounce of my strength, I pushed on.

The old man was ahead and, between us, the woman. When they got to the ladder the man handed his child to the woman while he climbed up and opened the manhole cover. I did not care what waited for us above now, for in another minute we would be drowned for certain. I reached the ladder as the woman screamed; the second child had been pulled from her grasp by the current. I lunged forward and just got a grip on an ankle before he was swept away. The kid coughed and spluttered as the woman and I held him against the ladder, our arms around each other to keep ourselves steady.

Finally, the manhole cover was thrown back above us. It was a dull grey sky, but to me that circle of light was as bright as the sun compared to the darkness we had endured. I gave a small sob of relief at the sight of it. Then the boy was hurrying up the rungs after his grandfather, the woman with her other child hot on his heels. Before I lifted myself up on the first rung, the water had been up to my armpits, the child on my shoulders screaming as the waves crashed into her. You cannot imagine the relief as the weight of that current fell away beneath me and I emerged once more into the world above.

We all sprawled out, spluttering on the wet cobbles, the girl from my shoulders crawling to her mother for comfort. It was still pouring with rain, but I did not care a jot about that; I could not have been any wetter. Then at last I began to take some notice of my surroundings. The first thing I saw was the end of a barricade a bare three feet from the manhole cover. I gave a shudder of horror, for had those sandbags extended just a little further over the metal hatch, we would all now be dead for certain. We were in a wide boulevard that had been well fought over, the buildings struck by bullets and shells that had left their scars. Two houses nearby were still smouldering, the flames being slowly doused by the rain. Then I noticed the soldiers. There were six of them sitting inside a ruined shop front, a kettle steaming on a fire between them. They were watching us with idle curiosity rather than any hostility. A half-drowned family emerging from the drains did not seem worth disturbing their coffee for. The old man saw them too and was not taking any chances. With an effort, he got to his feet and, marshalling his brood, he headed off in the opposite direction. The woman was about to follow, but seeing me still sitting on the ground, came back to grip my hand. She thanked me and wished me well. Then I was left alone in the middle of the street.

I probably sat there for a couple of minutes, just enjoying the sensation of being alive, under a sky and not having shit or rats washing around me. I wondered if the soggy wad of papers in my pockets would be remotely legible if the soldiers demanded to see them. Fortunately, they had now poured their drinks and were talking among themselves, having lost interest in me. I got to my feet and looked about. Now I could see one end of the street over a partly demolished barricade and realised I was in the Rue de Rivoli, the wide street that ran from Concorde to City Hall. I made to move off, but at last one of the soldiers shouted at me. "Put that manhole cover back," he ordered. I did as I was bidden. The soldier nodded in approval and then jerked his head to indicate that I should disappear.

Chapter 30

"Good God, Harrison, we thought you were dead." Stanley greeted me in the entrance to his hotel, after the concierge refused to let such a disreputable character into the premises. As he got closer the colonel's nose wrinkled in distaste, "Where the hell have you been? You smell awful."

"I will tell you everything," I promised, shivering. "But first, is there any chance of a hot bath and some clean clothes?"

Half an hour later I emerged from his bathroom feeling much more comfortable. Stanley was waiting in his living room with a large brandy, and to my surprise, Hoffman, his American friend.

"We have bad news for you, Harrison," warned the colonel, pressing the glass into my hand. "You had better sit down."

"Is it about Justine?" I asked, feeling a sense of foreboding as I settled into an armchair. The joy at my survival evaporated at that moment. I suppose in my heart over the last few days I had begun to accept that she might be dead, but I always retained that glimmer of hope. I suspected now that this small flame was about to be snuffed out.

Stanley reached down and put his hand on my shoulder, "It is the worst news, I'm afraid. I asked Hoffman over as he saw it happen."

"I'm terribly sorry, Harrison," started the American. "As you know my apartment overlooks the Place de la Concorde and so I had a view of the fighting there. It was back on Tuesday, when the reds were trying to defend the barricade at the Rue Saint-Florentin corner. They had been fighting hard all day, setting fire to nearby buildings and defending their position against attacks from the west and the north. Their defences had taken a terrible punishment, but they knew that holding that square was essential to keeping the centre of the city. I did not see Justine among the fighters then, but she must have been there as the shells fell. It was as the defenders finally began to waver that she emerged from the smoke. I watched as she shouted to those about her to hold fast, then she did the bravest thing I ever saw. Picking up a red banner from the ground, she ran to the barricade. Scrambling to the top, she began to wave the flag above her head to show that the position was still held.

The defenders found extra courage then. They turned back and took up their weapons once more. Soon they were blazing away again at the soldiers before them. I can picture Justine clearly now, her dark hair trailing in the breeze, the red silk rippling in the air above her and in the background the roaring flames of burning buildings."

"What happened next?" I asked, imagining the horror of the scene.

"It was a rifle shot, I think," Hoffman almost whispered the answer. "One moment she was standing there rallying the defenders and the next she sort of crumpled, dropping backwards down the barricade and making no effort to break her fall. I watched it all; when she hit the ground, she did not move. If it helps, I do not think she suffered."

"Thank you," I said, feeling suddenly empty. "At least I know what happened." She had heard Stanley and I talking about the importance of holding Concorde. She must have known that retaining it was their only hope and had risked everything for the cause. I had thought I could save her by bringing her to Stanley's hotel, but ironically, I might have hastened her end. "Do you know where they have taken the body?"

I saw Hoffman and Stanley exchange a worried glance and realised more bad news was to come. "I am afraid that she is already buried where she died," the American replied.

I frowned, puzzled, "I don't understand. I thought you said that she was killed in the street."

"The army was desperate to open up a field of fire for their artillery to attack red positions down the Rue de Rivoli," explained Hoffman. "That meant they had to quickly demolish the barricades. I am afraid that they just lay the bodies in the holes that the reds had dug to build their defences. They emptied sandbags over the top and then re-laid the paving slabs so that they could move their guns down the street."

"Are you saying that she is buried under the road?" I asked in astonishment. Their silence was all the confirmation I needed.

A few minutes later we were standing at the bottom of Rue Saint-Florentin where it joins the Rue de Rivoli, staring across the Place de la Concorde. I did not need Hoffman to point out the location of the barricade, for I remembered going there myself with Justine. We had put our supplies in one of the chest-deep holes, perhaps the one she had been buried in. The sizeable fortification around this key junction had now been demolished, but there were plenty of reminders attesting to its previous existence. There were still piles of sandbags and stone slabs lying about, and the square itself was still missing large areas of paving. The once flat road now undulated before us where the earth had not been compacted before the road stones had been roughly replaced. The weight of guns and other traffic was already creating ruts. I wondered if they would excavate the bodies when repairing the road, or if Justine was destined to have no marker on her grave. Yet in some way Paris itself was now her memorial, for she had given her life for the city and its people. Perhaps her body would lie permanently at its heart.

A couple of soldiers nearby were watching us, curious at our interest in this spot. From the British and American cut of our clothes, they might have guessed we were foreigners. As we had removed our hats out of respect, they may even have surmised our purpose, yet they showed no intention of intervening. Distant gunfire from the east of the city intruded on my thoughts. The sound indicated that the army was still closing in on the final red strongholds around Belleville. Yet here in the west of the city, life was already returning to normal. Shops were reopening and an omnibus was gingerly weaving its way over the remaining paving in the square. A couple of street sellers had reopened their stalls to ply their trade and I wandered over to one with coins in my hand.

I laid the flowers roughly at the place where I remembered one of the holes to be. Justine was not religious; she would not have appreciated a prayer. Yet if there is such a thing as a spirit, she would have sensed the grief in my heart. As I stood back on the pavement a cart rattled past, its metal-rimmed wheels crushing the small bouquet. Stanley shouted angrily at the driver for his carelessness, but I told him not to bother. The delicate beauty of the petals, crushed by the iron and falling between the stones, was strangely appropriate somehow.

Forbes found me at the apartment above the bakery the next day. He had come in with the army and knowing nothing about Justine's fate, was in fine spirits. He had not forgiven the mob for his beating and thought they were getting nothing less than they richly deserved. Yet

298

even he had to admit that the reds were fighting better than expected. They might have been forced to concede most of the city, but Belleville was still defying the might of the entire army. Surrounded now on all sides, the defenders still fought bitterly for every inch.

When I told him of my recent experiences, including my escape through the sewers and discovery of Justine's death, he was sympathetic. But he moved swiftly on to congratulating me for being on hand for another great story. Since Justine had gone missing, I had not given a single thought to the *Daily News*. "You cannot be serious," I replied. "I am in no mood to write now."

"You are a newspaper man," he barked at me, quite harshly I thought. "This is why we are here. I told you not to get attached. Anyway," his voice softened, "if you don't tell their story, who will?"

Most correspondents, like Forbes, had felt safer in Versailles and had been reporting the government's version of events. Yet even someone as cynical and experienced in war as my colleague, had been shocked at the reprisals inflicted by the army. Forbes had seen men, women and even children executed in the street, while any stragglers in the columns of prisoners being marched away, were similarly dealt with. General Gallifret, a hero of the cavalry charges at Sedan, had been particularly harsh. He had taken all of the grey-haired men from one column and had them shot on the grounds that if they had not participated in this uprising, they probably had in the 1848 one.

I knew that Forbes was right about the story, but as I sat at the table that afternoon the words would not come. My thoughts kept returning to Justine. It was not surprising, really, as I was in her rooms, surrounded by her possessions, and that night I slept in her bed. It was a warm summer night and I left the window open. In the distance the sound of gunfire continued. I wondered if the father of the children I had helped get out of the eastern suburbs was still alive. Perhaps even the rest of the family had been captured and marched away. I just hoped that the grandfather who had done so much to save his family – and me – had not come across General Gallifret.

The next morning I went for a walk to clear my head. I found a café open and stopped there for a coffee and some breakfast. The patron watched me guardedly, perhaps unsure of my sympathies. Then as he poured my second coffee, he grunted that the gunfire had stopped. I listened – he was right. After a week of constant fighting the silence was almost eerie.

Then after an hour there were a few crashing volleys of distant rifle fire, before the quiet resumed. Without any conscious thought, I found myself a short while later striding up the Rue de Rivoli. As I stood again at the fateful spot, I suddenly remembered the article that months ago I had promised to write on the people of Belleville. It was an obligation I was still to fulfil, although it would be a very different piece now. I stopped a boy selling newspapers and bought one. The masthead revealed that it was Whitsunday, the twenty-eighth of May, 1871. Those who had finally succumbed in Belleville that morning had been fighting the army for seven straight days. The newspaper described the battles of the previous day when hundreds of reds had made a final stand in the Père Lachaise cemetery. Having fought among the tombstones until they ran out of ammunition, many were killed. Shocked troops had discovered in the cemetery the body of the executed archbishop. Over a hundred reds were executed in reprisal near where the body was found. The dead in the cemetery, I knew, were just the tip of the iceberg, for there were thousands of corpses all over the city. They lay shot and discarded, just like their hopes.

I walked back the way I had come, but instead of going up to the apartment, I walked into the bakery below. There I found the workbench still dusted with flour and a peel used to remove loaves from the oven. Its handle gleamed like polished mahogany from years of use. In a chair by the range was a sewing basket and a half-darned sock that would now never be finished.

I found some paper and a pen, and finally sat down to write. Fuelled by brandy, I worked through the night to tell the story of the Commune, much as I have told it here; the good, the bad, the visionaries and the deluded. I described its hopes and ideals, as well as its naivety, as it failed to prepare for its inevitable end. My tale ran to many pages, but even Forbes said it was my best work yet. It would cost a fortune to transmit and given the chance, Versailles would have censored most of it. They would not get the opportunity, though, for Forbes knew of someone with a pass out of the city, travelling to Brussels. They would carry my copy in their jacket lining and arrange for it to be couriered to London from there.

I did not care if the authorities expelled me from the city once they read my article, in fact I wanted to leave. Paris was no place for me anymore. The centre of the city was half destroyed by shells or fire; the streets were still piled with rubble, partly destroyed barricades and other reminders of the struggle, such as blood-spattered walls pockmarked by bullets. Carts still carried the dead to mass graves outside the city, while soldiers in their blue coats and red trousers stood guard at every street corner. This army had at last been victorious, but against their own people rather than some foreign enemy.

With Justine gone the city felt empty to me now, although the reality was far different. The streets were full of the *bourgeoisie* back from the suburbs and from Versailles, roaming the shattered ruins as though on a Cook's tour – and I did not doubt that some of Thomas Cook's genuine customers would be embarking for France within days. There was hardly a working person to be seen, just the young and the old. A few feral children were hunched in doorways trying to make sense of the madness around them, while some old crones picked over the rubble for anything of value. They must have seen a few revolutions in their time and appeared to be taking this one in their stride. One enterprising soul was even selling spent bullets as souvenirs.

Two days later Forbes called in at the apartment where he presented me with the latest copy of the London *Daily News* to reach the city. On the front was a headline, *News From Paris*, with directions to a page inside. I was curious to see how much of my recent scribblings had escaped my uncle's editorial pencil. In the cold light of day, I thought a lot of it was sentimental rubbish that any newsman would normally strike through, but to my surprise it had been printed in full. Forbes must have sent his own note to explain, for even my final line was there: "Tread softly if you ever walk over the end of the Rue de Rivoli, for dreams lie buried there."

Historical Notes

I have used a variety of sources to ensure that Harrison's account is as accurate as possible. These include the definitive work on the Franco–Prussian War published in English, written by Michael Howard in 1961. I have also toured the battlefields in the company of Major General John Drewienkiewicz, a leading authority on how they were fought. Also in our group was author Grenville Bird, who, at the time of writing, is publishing a three-volume work on the conflict. Judging by the maps, photographs and other information Grenville brought on the tour, I have no doubt that it will be a very comprehensive piece of work.

Archibald Forbes

Forbes was the real correspondent for the London *Daily News*, whose editor at the time this book is set was Frank Harrison-Hill. Forbes wrote a detailed two-volume account of his experiences as a correspondent during the Franco–Prussian War. As Harrison recounts, he spent most of his time with the German forces, but also mingled with French officers in Saarbrücken in the days after the battle there. Under orders from Harrison-Hill to get articles back as quickly as possible to beat *The Times* (when the *Daily News* had introduced its new pricing) Forbes made extensive use of the telegraph to do just that and invariably beat his rivals with the news. He was also nearly killed when beaten by a Parisian mob after raising his hat to a German prince during the victory march through the city. Other incidental details are also confirmed in Forbes' account, such as the queues outside the Prussian embassy in London and his claim to have slept in Napoleon's bed the night after the emperor left Sedan.

Other Correspondents

Many British papers including *The Times* and the *Daily News* had correspondents on both sides of the conflict, whose accounts of their experiences appeared in articles that are now available in the British Newspaper Archive. Despite the efforts of the Paris imperial authorities, several managed to witness the French army in action. Intriguingly, there is even an account of the *Times* correspondent being arrested in Metz as a potential spy, at the same time Harrison was apprehended masquerading as Chalmers.

There is also an account of a British journalist's encounter with the *franc-tireurs*, where he was sentenced to death in a bizarre kangaroo court that was almost identical to Harrison's experience.

Background to the War

The build up to the Franco–Prussian War was largely as described by Harrison. Bismarck and von Moltke, the army commander, had been preparing for the conflict for some time. Treaties had been signed for assistance from the southern German states should Prussia be attacked, while potential allies for France, such as Austria, were forestalled by agreements with Russia. Prussia had learned from its earlier conflicts with Denmark and Austria and understood that the nature of war was changing. New tracks were laid to the frontier area in advance; detailed rail timetables prepared for every unit to get men and supplies quickly to the front; artillery training courses were rolled out to improve gunnery from their new steel guns and a rigid clear chain of command was established.

When the Spanish succession issue arose, Bismarck deliberately re-wrote the Ems Telegram to make it appear more dismissive of the French representative than the original. He then leaked it around the world via Prussian embassies. He wanted to provoke the French into declaring war on Prussia and they proudly took the bait. Confident in their superior weaponry, the French launched themselves into a war without a coherent plan, no firm allies and a command structure that, under the emperor, was lacking direction and energy. Yet even in their worst nightmares, they probably could not have predicted the string of catastrophes that would befall them.

Both armies failed to fully appreciate the changes in tactics necessary for their modern weapons. They persisted in using cavalry in battle (and would do so for over forty more years) when, with the modern accurate rifle, horsemen were only suited for long-range reconnaissance. Both sides saw cavalry regiments annihilated in battlefield charges. Prussian infantry commanders also persisted in advances over open ground that were near suicidal when faced with the long range of the Chassepot and Mitrailleuse. Harrison witnessed this at Spicheren. At Saint-Privat, (during the Battle of Gravelotte) the Prussian Guard lost most of its officers and eight thousand men in just twenty minutes. Eventually, the German army learned to rely more heavily on their artillery. This had a clear range advantage over the French and following their training courses, was more accurate too. While the German guns were breech-loading as opposed to the French muzzle-loading cannon, the rate of fire was not significantly different. Both types had to be realigned up on their targets after the recoil from the previous shell.

The Mitrailleuse
While a new journalist like Thomas may not have heard of the Mitrailleuse, there had been some articles in the press about an earlier thirty-one-barrel version three years earlier. These accounts had been critical of both the misfire rate and the accuracy of the weapon. At around the same time that Harrison was framing Chalmers (an article on the gun did appear in *The Times*), a French newspaper carried the story of a trial of the new version of the weapon. It described how five hundred horses were taken from an abattoir and shot at by a Mitrailleuse from a distance of a mile and a half away. The journalist claimed that all of the horses were killed, although did not mention how many times the gun was reloaded. Whether such a trial really took place is doubtful. The story was widely mocked in the international press as a wild exaggeration. Most saw it as an effort to intimidate the Prussians. One German newspaper commented that the Mitrailleuse might be a good tool for a slaughterhouse, but they doubted it would be much use on the battlefield.

As it turned out, the weapon did have great potential, but this was not fully exploited. The main disadvantage for the French was that so few soldiers were trained in its use. There are several recorded incidents of the guns and ammunition being available, but no soldiers who knew how to fire them. Instead of giving them to infantry for close support like a modern machine gun, the French army tended to use them in tightly formed batteries like artillery and fired at extreme range. One of the exceptions was at the Battle of Gravelotte, where the guns were used at closer range to devastating effect.

Battle of Saarbrücken

This took place largely as Harrison (and Forbes) described, although there was a huge variation in the accounts reported in the English press. French-based correspondents wrote that the smallest number of Prussian defenders was around eight thousand. This ranged upwards to three divisions, with additional claims that Saarbrücken had been destroyed in the battle. The Prussian sources on the other hand quoted that just three companies of their fortieth regiment were involved. Forbes was with the defenders watching the French approach and narrowly escaped being shot as he made his escape.

It was an extremely one-sided affair, with the young prince imperial blooded in battle by firing an artillery piece towards the town. This young man was later to meet his end fighting with the British in South Africa, when he was ambushed and killed by Zulus in 1879.

The St Johann's telegraph was not cut by the French, nor the railway line that ran north to south along the river, which was heavily used by the Prussians as soon as the French left. The Prussians were the first European army to use dog tags, which had been introduced in the American Civil War. They also introduced innovations in rations such as the pea sausage, or *Erbswurst*, which the Knorr company only discontinued making in 2019!

Spicheren

When you stand atop the Spicheren staring towards Saarbrücken, it is hard to believe that the Prussians would even attempt to take it by a frontal assault. Perhaps the first attack was forgivable if they thought the position had been abandoned, but not the second much larger attack. The sides of the hill are so steep that you cannot climb it without using your hands for grip, making it impossible to shoot while you struggle up. Now the Spicheren slopes are partly covered in thin forest with tree roots trying to get purchase in the sparse earth and rock, but contemporary photographs show that back in 1870 it was a grassy hillside with barely any cover at all. Prussian troops would have been swept away by Chassepot and Mitrailleuse fire, but incredibly some did manage to climb a corner of the escarpment known as the Rotherburg Ridge. Not that it did them much good. The grave of the commander of that attack is still where he fell at the summit. When his men discovered that their new vantage point was easily suppressed by fire from French troops further back on a higher point on the ridge, they were unable to advance further.

General Frossard had reasonable grounds to hope for assistance from Bazaine to block any attack from the north. Confident that the Spicheren was unassailable, he had stayed throughout the battle by the telegraph office in Forbach, updating his chief and other nearby commanders on developments. As enemy troops began to advance on his position from the northwest, though, his increasingly desperate pleas for assistance were ultimately made in vain. Bazaine had sent reinforcements, but orders went by courier rather than telegraph. Further confusion in the chain of command meant that none of these arrived in time.

Failed Breakout from Metz

The fallback of the French army on Metz after Spicheren, combined with news of the defeat at Frœschwiller, damaged French morale and handed the initiative to their enemy. Both Napoleon III and Bazaine lacked both a clear vision of what to do next, and the force of personality to impose a strategy. In contrast, von Moltke quickly saw the opportunity of encircling most of the French army and was soon issuing orders to do precisely that.

Ironically, Bazaine's one victory at Borny gave the Prussians more time to work their forces around the city to seal his fate. Yet he also contributed to his own difficulties. The emperor did leave as described and was nearly intercepted by Prussian cavalry. Meanwhile, Bazaine insisted on his entire army using a single road to Gravelotte, which caused delays. He seemed to have no sense of the urgency of the situation and had allowed his forward units to stop and cook lunch when they were intercepted by the Prussians. Most of the German forces were by then to the west, in anticipation of the French army having made more progress. During the first attempt to break out of Metz, instead of punching through the still forming Prussian defences and moving on to Verdun, Bazaine dithered and prevaricated, making little progress at all. Two days later, on the eighteenth of August, the French fought again at the battle of Gravelotte. This time Bazaine had chosen an excellent defensive position and his army fought well. All along the line the Prussians could make no progress. They then tried to turn the French right flank at the village of Saint-Privat. This was when the Prussian Guard suffered huge casualties. If Bazaine had sent the Imperial Guard, held in reserve, to support the position, a French victory would have been almost certain. Instead, the finest troops in his army remained unused for the entire day.

With their flank finally turned, the French retreated to Metz. Apart from a few sorties for supplies, they made no serious attempt to break out again until their surrender at the end of October.

The Army of Chalon
The orders given to this new force were more to do with political expediency than military strategy. Politicians in Paris facing the public's shock and anger at their earlier defeats, knew that only a major victory against the Prussians, with the emperor at the head of his forces, would save the regime. MacMahon's army had already been beaten by the Prussians at Frœschwiller, his veterans enhanced by barely trained new recruits. Bazaine had given mixed signals on his ability to break out of Metz, while politicians were passing intelligence based more on wishful thinking than firm facts.

MacMahon was ordered to relieve Metz but must have known that the chances of success were slim. They became even slimmer when a Paris paper revealed his plan of attack. The Prussians monitored his progress and had little difficulty blocking the main crossings of the River Meuse to drive his army north. When the marshal gave orders for his army to rest for a day at Sedan, he can have had little idea of the overwhelming enemy forces that were converging on his position. The Prussians had released part of the army besieging Metz to join the

307

pursuers of the Army of Chalon, to give them an overwhelming advantage.

It may not have felt like it at the time, but MacMahon was fortunate to be wounded early on the day of the battle. According to some accounts he was shot in the thigh, whereas others hint at the groin or the buttock. Regardless, he was able to use the injury to escape responsibility for the debacle of French arms that followed.

Due to key bridges not being destroyed and vital passes not being blocked, German guns were able to surround the French. De Wimpffen did assume command of the army at this point. However, instead of using the brief opportunity to escape the trap, as General Ducrot suggested, he launched a series of hopeless attacks. It was the German artillery that beat the French at Sedan, with great rolling barrages that gave the defenders little shelter. There were accounts of the emperor wandering among the shell bursts, apparently seeking oblivion, but he was not to be spared the humiliation of surrendering his army to the enemy. In Paris they refused to believe such a disaster could have happened until the emperor was allowed to send a telegram to his empress confirming the scale of the defeat.

The Third Republic

The scale of their victory presented the Prussians with a problem; with the enemy head of state a prisoner, who could they negotiate a peace with? The German public (partly encouraged through the press by Bismarck,) was determined that France would never be a threat to the German states again. Its peace demands in terms of financial reparations and territory were almost impossible for any French politician to accept. The French public were still trying to come to terms with how their proud and well-equipped army had been so comprehensively beaten. In a bloodless coup the people of Paris broke up proceedings in the Chamber of Deputies and then went to City Hall to demand a new government. The Third Republic was born, with predominantly moderate left-wing ministers. Only days later, however, this new government found itself besieged in its capital and as the telegraph cables were cut, unable to reach the provinces.

Gambetta's escape by balloon and his assumption of both interior ministry and military briefs made him effectively the head of the republic. Harrison's (and Forbes') account of travelling through French towns with the Germans shows the difficulties the locals faced. With no army to protect them, most chose to take a pragmatic approach and live peaceably with their occupiers. Few obeyed demands from Gambetta to institute a scorched earth approach, when it was their own farms they were being asked to 'scorch', leaving themselves homeless and without income in the depths of winter. *Franc-tireurs* would attack lone German sentries or small patrols, but were rarely around when the Germans were searching for someone to execute in reprisal. Consequently, locals were often caught in the middle of these conflicts instead. Areas not occupied were faced with increasing demands to raise and equip new regiments for the army. With provinces competing for arms and supplies, prices rose and the quality of weapons obtained fell. Many were forced to go to war against experienced veterans with little to no equipment and weapons that verged on useless.

Both Freycinet and Gambetta were committed Republicans doing all they could to save France. However, neither had any military experience and they did not trust most of their officers, who had supported the imperial regime. Ideas that looked good on paper, such as doubling the size of companies to reduce the need for officers, were not practical on the ground. They also did order the advance of the army of the Loire based on confusion over which place called Épinay had been occupied by the National Guard.

The Commune Uprising

There are various accounts of the Paris Commune uprising from British and American residents, including Colonel Stanley and Wickham Hoffman. Stanley did have a hotel overlooking the Place Vendôme, while Hoffman described the death of Justine. He does not mention a name, yet he wrote about a very attractive, dark-haired woman seizing up a banner to rally the troops at the barricade before being shot dead. He later witnessed Communard bodies being thrown into a ditch dug to construct the barricade, covered in quicklime and soil from sandbags, until paving slabs could be laid over the top.

The causes of the uprising were as described by Harrison. If the National Assembly was trying to provoke the people of Paris, they vastly underestimated the resolve of its citizens. Some later claimed that Karl Marx and his band of internationalists were organising the uprising from London. This was not the case; there was no single faction behind the movement, which was perhaps the reason behind its lack of focus. The largest group were the Jacobins, who looked more to the first French Revolution for guidance, instead of Marx.

Justine's friend Louise was likely Louise Michel, who did walk to Versailles to prove that her suggestion of shooting Adolphe Thiers could be done. She survived the uprising and even dared a subsequent military court to sentence her to death. Instead, she was sentenced to transportation to New Caledonia, returning to France in 1880. She continued to mix in anarchist circles and gave speeches in London and Paris before dying in 1905.

The attacking army came mostly from the provinces and had a historical distrust of the capital. Many will have resented the recent republican government under Gambetta, voted in by the Paris mob, which had imposed such hardship. The government and commanders did much to heighten this feeling of hatred, convincing soldiers that the reds wanted nothing less than the ruination of France. Certainly, they were in little mood to show mercy when they attacked. Fires started deliberately and carried by cinders on the breeze, helped convince many that the Communards were burning the city. Many key buildings such as part of the Tuileries and City Hall were destroyed, as were the city's tax records and other archives. The story of women with petrol bombs, the *pétroleuses*, was widespread. There is little evidence such a group existed, but many innocents were shot on suspicion.

The death toll from the Commune's suppression has been a matter of much debate, with estimates ranging from 6,500 to 40,000. Reliable French historians today have settled around 20–25,000, based partly on records from the municipality that covered the costs of disposing or burying 17,000 bodies. A further 40,000 were held for trial and some of those were exiled overseas, notably to penal colonies in the South Pacific. A few of the leaders escaped capture, some even returning after pardons to resume careers as politicians. One of the more interesting was Brunel, who had commanded at the Concorde barricade and burned the Rue Royale. Despite being wounded in the fighting, he managed to avoid arrest and get to Britain. He later became a French teacher at Dartmouth Naval College, teaching, amongst others, the future British King George V.

Bazaine and MacMahon: Aftermath

The fate of these two French marshals after the war could not have been more different. After the Commune was suppressed and peace settled over France again, citizens began to reflect on the recent war. They found it unpalatable to accept that their great army had simply been out-fought and out-manoeuvred by the now hated Germans, and instead looked for someone to blame. Marshal Bazaine was an obvious candidate. Many could not understand why he had failed to break away from Metz. He had not recognised the republican government under Gambetta and had even conducted some negotiations with the Prussians himself, suggesting, they thought, treason. Even though his generals had agreed to surrender when they did, after a siege of two and a half months, he was blamed for releasing the besieging Prussians which prevented the Army of the Loire from relieving Paris. As this book depicts, it was highly unlikely that the Army of the Loire was ever going to relieve the capital, regardless of these reinforcements.

There were, as always, political factors at play. Blaming Bazaine exonerated the Republicans for their failures. Some Bonapartists were happy to pass any blame from their emperor's shoulders onto those of the marshal, while the royalist faction had no interest in saving this soldier who had risen through the ranks.

The result of the trial was a forgone conclusion. Bazaine was sentenced to death for treason, although an appeal for clemency was immediately presented to the president of the republic, none other than Marshal MacMahon, whose career had taken the opposite direction to his former colleague. MacMahon commuted the sentence to life imprisonment. Bazaine was incarcerated on an island prison in the Mediterranean, but with the help of his wife and others, managed to escape in 1874. After stays in Italy and London, he eventually settled in Spain and died in relative poverty in 1888.

MacMahon had become a hero to all but the left-wing Republicans for his suppression of the Commune and returning law and order to France. He was persuaded to take on the Presidency after Thiers lost a vote of confidence in 1873. As President, his moderate rule allowed the republic to become firmly established and under him, France saw prosperity that allowed her to repay Prussian reparations early. He also strengthened the army. He resigned in 1879 and received a full state funeral when he died in 1893.

Thank you for reading this book and I hoped you enjoyed it. If so I would be grateful for any positive reviews on websites that you use to choose books. As there is no major publisher promoting this book, any recommendations to friends and family that you think would enjoy it would also be appreciated.

This is the first of the Thomas Harrison series, there will be more of his adventures to come. If you have enjoyed this book and have not already read them, there is also an eleven book series by the same author featuring the adventures of Thomas Flashman from 1800-1838.

There is a Robert Brightwell Books Facebook page and the www.robertbrightwell.com website to keep you updated on future books in the series. They also include portraits, pictures and further information on characters and events featured in the books.

Also by this author

Flashman and the Seawolf

This first book in the Thomas Flashman series covers his adventures with Thomas Cochrane, one of the most extraordinary naval commanders of all time.

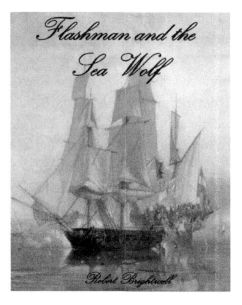

From the brothels and gambling dens of London, through political intrigues and espionage, the action moves to the Mediterranean and the real life character of Thomas Cochrane. This book covers the start of Cochrane's career including the most astounding single ship action of the Napoleonic war.

Thomas Flashman provides a unique insight as danger stalks him like a persistent bailiff through a series of adventures that prove history really is stranger than fiction.

Flashman and the Cobra

This book takes Thomas to territory familiar to readers of his nephew's adventures, India, during the second Mahratta war. It also includes an illuminating visit to Paris during the Peace of Amiens in 1802.

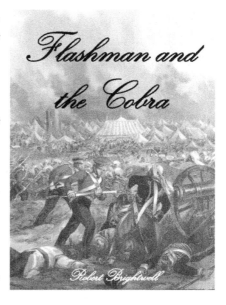

As you might expect Flashman is embroiled in treachery and scandal from the outset and, despite his very best endeavours, is often in the thick of the action. He intrigues with generals, warlords, fearless warriors, nomadic bandit tribes, highland soldiers and not least a four-foot-tall former nautch dancer, who led the only Mahratta troops to leave the battlefield of Assaye in good order.

Flashman gives an illuminating account with a unique perspective. It details feats of incredible courage (not his, obviously) reckless folly and sheer good luck that were to change the future of India and the career of a general who would later win a war in Europe.

Flashman in the Peninsula

While many people have written books and novels on the Peninsular War, Flashman's memoirs offer a unique perspective. They include new accounts of famous battles, but also incredible incidents and characters almost forgotten by history.

Flashman is revealed as the catalyst to one of the greatest royal scandals of the nineteenth century which disgraced a prince and ultimately produced one of our greatest novelists. In Spain and Portugal he witnesses catastrophic incompetence and incredible courage in equal measure. He is present at an extraordinary action where a small group of men stopped the army of a French marshal in its tracks. His flatulent horse may well have routed a Spanish regiment, while his cowardice and poltroonery certainly saved the British army from a French trap.

Accompanied by Lord Byron's dog, Flashman faces death from Polish lancers and a vengeful Spanish midget, not to mention finding time to perform a blasphemous act with the famous Maid of Zaragoza. This is an account made more astonishing as the key facts are confirmed by various historical sources.

Flashman's Escape

This book covers the second half of Thomas Flashman's experiences in the Peninsular War and follows on from *Flashman in the Peninsula*.

Having lost his role as a staff officer, Flashman finds himself commanding a company in an infantry battalion. In between cuckolding his soldiers and annoying his superiors, he finds himself at the heart of the two bloodiest actions of the war. With drama and disaster in equal measure, he provides a first-hand account of not only the horror of battle but also the bloody aftermath.

Hopes for a quieter life backfire horribly when he is sent behind enemy lines to help recover an important British prisoner, who also happens to be a hated rival. His adventures take him the length of Spain and all the way to Paris on one of the most audacious wartime journeys ever undertaken.

With the future of the French empire briefly placed in his quaking hands, Flashman dodges lovers, angry fathers, conspirators and ministers of state in a desperate effort to keep his cowardly carcass in one piece. It is a historical roller-coaster ride that brings together various extraordinary events, while also giving a disturbing insight into the creation of a French literary classic!

Flashman and Madison's War

This book finds Thomas, a British army officer, landing on the shores of the United States at the worst possible moment – just when the United States has declared war with Britain! Having already endured enough with his earlier adventures, he desperately wants to go home but finds himself drawn inexorably into this new conflict. He is soon dodging musket balls, arrows and tomahawks as he desperately  tries to keep his scalp intact and on his head.

It is an extraordinary tale of an almost forgotten war, with inspiring leaders, incompetent commanders, a future American president, terrifying warriors (and their equally intimidating women), brave sailors, trigger-happy madams and a girl in a wet dress who could have brought a city to a standstill. Flashman plays a central role and reveals that he was responsible for the disgrace of one British general, the capture of another and for one of the biggest debacles in British military history.

Flashman's Waterloo

The first six months of 1815 were
a pivotal time in European history.
As a result, countless books have
been written by men who were
there and by those who studied it
afterwards. But despite this wealth
of material there are still many
unanswered questions including:
-Why did the man who promised
to bring Napoleon back in an iron
cage, instead join his old
commander?
-Why was Wellington so
convinced that the French would
not attack when they did?

-Why was the French emperor ill during the height of the battle,
leaving its management to the hot-headed Marshal Ney?
-What possessed Ney to launch a huge and disastrous cavalry charge
in the middle of the battle?
-Why did the British Head of Intelligence always walk with a limp
after the conflict?

The answer to all these questions in full or in part can be summed up
in one word: Flashman.

This extraordinary tale is aligned with other historical accounts of the
Waterloo campaign and reveals how Flashman's attempt to embrace
the quiet diplomatic life backfires spectacularly. The memoir provides
a unique insight into how Napoleon returned to power, the treachery
and intrigues around his hundred-day rule and how ultimately he was
robbed of victory. It includes the return of old friends and enemies
from both sides of the conflict and is a fitting climax to Thomas
Flashman's Napoleonic adventures.

Flashman and the Emperor

This seventh instalment in the memoirs of the Georgian rogue Thomas Flashman reveals that, despite his suffering through the Napoleonic Wars, he did not get to enjoy a quiet retirement. Indeed, middle age finds him acting just as disgracefully as in his youth, as old friends pull him unwittingly back into the fray.

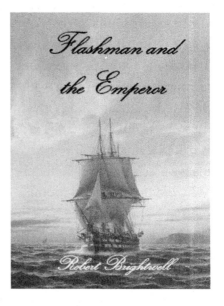

He re-joins his former comrade in arms, Thomas Cochrane, in what is intended to be a peaceful and profitable sojourn in South America. Instead, he finds himself enjoying drug-fuelled orgies in Rio, trying his hand at silver smuggling and escaping earthquakes in Chile before being reluctantly shanghaied into the Brazilian navy.

Sailing with Cochrane again, he joins the admiral in what must be one of the most extraordinary periods of his already legendary career. With a crew more interested in fighting each other than the enemy, they use Cochrane's courage, Flashman's cunning and an outrageous bluff to carve out nothing less than an empire which will stand the test of time.

Flashman and the Golden Sword

Of all the enemies that our hero has shrunk away from, there was one he feared above them all. By his own admission they gave him nightmares into his dotage. It was not the French, the Spanish, the Americans or the Mexicans. It was not even the more exotic adversaries such as the Iroquois, Mahratta or Zulus. While they could all make his guts churn anxiously, the foe that really put him off his lunch were the Ashanti. "You could not see them coming," he complained. "They were well armed, fought with cunning and above all, there were bloody thousands of the bastards."

This eighth packet in the Thomas Flashman memoirs details his misadventures on the Gold Coast in Africa. It was a time when the British lion discovered that instead of being the king of the jungle, it was in fact a crumb on the lip of a far more ferocious beast. Our 'hero' is at the heart of this revelation after he is shipwrecked on that hostile shore. While waiting for passage home, he is soon embroiled in the plans of a naïve British governor who has hopelessly underestimated his foe. When he is not impersonating a missionary or chasing the local women, Flashman finds himself being trapped by enemy armies, risking execution and the worst kind of 'dismemberment,' not to mention escaping prisons, spies, snakes, water horses (hippopotamus) and crocodiles.

It is another rip-roaring Thomas Flashman adventure, which tells the true story of an extraordinary time in Africa that is now almost entirely forgotten.

Flashman at the Alamo

When other men might be looking forward to a well-earned retirement to enjoy their ill-gotten gains, Flashman finds himself once more facing overwhelming odds and ruthless enemies, while standing (reluctantly) shoulder to shoulder with some of America's greatest heroes.

A trip abroad to avoid a scandal at home leaves him bored and restless. They say 'the devil makes work for idle hands' and Lucifer surpassed himself this time as Thomas is persuaded to visit the newly independent country of Texas. Little does he realise that this fledgling state is about to face its biggest challenge – one that will threaten its very existence.

Flashman joins the desperate fight of a new nation against a pitiless tyrant, who gives no quarter to those who stand against him. Drunkards, hunters, farmers, lawyers, adventurers and one English coward all come together to fight and win their liberty.

Flashman and the Zulus

While many people have heard of the battle at Rorke's Drift, (featured in the film *Zulu*) and the one at Isandlwana that preceded it, few outside of South Africa know of an earlier and equally bloody conflict. Under a tyrannical king, the Zulu nation defended its territory with ruthless efficiency against white settlers. Only a naïve English vicar, with his family and some translators are permitted to live in the king's capital. It is into this cleric's household that  Thomas Flashman finds himself, as a most reluctant guest.

Listening to sermons of peace and tolerance against a background of executions and slaughter, Thomas is soon fleeing for his life, barely a spearpoint ahead of regiments of fearsome warriors. He is soon to learn that there is a fate even worse than his own death. He is pitched in with Boers and British settlers as they fight a cunning and relentless foe. Thomas strives for his own salvation, before discovering that chance has not finished with him yet.

Flashman's Winter

This book fills in two gaps in Flashman's career, hitherto uncovered by his memoirs. The bulk of this volume is taken up with Flashman's adventures in what was then Prussia, but which now comprises Poland, Russia and the Baltic states. In 1806 Prussia declared war on France and in a disastrous campaign lost most of its territory. Russia was forced to come to its aid and Britain too sent observers to assess how to help. Flashman joins this mission in what should have been a safe diplomatic visit – but of course was anything but.

From bloody, frozen retreats to battles in blizzards, he is soon in the thick of the action as a country fights for its very survival. Diplomatic intrigues follow and, with the aid of a Russian countess, our hero uncovers the enemy's plans – and works to frustrate them.

Also included is the short story Flashman's Christmas, set in Paris a few months after the battle of Waterloo. As royalists conduct vindictive purges on former Bonapartists, Flashman is embroiled in a notorious eve of execution jail-break as he is reunited with old friends to outwit old enemies.

Printed in Great Britain
by Amazon

29656265R00189